STONE FEVER

EREBUS TALES: Book I

Norman Westhoff

IGUANA

Publisher: Meghan Behse
Front cover design: Ruth Dwight

Araceli del Rosario Suárez ©Marco Vernaschi. Used by permission.
Bison buckle image used with permission from Montana Silversmiths.

ISBN 978-1-77180-456-1(paperback)
ISBN 978-1-77180-457-8 (epub)
ISBN 978-1-77180-458-5 (Kindle)

This is the second edition of *Stone Fever*.

STONE FEVER

EREBUS TALES: Book I

Although I started writing this story before any of my grandchildren were born, it has always been with them in mind:

Olivia Reed Senter
Paul Martin Westhoff
Daisy Elizabeth Senter
Luther Reed Westhoff
Catherine June Senter

CONTENTS

I

ROUGH LANDING

I'm sardined into the left back seat of the Bailey Voyager. It's a good thing I'm short; this cell they call a cockpit is way too tight to fit four people. And these overstuffed flight suits — I feel like a mummy in a marshmallow. Still, I'm the newbie — Keltyn SparrowHawk, rock-smith savant — and they didn't ask me when they designed this craft.

Buck Kranepool, our big pilot, likes to boast about aeronautical advances of the past four centuries, but ask him why cockpit innovation hasn't kept pace and he'll just mutter. He's parked directly in front of me, yet all I can see of him is a wave of blond hair. He's taken advantage of the legroom I don't need to push his seat backward and hog more for him.

The view of my fellow-scientist Orfea Del Campo is no better. Fay sits right next to me, a fellow mummy. Aside from her marshmallow cocoon all that shows are her gray-tinged auburn curls. She peers out her window, lost in thought. She's got a lot riding on this mission — her reputation, perhaps her whole career as an anthropologist — yet you sure couldn't tell now. It's like she's in a trance.

The only person whose features I can see is the other front seat occupant, kitty-corner from me. His profile is telling: double chin, receding curly gray hairline, gold-rimmed dialups. That's Harry Ladou, our crew chief. Mr. Suave Quebecois. Pet name for me: "*ma chère.*" He, too, seems to be in a daze until Buck turns to him.

"Funny how we've lost radio contact with the Space Station. No big deal now, but I'm gonna have to check that out once we land." From the way he keeps tapping the dead radio connection, I suspect Buck is more worried than he's letting on, but his voice stays as smooth as silk. "Soon as we find the site matching this spot on the simulator, I'll slow 'er down and open the vertical landing gear."

Ten minutes elapse in silence. Unsettled, I find myself staring out the window too. Whizzing over the endless water below makes me dizzy. Gradually, the flat blue turns to waves, lapping up to the beaches of Antarctica.

Buck makes a few adjustments on the console, then sits back. "Now let the processor do the steering." He aims another speech at Harry. "First thing you learn in flight school, never trust your sensory cues. Mess you up every time. Vestibular disruption. Four hundred years of manned flight, but amateur pilots still crash when they forget that. You've got to curb your instincts and rely on your instruments."

Someone who didn't know Buck's track record might call that bragging, but this guy is a test pilot. He's walked away from more than one near-crash after a new gadget malfunctioned.

We approach a mountain. I recognize the domed shape with the saddle on one side: it's Erebus, our destination. By craning my neck, I can see a mark on our route console, a flat spot to the right of the mountain. That's the landing spot I picked, back in Canada when we planned this mission. I've never been anywhere near here, but then, neither have the others. The newbie gets to choose the target because a geologist is supposed to know about different terrains. I better be right; there weren't any other options.

Are we really here? Seems like we should have to pass through a time warp or something. I squeeze my cheek, just to make sure I'm not dreaming. Buck eases up on the throttle. When the plane gets to within five miles, he pulls a grip.

"Speed throttle, vertical stabilizer. In a few minutes we should point straight upward, right at the moment of zero velocity. Fire retro rockets for ten seconds while the VLG deploys, and bingo, the proverbial soft landing for Bailey Voyager." Buck peeks over his shoulder. "Harnesses, y'all."

I snap together the metal clamps that secure my body to the seat and take a deep breath; two years of prep have come down to this moment.

The ship reaches her climactic vertical position, poised just as it was at liftoff. Buck pushes one button to keep airborne before flipping the VLG switch.

Then... nothing happens. "No display on the panel." Buck angles one ear. "I should hear the hydraulics, even if the panel sensor is out."

There's no sound at all.

"Damn," says Buck.

Uh-oh. I hate it when your pilot says damn. A damn from him packs a lot more weight than if someone like me says it. We're so close to touchdown that I can already feel my boots crunch on the rocks, and now Buck can't get his friggin' plane to sit on its fanny.

Buck's tone rises. "The vertical landing gear won't deploy. It worked when we docked at the Space Station." He flips the switch again. Nothing. He turns to Harry. "Are you thinking what I'm thinking?"

"Human factors?"

"But how?" Buck mulls over this possibility. "I didn't leave the hangar the whole time we were docked. Maybe it's just radio frequency jamming from all that static earlier."

"So, what's next?" The chief's voice cracks.

"If this were a flat surface, preferably paved, I might try to land vertically by cutting the retro rockets slowly."

Harry, Fay, and I each peer out our windows again. It's late in the day; visibility is dropping, it's hard to see details, and anyway, we all just want to get out of our marshmallow suits and stretch our legs. To say nothing of other bodily functions.

Buck better pull us through, because he's the only one who can. I start to feel it, the sensation that always hits me when I'm utterly powerless: I'm engulfed to my chest, arms flailing, as I'm pulled down by quicksand. My lips start to tingle. I have to slow my breathing.

Buck seems to know what we're all thinking. "Forget it, you guys. I'm not going to risk it. Too steep. We'd fall on our collective fanny. Not lethal, but believe me, not pretty either. Might damage the shell. We'd burn up on the way home."

"Okay," says Harry. "You've talked me out of it. What's your contingency plan?"

"In the good old days, before VLG's and vertical stabilizers, we used to do a plain old horizontal landing. They even built wheels into Bailey Voyager's landing gear, just in case. One small problem, mates."

"What's that, Buck?" Harry rubs his temples.

"We need a runway."

Harry forces a smile through clenched teeth. "Maybe the folks here heard we were coming and built one." He peers over his shoulder at me, wondering if I'll bite. I don't. He can't see Fay behind him. I suspect his attempt at humor was really aimed at her.

Fay closes her eyes, shakes her head. "You're a hoot, Harry."

Buck turns halfway around. "Look sharp, everyone. We're gonna make it. Just keep an eye out for a few hundred yards of reasonably flat terrain, preferably bare."

You've gotta love Buck. I wonder if positive psychology is part of their flight school training. He eases back to a horizontal axis, while keeping the retro rockets on full. After a minute, the engine kicks in and the plane again inches forward. Daylight is fading fast. Buck turns a knob and the nose projects a bright headlight. He steers a spiral course around the perimeter of Mt. Erebus, gradually widening the radius with each lap, searching for a place to land. We're barely skimming the ground.

I brace for the worst. With light failing, what if a steep hill shows up? Buck won't be able to do anything until it's too late.

I hope the others can't tell how wildly my heart pounds.

Wait a minute. I lean forward to tug on Buck's shoulder and point below to the left. Two miles away, a wide, shallow pocket indents the flat scrub terrain. It looks to be about a mile in diameter.

"I think it's a crater," my voice croaks. "They generally don't have much growing in them."

"Score one for Missy," says Buck. "Wide enough, flat enough. The question for our wunderkind is, how smooth? Lots of rocks, we're liable to puncture a tire."

I do a quick mental inventory of crater surfaces.

"If you're not sure, Missy, just say so. I can do a vertical landing in the dark if we have to," Buck says.

"No, it'll be smooth enough for the tires," I blurt. Why do I sound so certain when I'm just guessing? I should have studied maps of the wider terrain beforehand, not just Erebus. But hell, who could have predicted this quandary?

"You're sure?" The edge in Buck's voice feels like he's staring me down, even though he can't see my face.

"Yup. Go for it." I try to sound confident.

"Everyone ready?" Buck looks around at the others. Harry nods, but his eyes jump hither and yon. He grits his teeth as he grabs the door handle with his right hand and the seat frame with his left. Fay nods too, but her cheeks have turned a pale gray. Eyes still closed, hands clamped together across her chest, she silently mutters what must be a prayer.

I grasp the handholds on the back of Buck's seat, my lips clenched.

"Here we go." Buck pushes another switch. The humming noise of landing wheel hydraulics brings forth a "Yes!" He eases up on the speed throttle and pulls the nose into a slight uptilt.

My eyes squint in the gathering gloom, trying to survey the ground as we prepare to make contact. Just before touchdown, I spy the worst-case scenario: jagged pieces of lava litter the ground, scattered at random like sleeping porcupines. Holy Buckets!

I sit bolt upright, gaping out the window. How can that be? What are chunks of lava doing in a crater? Then it hits me. Of course. We're five miles from a volcano. Why didn't I think of this before? Hell, our goose is cooked now.

The Bailey Voyager makes contact and bounces along until an explosion rocks its left side. The craft veers back and forth. My body jerks on its harness like a trapped lab monkey, but it's all reflex.

As if in slow motion, a compartment door over Buck's head jars open, and out drops a metal case. A crunching, dull thud echoes through the cabin as the container whacks Buck's skull. The plane swerves.

Harry's eyepieces dangle as he gapes at the stricken pilot. "Buck." No answer. Harry whips around toward the rear seats. "His head is bleeding. He's unconscious."

"Do something, Harry." Fay's eyes saucer. The plane reels jaggedly.

Sheesh. I'm scared too, but stopping the plane isn't rocket science. I have to shout at Harry to be heard above the bouncing clatter. "Slow the throttle with your left hand."

Harry reaches across and eases the handle forward. After lurching back and forth for a few seconds more, the plane skids to a stop.

We all sit stunned, breathing hard.

Harry is the first to break the silence. "That bang?" He turns to me, frantic. "Keltyn?"

I glance out the left side. The ground, horizontal to us a few minutes ago, now seems to slope up. "The left tire blew." I turn to Harry. "Know what that means, don't you?"

"What?" His white face sweats like ice in the sun.

"You want the good news or the bad news?"

"I dunno. Bad news first, I guess." He fumbles with his dialups, hanging off of one ear.

"Unless we can patch the tire, no horizontal takeoff. And unless Buck can fix the VLG, we can't do a vertical takeoff. Then..." My finger draws a line across my throat. It feels naughty to make the chief squirm, but he's acting like such a wuss.

"Then *what*?" Harry tries to focus.

"We're stuck. On top of that, we're miles from Erebus." I punch the back of the seat. The blood rushes to my head. I feel more worked up now that we're out of immediate danger.

Silence. Fay leans forward toward me. "So, what's your good news, honey?"

"We're here. We made it." But I keep a hawk's eye on Harry, whose eyeballs now drift up in their sockets. I shouldn't have baited him. He's losing it fast. "Fay, can you get the cockpit door on your side open? Better make it quick."

Fay reaches around the side of Harry's seat and wrestles with the latch. She's able to loosen it and push the door ajar, just in time for Harry to stick out his head. His dialups fall off his nose and he pukes, right on them.

When Harry collects himself, I help him and Fay haul Buck out of his cramped seat and lower him gently to the ground. He's in no shape to help himself, which is too bad since he's so big. Still, judging from his mutterings, he's coming to.

The only guy who can bring us back home is no longer in a coma. I should count my blessings, but instead, I'm haunted by the exchange between Buck and Harry, trying to explain the VLG malfunction. What did Harry mean by "human factors?" Likely a mental lapse by one of the mechanics at Chimera Space Station. Yet, I know that a pilot is compulsive about his plane, and Buck would have watched the mechanics' every move like a hawk.

But there's another possibility, isn't there? The thought creeps through my mind, as silent and deadly as a viper. Sabotage. How? Easy. One mechanic engages Buck as he checks the fuel, while his accomplice on the other side of the plane loosens a few bolts. It would take less than a minute.

We set up our two tents in the dark and make Buck comfortable. Now that Harry is over his initial panic, he has taken to giving me a sullen stare whenever our eyes meet. I think he blames me for the mess we're in. Get over it, Harry. Stuff happens, especially when you're out in the middle of nowhere.

Fay avoids any conversation. She's usually upbeat, so her silence bothers me more than Harry's stare.

As we settle in, I'm left to wonder if the break in sound transmission to the Space Station has anything to do with the VLG malfunction. Planned together, or just coincidence? Did my Chinese contacts have anything to do with this? If so, I've been set up.

I try to shrug off our predicament. This mission is the chance of a lifetime. I'll find a way to Erebus, even if I have to hike.

2

FLASH AND BANG

If Joaquin hadn't glanced up at just that moment, he would have missed it. Just as he lifted his head, a flash of light pierced the valley rim. Five seconds later came a muffled bang. He froze, waiting for something else to happen. Nothing, not another peep.

He eased back onto Cisco and let the pony walk downhill at his own pace. Meantime, Joaquin squeezed his temples hard, trying to focus. Could it be a shooting star? Maybe a trick from the setting sun? But neither of those would explain the noise.

The sun was close to setting on the northwest horizon. Joaquin had spent the past hour on foot in the hills above camp, squinting for signs in the dirt. Thirsty and tired, he struggled to lead his pony and ignore the aching drag of his clubfoot.

He felt proud that the gaucho jeaf Aldo had sent him on a meaningful job, to seek out traces of four missing heifers. He found cattle tracks, but they were laced with horseshoe prints, which troubled him and could mean only one thing. Aldo figured as much: rustlers. Did the rustlers have rifles? Was that what made the noise? The thought made Joaquin shiver.

Didn't matter. He couldn't track more tonight anyway. He'd just have to tell Aldo and let him decide.

By the time Joaquin got to the outskirts of camp, it was full dark. He pointed Cisco toward the largest fire, where the other *charros* were sure to be eating supper. Near the edge of the herd, he came upon the blowhard Nestor at guard duty. Leaning forward on his saddle horn, he seemed half asleep, but when he spotted Joaquin, Nestor jerked up straight, turned to his right and fired off three high-pitched, loud whistles.

What's up with that? Nestor liked to pull crazy stuff just to taunt Joaquin.

The charro rubbed his scraggly whiskers. "Well, look who's here. Whaddya know, gimp?" That raspy voice sounded like grating metal on stone.

Joaquin's intuition told him not to mention the shoe prints, but he needed to say something to keep Nestor off that scent. "I saw a strange light drop down from the sky. A few miles away."

"Oh, you did? A fine scout you are." The snaky mouth twisted into a smirk.

"Don't you joke with me 'bout this stuff, charro. I'm gonna see what Aldo says." Joaquin huffed and spurred Cisco on toward the campfire.

Nestor shouted after him, "If he asks, I shall avow your diligence." The sarcasm made Joaquin's ears burn.

He found the rest of the gaucho crew scattered on the ground, backs propped up against their saddles, wolfing down their asado stew, tortillas mopping up the gravy. From the shouts, he could tell they already dipped into the pulce brew. Didn't matter. He had no plans to confide in them, not after Nestor's reaction.

Joaquin edged his way over to where Aldo sat hunched on his stool, apart from the younger charros. Already done with supper, he puffed on his pipe.

"Seir Aldo, I have important news to share with you." Joaquin's heart pounded like a runaway bull.

"It is good of you to show up, boy. I was beginning to worry." Aldo checked him up and down. "Plenty of time to recite your discoveries. Go fetch your share of stew before those pigs gobble it up." He pointed at the cauldron hanging over the fire.

Joaquin took a deep breath, then pulled the water gourd from his saddle and tossed a few spoonfuls of stew on the plate. He found a rock to sit on and tried to eat a nibble while watching for Aldo's signal.

The jeaf scrutinized him through a haze of smoke before speaking in his tight, throaty near whisper. "OK, kid, what has got you so worked up? Did you find the heifers?"

"I found their tracks, but something else happened. As the sun set, I saw a light just above the southern horizon." Joaquin pointed in the direction of Mt. Erebus. "The light moved along for a few seconds afore it disappeared ahind a bluff. Then I heard a bang." The story seemed to rush out of his mouth.

Aldo stuck out his lower lip, nodded. "Quite an account. What do you make of it?"

Ah. Aldo's interest was piqued. "I do not know, jeaf. I told Nestor on the way in. He laughed it away."

Aldo spat. "Nestor would joke about the death of his own mother."

"What do you think it is, seir?"

"Perhaps a heavenly body, a small meteor." The smoke around his face cleared. He knocked embers out of his pipe. "Nothing to worry about."

Joaquin shook his head. This was his chance. "What of the heifers, seir? Their tracks was mixed with hoss-shoe prints. They was all pointing that same direction."

"Oh, they were, eh?" Aldo gave him a hard stare.

Joaquin bobbed his head.

The jeaf slapped his thigh. "All right. Tomorrow morning, first thing. You shall guide the three of us to the spot."

"Three?" He nearly gagged, hoping he had Aldo's meaning wrong.

"You, me and Nestor. You already told him, remember? He has a rifle, in case we need a second one. And, I wish to see his reaction if we find any trace of those beeves."

Joaquin cursed himself again for having mentioned anything to Nestor. Allowing that blowhard to come along could mean nothing but trouble, extra rifle or not. And how did Nestor get a hold of such a treasure as a rifle? He told everyone he traded with his cousin, but what did a punk charro have to trade that was worth anything? Joaquin was not the only one to speculate.

Aldo pushed his big butt up and stretched. "Say nothing to the rest." He nodded toward the rowdy gauchos. By now, they were in a loud contest of after-dinner noises.

"Of course, jeaf." The thought of Nestor accompanying them on the morrow poisoned Joaquin's appetite. He stood up to empty his plate into the slop bucket. He expected that the charros were too far gone in their pulce fog to pay him any mind. No such luck. Behind him, he heard a jibe.

"What's the matter, kid? You look uptight."

Joaquin turned. The brothers Gabino and Soriante lay back on their elbows, at the edge of the campfire.

"Take a load off, boy. Here, have a shot." Soriante's arm waved the gourd holding the sour brew. "Tell us about your adventures today." Both of them guffawed.

Should he? Joaquin was half tempted. For only his second season on the range, Joaquin was already used to the gaucho routine. The challenge was to stay on good terms with the charros without slipping into their bad habits, drunkenness being only the most obvious.

He thought back to his state just last year, a skinny orphan with a clubfoot. No horse, but an acute yearning to ride one. During the winter off-season, he became the idle charros' gofer. Go fer this, go fer that. He made it his business to learn each of their habits, run their errands.

By the spring of the year he turned thirteen, he was desperate for a change. As the band of gauchos readied for the grazing season, he decided he could not face another long summer stuck at home in Nomidar with the young, the old, the lame, a few pregnant women, and the uncle who raised him. Yet he had no other prospects.

Then his luck turned. A neighbor boy who died of consumption willed Joaquin his pony. As he groomed Cisco a few days later, Aldo Correon rode up. The jeaf offered to let him ride with the herd, to be his "eyes and ears," as he said. Joaquin figured that Uncle Fermin would object, or at least expect Aldo to pay him. Being the gaucho jeaf, he must be loaded. Instead, his uncle just swiped his hand, like shooing away a stray dog.

Sure, the charros picked on him with no mercy, but Joaquin thanked his lucky stars each night to be among them. Yet his relationship with Aldo was key, and he would do nothing to jeopardize that.

"Thanks for the offer, fellas, but I better turn in." He faked a yawn. "I'm bushed."

She had been obsessed with the ring of violet running along the rim of the crater ever since first dreaming of it months ago. The crater, however, was tucked on the west side of a neighboring valley, and by the time Luz arrived, it was too dark to make out the subtle details of the peculiar layer of rock that she sought. Yet another roadblock. Luz whipped the horse's reins around and headed back. She would have to return in the morning to get a good look at it.

***

Today, Luz left camp at dawn, before her mother could awaken and stop her. Riding through the morning chill, Luz yawned, the effects of a sleepless night. All the hills slumbered in darkness, save for the western peaks. Not a sound but for that of her heated mare, swatting through the brush. Quintara's nostrils steamed as Luz pushed her up that last stretch to the crater rim.

Scruffy Flaco ran alongside, bounding ahead as fast as his measly little legs would take him. He showed no interest in small game, but then he was getting too old to give chase. Every thirty paces or so, the dog froze and stared. But at what? Nothing moved beyond fluttering stems of grass.

Luz felt only a teeny bit guilty filching a small stone hammer and cast-iron chisel from among her mother's tools. She needed enough time to explore the ring, to whack out pieces of the violet stone and compare them to the samples in her mother's scant supply.

At the crest of the hill, Luz paused to scour the outline of the crater. "Splat," she called it, like when a drop of water struck dry ground. Perhaps as much as a mile across, different layers of rock stretched on edges at least three times as tall as she. The one she was after was her own length, however. All the layers angled upward, but this one shone with a darker, more distinctive luster.

Luz held her breath as the first light crossed the mountaintops to glisten on the crater. Where the other layers appeared just as brighter shades of blue-gray, brown, or orange, this violet layer slowly altered, revealing a rainbow-like quality, sparkling with color. Its multi-hued effect mimicked the iris stone.

Could this really be the source of the piedra de yris? Luz needed to inspect the rock closer, but then Quintara jerked at the bridle, and Luz realized that, in her eagerness, she tightened the reins too hard. She loosened her grip and patted the mare's flank.

As she scanned the shade along the crater floor for a spot to dig, she noticed something out of place. Three-quarters of a mile away, toward the far end of the crater, sat a large object, the shape of a giant bird. Despite the dim light, the object shone like silver.

Luz could hardly believe her eyes. It definitely was not there yesterday. Next to the giant bird stood two other objects, roughly the size and shape of yurts, but glistening too much to be made of skins.

The bird-like thing did not move. Just sitting in the gloom, it seemed spooky strange. If it were alive, it must be a kind of monster, taking a moment's rest. Was it even breathing? Luz chewed her lip, waiting for the monster to exhale. Any kind of movement at all, and she would jump onto Quintara and hurry back to her camp.

But did monsters come in the shape of birds? If so, it would be useless to try and escape. Luz pictured the silver bird's hawkish eyes spotting her, raising its wings, and soaring off the crater floor, then swooping down seconds later to grab her, Quintara and Flaco as they tried to flee. They'd be trapped like mice in its mighty talons.

Luz shook her head and glanced down at Flaco, but he just wagged his tail. She must be losing it. Bird monsters!

Yet, if the thing was not a living creature, what else might it be? The stories told how the land used to be covered with ice, inhabited by flightless black and white birds. Yoka Sutu, the old woman who recited these tales, knew of other lands as well where people used to travel long distances before the Great Migrations, using machines instead of horses. Certain of these machines even flew through the air.

Could this be such a flying machine? If so, there would be people nearby. The thought of other people propelled by this, their creation, excited Luz; better an engine than a monster, but what race of people could fashion and navigate such a thing?

Just as this idea occurred to her, she spotted movement. The giant bird made the figures appear as teeny as mice, somehow balancing on their hind legs. After walking around in a seemingly random pattern, they convened together face to face.

Luz dismounted from Quintara, led the mare a way back down the hill, and tied the reins to a branch. She sat down and took a drink from her gourd. Her bravado of a moment ago dissipated in a cold shiver. Should she skirt around to the far edge of the crater for a closer look, or just go back for help? In any case, she wasn't going to let these aliens find her here alone.

As she turned back to untie Quintara, she spied three riders approaching from the direction of camp. A quarter mile away, Luz could make out the barrel-chested form of Aldo Correon. She thanked the Spirits in silence. Aldo would discern what to do. But then she recognized Nestor and shivered again. Why were they here so early in the morning? Surely not searching for stray beeves.

The third figure, smaller and riding a pony, must be Joaquin. The gauchos still treated him with disdain, but he seemed used to that. To the rest of the tribe, he was their mascot, being an orphan and all. Luz's Uncle Ariel made him a pair of fine studded boots, customized to fit his clubfoot, for the price of Joaquin's paltry first-year's earnings, half of what they were worth.

Joaquin spied Luz before the others, waved, and trotted his pony toward her.

"What's up?" Luz noted that Aldo and Nestor packed their rifles. "Are you hunting?"

"In a way, yes. I saw a light last night."

"A light? In the sky or on the ground?"

Joaquin rocked his head back and forth. "Both, sort of. And I heard a bang come from over this hill."

They all pulled up in front of Luz but remained mounted. Aldo reached for his gourd and took a long swallow. Beads of water glistened on his graying mustache. Nestor ogled Luz with his usual leer, made all the more grotesque by a new growth of scraggly whiskers.

Luz tried to ignore him. They were on her turf now. "Yesterday, I visited a crater on the other side of this hill. I came back this morning to hunt for a certain kind of rock." She pursed her lips. Enough said in front of Nestor and Aldo. Nestor could never keep his mouth shut, and what spilled out of it would be as twisted as a snake.

Aldo was more complicated, more intriguing. She admired his horsemanship, of course, but also his respectful bearing. He assisted her numerous times with Quintara, once having spent several days using herbal poultices to treat the mare for a bout of pneumonia. Yet, it seemed to Luz, Aldo kept his thoughts and feelings in reserve. She sought to emulate his proud air on horseback, but despite observing her often, he never offered a compliment.

The jeaf spoke. "Well then, you shall be our guide, Seirita Luz." No trace of sarcasm. "With your permission." The words came out surprisingly soft for such a big man. Lately, one must strain to hear him.

"Of course." Luz felt relieved. "But listen, you must be careful." Nestor grunted and patted the stock of his rifle. What an idiot. Aldo's frown told her he must have the same thought.

She met their eyes, one by one. "Dismount before you go any farther. Walk up to the crest and look toward the far end of the crater."

Aldo regarded Luz for a minute, then arched his brows and nodded for them all to dismount. She held the horses' reins. Joaquin scrambled up the hill first, followed by Nestor. Aldo panted, bringing up the rear.

"Oh, wow." Joaquin scanned the crater. "I see what you mean. Look how shiny..."

"Keep your voice low." Nestor pulled him down to a squat. "It may hear us."

Aldo alone remained standing as he watched, leaning one arm on a boulder. His coarse whisper sounded even more strained. "It cannot hear a thing. It is not alive. But those small figures moving around, those are human and they may have weapons." He stared for another minute. "They definitely are not of our people. And it, that thing that looks like a giant bird, must be a flying machine. Look how it gleams silver as the sun catches it."

Luz tied the horses' reins to a bush and scrambled to the top of the hill. What she saw now in full light took her breath away. "See, it gleams as bright as the ring of purple on the crater's rim." She tried to keep her voice calm.

"And what might that mean, seirita?" Aldo removed the floppy wool boina from his head and wiped his brow.

"I... I'm not sure. That purple ring contains the rock that I am hunting for. I, we, think it might be the same stone as, as..." Her stammering left both Aldo and Nestor staring.

"As what, Luz?" said Aldo. "And who is 'we'?"

"My mother and I. The same as she uses to fashion her jewelry."

"Ah, the stunning iris stone." Aldo shielded his eyes as he scanned the crater again. "That ring on the rim of the crater, it would not surprise me if it were the same as your mother uses. But she trades for it, no?"

Luz nodded and averted her gaze, not wishing to mention the trader's disappearance.

Aldo watched Luz for a moment before turning back to study the crater. "So, who cares to venture a guess about this flying machine? What makes it shine so brightly? Who are these Sky-Borne strange ones who flew it here? What do they want?"

No one answered. Nestor shook his head slowly, keeping his eyes on the ground. Joaquin's gaze jumped from face to face, but he just shrugged. Luz stayed silent, too confused to speak.

Aldo stood up straight. His breathing slowed. "Alright. Here's what we do. Joaquin, you stay here with Seirita Luz for now."

Joaquin pouted, glaring at him.

"Listen, kid," said Aldo, "your job is just as important as Nestor's and mine. If harm befalls us, you two must ride back to camp and warn the others. Got that?"

"Yes, seir."

"You can watch us from here, but keep low so the Sky-Bornes do not see you. Once we meet them, wait fifteen minutes. If you do not hear any gunshots, we should be safe, and you may both approach with caution."

Joaquin started to mutter his objection, but Luz nodded and motioned him to hush up. He might wish to go greet these aliens, but she felt content to leave the initial confrontation to armed men.

Yet, as Aldo and Nestor stepped down the hill, Luz's heart pounded again. She pictured Aldo and Nestor being drawn by an invisible force toward this giant bird monster, so powerful that it could reel in its prey without even the need to chase it. As if awaiting this fate, Nestor now sat slumped in his saddle, shoulders hunched, eyes darting to and fro. Aldo alone remained ramrod straight.

When they came within a hundred yards of the flying machine, the standing figures stopped moving their bundles to gawk at the riders. Luz counted four people. Aldo and Nestor slowed to a walk. At fifty feet, they stopped. No one moved for several moments.

Joaquin sucked his breath in. "What'll they do now? Them strangers, do they even speak our tongue?"

A big lump filled Luz's throat. "If they are smart enough to build a flying machine and come here from afar, they must have thought about meeting people like us. Either they have a plan of how to communicate, or..."

"Or what?"

"Or... let's not talk about it." She squeezed her eyes shut.

"Don't be scared, Luz. Aldo will find a way."

"Oh yes, I'm sure he will, if Nestor doesn't do something stupid first." They both tried to laugh.

As if in response, a gunshot rang out. Flaco's ears shot up. Luz and Joaquin froze, then glanced at each other.

Joaquin made to turn and head for their mounts. "Let's get out of here."

shoes were equally sturdy, as if ready for outdoor work. She sat on the ground by herself in the shadow of the flying machine, mug in hand, posing a slightly bemused expression. Though her posture made no effort to act welcoming, neither did she seem afraid or hostile, just... detached.

Well, then, let her be. Luz turned her attention to the tall, broad-shouldered, tanned and square-chinned man closest to them. His wavy yellow hair crowned a bandage wrapped around his forehead. He sat leaning forward, arms resting on his knees, a mug also in his hand. The others pushed their wraparound sunshades up to their hair, but the blond man kept his perched on his nose, like a giant insect. Finally, he fixed his gaze upon Luz and removed them.

She gasped. Squinting into the sun left deep creases around his eyes, but the color: deep blue, you could drown in them, just like those of her boyfriend, Ian. On instinct, she fingered her onyx belt buckle, Ian's pledge offering from when last they met at the Rendezvous. But that only brought up bittersweet memories of the scant days they could spend together, all of one week a year. They were, in truth, from different tribes on opposite sides of the continent. She blinked hard, trying to put Ian out of mind, trying to force her gaze away from his lookalike.

Peeking at the blond man from the corner of her eye, Luz guessed that he must have been the one to rile Nestor. His stare could be unnerving, but every few seconds, the stare wandered off, as if his mind could not concentrate. That, plus the bandage, suggested a recent blow to the head.

Luz and her companions dismounted and approached on foot. Flaco stayed by the horses, tail pointing straight back. The strangers and Aldo sat on a mat in the shade of the flying machine, Aldo puffing on his pipe to put them at ease. Luz realized he must be nervous, but he acted the soul of calm. She waited for Nestor to pick a spot before finding her own, a good distance away.

The other woman noticed Joaquin's limp and fetched another stool. She carried it like poles fastened to cloth, but when she opened it, it became a seat. How handy. Before Luz knew it, this woman whisked out another stool for her as well. She nodded her thanks.

Unlike her mate, no one could mistake the sex of this woman. Curvy but nimble, she seemed like the only one of the bunch who cared about her appearance: a wide-brimmed straw hat and a dark half-sleeved yellow dress of the same fine texture as the men's clothes; a wide reddish-brown leather belt that matched her sandals; a shiny oversized crimson bracelet dangling on her left wrist; with fingernails, toenails and mouth painted red.

The woman's eyes flitted back and forth between her guests, and her hands beckoned them. She gave the impression of a party hostess, grossly out of place among her wary comrades.

As much as these people transfixed Luz, she could not help but notice their tents as well. They stood at an angle to each other, their material shiny but thicker than the Sky-Bornes' clothing. One tent glimmered blue, the other orange, both brighter than any pigment Luz ever saw. They seemed out of place against the muted tan of the crater floor, like the banners of an invading tribe. Was that the goal of these four aliens, to scout out this land for some advancing army? If so, they seemed an ill-fitted lot.

Just then, a passing breeze billowed the sides of the orange tent, overlapping any number of small packs tucked close by. Now it reminded Luz more of a mother hen protecting her brood. She let her suspicions relax, for the moment.

The second man, despite having no wounds, seemed less healthy than his companion. Older, average height, and stocky, he stood crookedly, as if on mismatched legs. A golden strand of wire sat on his nose, split around each eye and ran back to his ears. Within the wire were magnifiers for the eyes, but even with these, he squinted in the bright sunlight. Despite the early hour, this man's skin shone bright pink. Clearly, he was not used to the outdoors.

His gaze darted back and forth between the faces of his own foursome and these strangers, as if he expected more trouble and might have to head it off in a hurry. Though none of the Sky-Bornes brandished weapons, and Aldo had stashed both his own and Nestor's rifle in his pack, Luz suspected that the older man's brain busily gauged the chances of this friendly encounter turning hostile. Several times, she caught him glancing at the small-busted woman, and each time he did so, the corners of his mouth turned down. Regardless, the small woman paid him no attention. Luz smiled to herself.

The older man brought out more mugs and a steaming pot, which sat on a flame inside a metal container on the ground. He poured a brown liquid from the pot into the mugs, which released a strange but inviting smell. After adding white crystals and stirring, the man passed a mug to Aldo. The jeaf studied the brew and sniffed for a long time before lifting his chin at the curly-haired man, daring him to drink first, which he did. At this, Aldo took a sip, nodded, and took another.

The curly-haired man smiled, handing mugs to his other three guests. Joaquin took a sip, grimaced, and stuck his tongue out. The woman in the dress laughed.

"Joaquin, that is not good manners," Luz said, frowning. She tried a sip of the strong brew. More bitter than yerba maté, the white crystals acted as a sweetener and partly masked the taste. She tried more out of politeness, forcing herself to swallow. Perhaps these people needed a stimulant, but why drink such a disgusting beverage socially?

As she sipped, Luz stole another glance at the flying machine. Its weight sagged on the left side. That wheel appeared considerably flatter than the wheel opposite, and its black surface duller. These people must have had a mishap. Between the flattened wheel of their flying machine and the bandage on the blond man's head, these people were already in trouble. No wonder their curly-haired leader acted worried.

This same cautious man brought out a plate of biscuits and passed them around, careful to let everyone see him eat one first. Joaquin hesitated with his first bite, but then grabbed several more before the plate passed from his reach. Luz just grunted her disapproval.

The bold, dressy woman sidled close to Aldo, squatting to face him as she held a small metal box. Its top shone with tiny red dots that changed shape every time someone nearby spoke. She tried several short phrases on Aldo, who nodded with his sly smile, as if he understood. But Luz knew Aldo's reputation as a ladies' man, and she suspected he was just egging the woman on.

The brash woman pointed to the sun, the domes, the flying machine. After naming each of these things in her tongue, she invited Aldo to say their names in Onwei. He obliged. Each time he would say a phrase, she would study the face of her box hopefully, but whatever shape she wished the red dots to assume, it continued to elude her.

She walked to Nestor, Joaquin, and Luz in turn, bidding them to name other objects using the Onwei tongue, but none of them could make the box sing the dressy woman's tune. Finally, she lay the contraption aside, took off her straw hat and tossed her head back and forth, shaking her graying, reddish-brown curls. A moment later, she straightened up and beamed. She reminded Luz of those young charros on the hunt for pretty girls at the Rendezvous. Don't be put off; sooner or later your reward will come.

Now the stylish woman pointed to herself and said what sounded like "Orfea." She gestured to her older companion to do likewise. He said what sounded like "Harry." That sound was hard to mimic. When the blond man's turn came, he poked himself in the chest and barked: "Buck." That one was easy.

Last came the turn of the small woman, sitting there as quiet as a mouse. Her eyes flitted around as she pointed to herself, whispering, "Keltyn." Luz and her mates practiced this beautiful sound, though Nestor managed to botch it into a mumble.

Orfea gestured to her guests, their turn. When it came around to Aldo, he tipped his boina with a flourish. Orfea threw back her head and grinned. She pointed to Luz's dog. By now, he was busy sniffing the tents.

When Luz said "Flaco," Orfea laughed. She spoke to the three others, pointing at the scrawny mutt until they too laughed. "Flaco" must be a funny word in an old tongue that she knew.

Aldo turned to his three younger companions. "This woman Orfea, I think that she has a gift for tongues and could learn ours, even without the help of her worthless machine. What a shame that no one can interpret."

Luz jumped in. "Yoka Sutu might be able to understand her. She has studied languages used by the ancestors."

None of the charros gave the old woman any respect. Even as Luz mentioned her name, she had misgivings. For the past five years, Yoka had tried to recruit her as a disciple for her strange and demanding Venga ritual. Luz feigned interest, and, truth be told, wanted to experiment on her own, but Yoka insisted on proper training or not at all, so there the matter lay.

True to form, Nestor smirked at mention of the crone. It was all Luz could manage to stifle a scowl, for fear of egging Nestor on. She turned to Aldo. Unless she could convince him, they would never learn the purpose of the Sky-Bornes' appearance.

Aldo hesitated. "You may be right, seirita, but Yoka is too old to ride here on horseback. Besides, we must escort these people to our camp. Whatever the reason for their journey, the others will need to hear about it." He put his hand on his hip, tilted his head back, and sniffed. "I can see Yoka divining her Venga potions now, trying to decipher this turn of events."

He turned to Nestor. "Head back to camp, borrow four mounts, and bring spare packs. Do not tell anyone of our Sky-Borne visitors, understand?"

Nestor didn't move. "What about my rifle, jeaf?"

Aldo stood, jaw clenched, staring Nestor down for a long minute. "Take it, but mind you, no more idle threats." He peered at Buck, fidgeting in his seat, adjusting his squint. "That one looks to spook as quickly as you, charro."

Nestor stalked over to Aldo's stallion, retrieved the gun, and shot a mocking glare at Buck. The large blond man slipped his hand into his jacket pocket. Luz stiffened. Did he have his own weapon?

Harry leaned over to grab Buck's arm. He said something under his breath as they both kept a hawk's eye on Nestor.

Nestor jerked his head toward the jeaf, as if to say, "I told you." Without another glance, he stashed the rifle in his pack, mounted, and spurred his horse back the way they came.

Luz let out a long, deep breath. The morning's events were more than she bargained for. Her instincts about this crater were right, but not for the reason she supposed. What's more, Aldo listened to her advice. Something important was going on here, and she intended to stay in its midst.

5

MIXED COMPANY

That creep Nestor is supposed to bring back extra horses. Good. I'm gonna need one to scout the volcano. I have to bide my time, though. First, big Aldo has "invited" us to visit his camp. Fay's our social director, excuse me, our liaison for the locals. If I didn't know better, I'd swear that all her banter naming things was an excuse to flirt with their leader. She seems to think we all need to meet the rest of the tribe. Thanks, but no thanks. Whatever mount they bring me, I have a mind to point it toward Erebus first thing tomorrow.

For a few minutes, we just sit and drink coffee. Then the tall girl, Luz, catches my gaze, a gleam in her eye. She gets up and rummages through her horse's saddlebags, pulling out a hammer and chisel. Well, I'll be damned! Is she a rock-smith too? I jump up and whip off my sunshades for a better look. I head back to the blue tent — Fay and I share it — and pull out my own tools, specimen bag, and several chunks of stone that I chipped off the violet ring on the crater's edge this morning. It was iridium, all right, just not metallurgic grade.

I hand them to the girl and she stares at me, mouth agape. She turns over the rocks in her hands, holding them up, then points toward the ring on the crater's edge. I nod.

So, she's interested in iridium, too. What on earth for? Can there be any kind of industry around here? It's different for us; our plane's shell is layered with the stuff to resist the caustic chemical soup of the Hurricane Belt. It reflects the sun's rays like a mirror.

I point to the silver-colored hull and hold up the rock. Luz nods slowly. She seems to get it. She pulls out a small amulet, with all the facets of a gem. So that's it. One of her people is a jeweler and has managed to separate the ore and burnish the pure stone until it sparkles.

Wow. I never would have guessed that the stone could be used for jewelry. It's so brittle. How do they do it? I take the gem and bounce it between my hands, like it's just been retrieved from the fire. Obviously, this rock is purer than the stuff I chipped off the edge of the crater.

Harry wanders over to have a look. He turns the amulet back and forth several times, raising it to the light.

I need to seize the moment. "Harry, this is the real deal. It's not from this crater. It must have come from Erebus."

He hands the gem back to Luz, but his mood is no brighter. "Maybe it is, but we're stuck here..." He glowers at me, and my mind finishes the part he doesn't say: "thanks to you."

Luz's eyes light up. She raises both hands, points toward Erebus, points at the rock specimens, points at me and then at herself. She mimics the motion of riding a horse toward the volcano.

I chew my lip and think, then hold up my palm toward Luz, trying to keep her from getting her hopes up. No question, Erebus is the place to look, but pairing up with a teenage girl I can't even talk to? That would just be asking for trouble. I do better work solo.

After a minute, the girl's enthusiasm seems to wane. Her shoulders slump as she goes to deposit the rock back into her pack. She can't be more than seventeen. Probably needs her mother's permission. Mama knows best.

Harry plops down, digs in his pack for a pain patch, and reaches under the back of his shirt. He shifts around on his stool, adjusts his eyepieces. The circles under his eyes have deepened. He projects unease, like a cow separated from the herd.

What does he liken this place to? Black lava litters the sandy crater floor. Multicolored layers of rock line the crater's edge. Hills on every horizon, the panorama dominated by the bulk of Erebus, itself capped by wisps of smoke floating into the cloudless blue sky. It's not your green homeland of Quebec, Harry.

Do I dare run off to scout Erebus without Harry's permission? If only we landed on target. I have to play it by ear, learn the lay of this land.

Truth is, this place is like nowhere I've ever been, and believe me, I've been to some strange places. Here, in the midst of this desolate crater in the middle of nowhere, Luz still juggles my stone samples.

Soon, Nestor returns with four more horses. Buck insists on staying behind to rest. Aldo doesn't object, probably figures that anyone acting as weird as Buck might provoke others besides Nestor.

Getting bonked hasn't done much for Buck's analytic skills. He stumbles over to the broken wheel, baffled, twisting toward his left, studying the damage like a little bird fretting over a bigger one, both of them wounded. Right now, he's way too unsteady to perform any task. Who knows how long that will last?

Harry catches me studying Buck and scowls again. Yeah, you could blame the whole crash on my wrong advice. Just let me go crawl into a hole. No such luck. Now Fay scowls at me too. I guess it won't do to leave half our party behind when we're supposed to present ourselves to the locals. Reluctantly, I mount up with the rest of them.

***

We near their camp by early afternoon, the three of us in the company of four of them. We're not hostages, not prisoners. I don't know what you would call our status now, but we do have an escort. Fay and Harry don't seem concerned, so I guess I shouldn't be either. I'm along for the ride, doing my social duty, waiting for the right time to break off.

But, there's a glitch. The way Nestor fussed when he handed us the reins — it's clear that they belong to other gauchos who weren't too thrilled to lend them out, even for a few hours. So, I can't just take off on my own. They would track me down pronto, and then we'd all be toast. I need to find someone who can spare a horse for several days.

Right now, though, this sun is way too bright, and there's precious little shade. I turn to Fay and hold up my sunshades. "Okay to put these back on?"

She shrugs and fishes her shades out too. So what if they make us look like giant flies?

"What do you figure Aldo's got planned for us, Fay?" She's the anthropologist, so she ought to know.

"Oh, I expect he'll parade us through camp, let his people see that we're not dangerous, make introductions. No doubt there will be a meal involved."

"He's not planning to keep us overnight, is he?"

"I doubt it. We didn't bring gear."

Up ahead, Harry begins grunting. He's having a tough time controlling his stallion. Its head bobs from side to side. Aldo rides close enough to Harry to steady his horse if need be, but his only reaction to Harry's clumsiness is a twitch at the corner of his mustache. He must aim to let the poor guy learn from his own mistakes.

After several minutes of watching Harry make a fool of himself, I can't stand it anymore. "Loosen up on the reins, chief." I learned how to ride years ago, but never dreamt I would need to get around Antarctica on horseback.

Fay, Luz, and I trail behind the men, with that mutt Flaco alongside. Luz points out various objects as we pass, phrasing them in her strange tongue. Fay repeats each word several times, making it sound like a song.

The first person we run into is another big gaucho — a younger version of Aldo — walking his horse around the edge of the herd, rounding up stray beeves. Joaquin calls out to show off his new buddies. The big guy sits motionless. Whatever he mutters doesn't sound complimentary. We pass other gauchos, their faces running the gamut from wild-eyed to sullen. No one challenges us, thanks to Aldo.

I'd feel embarrassed if I were in their shoes. There's no escape from the smell of manure. It hangs over camp like a blanket of ripe hollow fog. Horse manure or cattle manure, my nose might tell the difference up close, but elsewhere they blend like bad relish. I suppose you can block it out if you stick around long enough, like ignoring the crick in your back from sleeping on a canvas cot, or the fine layer of dust caked on your skin. The difference is, here you won't be rid of the crick or the dust until the season is over.

Harry turns his head to avoid the stink. Fay yells, "Breathe through your mouth." A moment later, he starts flailing at a swarm of flies. The horses' tails swoosh nonstop. This encampment is one dusty, smelly mess.

The sun disappears behind a cloud, and I start to shiver. We splash across the creek that separates the gauchos from the camp followers. The women stand in front of their yurts, chattering to each other. A few run forward to get a better look.

Aldo motions for Nestor and Joaquin to stop as we pull up at a shady grove of cottonwoods. As Aldo explains the turn of events, gauchos, women, and children inch closer. Fay signals for us to remove our sunshades, the better to be inspected.

It's a strange feeling to be the "other." I should be used to it after living in China for two years, but it's still unnerving for someone who wants to fly below the radar. Social isn't my normal thing, I'll admit it. I'm taking it all in, but not going out of my way to be friendly.

What are they thinking? Some react with cautious smiles, others with hard stares. A feebleminded woman catches my eye and sticks out her tongue. Young children giggle and point. What's the matter, kid? Never seen a monkey in the zoo before?

Luz starts using gestures, trying to coax me away from the others, wants me to follow her. Sure. Anything's better than this.

We pass a bunch of sourpuss older women. They turn away, but not before sizing me up. They're icy toward young Luz too. Maybe she skipped out on chores. I gather we're heading toward her place. Perhaps her family will have that extra mount I need.

The women keep their modest hide yurts tidy in comparison to the gauchos' mess. Most of them string ropes between yellow willow tree branches to hang the wash. Coarse gray wool rugs hang everywhere. Several hefty old gals swat them with brooms, raising more dust.

We approach what I assume is Luz's yurt at the end of a row. Washed sheets hang out to dry. Rugs have been dragged out and a broom lies beside the open door. Amidst all this stands a middle-aged woman, frail, much shorter than Luz, and dressed in a tan hemp shift. She squints at Mt. Erebus. Is she daydreaming or just tired? A bone barrette anchors her gray-streaked hair. Her face darkens as she spots Luz, and she lets into her daughter, pointing at the rugs. Her hands make this brushing-away motion. Yep, Luz was supposed to clean house this morning. She's in for it now.

But the girl seems prepared. She jumps off and rushes to embrace her mother. Spills her story a mile a minute. The woman's squint shifts to me.

Exactly her height, I stand in front of her and bow my head. She points to herself and says her name, sounds like "Trieste." Too wound up to make the introduction, Luz keeps on reciting the morning's events. I look around. No sign of a man in this family.

Trieste claps her hands to her ears and makes us sit. She looks at me, pulls her hand toward her face, and opens her mouth. I nod. She retrieves food from a storage tent nearby, spreads out a bundle of what might be cow's tongue, tortillas in which to wedge the meat slices, and a dish of salsa. An earthenware jug with fresh milk stands nearby.

Can't say that I have a taste for exotic foods, but I learned to adapt as a grad student in Siberia. This looks fresh by comparison, but Trieste serves it cold. No sign of firewood. The gauchos have a campfire going with what smells like dried cow dung. Of course, they're stuck on the other side of the creek.

Luz picks at her food. Trieste's head bends down as she nibbles, but she keeps peeking at me. I pretend to be engaged in my tortilla wrap. Does she wonder how I managed to hook up with this expedition? I don't look that much older than Luz. I'm sure they also want to know why their gemstone is so important to us that we would risk our lives to find it. Good thing I can't speak their language — how could I explain it? Would I even try?

After the meal, the three of us sip our milk until Luz abruptly sits up straight, all serious. Trieste stares at her, arches her brows, mutters a phrase. Sounds like what Luz called the stone earlier: piedra de yris.

Sighing, Trieste eyes me and taps her skull, like she's got her daughter all figured out. Luz flushes, turns toward me. Then she slowly faces her mother with another plea, reaching her arm toward me.

Trieste throws me a glance halfway between icy and curious. Keeps eyeing me as Luz continues her pitch. Luz says something that makes Trieste gape. She points to the volcano with a questioning look at her daughter, who barely manages to nod.

Still pointing at the mountain, Trieste turns to me to confirm this insane request.

I've got to humor her, act like the voice of reason. Why would I want Luz along on this expedition? I look Trieste in the eye and run one pointer finger over the back of the other, hoping she understands that signal of naughty behavior.

Luz slaps her hands on her hips, aghast, and lapses into a pout.

"Hmph." Trieste smirks, bends down to remove the food. She stands with her hands full and shakes her head slowly. No dice, Luz.

Abetting the whims of a teenage kid against her mother's wishes is the last thing I need to get mixed up in right now. If anything goes wrong up there, it's not just her mother who'll be pissed, it'll be the whole tribe. Another screw-up, after misgauging the landing conditions, and Harry will ground me for sure.

Besides, I just met the girl today. Now, about that horse...

6

ASADO

Fay and Harry, both still mounted, followed Joaquin through camp, past the stares of women and children. From her years of field anthropology, Fay was used to this sort of reaction. She kept her head high, beamed a smile and tried to make eye contact. She had been right all along; here was a whole race of people who had survived global warming by moving south. She resisted the temptation to gloat.

The first step was to establish communication. She hoped that the person Joaquin was leading them toward would be that link. They passed through the cottonwoods into a clearing. On its far edge stood a modest yurt. A shrunken Black woman sat on a stool in front of a loom. Fay sucked in a breath. Surely this old hag wasn't the intermediary whom the chieftain Aldo had in mind.

The crone lumbered to her feet. By way of greeting, she clapped her palms together slowly. The corners of her lips turned up ever so slightly as Harry caught his foot in the stirrup while dismounting and almost tumbled on his face.

Fay stepped down carefully, approached, and made a slight bow. She bent to pet the old black setter spread out at this woman's feet. The hag stood with her hands clasped until Fay bid her to lead on. She glanced at Harry, his face still beet-red from fighting his mount. He dropped onto the nearest stool.

Fay pointed at her own chest and mouthed her name. The crone responded with what sounded like "Yoka." No teeth behind those shriveled lips.

Fay waited for Yoka to make the next move, but the old woman remained standing. Fay spread her palm until Yoka signaled her to follow. As they wandered around, Joaquin tagged along behind, his hands clasped behind his back. Was the boy just curious, or did he feel important for having brought the two of them together?

Fay pointed at the yurt, the rocker, the smoldering campfire, and Yoka named each of these things. They stopped in front of the crone's hemp loom. She gestured between her frock and the loom, eyes shut with a smug nod.

Fay noticed the color of her sandals matched her purple frock, and wiggled her finger between the two. On a hunch, she uttered "*morad,*" the Spanish word for purple. This provoked a startle from Yoka, and the same response when Fay named the color of her yellow dress and brown belt in Spanish. Yoka stopped, deep in thought. She pointed to her black skin and Fay's white skin. Hearing the names for these, the crone exposed a toothless grin. She motioned Fay to sit on another rickety stool, and then brought out sun tea, biscuits and a spread before plopping down into a creaky rocker.

Good, I've stirred her interest, thought Fay. She reached into her bag for the lang-synch machine.

***

Joaquin was intrigued by this shiny little box of Orfea's, but her failure to get any results earlier that day suggested it would take some time here, even though Yoka knew languages other than Onwei. He might as well report back to Aldo. When he rose, Fay beckoned him, handed him a pouch, and let him sniff it. He reeled back as a shot exploded in his nostrils, rousing some deep part of his brain more profoundly than could the brightest flower or the loudest thunder. The likes of this potent magic he had never imagined, let alone sampled. How did she plan to use it? She laughed, wrapped up the pouch, handed it to him. "For Aldo."

He found the jeaf telling his story to Efrain, his big gaucho nephew. Joaquin showed him the pouch. "Seir, this is from the woman Orfea. Would she wish to poison us?"

Aldo stuck his big nose in, shot up his brow. "Some strange concoction, perhaps her offering with which to season the veal." A twinkle flashed in his eye. "Let us prepare two cuts of asado and let the Sky-Bornes sample theirs first."

Joaquin hurried to the firepot. The yearling picked by the charros was slaughtered and already prepared for the feast. Three of the quarters they rubbed down with the regular chimichurri relish: parsley, oregano, garlic, salt, chili pepper, onion and paprika. Now they kneaded the last quarter with the exotic blend from Orfea's pouch, then skewed all the meat on asadores. They staked the crosses of metal rods high over the coals to keep the grease from spattering, then sat back and passed the pulce jug around. Joaquin whittled sticks at his tent, biding his own time. He could hardly wait to see how the charros reacted during this feast, and how this potent rub would affect the Sky-Bornes.

A thick layer of clouds hung over the sky by the time the gaucho sampling the veal finally okayed it. In line to get their share, each of the charros stuck with the chimichurri version. Soon, loud belches of satisfaction echoed around Joaquin.

Harry and Orfea each carried a plate full of their own meat, along with root vegetables. They sat on stools next to Aldo around one side of the campfire. Joaquin watched as they nibbled, waiting for signs of unease. If the mixture in Orfea's bag contained some kind of poison, and she had wished to trick them into rubbing on all the meat, Aldo had called her bluff. Yet they seemed to enjoy every bite. Presently, Aldo arose to sample this last quarter of veal himself. He nodded his approval until Joaquin himself could resist no longer. An intoxicating tingle greeted his palate on the first bite, and his suspicions gradually relaxed.

Orfea tried just itty-bitty sips of the pulce brew before hiding her mug away, but Harry was a different story. Gabino sat himself next to Harry and kept refilling the poor fellow's mug before raising his own to toast anything and everything. Harry kept bending his elbow, clueless as to what they were toasting. He'll be sorry, thought Joaquin. That stuff packs a punch.

The younger charros, watching Orfea from a bit farther away, made sly jokes to each other, punctuated by hoots and snickers. As far as Joaquin could tell, the jokes didn't bother her a bit. In fact, her playful gestures made it clear that she relished the attention. So different from most of the women who Joaquin knew. What was she after? Not compliments. He sensed that her behavior was a way to defuse the tension, as if opening herself would make them feel more comfortable in her presence, just like at their first encounter in the crater.

Around the time raindrops started to fall, the windbag Soriante took up a yodel.

> *"A charro's life is rough but sweet,*
> *He swings a rope and lands on his feet*
> *He walks bowlegged, his knees never meet*
> *O bolo leh, eh ee oh, eh ee oh,*
> *O bolo leh, eh ee oh.*
> *A charro he loves to sleep on the ground,*
> *The bawling of cows is his favorite sound,*
> *A crazier job will never be found."*

This time, Harry joined in on the yodel refrain. Soriante flashed a wolf's grin at the boys as he started the third verse, much slower.

> *"When out of the saddle he's ready to fall,*
> *A pretty young girl does turn to his call,*
> *And together into the sack they do crawl,"*

Now he ran with it.

> *"O bolo leh, eh ee oh, eh ee oh.*
> *O bolo leh, eh ee oh."*

More guffaws, more swags of pulce for the gauchos. Aldo's half-brother Ysidro, perched on a log off to the side, got up and staggered to the middle of the circle. His fingers wiped his whiskers, the salt-and-pepper scrub that formed a shallow "U" on each side of his jaw, meeting above the lip but leaving his chin bare. He raised his mug and cocked his head in the direction of the Sky-Bornes. "A toast to our guests." His body rocked back and forth as he slowly lifted his head, addressing the rain clouds. "May they have nothing to fear from us, nor we from them."

He held his mug at arm's length and fanned it round at everyone. "May this encounter signal a season of good fortune for the Nomidar Tribe." His arm stopped when the mug pointed at Harry. Ysidro's face turned glowering. "But know that charros are no fools. Find a way to explain what business you have among us, or begone." He stumbled back and sat down; his jaw clenched.

Joaquin perceived a new set of mutters among the gauchos. Most of them, it seemed, echoed Ysidro's sentiments. Uh-oh. This could mess things up in a hurry. He watched Harry and Orfea shoot looks at each other. Yet even were they able to communicate in the Onwei tongue, how could they answer?

Now it really started to rain.

Aldo huffed his chest and pulled Joaquin over. "How did Yoka Sutu take to this Orfea?"

"Oh, they got along quite well, seir."

"Good. You shall escort her back to Yoka's yurt. It is obvious that returning to their camp tonight is out of the question." Aldo bent toward a huddled Orfea and offered his hand. Was it just Joaquin's imagination, or was this the start of an attraction? Aldo's strait-laced expression was hard to read, but Orfea definitely had a twinkle in her eye. She got up, nodded her thanks, waved to the rest of the gauchos, and followed Joaquin.

Aldo bowed and pointed Harry toward his own yurt: "It would be an honor to share my humble lodgings." Harry bobbed his head back and forth and groped around to find his pack.

Joaquin lay awake in the dark as the rain kept coming. The light from the campfire bounced around the walls of his tent. The laughing charros kept it up for a good long time. Between Orfea's choice of clothing and Harry's bumbling try to fit in with the singing, they milked the quirks of those two strangers for all they were worth.

No one ever taught Joaquin niceties, but he knew it was mean to mock strangers behind their back, especially your dinner guests. He felt especially ashamed of how Orfea was now ridiculed, especially after how hard she tried to charm those boys. As an orphan growing up in solely male company, he often imagined a mother. This Orfea, he could take a liking to her. He was glad she entrusted him with her blend of spices, and that Aldo approved their use. Despite the charro's mocking and Ysidro's not-so-veiled threats, the ice was broken, and Joaquin helped that happen.

He suspected that, so long as Orfea remained at the Onwei camp, she would be the best source of clues for what the Sky-Bornes were up to. Aldo wanted Joaquin to serve as his eyes and ears. This assignment was at least as important as finding missing heifers. If these people were an advance party for some other tribe that could threaten the Onwei, the sooner they were exposed, the better.

Joaquin finally fell asleep. He dreamt, with a mixture of elation and unease, of the flying machine taking off with him on board.

7

SPEAKING IN TONGUES

Fay felt good, not only in confirming her prediction about this hardy race of people, but that she and her crew had made peaceable contact with them. Now everyone just needed to keep a level head. To that end, she convinced Harry to spend more time with the gaucho chief Aldo, even if it meant that Aldo would parade poor Harry around camp on horseback.

Finding this shaman, Yoka, turned out to be a stroke of luck. Fay expected that she would need to coax someone for hours and hours in order to decode the Onwei tongue, but Yoka proved to be neither shy nor encumbered. The gift of dialups helped. For now, they could get by, as Yoka, like Fay, spoke passable Spanish.

This morning, Fay and Yoka sat on stools in front of the crone's yurt. As Yoka gummed her tortilla and washed it down with maté, she kept switching looks between downward, near, and distant over the top of the rims of the dialups, stuck on the end of her nose.

Then she spotted someone behind Fay and waved him forward. Fay turned to see the boy Joaquin standing a few feet away, his hands clasped behind his back, his standing posture skewed to one side. Wasting no time after Yoka's beckoning, he scooped up a plate.

Plopping cross-legged on the ground, he ravaged his tortilla with its spread of dulce de leche.

If he was bold enough to join the company of two older women, he couldn't be too shy to answer a few questions. Fay started with his age. Fourteen. She asked about his limp. He shot her a quick glance before taking off his boot to display a clubfoot. He watched her face. Perhaps he expected her to flinch or exhibit some type of mock sympathy. Instead, she instructed Yoka to praise the boy's riding skills, and inquired after the pony's name.

When she got around to asking about his family, Yoka answered on her own. "He is an orphan."

Oops, wrong question. Fay reflexively clenched her lips, which Joaquin noted right away. There followed a tense exchange between Yoka and the boy. He lapsed into a sulk, swirling and studying the crumpled tea leaves in his cup.

Yoka broke the silence by diving back into what seemed to be her favorite subject — the history of the Onwei people. Fay listened with one ear while continuing to adjust the lang-synch. The forebears of the Onwei were refugees from lands of the Southern Hemisphere. Their green fields withered from the heat, forcing people ever southward, finally pushing them and their stock into a dangerous open boat trip to Antarctica. The frozen waste here thawed, leaving huge patches of green and yellow, begging to be grazed.

Truth be told, Fay was more interested in the boy than in Yoka's ramblings. This history lesson, after all, was but icing on Fay's own cake, the stuff she preached for years to the skeptical folks back home. A few details still needed to be cleared up, though.

"Why did your people become nomads?"

The crone seemed perplexed by the question, gesturing to the open grassland that surrounded them. "Because it suits this land."

"I meant, how do you cope with the months of darkness?"

"Ah, the time we spend in our village. We fashion the tools we need for the grazing season." Yoka pointed to her looms, the axles and wheel staves on her wagon. She passed Fay her wrought iron knife to examine, then rose to set up her loom.

As Fay cleared the breakfast dishes, another question weighed on her mind. She needed to phrase it in a delicate way.

"I don't see any others of African descent here." She already feared the answer.

The crone peered over the rim of her dialups. She translated the question for Joaquin, addressing him with the back of her hand covering one side of her mouth, before answering Fay. "That's because there aren't many of us. My ancestor M'Bine came from Kenya. She was lucky to have a special gift and learned how to barter it to help herself and her family, but few others of my people survived. Their tribes were already beset by false prophets, mass suicides, riots and famine." Yoka pulled in a deep breath, set her head back, hand on her heart. "The government troops slaughtered them like dogs."

Fay buried her face in her hands. Those rumors of genocide were correct. No survivors, just official denials. Finally, the truth. By the time she lifted her head, tears ran down her cheeks. She noticed the boy give her a blank look.

"Come now, woman." Yoka made a clucking sound. "These things happened hundreds of years ago, far away from here. Why do you take it personally?"

Fay reached in her dress pocket for a tissue and blew her nose with a honk. The unrelenting drumbeat of the strong trampling the weak, the same story repeated generation after generation. All that she and her colleagues could do was dig up and catalogue the remains of these once-vibrant cultures, whose main flaw was to foolishly believe in the ennobling powers of civilization, the perfectibility of the human condition. There were times she wanted to scream the line from that old song: "When will they ever learn?"

She needed to keep her composure here, though. "If you were an anthropologist, you would understand."

Yoka guffawed and sneered something toward Joaquin, something to the effect that Fay's calling was to meet people from strange clans and study them. Fay could comprehend enough of the rebuke to flush and bite her lip.

Her moment of humiliation was saved by Joaquin, who began to fidget, drawing Yoka's attention. The two spoke briefly before Yoka explained to Fay, "He wishes to know more of his family tree. He knows they were gauchos, who once occupied large dwellings all year round."

Fay finished wiping the tears off her face. She sat up, tilted her head at a sympathetic angle, and addressed Joaquin directly. "You and I may have something in common. My people, the Del Campos, lived in Buenos Aires for a hundred years, but when it became too hot and humid, most of them couldn't adapt to the pampas or the rugged mountains. So, they sailed back to their ancestral homeland in Europe."

Yoka sniffed as she translated this for Joaquin, belittling the chance of family ties between Fay and an orphan like himself. The lines on her prune face deepened as she turned back to Fay. "Forgive my bluntness, Orfea, but how long do you plan to stay?"

Fay clenched her teeth. "No longer than a week, assuming that Frank, our pilot, can repair the flying machine." Despite herself, she cringed. Had she worn out her welcome so soon?

"Ah. I'm sure your pilot is capable. He brought you safely here, to the end of the earth." Yoka threw her arms over her head.

"Oh yes, he is the finest product of genetic engineering." Fay drew out *finest*. "His brain is enhanced by the latest computer. He can see shades of light and hear tones that none of the rest of us can. His body adapts readily to any climate. But," she shrugged, "none of that matters now. Until his head clears, all of those survival traits are for naught." She placed her hand over her heart, studied Yoka. "Tell me something. Yesterday you said that you were led to expect us."

Yoka's eyes stuck out over the rim of her vision aids. "Ah, that has to do with the prophecy."

Fay's eyes widened. Here was a new angle.

"Yes, your arrival will trigger momentous events."

Fay's mouth dropped open. She barely noticed Joaquin arise and take his leave, shaking his head slowly as he departed. "Trigger momentous events." What was that supposed to mean? This witch,

Yoka, carried an agenda, and Fay needed to discern and deflect it before any trouble ensued. Did she interpret their presence as a threat to her tribe? Would she use it to try and solidify her own prestige? Any number of scenarios flitted through Fay's imagination, most of them with unhappy outcomes.

And the boy, she didn't wish to put him off. He was bright and he was fresh. She jumped up and ran after him. When she reached him some distance away, she grabbed his hand, reached into the pocket of her skirt and produced an earpad. She pointed to one just like it in her own ear and beckoned him to insert it.

She tried out a phrase. "How do I sound?"

The boy's brow furrowed for a moment, but then he managed to say something that translated back as "very well."

Fay frowned. The lang-synch needed more refining on the grammar end, but in another day she would surely have it. She nodded to Joaquin. "We won't tell Yoka yet. Our little secret, okay?"

The boy's conspiratorial smile told her all she needed to know. He turned and resumed his awkward gait back toward the gauchos' camp.

8
FLACO'S FIND

I've spent a rainy night at the yurt of Trieste and Luz. At first light, I leave, alone, with an old mule that Trieste has grudgingly lent me.

The girl sulks to be left behind, but we have no way to communicate except by sign language, which can get pretty frustrating in the details. It's fine for pointing to things, you can learn how to say simple phrases if you're patient, but that gets old in a hurry. If only Fay would get her lang-synch gadget to work.

Luz spent a good part of last evening using hand signs, trying to convince me that I would need her as my guide. I pretended not to understand. I've scouted plenty of new spots before, without anyone's help.

It's a gorgeous morning, even slogging along on this mule, Cozuel, they call him. The chaparral gleams, fragrant of mint from last night's downpour.

I pass through clumps of a fiery bush with a blazing red flower. Maroon manzanita scrub and an intense violet floor of sweet pea stretch across the valley, leaves moist with morning dew. A few bumblebees make their rounds, but there's no sound save the twitter of a meadowlark perched on a tall stem of pampas grass. It sings, "A mate, I want a mate." Good luck, buddy.

A ground squirrel stands upon its hind legs and whips its head around, quickly racing back in its hole at the sight of intruders. A jackrabbit darts ahead of us in a zigzag pattern before it disappears into the spindly pink-white burro grass. Despite being stuck on this mule, I do feel animated again.

This land has a stunning variety of shapes and textures, like the valley I ride through now. The line of hills climbs for miles, up to the steady plume of smoke that trails from snow-capped Mt. Erebus. If I want to find prime-grade iridium, that's the place.

Still, getting there will take planning. Trieste's emphatic gestures made it clear last night that I'm only to use the nag around here, not under any circumstances to ride up the mountain. Dare I try anyway? How would she find out if I did? The whole thing would be so much easier with one of the horses that brought us to camp yesterday, but Nestor has already rounded them up for their owners.

At the edge of the crater, I pull out some tools and start hacking away at the soil. It's frustrating. The ore here is useless, so instead, I run soil tests — moisture and acidity. But those results show the same story as in the Northern Hemisphere: global warming has not yet peaked.

I pack the instruments away, cursing under my breath. Nothing is panning out. Why, oh why, couldn't we have landed on target?

Might as well test for other minerals, see if there's anything else here worth mining. I chip away samples from various cracks and fissures, stuff them in my specimen bag to assay back at camp.

After messing around for twenty minutes, I look up and there's Luz. She obviously followed me at a distance. Skipping out on your chores again, kid? She comes up and starts to paw through my bag, holds the samples up with a jeweler's eye, checking at different angles for any sparkles.

Damn, I wish we could talk to each other. I'd have to tell her: Sorry, girl, not interested. Instead, I shake my head, hold out my hand for the specimen bag, tie it up and stuff it in my pack. I mount and pace along the crater rim, my back to her. The slight doesn't seem to bother her, though. She jumps on her horse and rides ahead. Fine, I'm not going to chase her away.

I'm jealous of her high-spirited mare. She responds to the slightest cue, needs barely a nudge to change her course or pace, like she's ready to sprout wings and fly if need be. Makes poor Cozuel look even feebler, if that's possible.

Luz must feel me watching her. She sits up straighter, quite self-aware now. She wears her long black hair in a braid. A full-length wool blanket, rust colored and fringed with black and white stripes near the edges, spreads in a cape across her shoulders to keep off the morning chill. Her leggings are a thicker weave of the same off-white hemp as her tunic. Her wide-brimmed, tasseled felt hat looks well made too, plus boots stitched with a lattice pattern around the ankles. It costs her mother plenty to keep the girl dressed and shod. The jewelry trade must be good.

I slow to a walk, circling the crater's edge, looking for one more spot to pick off a sample. I stop at an outcropping, dismount, and chisel off this last piece with a few well-placed whacks.

Now that mutt Flaco spots something in the dirt and jumps on it, digging frantically. We wait, but he persists. Luz shouts at the dog, even kicks a rock toward him, but fails to get his attention. When she turns toward me, she's flushed.

Luz strides over to where Flaco paws in such frenzy. A smooth yellow-white edge sticks out at the spot. She bends down, nudges him away, and tries to pry the edge free with her knife, skimming off wet flakes. She glances over her shoulder at me, raises her hands. I shrug and head over to help.

We take turns digging more slowly. My tools aren't effective. The stuff is much softer than rock and chips off if we use any force.

After fifteen minutes of careful excavation and wiping off mud, I can see its shape, roughly two feet in each dimension. One edge is smooth curves and three sharp ridges. Each points in a different direction. On the fourth side, the material becomes denser, rough but flat edges on top and bottom. In the middle, between the dense part and the curvy spiny part, there's a hole, ten inches in diameter.

Are you kidding me? That's impossible. Luz and I stare at each other. The shape of the bone is clearly a vertebra. The largest animal bone I've seen is from a cow, but a full-grown bull's vertebra core hole measures four inches, tops. What kind of creature did this bone belong to? This giant, whatever it was, no longer exists, of that I'm sure. She's stumbled onto something *big*! I don't want her to think I'm too excited about it, yet an involuntary smile escapes me: the joy of discovery.

Flaco scampers around the bone, finders-keepers, until Luz ties it to the back of her saddle. She motions to me that we should take it back to her camp.

Hey, kid, this isn't my field. Do I want to get sidetracked on the ID of an ancient bone? I hold up my specimen bag to show her I've got more pressing business, shake my head. But there's a gleam in Luz's eyes, a mixture of eagerness and innocence. She clasps her hands together and lights up this beautiful smile. How can you say no to that? Now I see how she works her mother.

I almost give in, until I remember the reason I'm on this mission. Unlike Fay, it's not to get chummy with the locals. It's to find a valuable mineral, and once I find it, let the chips fall where they may.

I shake my head, give the girl a brief wave, and head down into the crater toward our camp. Out of the corner of my eye, I catch the chagrined expression on the girl's face as she watches me depart. When I look back a bit later, though, she's already gone.

I cast another peek at the volcano and make a decision. Enough waiting around. There's nothing more worth doing at this crater. If I'm going to get to Erebus, I need to make it happen myself. It's not as if some genie will show up to grant me three wishes. Tomorrow, first thing.

What about a mount? If Harry's back, I'll "borrow" his before he awakens.

9
A SÉANCE

Once again, Luz sensed the scornful looks of the older women as she rode in, but when they spotted that giant bone, she noted a few raised eyebrows too. Let them snicker now. Luz felt sure that finding this giant bone portended more than its taxonomy. It must signify some kind of omen. She convinced herself of this much by the time she reached her yurt. There sat her mother among her wares, stringing small pieces of the iris stone onto a necklace.

"Mama, look at what I found." Luz tried to hand the prize over to her mother, but Trieste drew back.

"Where did you come upon this?" Trieste's eyes fixed on the bone like it was a viper ready to strike.

"Near Splat." Luz pointed in the direction of the crater. "Why? What's the matter?"

"Just sitting on the ground?" Trieste's arms encircled her chest as she continued to study the vertebra at a distance. A few of the neighboring women treaded closer.

"Flaco dug it up." Luz nuzzled the rusty mutt.

"It is clearly a backbone, but so much larger than any animal I have ever seen." Now Trieste eyed Luz. "They say that huge beasts roamed the earth long ago. Dinosaurs, they were called."

"You mean that the ancestors contended with these dinosaurs? They must have needed powerful weapons." This was getting weird.

"Well, no, they roamed long before humans." She didn't sound too sure on the details, but her next words were emphatic. "They say ill fortune will befall those who disturb these bones."

Would it? Luz weighed her mother's words. Had Trieste not been superstitious by nature, Luz might take more heed. For her, any little thing out of the daily routine seemed to be an omen. Luz was sure she had already configured the Sky-Bornes' arrival into something apocalyptic.

Ignoring her mother's glare, Luz picked up the treasure again, holding it in her palms, expecting it to reveal secrets. What was the shape of this dinosaur? Like a giant bull, or more like the bird monster that brought the Sky-Bornes?

After another minute of holding the trophy, Luz knew what her next step must be. It involved Yoka, and it would best be done while her mother napped. For now, she wrapped the vertebra in a hemp cloth and led Quintara to get water at the creek.

Not a cloud remained in the sky that afternoon. Waves of heat shimmered from the ground. Luz carried the wrapped vertebra in both hands, marching toward Yoka Sutu's yurt. Flaco ran beside her and sniffed every scrawny shrub that he passed, finally settling on a stand of goldenrod.

Orfea was there, struggling to help Yoka drag her hemp loom into the shade. Warm days like this were a boon, and Yoka shed her serape to reveal a short, swaybacked figure topped with a clump of frizzy white hair. She wore a sleeveless purple shift of her own creation. As she sat down on her stool to weave some more, her wrinkled ebony skin reminded Luz of an aged lizard sunning on a rock.

Orfea replaced the metal box on her lap. She listened intently as Yoka prattled on. It dawned on Luz that the old woman now spoke to the stranger in Onwei. Did she finally get her machine to work?

Yoka's old setter, Mugabe, lay there in the sun. He lifted his ears as Flaco ran up and they sniffed each other. Yoka turned her whole body to watch Luz draw near. Vision magnifiers sat on the old woman's nose, no doubt a gift from Orfea.

"Good afternoon, Auntie Yoka," Luz said. "It is a warm one, no?"
"Ah, but it does my old bones good, dear Luz. Pull over a stool." The mention of bones made Luz smile. "I have brought something to show you."

"Have you now?" Yoka sat with her arms folded, her squinty eyes on the bundle.

Luz unwrapped her prize and laid it on the ground. Flaco wandered closer, wagging his tail, but Luz shooed him away.

Yoka stuck her neck out, looking all the more like a lizard. "My, my. Look at that." She leaned forward to study the artifact.

"I found this today, while exploring near the crater. Mother told me it might be a vertebra from a dinosaur. She could not tell me much, except that dinosaurs walked the earth long before humans." Luz stopped. "I hope you don't mind me asking you. Mother appeared stumped."

"Of course not." Yoka leaned farther and pushed the bone over. She raised her head with a little twist. "Dear girl, you may be onto something here."

"What does it mean, Auntie?"

She stroked her throat. "I recall a prophecy having to do with dinosaurs. When their remains are found, it will portend changes."

Luz's heart began to race. "Ooh, what kind of changes?"

Yoka shuddered. Her eyes closed tight. "The earth will move." She concentrated, finally opening her eyes to stare at the Sky-Borne woman. "And we shall have visitors, from another time, another place."

Luz grasped her hands together and shook them. She glanced at Orfea. "How exciting. And here they are!" She waited for Yoka to continue, but The Inscrutable One just sat back and picked up on her weaving.

Luz exhaled, made her voice calm. Surely this couldn't be the whole story. "Please tell me more, Auntie."

Yoka stopped and put her hands on her lap. "If this so fascinates you, we will need to consult a more reliable source."

Luz frowned and said nothing, fully aware of Yoka's meaning: Venga, her African inheritance.

Smiling patiently, Orfea fumbled in the pocket of her dress and pulled out a metal disc, about the size of her fingernail. She handed it to Luz, who had no idea what it was for. Orfea turned her head to show her own disc, stuck to her scalp just behind the right ear.

"How does that sound?" Orfea's voice came through as Luz placed her earpad. Her eyes stretched wide.

"Yes, I finally made the connection to the Onwei tongue." Orfea sounded so happy, her auburn curls bobbing up and down. "I programmed one for Keltyn too. I thought she was with you." She glanced about.

"She is still scouting for rocks. I'm supposed to meet her again later." Luz hoped the lie didn't sound too implausible. If they both possessed earpads, it might be her last and best chance to team up with Keltyn. She reached out her hand.

Orfea handed her a second earpad. "Now you and Keltyn can understand each other. It has a built-in transmitter," she spread her arms apart, "so you can even reach across the length of this camp." She turned back to Yoka. "So, what is this 'more reliable source,' if you don't mind my asking?"

Luz squirmed as Yoka answered. "It is a ritual where we each ingest a wafer made from an ancient herbal recipe. Under its influence, we summon our ancestors for comfort or wisdom."

Orfea's eyes widened. "Really! Would you... would it be a bother?"

Yoka blew out a quick breath. "No bother at all." She pushed herself up and shuffled over to her pantry tent, reappearing with a tray of crackers, a crock of sun tea, and three cups. After pouring the tea and handing the cups around, she selected a medium-sized bead from the several dozen on her necklace. Her gnarled fingers took the bead; she used a hand press to crack its shell, then spooned the syrupy contents into a small bowl and dipped each cracker.

She kept her chin up as she passed the tray around. Luz hesitated, took one, but turned her head away as her fingers made contact. Must she really do this?

The crone placed the tray next to her feet and sat down in her rocker. Next, she held up her cracker, dipped it in the tea, opened the little hole of her mouth, and swallowed the morsel in one piece. She closed her eyes and bent her head in deep meditation. Luz and Orfea followed.

Yoka warned them that the effect would be gradual. After ten minutes of silence that felt to Luz like an hour, she felt a tingle in the back of her neck.

Yoka lifted her chin and opened her eyes. The lips over her toothless gums moved as she stared at the dinosaur bone, sitting on its wrapper. When she opened her mouth, she spoke with a more resonant voice that made Luz gasp. How did it arise from this same tiny body?

The voice became a force of its own, demanding, "What is it you wish to know, girl?"

Luz blurted out, "Tell us about the visitors."

Yoka puckered her lips, as if sucking on sour grass. "The Onwei have been a people unto themselves for hundreds of years. No good can come from the arrival of these Sky-Bornes. I see calamity ahead." Her frizzy mop of hair shook side to side.

"I'm sorry, Auntie." Luz cleared her throat and tried again. "What about dinosaurs?"

"Ah, much better." The old woman's mouth settled into a sly smile. She took a deep breath and concentrated with her eyes closed. "A man named Jonas Tofala cast a bright light in southern Africa's darkest time, one of the few voices of reason during an era of mass riots and famine. He taught paleontology at the University of Pretoria. That means," her eyes snapped open, "he was an expert on dinosaurs. He was also," she intoned smugly, "my great-great-great-great-great-grandfather."

As the old woman spoke, the fuzzy image of a man's head appeared to Luz, with wrinkled ebony skin, long face rimmed with short-cropped wiry gray hair and beard. He wore the same kind of gold-rimmed vision aids as Harry.

"So," Yoka's breath blew out, "what question do you have for him?"

"Please, tell us what kind of creature this bone belonged to." Luz reached down and turned it at a different angle.

Another minute of silence. When Yoka spoke again, her voice rang deeper. "It is, indeed, the vertebra of a dinosaur, as you surmised. To be precise, it anchored the rib of a sauropod called Glacialisaurus." Another pause. "A giant fat lizard. It ate massive amounts of plants."

Luz gazed toward the dry hills, puzzled about how this terrain could have supported such a beast.

"In this arid terrain there once thrived a teeming swamp," Yoka continued. She studied the vertebra again and raised her arms. "Dinosaurs came in all shapes and sizes. Mostly they were big, with voracious appetites."

Luz sat up straight, wide-eyed. "What happened to them? How did they die out?"

Yoka shut her eyes again. Her breathing slowed. Luz wondered if the old woman fell asleep.

She finally opened her mouth and said, "Craters." Her eyes flicked wide to see the reaction.

Luz glanced back and forth from the bone to Yoka's blank face. "What do the craters have to do with the dinosaurs?"

"What indeed?" Yoka's face showed more prune-like features than ever, deep in concentration. Her voice betrayed a hint of exasperation. "Jonas cannot help us with craters. He suggests going to another source, closer to the earth."

Orfea flayed her arms out. "Who else would know about craters?"

Flaco gave chase to a crow that lit nearby. Luz ventured, "Perhaps someone on my grandfather's side. His line descended from the original peoples of Australia. They stayed close to the earth."

Yoka's jaw stuck out. "Indeed, they did, and you are fortunate to have this bloodline. Are you willing to tap it?"

Luz bit her lip. "If I must." She hated having to submit to the crone's hocus-pocus, especially in front of this stranger.

The crone twisted her necklace once more, picked one of the smallest beads, crushed it, emptied the insides into another bowl. She reached into a fold of her shift and pulled out a red cloth packet with a bunch of bone needles. She picked one of the larger needles and held the point up for Luz to inspect.

Luz squeezed her eyes shut.

"Well?"

"Do what you must do." She gave up her right hand and turned away.

"Pull your stool closer," said Yoka. She deftly poked Luz's middle finger with the needle. Luz grimaced as Yoka alternately squeezed and released pressure, until several drops of blood fell into the bowl. She whisked the blood through the liquid contents of the bead, placed the bowl on the tray and added three more crackers beside it.

They followed the same ritual: dip and swallow the crackers, sip tea and wait.

Ten minutes of silence passed, but Yoka was not dissuaded. "Naturally, a spirit would be easier to summon if you knew its name, but," she winked like an ancient owl, "often you can get your answer simply by concentrating hard enough on your question. Meditate harder, girl. Try to picture Splat, down to the finest detail."

Centered in her mind's eye, Luz focused on the violet stripe, glistening in the morning sun. After another five minutes, her neck tingled once again. As she stood on the edge of the crater and peered over, she became aware of another old woman standing beside her. Wearing nothing but an untanned animal skin and a belt of coarse fiber strands, the creature's bare feet were callused, her skin brown, but not as dark as Yoka's. Her thick pleats of gray hair stuck a foot straight out, pointing away from all sides of her head. Her deep-set brown eyes glistened like drops of resin on a gnarled tree trunk. She wore a loopy grin.

Luz drew her breath in, trying not to be frightened by this apparition. "Auntie, do you see what I am seeing?"

"Yes, girl, we all share the same vision."

"Can I talk to this person?"

Yoka let out a short laugh. "If you know her tongue."

Luz's shoulders sagged; the crone had landed another jibe about her missed Venga apprenticeship. She swallowed. "Can you get through to her, Auntie?"

Yoka glanced at Orfea and pointed to the tool on her lap. "Your magic is stronger than mine."

The Sky-Borne shook her head. "No magic, I'm afraid. This works as a decoder when you hear the other person speak directly to you." She turned to Luz. "I played with these dials for hours while listening to Yoka before finding the right settings for Onwei."

Yoka blew a gust of air. "You're asking a lot of an old woman. Aboriginal Australian includes a dozen different dialects." She squeezed her eyes, readjusting some mental signal. Finally, she spoke. "Her name is Kapujeena. She consents to take your questions. What do you wish to ask, girl?"

Luz frowned in concentration. "What is the connection between craters and dinosaurs?"

Another period of silence, until Kapujeena threw her hands into the air. Yoka spoke again. "She says the craters were made by giant rocks. The rocks rained from the sky and changed the earth in such a way that the dinosaurs could no longer survive."

Luz's heart began to pound. "Changed how?"

Kapujeena's hands darted to and fro as Yoka continued. "The rocks stirred up giant clouds of dust. The dust storm lasted so long that it starved the dinosaurs, first of sunlight, then of plants to eat, finally of air itself. As the dinosaurs died out, the whole face of the earth changed."

Luz tried to envision the scene that old woman described. "Are any of those rocks around? All I have seen are the craters."

Another long pause. "She says that even rocks wear down over time. They become part of the earth on which they land. If you look around the rim of the craters, you may be able to see telltale signs of this period. The giant rocks contained a dense substance. It left streaks of deep color around the edges of the craters."

Luz gasped and opened her eyes. "Is the color violet? Is this the color?" She touched her mother's rainbow studs on her earlobes.

Yoka opened her eyes and adjusted her vision aids to study the earring. "Perhaps it is."

Luz jumped up, eyed the crater, and started pacing in a circle. "I have seen the deep-colored streak that you speak of, on the rim of the crater." She slapped her thigh and turned back to Yoka. "Ask her if the violet rock is to be found on the mountain."

"What makes you ask such a question?" Yoka's frizzy brows knotted up.

"Just ask her!" Luz could not explain the feeling of urgency that stirred her. It must have been the combination of discovering this prophetic bone and of having someone like Keltyn, someone who knew about the piedra de yris, so close at hand. Now was the time for Luz to act. She could not bear to wait any longer for the right moment that might never come. She felt her fingers lock into claws from the tension. "Please!"

Yoka frowned before resuming her meditation. After a long pause, she announced, "Great quantities of the stone are spewed forth from the earth each time the volcano erupts." Another pause. "But you must bide your time, she says. It may erupt again soon."

Luz leaned forward, her fists now clenched. "How soon?"

After another interminable period, Yoka opened her eyes and shrugged. "The Venga is wearing off. We've lost her."

Luz stopped her pacing. "How soon? Yoka, I must know." She grabbed her hair with both hands. "Do we need more Venga?" She needed to tap the wisdom of her distant cousin, even if it meant playing at more of Yoka's rituals.

Yet the crone just shook her head.

The tingling in the back of Luz's neck was gone. She felt spent by the vision, but there were so many unanswered questions. An idea came to her in a flash as she bent down to wrap up the bone.

She needed to question Kapujeena herself. The woman was her own kin, for pity's sake.

Luz cursed, dropped the package, hurried over to the bowl lying on the ground beside Yoka, and scooped up a handful of Venga nuggets.

The old woman scowled and plodded to her feet. Orfea remained seated, slowly shaking her head. Luz shoved the nuggets in her pocket as she hurried back to pick up the bone.

"Now girl," Yoka hissed. "You would be wise not to attempt anything foolish. Look at me."

Luz avoided her gaze and marched off as fast as her legs would carry her. Yoka kept shouting her name.

She swept through her mother's yurt, collecting chiseling tools, bedrolls, and layers of clothing. As expected, Trieste protested her sudden departure, but Luz had practiced her story.

"Not to worry, mama. I'm going to spend the night with Keltyn in her tent, the better to search for the piedra de yris on the rim of the crater in the morning light. I'll be fine. See you later tomorrow." She gave her mother a peck on the cheek and hurried out. As she saddled Quintara, Luz glanced across the landscape at her real destination. The plume of smoke still trailed from Erebus' dark summit.

Now she must convince Keltyn to take on a partner. That attempt had failed this morning. She hoped that use of the earpads would provide more ammunition. If not, she had a riskier plan.

10
SUSPICION

The Sky-Bornes' flying machine cast a long shadow as Luz approached. She could glimpse only Buck's legs; his head, arms and torso were hidden inside the large hole at the tail of the flying machine. A chorus of mutters escaped like so much hot air.

Keltyn was sorting gear outside her tent. "Buck, we've got company," she barked as Luz dismounted.

He stuck his head out. His eyes were glazed, his sweaty face and the bandage tied around his forehead stained with grime. He kept blinking, trying to focus, then pulled a rag out of his back pocket and wiped his cheeks and hands, all the while lingering on a detailed inspection of Luz. She tried to maintain her poise by standing erect beside her horse, but his burrowing gaze made her feel like a sale item at an auction.

Buck reached for his sunshades. "Whatchoo two birds up to now?"

Keltyn eyed Luz. "I'm itching to go visit Erebus, and I suspect Luz is still hoping she can tag along."

"Damn landing gear." Buck cocked his head at the defective equipment. "If it wudda worked, we shoulda come down right at Airbus."

"If your grandma had wings, she could fly."

Though Luz's earpad translated all their banter word for word, she could not grasp the meaning behind their sparring. She tried to tune out the rest until she could draw Keltyn away to pitch her proposal.

Now Buck attempted to laugh, but instead drooled a mouthful of spittle. It must be his head injury.

Keltyn said, "If we came down on target, we never would have met these people."

"Does she savvy?" Buck nudged his chin toward Luz.

"Nah, not until Fay gets her lang-synch to work."

Buck said, "You got to admit, them being around does complicate things."

"Maybe, maybe not," said Keltyn. "Has it occurred to you that, one, they can guide us around this terrain, and two, we have a real problem if you can't fix the landing gear?" She stared Buck down. "We just might need help."

"Oh, I'll fix it, Missy." His head rocked back and forth. "Dontcha worry none." He turned to pack up his tools. "Takes more than a little bonk on the noggin to keep old Buck outta the game." He resumed muttering to himself.

Luz gestured to Keltyn that they should go into her tent. Keltyn seemed reluctant until Luz flashed the earpad between thumb and forefinger. That got her attention pronto.

They sat on packs across from each other as Keltyn fit the device into her ear. "I suppose you figure this puts a whole new spin on things." She did not seem as thrilled as Luz hoped.

"You have to admit that hunting for the stone will be easier if we join forces."

"I don't know about that. I like to work alone, or didn't you notice?"

"But... you don't know this terrain," Luz sputtered.

"Listen, sister. The only reason I haven't headed out to Erebus already is that I promised your mother I wouldn't take her mule too far. I would borrow Harry's mount, but he hasn't returned from your camp."

Luz brightened. She was waiting for the moment. "Mother changed her mind. She said to tell you that, so long as the two of us look out for each other and we're back by nightfall, you can take Cozuel." She hoped that her feigned sincerity sounded convincing.

Keltyn seemed skeptical. "Why this sudden change of heart?"

"I explained how you are an expert in the piedra de yris, and you are convinced it is to be found on the mountainside. She, too, needs a new supply of the stone for her craft."

"Hmph. So, according to you, your mother will allow me to ride her mule up the mountainside, but only if you escort me."

"... and we must share whatever we find." Luz nodded for emphasis.

"Oh, I'm sure there will be plenty to go around." Keltyn studied Luz for a long minute. "Let's get one thing straight, though."

Luz waited.

"No more side trips. We go where I say."

"Of course. You are the boss."

"I see you left your mutt behind. That's a good start."

Luz smiled to herself. So far, so good.

***

I bring the girl with me to see Buck. He's sitting on a stool in front of his tent, sipping coffee, a vacant look in his eyes.

"It's settled. The girl and I are heading over to scout Erebus, first thing in the morning."

He turns his head toward me but says nothing.

"We're going to need a share of the provisions."

"Fine."

"And I want to take a radiophone. Just in case anything happens."

"Go ahead."

"That means you or Harry need to be near one, if I have to call."

Buck straightens up with a ragged smile. "I'll be waitin' for your call, Missy. First time your horse stumbles."

"I'd hate to disappoint you, big guy." I start to flush. Before it shows, I whip around and stride back to the blue tent, the girl behind me. Inside, with the flap closed, I stick out my left arm in Buck's direction and slap the upper arm with my right hand: a good old-fashioned Bronx cheer. He can be such a jerk. Why do I even bother to talk to him?

Not to be outdone, Luz sticks her tongue out in Buck's direction.

You got it, sister," I say. "And don't feel sorry for him. Bonking his head didn't make him arrogant. He's always like that."

She cocks her head, thinks about that. "How did he get hurt?"

"We almost crashed the plane trying to land."

"Oh." The girl's eyes widen. "Does that mean you're stuck here?"

We're stuck here unless or until Buck's brain gets to working right. It's as simple as that." I try to sound matter-of-fact but end up with an involuntary gulp.

I busy myself with preparations to try and forget the dilemma we're in. Retrieve more equipment from the plane, set up a lamp for inside the tent, stuff my windbreaker and wool cap into my pack, heat water. The girl's eyes follow my every move, but I don't care to engage her any more.

Despite Buck's passive behavior, I'm still worried that he'll challenge our plan in the morning. All he has to do is radio Harry, who's still hanging out at the Onwei camp, and the chief will put the kibosh on our little expedition.

I hand Luz tea and biscuits and nibble my own portion in silence. Soon I'm ready to tuck into my sleeping roll. Luz still sits there, pouting. "Now what's the matter?" This adventure must not be going the way she imagined.

"I... I want to learn more."

"More? Like... everything? Tonight?" I huff a breath. "Big day tomorrow. Get some sleep." Why did I agree to chaperone a teenage kid?

***

Luz and I arise as the first light of morning shines through the tent. I heat more water, this time for coffee. Biscuits on the side, that's all we've got for breakfast. Funny, we've got earpads now; we could chat about anything and everything, but she senses that I'm still not in the mood. Good girl.

As I stuff a sweater in my pack, I hear Buck muttering outside, his speech choked and guttural.

I shoot a quick glance at Luz. No sooner have I opened the tent flap than Buck's voice rises another notch. He stands near the plane, pawing a piece of my equipment, a box painted yellow. "Dontcha forget this gadget now, Missy."

Uh-oh. He found the Chinese meter. An ear-splitting alarm goes off in my head. Blinding red lights flash in every corner of my brain. Now the shit is gonna hit the fan. I face off from him at ten feet, my arms crossed. "It's really none of your business what I take along, Buck."

"No, course not. I found it lying on the back seat."

"Had to move it last night in the dark, to get at other gear." It's all I can do to keep my voice even. He's just waiting for me to crack.

Buck turns the box over, checks the markings. "Just my addled brain, or are these Chinese characters?"

I stand my ground, keep my eyes shut, shake my head slowly. "Buck, you have a hell of a nerve pawing my stuff."

"Why would our prize geologist need Chinese equipment for this mission?"

"Now's not the time to deliver a report. I'm heading out to do a job. We came to the other end of the world to explore for iridium, am I right?"

"Things don't add up here, Missy."

I feel my lips tighten and shoulders hunch. "For me to explain each piece of my gear is like you trying to show me how to fly this plane." I hold my hand out.

Buck hesitates before tossing me the little monitor.

"Thank you. Now if you'll excuse us, we have work to do." I whip around, realize Luz has witnessed the whole scene. I sigh, motion for her to follow.

The two of us head back into the tent, where I bury the monitor in a larger case holding other tools. I slam the case closed and snap on a hefty padlock, yank it to make sure it's secure. "I should have done all this beforehand. No sense asking for trouble from snooping eyes."

"Can't you trust your own people?" Luz asks.

My skin feels on fire. "My own people are Indigenous Peoples from Canada. Come on. Let's saddle up and get out of here."

I lead the way out of the tent, gear stuffed under both arms, heading toward the mounts. We take pains to avoid direct eye contact with Buck. He leans against the flying machine with one arm, legs crossed and the other arm resting on his hip. Mouth wide open, his tongue balances a toothpick on end. He deftly flips the sliver so it lies flat on his lower lip.

Luz follows me with her pack. Out of the corner of my eye, I see Buck flash the girl a wicked smile. He looks grotesque with his dialup sunshades perched on his nose, like a predatory yellow insect sizing up its next meal.

We saddle up and head toward the crater's edge.

Buck doesn't know it yet, but I found a little secret last night too. I rifled through the bags we left on the plane, looking for more provisions to take on this little jaunt today. The dome light in the cockpit was dim, so it was hard to ID the bags. I opened zippers at random, using touch to tell what was what. I must have opened one of Harry's, and my hand felt a crumpled piece of paper just inside. That made me wonder. If it was just trash, why did he keep it?

I spread it out, held it up to the dome light, and started cussing to myself as I read it. When we were refueling at Chimera Space Station, someone overheard me talking with a Chinese technician, suspected the worst, and scribbled a note to Harry.

Has he shared this with anyone? Doesn't matter. As soon as he gets back to camp, Buck is gonna clue him in about the meter, and then Harry will shut me down, period.

I'd better make hay while the sun shines.

II

GORED

The wind whipped Joaquin's face, shaking the cobwebs out of his brain. He stuck his left heel into Cisco's flank, prodding his pony as fast as it could run. As the jeaf's "eyes and ears," what he had to report now was every bit as vital as tracking missing heifers. What's more, Joaquin suspected that the jeaf would need him to help resolve this mess.

Directly behind Aldo, the morning sunlight bounced off the rock face of a distant hill. This made the big jeaf appear even larger. He sat on his stallion atop a rise, half a mile from the herd. Joaquin squinted to make out the mounted figure beside Aldo. Sure enough, Harry was still trying to fit in like one of the boys.

Joaquin pulled up, out of breath. "Jeaf, come quickly. Heriberto's mount has been gored."

Aldo's weather-beaten face betrayed nothing. He handed down his water skin. Joaquin pulled a deep swallow, glancing at the grim picture of Harry. Effects from the fiesta of two nights before still lingered; his figure slumped, his chubby face now sprouted gray stubble, and bags sunk heavy under his eyes.

Aldo took the pipe out of his mouth, spat, wiped off his graying mustache. He nodded toward the herd and took off at a canter. Though getting on in years, the jeaf still rode effortlessly. His palomino stallion, sixteen hands tall, carried his massive bulk with ease.

Harry, by contrast, grabbed the saddle horn with both hands, hanging on for dear life. Having pulled too tightly on the reins the first time he rode the stallion, now he appeared afraid to rein it in as it matched the pace of Aldo's steed. Joaquin followed discreetly, trying to imagine what it must feel like for a full-grown man to be a novice on horseback. By the time they stopped, Harry's face mimicked the pale yellow-gray color of tallow, his forehead beaded with cold sweat.

They found Heriberto Paz's bony frame bent over, trying to soothe his sorrel mare. Lying on her side, she struggled half-heartedly to stand back up, neighing in agony. A foot-long wound gaped from her left haunch, a dark-red blotch pooling in the dirt beside her. Several of the other gauchos loitered around, their hands soaked with blood from stuffing rags into the hole.

Aldo took his time dismounting, his face still a mask. Heriberto turned his head toward the jeaf, but Aldo paid the man no mind. The charro held a shaking hand over his mouth, not seeming to notice the hand was full of blood. A charro who lost his mount during the season counted worse than useless. He became a burden to the others, to the whole tribe.

"Jeaf, can you help?"

Aldo shot the man a brief, dark stare. "As if you deserve any help." It came out a near-whisper.

Joaquin knew that Heriberto feared for more than his horse. He had fallen asleep on his watch more than once, which stuck him on Aldo's slacker list. He was half Aldo's age, but thin enough that one good smack would floor him. Heriberto avoided Aldo's glare up to now, staying clear of the jeaf as much as possible.

Like all of the gauchos, Heriberto was bred too proud to ask forgiveness. Yet, unless he showed some sign of remorse for his past behavior, the jeaf was not likely to salvage his mount. Aldo, for his part, was bound to teach this stubborn charro a hard lesson. Joaquin glanced from Heriberto's face to Aldo's, both of their expressions unyielding.

Joaquin could think of only one thing to do, but it was risky. Aldo might interpret it as crossing him. But Joaquin also knew the mare's life was at stake. He had to make Aldo see the moment in those terms.

The other gauchos stood frozen. Joaquin felt all eyes on him as he removed the canteen from his saddle and walked toward the wounded horse. He bent down and poured water into a cup. After failing in her efforts to stand, the mare lay still on her side, deathly quiet. Now she turned her head awkwardly, struggling to drink.

The horse's renewed agony seemed to shake Aldo out of his funk. He gave Heriberto one last withering glare, then bent down to inspect the wound. Mangled from the steer's horn, it stretched six inches deep into the muscle, bleeding in little spurts. Aldo smoothed his hands along the mare's flank, trying to calm her. The other gauchos gathered closer.

"Nasty gash. Perhaps tendons torn." The jeaf took a deep breath. "First, we must stop the bleeding." To Ysidro, his next in command, "Fetch a large basin. Lots of water. Soap. Clean rags." Ysidro in turn barked at his nephew Gabino. They hustled up their horses and sped for camp.

Aldo pulled his cape and a small wrapped packet from his saddlebags. He laid the cape on the wet ground, carefully opening the bundle on top. The inside lining held small pockets, with a surgical tool in each one: several sizes of bone needles, each with a sculpted eyelet; a whittled bone blade; hemp threads of different thicknesses, each piece wrapped around a bone spool; a dozen pieces of gauze.

The jeaf returned to the downed mare and knelt with the effort of a large man used to riding high. Having settled down, the horse now started to buck again as he ran his hands closer to the wound.

Aldo made little clucking noises as he stroked the horse. Joaquin stood beside him, half-afraid that Aldo might wave him away, which meant losing the chance to learn crucial *curandero* skills. Instead, the jeaf motioned for him to squat alongside. "Remember, you need more than the right equipment; you must gain the horse's trust. She may be smart, but she is scared and you cannot sew up a moving target."

The jeaf opened a packet of coca leaf, crushed a half dozen pieces onto a large gauze, then wrapped and moistened it from a small gourd of liquor to make an elixir. He passed the poultice to Joaquin, who had no idea what to do with it.

"Go ahead and stick it deep into the wound."

Joaquin pushed up his sleeve, scrunched his face and did as he was told. For some reason, he did not expect that a curandero would need to get his hands bloody.

"Now hold it with steady force," said the jeaf. He remained in his squat. Every few minutes, he motioned for Joaquin to twist his arm and apply pressure in a different direction. Joaquin was sure his arm would fall off by the time Aldo bid him to remove the sopping rags and watch. Blood still oozed, but no longer spurted.

Ysidro and Gabino showed up with supplies. Aldo poured water onto a rag, rubbed in soap to make lather, and nodded as Joaquin cleaned the matted blood from the edges of the wound. He crept his hand inside the hole, held the wet rags in place, and followed the same sequence as with the poultice.

"Well done, boy. Take a breather," said Aldo.

Joaquin scooted back, kneeling close by. The mare lay calmer now. Aldo pulled out his knife, cleaned it with the lather, and sawed out the mangled flesh. Breathing hard, he rested and spat every few minutes. He glanced at Harry, standing ten paces away, and held up his bloodstained palms. Harry flinched and turned away. Ysidro and Gabino glanced at each other, breaking into guffaws. Yet within a minute, Harry was back to watching again.

Finally done cleaning out the wound, Aldo turned to glare at Heriberto. "The tendon is gouged..." The jeaf paused until the poor charro squirmed, "... but not severed."

Heriberto, camped by the mare's front quarters, tried to calm the horse by whispering to it. He kept his head turned to avoid having to look at the huge gash.

"I will sew now." Aldo's words came out in a hoarse croak.

Heriberto cleared his throat several times. The jeaf showed compassion for his mount, and now the tall charro seemed contrite. "Do you think I will be able to ride her again, jeaf?"

"In due course. She will need a week of rest." Aldo motioned Joaquin to come closer and handed him a bone blade. "You will cut the thread."

As Joaquin knelt, his clubfoot began to cramp, but he dared not shift his weight yet. He sensed the jeaf was testing his capacity for tasks like this, ones that needed both mental and physical stamina. Though time dragged and his mouth felt parched, he determined to watch the jeaf's every move.

First, Aldo threaded a finger-sized needle with a foot-long string of hemp. He poked the needle through the muscle belly to grab a good bite of tissue, then pulled the full length of thread through the hole. He repeated on the other side of the wound then removed the needle and pulled up on both ends of the thread, careful not to yank too hard. Finally, he tied the ends in a double square knot.

Aldo nodded. "Cut close to the knot."

Joaquin used one hand to steady the other, sawed back and forth on the hemp fibers. Each cut took forever. They went through the step four more times until the size of the wound shrunk in half. Joaquin's bad foot throbbed like it had been stung with a branding iron.

Hands trembling, Aldo put the needle and thread aside. He leaned back and took a long draw from his canteen, then removed his hat and ran his arm across his brow. Near to fainting from the pain in his foot, Joaquin discreetly switched to a kneeling position.

Sweat soaked through the jeaf's shirt, despite the breeze. He washed and wiped his hands before eyeing his tools again. This time, he picked a smaller bone needle, a finer strand of hemp to sew the skin. The beast relaxed, breathing slower and more steadily, with but few passing spasms.

The wound's edges appeared much closer. Joaquin thought the hard work must be over. Aldo placed the skin stitches just so, half an inch apart.

"Cut this far above the knot," motioned the jeaf.

Craning forward, Joaquin barely saw the thread as sweat dripped from his own brow and clouded his vision. He expected just a few more stitches, yet it turned out they were far from done. After sixteen painstaking stitches, Aldo unwrapped a second spool of thread to finish the job. Joaquin's clubfoot started to cramp again, but he ignored it. Keeping his concentration was now a point of honor.

After twenty-nine stitches, Aldo put his tools down. "There." He struggled to his feet. "The rest is out of my hands. Fortunately, the wound is far enough back that her tail can swat the flies off."

He stared down at Heriberto. "You must clean it carefully with a wet soapy cloth each day. I will make a poultice for you to apply to the wound. The skin stitches will come out in a week."

"Jeaf, how can I thank you?" Heriberto stood, head bowed.

Aldo turned and spat. "You can thank me by nursing your steed back to health." The young gaucho's face turned white. Aldo grunted and turned away.

He spied Harry and his features quickly softened. The Sky-Borne leader bent forward, hands on his knees, alternately gulping and gritting his lips. "Come, my pale friend." Aldo took Harry's elbow and led him away. He turned back to the other gauchos. "Let us brew maté. After that, I wish to see the beast that gored Heriberto's mare."

Joaquin almost jumped up then and there. He had been the one who saw the deed most clearly, and he was in the best position to identify the offending steer for Aldo. He still shook from his ordeal of trimming the stitches without squirming, and never needed a lift like he did now, yet it was all he could do to sit still.

Ysidro and Gabino knelt to build a fire from scattered chips of cow dung. They laughed as Harry winced and turned away from the smoke. As water heated in a small iron kettle, Aldo retrieved the gourd-like maté cup and bombilla metal straw from his pack. He dropped several leaves of yerba in the gourd, and Gabino filled it with boiling water. Aldo fished out his pipe, went through his routine of cleaning, filling and lighting it, then leaned back.

Joaquin pulled his boot off and massaged the cramp in his clubfoot, glancing at the jeaf from the corner of his eye. He expected that he could master the curandero part — herbal poultices, sewing technique and the like — if he remained in Aldo's favor. Yet that which went with it, the aura of command, the demand for respect, how could he ever earn such a thing?

Gabino passed the cup around. Harry squatted at the edge of the group, taking his turn at the cup by sipping token amounts. His complexion remained pasty. After a few minutes, he excused himself and rose, pointing in the direction of the crater. The task of hoisting himself onto the stallion's back took several tries. Still jerking the reins around, he headed off. His behavior got the charros muttering once again. Unlike the night of the feast, by now Joaquin felt only the smallest twinge of sympathy. A man needed to learn these lessons, or else one would quickly perish out here on the range.

Aldo shrugged. "He is not used to our ways."

Ysidro guffawed. "Not used to riding horseback, you mean." Then he turned serious. "How do the Sky-Bornes get around in their homeland? Surely not on foot?" He turned to the other charros, but they could only shrug.

Joaquin was intrigued. Did each of them own a personal flying machine? How often did they crash?

Gabino refilled the gourd several times.

Finally, Aldo sat up and turned to Ysidro. "Any idea what spooked that steer?"

His half-brother shrugged. "Who knows? None of the others have been acting up."

"Hmm. Who saw this happen?"

Ready, Joaquin jumped up. "I can show you the beast, seir."

"How did I guess?" Aldo lumbered to his feet and headed toward his palomino. As the two rode through the herd, Joaquin noticed that none of the other beeves appeared troubled. Strange, he thought, since one jumpy animal typically affected them all. The rare thunderstorm could be a disaster.

Then he spotted the culprit. "There. That smaller one." Joaquin pointed toward a younger steer ahead. It stood off by itself, pawing the ground, shaking its head back and forth and snorting every few seconds.

Aldo tried to get a good look without getting too close. "See the eyes, boy? The pupils are dilated. And what can you tell from the skin?"

What could he tell? Joaquin thought fast. "It is dry."

"Exactly. All that thrashing, but not a bead of sweat." He raised his head. "There is a pattern here. The steer will be better in a few hours."

What made the jeaf so sure? That was what impressed Joaquin: not just Aldo's vast knowledge, but the casual assurance with which he wielded it. "Did a snake bite it?" Joaquin ventured.

"No, it would have fallen by now." They rode slowly. Aldo focused on the ground. He stopped, dismounted, and picked the purple cone-shaped bud of a leafy plant. He held it up. "Know what this is, boy?"

Joaquin stuck out his lower lip. "Just another weed, no?"

"Hardly." Aldo held the stem at arm's length, pointed the way they just came. "If you eat this weed, it will make you act crazy, just like that steer. The poison will speed up your heart and your breathing, give you a fever." He sniffed it. "No smell. The older ones learn to avoid it, but this one did not know any better."

The corners of Aldo's mustache perked up. A twinkle shone in his eye. "If you are young, you will recover."

Joaquin dismounted and bent down to study the harmless-looking plant. He reached out to pick it, but Aldo rasped, "Do not touch the leaves. If you later rub your eye, your vision will blur just the same as if you ate them."

Joaquin jerked back, heart racing without even touching the weed. So much to learn — plants that cured what ailed you, others that could just as easily poison you. How long did Aldo spend as some other jeaf's apprentice, or did he just pick all of this up the hard way?

Aldo sniffed again. "I call it locoweed. Crazy charros who spurn the little sense God gave them might chew this weed on purpose, claim to see visions." As he prepared to mount, Aldo studied him. "If you find yourself in the company of these morons, you will need to avoid such a lure."

Joaquin stood straight and touched his boina in a mock salute. The jeaf's point was clear. Joaquin could now spot a poisoned steer. Who knew when that might happen again? What's more, Aldo gave him more responsibility today than ever before. Every new task was a test. If he could stay alert, he would yet win Aldo's respect, but would that be enough to make it as a gaucho? He needed to show that he was tough enough to handle cattle. The next time such an opportunity arose, he would be ready.

12

THE MOUNTAIN

Cozuel trudges along at his own slow gait, no matter how much I prod. I curse under my breath; I could have made better time on foot.

Luz has focused on a mounted figure skirting across the rim of the crater, half a mile behind us. "Keltyn, I think Nestor is following us." She points.

I can barely make out the horse, let alone the rider. "What makes you think so?"

"I can't be sure, but that horse looks like a piebald, and there aren't too many of those among our tribe."

Hope she's wrong. This could throw a monkey wrench into our plans. "Mr. Nosy, eh?" I turn back to her. "You worried?"

"He's a jerk. Lots of times I've caught him following me at a distance, when I'm out exploring. He hasn't threatened me or anything, but I can tell he's trailing me, and he knows I can tell."

"So, no big deal, right? And now there are two of us."

"I guess. But as you saw the other day, he owns a rifle."

And he's trigger-happy, we found that out. "If he gets closer, I'll still have time to call Buck, but I can't see any reason why he would threaten us." Still, why would he waste his whole day snooping? I ponder the risks. Should we call off our plans? Try to hide in some brush until he passes by? Confront him?

In the end, we decide to trek on, convinced that Nestor wouldn't know what to do with the iris stone if it stared him in the face. I feel like he's just one more obstacle to deal with, a minor toothache that, sooner or later, will either worsen or subside.

After leaving the crater, we pass through several miles of manzanita and holly scrub. Occasionally, a lone pine greets us like a drunken charro, growing at a stilted angle out of solid rock. From the hard, yellow earth, every step of the mounts' hooves stirs up a puff of dust.

Luz turns in the saddle to face me. "Who are the 'Chinese,' Keltyn? Why did that get Buck so upset?"

The girl's question jolts me. How much should I tell her? "They're the so-called bad guys, enemies, competitors, whatever you want to call them." I point my chin at her. "Don't the Onwei have another tribe that you don't get along with?"

She ponders that. "Not really. We have outlaws, but not a whole tribe."

"Well, imagine billions of outlaws. That's how my 'tribe,' Canada, judges the Chinese. I personally don't buy it, but I'm in the minority."

"And that tool?"

"Chinese geology equipment is better quality than anything I can find in Canada." I nod abruptly to signal that's all I have to say about the matter, then reach for my water skin and take a deep swallow. Luz turns forward again, but her knitted brow tells me she's got more questions. Too bad, sister.

The terrain is changing. Not just a steeper slope, but also the ground turns harder and more slippery. My nag has a low center of gravity, but I worry about Quintara's footing.

"Looks like we're not the first ones to come this way." I point downward. There are other tracks, and, judging from their depth and sharp contour, they're fresh. Most are shaped like cattle hooves, a few like horses.

Luz studies them. "That's odd. The entire herd grazes in the valley."

That makes sense. The grass this high is too sparse to feed large numbers, and the gauchos would curse the rough terrain. "You think there's someone else up here?"

Our eyes lock momentarily, then we both peer back in the direction we have just come. The trail is too winding to see if Nestor is still behind us, but I'm willing to bet he is, and that's why he's been following us. Does he think we're trying to spy on whatever's happening up here? What will he do to stop us from finding out? A man with a rifle who knows this terrain; I have a sudden feeling the odds have shifted in his favor.

We keep riding, but I'm warier, listening for any sounds from ahead or behind. Luz too has taken to scanning back and forth as her horse paces. After another half mile, the tracks take an abrupt turn to the right. Their path heads for a square-walled canyon half a mile distant. Glaciers, long since melted, have scraped its walls.

Now Luz sits ramrod straight, poised on the edge of her saddle horn. Her gaze flits all over the canyon. Even before she turns back to me, I know what's on her mind.

"We need to check this out." She nods for emphasis. "Four heifers have been missing from the herd ever since our tribe set up camp. Aldo will wish to know where they are."

I snort. Luz is just like her mutt. Any passing thing that nabs her attention, she wants to chase it. "Don't even think of taking a detour," I say. "Just keep riding straight." I study the canyon. "The cattle didn't just wander up here. Someone's with them, and, judging from how isolated this spot is, they likely don't care for visitors. That's got to be why Nestor's tailing us." I turn back to face her. "You can tell Aldo when we get back tonight."

"How can I tell him unless I have seen them?"

"And I'm saying we don't have time to get sidetracked, not if we're gonna scout the mountain and still get back by tonight."

Her eyes flash as she weighs her options. "We could split up. You keep going, I'll catch up later."

I'm starting to lose it. "Girl, don't you remember what your mother told you? We've got to stay together, otherwise we'll both be in trouble."

She flushes, making me wonder if her mother really did sanction this little excursion. Finally, she nods. "What about our tracks?"

"Like I said before, the rock gets so hard, pretty soon we won't leave any. Coming down, though, different story."

With the sun near its peak, light bounces from each leaf and blade of grass. We cross several ravines alternating with ridge saddles on the lower slopes of Erebus. Into the distance stretch jagged igneous volcanic rock, hardened lava from prior eruptions. Only the upper trunks of larger trees, above three feet high, have survived a prior volcanic bath.

Soon we run into lush pockets of green mountainside, fertilized from lava flow. We pass through a meadow ablaze with red passionflowers and purple lupine, and smell the tang of fresh mint. Sure enough, as the brush opens up and we can see half a mile back, there is no sign of Nestor. He must have taken the turnoff to the box canyon. It's good to have him off our tail, but now I'm dead sure that something rotten is going on in that canyon. I'm already checking the lay of the land to see if there's an alternate route for the way down. We'll need to skirt wide of Nestor and whoever else is holed up there.

The mountain's shadow makes it hard to tell which formations might be the iris stone. Several times, we dismount to get a closer look at a promising ridge point, but in each case, the rock proves too hard to chisel.

Cozuel tugs out clumps of grass to munch on at every stop. That's a mule's way to get extra fluid. Luz frets about water for Quintara, but just before the tree line, we find a spring with shade and break for lunch.

We munch on cheese, crackers and fruit slices from my provisions. Not as hearty as Trieste's *lengua* tortilla wraps, but they'll have to do. I scan every direction for signs of iridium. It must lie somewhere near. Now I begin to wonder if a one-day trip will be enough time to scout the slopes of Erebus. Was I naïve to think that the deposits of stone are strewn randomly, or do they favor certain terrain? Up here, as we close in on where paydirt should lie, my self-assurance starts to ebb.

I try to steel myself by flashing back to our last press conference, only a few days ago, the one where I project total confidence in our mission.

***

Three of us — Harry, Fay and I — are strapped onto plush chairs in the Space Station to keep from floating away. We watch a large cube, mounted on the far wall, which shines our blue home planet on a black background. The image of Earth on the screen fades, replaced by that of a man of indeterminate age. That's the thing about Sir Oscar; somehow there's no wrinkle lines to mar the smooth skin of his face. He strides up to a wooden platform. On the front of the platform, a sign, "The Face of Tomorrow," along with a sunflower logo, casts the emblem of Bailey Holdings.

Sir Oscar scans the twenty-odd faces of people all seated in straight chairs below him. Screens mounted on the far walls beam other images of faces, their features less clear. He raises his arms to signal quiet, regales his audience with an update of our progress, and entertains questions from the press.

Most of the queries have to do with political implications of the mission, stirring up the cold war with China, etc. He tries to deflect these: "I certainly do not pretend to speak for Canada about any political implications of this mission..."

I admire how smoothly Sir Oscar handles the media, but that's a tough blurb to swallow. Everyone knows that, since Parliament dissolved decades ago, there is really no one in government to speak for Canada other than the King, and he tries to stay out of politics. So, the press has a habit of hanging on to Sir Oscar's every word, trying to sift his folksy one-liners for deep meaning.

He rambles on. "I will say that the potential for finding natural resources in Antarctica is enormous."

Someone raises her hand, finger pointed. "Give us a for instance."

"Certainly. Perhaps Savant SparrowHawk would care to comment." He turns around to face the screen, which now flashes an image of me, his rising-star geologist.

I should have expected questions to head my way. It's not like the first press briefing, six months ago, when Sir Oscar announced the mission. I was tongue-tied then. Now, I keep a patient monotone. "We have reason to believe there are large deposits of iridium near Mt. Erebus."

Sir Oscar obligingly points a light at a spot on the white portion of the huge wall diagram.

Oops, I've lost them. Blank faces pepper the audience. Newbies.

Sir Oscar interjects, "Savant, for the benefit of those in the media who were not at your last briefing, could you explain the importance of the Erebus connection?"

I keep my hands folded on the table. "Certainly. You can find iridium near meteor craters, but the best quality ore comes from the slopes of volcanoes. All of these except one are in low or middle latitudes, inaccessible due to global warming. The exception is Mt. Erebus. Now that Antarctica's layers of ice have thawed, Erebus is our destination."

"Thank you, Savant. I hope you don't mind if I take this opportunity to make an announcement." Sir Oscar beams like a proud parent. "I have invited Keltyn SparrowHawk to join the Bailey team permanently as a Science Fellow, pending the outcome of this mission. At the tender age of twenty-five, she will be, by far, the youngest Fellow I have ever appointed, which should speak for her caliber."

He turns back to face me. "Keltyn, it humbles me to admit this, but the success of our mission hinges on your invention, the iridium field assay."

I feel my face flush, but I just nod and mumble my thanks. I suspected this was coming. A few weeks ago, Sir Oscar stopped by at one of our briefings. With the smile of a cat that swallowed a canary, he hinted at a surprise announcement in the works. I would be pleased.

Harry pats me on the back and Fay reaches over to hug me. Sir Oscar winks before turning back to his audience. He waits until the applause has subsided and deftly moves the questioning along.

***

Amazing how a person can act so confident when they're just blowing smoke. That's about all that Oscar and I have in common. At least he was smart enough to hold that Science Fellow position as a reward, to see if this dog will roll over before she gets the bone. The stuff is here. I know it. If I had a tail, it would be wagging.

13

FREE FALL

Fay clasped the mug of tea and tried to say "khosko," the Onwei word for mug, but that sound simply would not roll off her tongue. How frustrating. She was fluent in half a dozen languages, and passable in at least ten more. What was the problem here?

She spent all of yesterday with Yoka, tolerating the old woman's abrupt manners and trying as best she could to deflect her pointed questions. Now that her machine finally broke through to decode Onwei, they could have a decent enough conversation, but her pride would be shaken if she were unable to learn some rudimentary phrases on her own. Though she'd given up with next to no progress last night, this morning she dove back.

Yoka set up her loom, but Fay could tell that her questions aroused the crone's interest. Now she broke in. "No, no. Not 'gosco.' 'Khosko.' It's a more guttural sound. You don't have that inflection in Spanish."

"Must be the influence of other ancestors," Fay said.

"We Onwei are — what is the expression — a melting pot."

Another matter puzzled Fay. "Yoka, can I ask you a more personal question?"

"And what might that be?"

"This ability of yours, channeling."

"A strange term."

"Communicating with the dead."

"Yes? What of it?" Yoka's voice dropped a notch.

"Do only the women partake of Venga?"

"The charros believe I will try to cast a spell upon them. The tradesmen in Nomidar, the older ones, often they come. Especially when hints of mortality intrude."

"Yours must be quite a gift."

Yoka sniffed. "Not a gift. Just years of study."

"You must have had a teacher."

"Of course. My mother."

"But you... have no children?"

"I had a daughter, Addys. She died ten years ago." Yoka's voice dropped.

Fay took a quick breath, worried she might lose the old woman. "I'm sorry. Did she have an accident?"

"No, from the khokri, the wasting disease, all too common among our women since our ancestors first arrived on this continent."

Fay mulled that over. "I'm guessing she was your protégé as well."

"For twenty years. I taught her all the different tongues. We refined the Venga recipe. And weaving, of course, what you would call a useful trade. By the time she died, I was past sixty. Too old to lure another apprentice. What young woman would want to humble herself to me, I ask you?" Yoka's voice took on a whine. She pulled in a raspy breath. "So, you see my dilemma. No heiress."

"Aha." A switch snapped on in Fay's mind. "I have an idea."

"Pray tell."

"I think we can help each other, Yoka. You and I."

"What can you possibly do to help me?"

"Joaquin." She pronounced the name with a triumphant air.

"The boy?" The crone snorted. "What of him?"

"You tried to sway Luz to learn the Venga craft, but she acts too impatient for this sort of thing. Joaquin has the right temperament."

"Ha! You have not been paying attention. The Venga, only the women and a few old men show any interest." Yoka started back on her loom.

"Joaquin has curiosity. You planted the seed yesterday. He'll come around, I'm sure of it."

"Maybe he will try it once. So, what? You suggest that he would waste his youth learning an old woman's secrets? He wishes to spend his life herding beeves, the same as all the young men in our tribe."

"I believe that we can entice him, you and I."

"How? By mocking his clubfoot."

Fay winced at the crone's crudeness. "Young men have stubborn pride," she offered. "He rides a horse well, which I'm sure did not come easily for him."

"So? What do you suggest?"

"Play on his curiosity about his ancestors," said Fay.

"I see." The dialups slipped down Yoka's nose as she lowered her chin and studied her guest. She pushed them back with one finger. "You believe that a male diviner might allay the fears of the charros."

"Exactly."

"But the tongues of the ancients take years to learn. I'm afraid I don't have that much time left to teach him."

"This machine, Yoka." Fay held up her decoder. "It's perfect for your needs."

"Ah, yes, I'm sure your magic can teach this sort of thing." The old woman's prune face broke into a contorted smile.

Fay glanced up and spied a lone buzzard. How appropriate.

"Very well," said Yoka. "Supposing I agree, what is it you would wish from me?"

"You understand why we came?" Fay kept a singsong lilt in her voice. This usually had a soothing effect when she found herself dealing with a wary stranger.

"I gather that the others came to search for this precious stone. You, unless I miss my guess, came for a different reason altogether. Am I right?" Fay picked her words carefully. "Sort of. I came to find proof that humans have adapted to this side of the world. But officially, I am our liaison."

"Meaning, you deal with the locals."

The crone's piercing gaze seemed to cut straight through Fay, and made her eyes flutter. "You are too candid, but yes."

"You need me, for what? Let me guess." Yoka stopped handling her loom and hummed.

Another buzzard drifted into view.

"You need me to seal the deal between your people and mine, so you can acquire the iris stone from our land without resistance."

"Not the words I would have chosen, but... I'm afraid you're correct."

"Something else has been troubling me about the reasons for your so-called mission." Yoka's tone changed. She set hands on hips. Fay sensed an imminent trap. "You know, 'mission' is a funny concept. It brings to mind the word 'missionary.'" She said the word in English; the Onwei must not have such a thing.

Yoka pointed a finger. "Our people lost most of what you would call modern civilization when they fled to this continent amidst the chaos of environmental ruin. We have no mines, no factories, no printing presses, certainly none of the machines that perform your complex tasks." She waved her arms, dismissing all of these. "Our children receive rudimentary instruction at the feet of their elders. They have no history books, no concept of such things as colonies or religious conversions. But you and I, Orfea, we keep score."

"I... I don't follow." Fay fought to keep her voice from breaking.

"Oh, I think you do. You have fooled yourself that your own motives are pure." Yoka slapped her thigh with a dull thud. "Who sponsored your voyage here? To whom do you answer?"

"His name is Sir Oscar Bailey."

"This Sir Oscar Bailey, he is rich and powerful, no?"

"And perhaps immortal."

"Meaning what?"

"He keeps his age a secret, but it's well over a hundred. Rumor has it that he employs a team of scientists whose sole task is to tailor the latest medical discoveries for his brain and body." Fay regained the lilt in her voice. "Lotions to keep his face soft. He never needs to shave."

"Skin that never ages." Yoka stroked her own deeply wrinkled cheek. "Hmph. Such conceit." She paused. "This 'mission' that he funded, it must cost much in treasure. He expects a greater reward in return."

"No doubt."

"What do your people term such an undertaking?"

"You could term it an investment," said Fay.

"Quite so. Now, assuming he can procure a steady supply of the iris stone, how will this enrich him?"

"He will have what we call a 'corner on the market.'"

"A 'corner' indeed. Pray enlighten me, dear one." Yoka's voice oozed warmth with a touch of acid. "Of what use is this ore to your people, other than to protect your flying machines from harm as they travel through hazardous skies?"

"It's the key to produce cold fusion energy. But, as you say, he could also build many more of these flying machines." Then it hit her. Fay let out a long slow breath. "Is that what you think? That Sir Oscar wants a great supply of iridium, so he can build a lot of planes to fly to your land?"

The old woman barely needed to nod. Fay looked upward. The dozen buzzards now circling seemed more ominous than ever. Her voice felt strained. "Why didn't I put two and two together? I should have been able to figure this out. We walk around with blinders, expecting the world to go on as it is."

She paused, pressed a hand to her temple. "Oscar must envision ferrying people here to... to colonize. Our food supply is squeezed. The best climate for crops moves ever northward, but the land ends at the shores of the expanding Arctic Ocean, and the yield is constrained by shorter growing seasons."

Yoka's eyebrows arched high into her forehead. "The Onwei people faced this problem long ago and adapted."

A thought warmed Fay. She looked the old woman in the eye. "Yoka, think of all that your people could teach ours, about food production in this kind of climate."

Yoka grunted. "Remember your history books, woman. What did the European colonists do to all the native peoples they encountered in other parts of the world?"

"No, it won't be like that." But Fay slumped. Why wouldn't it? Who was she kidding?

"Hmph," croaked the old woman. Then, silence.

***

Luz and I pack up our lunch and move on. For some time, we stay in shadow before emerging into the sun's glare. I adjust the brim of my cap lower and pull out my sunshades.

I check my timepiece and the angle of the sun. It's well past noon. How much longer can we go on and still expect to return back to camp before dark? We didn't bring camping gear, and now I notice clouds gathering on the horizon. I catch Luz watching me mull this over. She frowns. Too bad, sister. If we don't get some clue soon, I'm going to have to call it.

The doubt creeps back. I begin to mull what will happen to my career if, after this vaunted expedition, the good stuff is nowhere to be found.

But there's a bigger question, one I don't even want to think about. What happens if I *do* find it?

Passing above the tree line, the footing turns rockier. I stop again, pull a spotter scope out of my pack, and survey the mountainside. Veins of quartz in a reddish-brown base and the occasional glint of fool's gold, but no sign of the I-rock. Could all my calculations be wrong? The cheese and crackers sit undigested in my stomach, weighing on me like a chunk of this ephemeral stone.

I'm just about ready to give up when something catches my eye. I gasp and hand the scope to Luz. "A quarter mile farther on this side, another five hundred feet up, take a look at that ledge." My heart races.

Luz peers through the scope and nods eagerly.

A mammoth outcropping awaits us as we climb onward with renewed gusto. Inching closer, we're almost blinded by sparkles of dark purple in its dull gray base. The footing becomes so hard that each hoof step grates with a loud scrape.

We tie the mounts and scale the wall on hands and knees. Reaching the top, I'm awestruck. Luz shakes her head, equally amazed. This is it, the jaw-dropping real deal.

I let out a "Yee-hah," and Luz whoops something that sounds like "Oleh!"

Without another word, we spread our tools and frantically chisel away to collect specimens. Chunk after chunk plops into the bags. I stop and pull a small camera out of my pocket, point it at Luz. She stops chiseling, but I motion for her to keep on. I keep shooting until she completely separates an egg-sized lump of ore and holds it up for inspection.

I show Luz the segment, using my body to shade the sun's rays on the camera. She watches a moving image of herself perform the whole three minutes of chiseling out the rock. Her brow furrows.

"Close your mouth. You're collecting flies," I say.

She keeps staring. "How... how does this thing work?" Before I can answer that one, she adds, "And how come you saved it until now?"

"To be honest, I, all of us, feared how your people would react to seeing their image. That's why none of us dared use this at your camp." I turn the camera over in my hands. "When the white men first used one of these on my people, it caused a lot of trouble. Of course, they used a big black box, with exploding powder for a light source, so no wonder. My people wouldn't let them do it, claimed that capturing the images would snare their souls as well." More of the white man's black magic.

Luz ponders this. "My mother and lots of others in our tribe would have the same reaction."

I lift my chin while eyeing Luz's bag. She empties it out, and we savor the texture of each piece. Nine multifaceted gem-quality stones, ranging in size from grape to egg-sized. Each reflects the light differently, a whole palette of color beyond the base violet.

"Not bad." I draw the phrase out. "Now check these." I pull out my own sack.

She can't stop her hands from shaking. She paws one plum-sized piece after another.

"They're from various points on the face of the outcropping," I tell her. "Look closely. See if you can tell the difference."

She holds them one at a time, trying to shade them from the sun.

"Each one is from a different spot, only a few steps apart, but you can see how they shine differently." For my own picky reasons, it's important that she understand this.

"Why would that be?" She keeps turning them over.

"Probably from altered rates of the magma cooling."

"Magma?"

"Sorry. Molten rock." I reach for the canteen and take another swallow. "This is, by far, the largest amount I've ever seen in one place." I rub my hands together, slowly nodding, taking in the entire scene. I try to envision an iridium mining operation on this spot. After a minute, I feel my lips tingle, and I realize that the excitement has got me hyperventilating. *Slow. Down.*

Luz must see the panic in my face. She moves closer, and we crouch together on the far end of the outcropping. Just then, the sun catches a larger seam of even brighter violet, shining another quarter mile higher on the mountain's slope. We both gasp in unison. Within seconds I'm panting. I try to sit but end up lying flat on the rock.

I can't tell if it's elation, altitude exhaustion, the bright afternoon rays, or all of those things. I will myself to breathe slower and shut my eyes, lips half-parted. I've found what I came for.

The girl also sinks back on the rock face and announces, "This will change my life. Of course, Mama will be relieved, and oh so proud. I can come back here anytime, and haul away as much as she can ever use."

"And down the line, when your mother becomes too tired, too frail to continue her craft?" I don't mention that Trieste doesn't look all that sturdy now. "Maybe she can teach an apprentice."

Luz laughs. "Not me, I can't sit still that long. My boyfriend, Ian, maybe one of his sisters will take up the trade. Or maybe Ian and I will come up here every year, collect a great big stash, sell the raw stones at the Rendezvous, to the highest bidders."

As if these thoughts are blasphemous, the earth starts to shake beneath us, jolting us both upright. A warm stream dribbles down my pant leg. I crawl over toward Luz, the color emptied from her cheeks, and we embrace in a shudder of fear.

***

Fay sat in a funk, her head bowed, hands digging through her hair, trying to discern the implications of what the old woman's shrewd deductions had just uncovered. Just then, the ground began to shake. Fay instinctively glanced toward Erebus and watched the spiral trace of smoke morph into a dense cloud. "The volcano. It's erupting, isn't it?" Her voice shook as she jerked around to face Yoka. "Just as you predicted."

"I did not invent the prophecy, simply recited it."

"You warned them not to go. Oh Lord." Fay chewed her lip.

"Who listens to the rants of an old woman? The young must chart their own course." Yoka groaned and shuffled her body. "Now if you will excuse me, it is time for my nap."

Fay's jaw dropped. "But... oh, geez." She gulped. Her cheery exchange with Yoka had ended, and she sat alone, glum, hunched over her stool in the shade, swirling her cup of sun tea like it could answer this riddle.

Ever since she and Oscar first met, Fay imagined, knew, that it was she who manipulated him. Now, faced with the shrewd insight of this cunning old woman, she realized that Oscar used her for his own purposes. She recalled their first meeting. What clues did she miss?

***

Muted sunlight from high windows filters into a hallway. Fay pauses in front of a door and pulls a hand mirror out of her purse. She wears a mustard-colored full-length tunic with a wide-patterned fabric belt that advertises her slim mid-section and an amber necklace meant to cover the wrinkle lines beneath. Her hand knocks, then splays open, casting her fate to the winds.

The man who opens the door stands erect; his head tilts in an expression of query. The contrast between his shock of white hair and wrinkle-free face unnerves her. Piercing steel-gray eyes, a pug nose, thin-set lips, prominent chin. The scent of verbena wafts through the doorway.

A velvet robe encircles his short, sturdy physique. Fay's eye catches a discreet white cross emblem sewn onto the left breast. The robe's deep crimson is set off by a cream-colored sash and matching scarf. A gold pin in the shape of a sunflower anchors the folds of the scarf.

"A pleasure, Savant Del Campo. Please come in." The man bows at the waist.

"Welcome to Zürich, Sir Oscar." Fay senses the greeting is superfluous for this man, who appears thoroughly at home already.

"Just Oscar, please." He flicks his wrist and escorts her to a sofa. "The 'Sir' is for king and media. Thank you. I do feel welcome in Zürich. Spend quite a bit of time here, actually." He holds up a decanter. "Care for a spot of Yukon sherry?"

"Thank you, Oscar."

"So!" He passes the glass to Fay and drifts into an armchair. "What would the effervescent Orfea Del Campo want from the curmudgeon Oscar Bailey?"

"A seat on the plane."

"Ha!" His eyes widen. "The Bailey Voyager, I presume. I had a hunch..." His eyes light on the wall before meeting hers again. "No, I think not, Orfea. May I call you Orfea?"

"Fay, please, Oscar."

"I envision this as a low-profile mission, Fay. Right now, Antarctic exploration is a pipe dream. I don't want to raise people's expectations prematurely."

"You think that my inclusion would generate extra publicity?"

Oscar's gaze narrows. "You're not the type to hide your light under a bushel, now are you, Fay?"

"Oh, I assure you, I'm a team player. What matters to me is finding out if there really are people living in Antarctica."

His free hand alternates between open and clenched. "You have to understand my position. The motive for the whole venture, I dare say for all my ventures, is profit. I make no bones about that. We have no idea what kinds of resources exist in Antarctica. No one has explored that land since the ice melted."

"I do understand that, Oscar, but we'll need to develop a relationship with these folks, if there are any."

"Of course. Even supposing I agree to include a liaison..." He takes a deep breath. "You must pardon me for being blunt, but I can easily find a dozen people as qualified as you, and none of them controversial. Give me one good reason why I should pick you."

Fay's eye wavers and catches the glint of sunlight bouncing off a crystal goblet on the mantel. She expected that it might come to this. She turns back to face Oscar. "Paul Buchschreiber."

"Paul who?" No glint of recognition in the voice. His ignorance seems genuine.

"My husband. He died five years ago."

"I'm sorry. What has that to do with me?"

"You killed him."

Sir Oscar chokes, seizes his breath with a retch. "Oh, please."

"You, corporate. Bailey Holdings."

A forced laugh. "We've been accused of many transgressions, but this is a first for homicide."

"Don't worry, no jury will ever convict you. However..."

"Yes?" The massive head tilts.

"The story could make for nasty publicity."

His lips purse. "So why have I not heard about this?"

"You pay people to do your dirty work, Oscar. To spare you the messy details."

He seems neither surprised nor angered by the accusation. "Pray share a few of these details."

She tilts her head and studies him first. "Paul was an industrial hygienist. Worked for I. G. Farben, one of your chemical subsidiaries in the Rhineland."

The head rocking stops. "And?"

"Paul's last assignment, part of the merger deal, was to inventory the residual toxic waste."

"Standard procedure for all our acquisitions. We need to find any closet skeletons." Oscar leans forward, hands between his knees, cupping the wine. "So, what happened to your Paul?"

"He did his job. Spent months sampling the layers of debris in the factory ruins. Prepared a report, two hundred pages. Tables of data, lab analyses, the works." Her eyes moisten. She hates reciting the details.

"And?" He watches her intently.

"No big surprises, at least not for anyone at Farben with half a brain. Sky-high levels of benzene, cadmium, dioxins, you name it. Stuff that hasn't been used for centuries, but it's still there. The grounds are saturated. It would take years, decades, to clean up."

"Which would have killed the merger. You're alleging that my staff kept this quiet?"

"Like I said, Oscar, you pay people to hide the nasties from you." Fay's jaw clenches, despite the time spent rehearsing this moment. "Paul's report never saw the light of day. He was told that it would be published in due course, not to worry. Then he was given a nice severance package."

"I have a feeling we're coming to the punch line." He cocks his head again, eyes locked into Fay's.

"A few months later, Paul's gums started bleeding, then blotchy sores popped up all over his body. His color turned pasty." Fay sniffles. The story doesn't come any easier no matter how many times she tells it. She struggles onward. "He was diagnosed with aplastic anemia. The doctors recommended a bone marrow transplant. He lasted three more years, miserable until the end."

Sir Oscar's face is blank. "Forgive me, Savant Del Campo, I don't see the connection."

"No, you're not a medical person." Fay pulls a hankie from her purse and blows softly. "Aplastic anemia is pretty rare. Almost all cases are linked to toxic chemical exposure. Benzene is a prime culprit."

"Ah." His leonine head lifts. "So, Paul was poisoned."

"You got it."

Oscar's bushy white brows beetle up. "Unintentionally, of course."

"Sometimes the difference between stupidity and malice is hard to discern. At least that's what I've told myself for the last eight years."

"A sad story." He shakes his head slowly and rubs his palms together, the stem of his glass twirling between them. "Too bad the report was buried. You could have a field day with that in the right hands."

"Well, funny you should mention that, Oscar. After Paul's death, I sorted through his papers. Guess what I found?"

Oscar's hands freeze.

"A copy of the report. Paul normally didn't bring his work home. He must have suspected that nothing would be done with the original."

His head slumps. "That does change things, doesn't it?"

Fay allows the moment to draw out. "Let's be clear, Oscar. I'm not after publicity for its own sake. I will never release that document to the media unless my back is to the wall."

"Meaning?"

"Put me on the mission and I'm a happy camper."

A long silence follows, then Sir Oscar rises to pour them each more sherry. He raises his glass and forces another smile. "To you, Fay."

***

After twenty seconds, the ground tremor stops. Luz and I hurry to pack our gear and the trophies. Wobbly, we skid back down toward the mounts, leading them on foot to where we first sighted the seam of iris stone. I pause to take a swig of water, trying to ignore the clammy feeling in my breeches. Luz fumbles to stick her specimen bag into her pack.

One of the stones slips out and rolls down the rock face ten feet, coming to rest at the edge of the dirt. Bending down to retrieve it, she spies something, kneels and paws at the ground. Another tremor rumbles, this time followed by a hissing noise that makes her look up.

"Lava, vaporizing the snow into steam." I try to play it down. "That's it. Time to go." I mount Cozuel, but Luz stays put, cries out, and holds up both hands.

I shake my head. "Honey, we have to leave. Now."

"No, wait." The girl tosses rocks aside in frenzy, grabs a small pick, and starts hacking away at the dirt that surrounds this mystery find.

"Are you nuts? Listen to me, Luz. I'm the boss, remember?" But the girl just ignores me and keeps chopping.

"If we get stuck up here," I start, then stop and shake my head. What can I possibly threaten this girl with? Muttering, I climb down to help. From the tip that attracted her notice, we gradually clear the margins of the target. Dull lavender with a grayish tint, vaguely rectangular, its longest dimension is six feet, while the other two are each a foot.

When at last we're able to move it, I give a start. "Is this what I think it is?" I mop my brow, try to describe it like we would in school. "A long bone. Characteristic grooves on one end, rounded on the other. Upper bone of an arm or leg."

"What kind of creature has bones that long?" Luz's gaze darts all around.

"Maybe another dinosaur." I slump backward as the words come out of my mouth. She stares at me, dumbfounded. I use a stick to trace a rough picture of an upright dinosaur.

Luz points to the half-freed bone and gives me a tentative look. Using our small array of tools, we go at it. After another five minutes of digging, I sit back on my haunches, panting, resting the backs of my hands on my hips.

I give her a look over my brows and bark out a laugh. "You want to haul this back to camp, don't you?"

"Of course. Yoka Sutu can summon her ancestor to tell us the story behind it."

"You think she'll forgive you for stealing the Venga nuggets?"

She mulls that over. "Yes, when she sees what we found. How much do you think it weighs?"

"Too much," I say. She's behaving like her nosy mutt again. Doesn't she perceive the risk of dawdling up here? But I can't force her, and I can't leave her here. Despite my better judgment, I shrug and return to the task.

It takes another twenty minutes of scraping and prying to loosen the whole relic. Luz grunts, trying to pick up one end. The thing must weigh as much as the cart that carries all of Trieste's wares. Heaving together, we manage to turn it over.

More grunting as we drag the bone and lash it to the mounts, tying each end of the rope to a saddle horn. The load drags between and behind Quintara and Cozuel. The two are clearly mismatched, but there's no other option.

Just as we start to tow this cargo, I feel another quiver, this one stronger than before. It vibrates through Cozuel's body. Rocks bounce all around us like so many jumping rabbits. Cozuel takes it in stride, but Quintara turns skittish, and Luz has to coax the mare to keep moving. The beginnings of a rumble in my gut echo the shaking all around us. We need to get down and find a safe haven. Pronto.

As we angle toward the tree line, a boulder the size of a newborn calf plunges down the hillside straight at us, with Quintara first in its way. The big rock bounces off an outcropping four feet up, then slams into the mare square on the left rear leg.

Luz hollers. Quintara buckles and collapses. The girl is thrown down and back. She screams. Her lower spine crashes into the edge of the boulder. She screams louder and slides into a heap at the base of the rock.

I jump off Cozuel and run to her, my heart in my throat. She yells and waves her arms, but she can't move her feet. She pounds her thigh.

Slowly, agonizingly, it dawns on both of us. If she can't feel or move her legs, her spine must be damaged. She may never walk again. She breaks into sobs, first a little bit, then in gushes.

I lift my head and slap my hands over my ears. After several minutes, I lay Luz down gently and pull off her boots. I pick up her feet and rub them vigorously. Opposing thoughts crash through my head in waves: "Poor Luz." "Damn my luck, I should have gone solo."

"Can you feel that, Luz? Please! Move your toes," I gasp, wiggling my fingers to imitate.

She stops sobbing long enough to see if her toes will move, but when they won't, she moans even louder.

"Your legs are paralyzed." I gulp as I say it. "Maybe a fractured lumbar vertebra. We have to get you back to camp but moving you may cause more damage." I put her feet down and stand myself up. "I'm gonna have to call Harry. He'll call Orfea at your camp to get help."

I grit my teeth and stumble back to the mule. The intensity of the tremor has slowed; all but the smaller rocks have stopped moving. I dig in my pack to find the phone, yank it out and jam on a button. "Come on, Harry, answer." I shake the dumb thing, growling at it.

Nothing, not a peep, nothing but silence from the phone, while behind me Luz alternates between wails and whimpers like a trapped animal.

***

Now, replaying that meeting with Oscar, it hit Fay. He sized her up on the spot and decided then and there to slot her into his grand scheme. He was using her, plain and simple. To think that she only bargained for the other way around. Fay swirled the dregs of her tea again, then tossed the remains onto the dirt.

As if to match her mood, the sky darkened. Soon, the mountain seemed to hover over them, its captive cloud turned thick and ugly. The wind picked up. Cottonwood leaves rattled as if they'd already dried and were ready to drop. The cattle started to bay. Gauchos, rounding up strays in the field, stopped to look at the sky. Neither could they figure it out. Even Yoka popped out of her yurt, muttered, and waddled around to collect loose stuff.

Fay stood and glanced about for a sign of what to do next. It felt like the end of the world.

She needed to enlist Keltyn's help. Together, they could devise some kind of monkey wrench to thwart Oscar. But Keltyn was stuck somewhere up on that mountain with Luz. Fay glanced at Erebus once more, her mood as black as the cloud of smoke hanging over its peak.

14

THE BISON BUCKLE

The girl lies there moaning, paralyzed from the waist down. I'm her only hope of survival, and she's known me for all of three days. I stand on that wooded slope, clenching the phone with both hands. There's no response. I poke the call button again and again, waiting for what seems like forever. Finally, a feeble beep.

"Hello, Keltyn. What's up?" It's the voice of our chief.

"Harry, thank God. Listen. There's been an accident. Luz is hurt. Bad." My eyes dart between her prostrate body and the mountaintop.

"Did the volcano erupt?" Harry's voice breaks. "The ground rattled here at the crater a bit ago."

"Erebus is acting up. It could be just letting off steam, or it could be getting ready to blow big time."

"What happened to the girl?"

"Thrown off her horse. A boulder smashed the mare's leg." I watch Quintara try to stand, but her three good legs can't support her weight and she sinks again. "I think it's shattered."

"That's awful. And Luz? Did she bust something too?"

"Worse. She fell hard on her back. Can't feel or move below her waist." "Oh, sweet lord."

"Harry, we need help to get her out." I tug at my hair. "I can't lift her, and even if I could, I don't dare sit her on the mule."

"You're right, we've got to get someone up there."

"You should be able to patch in to Fay at camp." I jab my finger to emphasize the point, even though he can't see me. "She can talk to Luz's people. She finally figured out the code to their language. I meant to leave you a note this morning before I got sidetracked with a stupid..." I halt abruptly, wincing at the memory. "Anyway, Fay can clue Aldo. He'll send muscle to help move Luz gently."

"Buck knows emergency response."

"Sure, but how's his head doing now?"

"There is that. Let me ask him." Several minutes of garbled sounds follow before Harry comes back on. "He says he's game, but I don't think so. You're right. We can't take any chances with Buck. He's got to fix the plane." After another minute, he chirps, "Hey, I could come."

I stifle a huge sigh and shake my head slowly. He is so pathetic when he tries to make light. I try to picture our out-of-shape boss moving Luz's weight in her fragile condition. "Just drop that idea, chief. Let Aldo send a couple of his own big boys."

"Anyone but Nestor," Buck growls in the background. Luz hears the comment and grimaces, jerking her back, and immediately starts to whimper. I tell Harry I need to go take care of her.

He says, "Give my best to the girl. We'll get you help. The fallout we'll deal with later." A click ends the chat.

I lower the phone and hang my head. What now? Try to make the girl comfortable. I remove the gourd from Cozuel's bags and hold it as Luz props herself on her elbows to drink. She still writhes in pain from the waist up, but her numb legs lay as stiff as a couple of logs.

I unroll a blanket and spread it under her, easing her to the side. I lift her shirt in back. An ugly sight makes me gasp.

"What is it?" Luz looks behind, but she can't see the huge purple welt covering her lower spine.

I make a fist to demonstrate. "One heck of a lump." Then I grab the edge of the blanket. "Hold on. Bouncy ride ahead."

Leaning back and straining for all I'm worth, I pull her weight toward the trees, pausing every few feet to catch my breath. Selfish thoughts about little me dragging her considerable dead weight run through my head, but the groans she lets out every time we hit a bump stifle them.

We're lucky in that the trees are a rare stand of tall conifers, all untouched by recent eruptions: a mixture of pine, fir and cedar. Their needles carpet the ground. I pull Luz to a spot far enough in to be soft all the way round, with a canopy of branches to protect us from the weather. We're close enough to the open rocky slope to see anyone approaching on this side of the mountain.

I rummage through my pack for a pain patch and hold it up for her inspection. "It will make you feel loopy, but we need to try something." I apply it to her arm and pat it. "Now lie on your side." I wedge my pack behind her to keep her from rolling onto that hideous welt.

Returning to the mounts, I remove the ends of the rope. After being freed from the saddle, Cozuel hoofs out a bare spot on the ground and does what mules like to do, roll on their back in the dirt.

I kneel beside Quintara's crumpled leg. The big mare lies helpless, heaving, no longer trying to stand. I grimace as I remove Luz's pack and saddle. It sticks in my mind that, for a horse, a broken leg means they have to be put down. No sense bringing that up to Luz, as if she hasn't guessed already.

It's not just her back and her horse's leg that lie shattered. It's her whole life. I close my eyes and shake my head slowly. It's the first time I've thought of her in those terms.

Clouds gather as the afternoon wears on. The pain patch seems to kick in: Luz's moans are less, but she also complains of feeling lightheaded and dry mouthed. I kneel beside her, offering water.

She shakes her gourd. "How much do we have?"

I walk off to check my own supply. The gurgle when I rattle the canteen means we'll be sunk if help doesn't get here by tomorrow, but for Luz I try to put a positive spin on. "We'll be fine so long as we stay put."

Before long, the sky darkens and raindrops wet the ground beyond the canopy. A whiff of pine scent dances amidst the sulfur. I gather rocks for a fire circle, then scavenge for twigs and branches of all sizes. I manage five or six loads, arms full of kindling first, then several more trips to drag fallen limbs.

That should be enough wood to keep us warm through the night. I kneel and prepare the kindling: small twigs on the bottom where they'll catch fire first, larger ones on top where hotter flames will grab them. Shading the bundle from the breeze, I reach deep into the middle and snap my lighter. The twigs crackle as they blaze, and soon the heady scent of resin wafts over us.

I retrieve more of the biscuits, cheese, and fruit, then squat in front of Luz and break the food into small pieces. She tries a few bites, then drops it, saying the pain has slackened her appetite. More likely it's the drug in that patch.

I scoot behind her, stroke her head, finger her braid, and pull its end around for her to see the motion of untwirling. She nods. It's something to do. I've never let my hair grow as long as hers.

Next thing, I'm shivering. This persists even after I put on a sweater and windbreaker. We did not expect to spend a night outdoors, let alone at this elevation. Oh, for a tent. The few drops of rain turn into a steady drizzle.

Lying now with her head in my lap, Luz gazes up. "Did you ever imagine that you would be here?"

I grunt. "Ha. Are you kidding?"

"How did you get into this project, anyway?"

"It's a long story, little sister."

"Please tell me. It will take my mind off the pain."

I avert my eyes and say nothing for several minutes. What's the point? Then it hits me. After what's just happened up here — finding this huge treasure of iridium, followed by this dreadful accident — it's going to be hell to pay when we get back down. I say "we" without having any idea if Luz will make it. But if she does, I'm going to need her for an ally, so maybe it's time to quit being so secretive. Plus, we're in for a long night.

"Sometimes it's hard work that gets you where you are, sometimes it's fate, and sometimes it's a strange combination of both." I pick up a twig lying beside the girl's head and trace patterns in the dirt. "Mostly, this is payback."

"Payback for what?"

"I grew up near a nickel mill owned by a rich man."

She looks puzzled. "What is 'mill'? And what is 'nickel?'"

"A mill is a place where people work together to make lots of the same thing." I pull off my belt and hold the buckle close for her to see. "Could anyone in Nomidar make this?"

The centerpiece of my buckle has the likeness of a great shaggy steer with a hump on its back, offset from the buckle's surface. Luz runs her thumb along the outlines of its body.

She shakes her head. "My people make all the things they need at home."

"To forge metal, you need a big operation. My father worked in the nickel mill. He took me through one day, how old was I? Eight, maybe."

***

The big man beside me holds my hand. We both wear yellow helmets. The man's tall frame is bent, clad in sooty gray overalls and laced boots. I look up at his weary face, the skin shriveled like a dried orange peel, deep creases sagging and lined with grime. His dark eyes try to smile down at me, but every few seconds, a barking cough intrudes.

We stand in the middle of a huge room, the ceiling at least thirty feet high, the nearest wall a hundred feet away. Scant light comes from scattered globes dangling down. I have never experienced a place so large, so dark.

Scores of other men scurry to and fro, their heads also covered by the shiny helmets. Even when they stand close together, they have to shout to be heard above the deafening roar. The small, soft, elastic things plugging my ears are a pain. I look up for permission to remove one, but the man shakes his head.

Abruptly, his eyes light up, and he points behind me. Sixty feet away, suspended from metal girders on the ceiling, a giant bucket ladle tilts, its broth a flaming orange liquid, brighter than the sun. Even as far away as we stand, I feel the heat. In seeming slow motion, the molten orange cascades down into a huge sluice, which divides and shunts the liquid away. As it rushes along, the cooling contents morph into a shiny gray.

The man leads me along the path of one of the smaller channels, its molten gray oozing along in silence, until it passes to another, less cavernous, room. There, he motions that I may remove the earplugs but must keep my hard hat on.

The channel divides into scores of small troughs, each steering its silver river into a pile of sand, six inches long, with a depression in the middle. Each trough sports a little gate, allowing a few ounces of the stuff to drop into the midst of the sand pile before it closes.

From above, a hammer's head stamps the gray pool inside its sand cocoon, releasing a hissing noise and vapors. Another man stands by, tending five of the sand piles at a time, using thick gloves and tongs to remove from each nest its contents, now hardened into a solid disc. He tosses the disc into a pile behind him. Seconds later, the gate opens and more of the molten gray pours into the sand.

The man guiding me lets go of my hand, puts on a thick glove, grabs a pair of tongs, and picks up one of the discs from the pile. He places the disc in the palm of his glove so I can get a close look. It's a belt buckle, with its centerpiece that same great shaggy steer. I reach to touch it, oblivious of the heat still shimmering from its surface.

With a gentle hand and a knowing smile, the big man in the gray overalls stops me. The twinkle in his eyes tells me that he knows exactly what I'm thinking. That's good. He's the only one who cares.

***

Luz shakes her head. "I can't imagine working in such a place."

"It's a grunge job, but you have something to show for it at the end of the day." I string the belt back onto my breeches, pick up the stick, and resume tracing patterns in the dirt.

Luz points her thumb toward the buckle. "You have those creatures in your land?"

"Bison. They once ran wild on the prairies near my home. Now they are gone... extinct." I grimace and squeeze my eyes shut.

"I have heard tales of flightless coastal birds, once lined up by the thousands along our shores, now vanished forever."

What can you say of extinction? I say nothing.

Silence seems to bother this girl. "You grew up near this factory?"

"Yeah. We were getting along okay, until my little brother died of the whooping cough. That took a lot out of my folks. They didn't try for another kid again after that, but I made do alone."

I picture the block of dingy row houses, the air reeking from factory smoke. Moms kept their kids indoors, but I acted so fidgety that my mother relented. "I became an outdoor brat. Don't ask why I got into rocks; maybe there wasn't much else to do. The different colors and feel of the stones: smooth and shiny, jagged and dull.

"When I was nine, the owner of the nickel mill announced massive layoffs. My father got kicked out the door after twenty-three years."

Luz catches her breath. "How cruel of them to take away peoples' jobs."

"Can't be helped, that's how they explained it. Harry Ladou," I pause and wait for the surprise to register on her face, "yes, our very own chief, he delivered the news to the mill workers."

"He does not act like one whose heart could be so cold."

"Not his decision."

"Whose then?"

"The man I work for now." It comes out as a growl. "The same person who sent us here, Sir Oscar Bailey."

She mulls that over. "How does it make you feel, to toil for one so ruthless?"

"A scientist needs a sponsor, someone to pay the bills. It's always been that way, unless the scientist was born rich." Hah. "After the layoff came hard times for my folks. My mother started cleaning people's homes. Dad tried to make ends meet by doing odd jobs, but his body failed him. A long-time cough turned out to be silicosis, from breathing the nickel dust, plus a bad lung infection, called tuberculosis." A shudder runs through me. "Do the Onwei get this too? Coughing, fevers, weight loss, eventually you start spitting up blood. That's the beginning of the end."

Luz shivers too. "It sounds like what our people call consumption. In our village, every night a fit of coughing from the hut of a neighbor will shake your sleep. That's another reason I don't want to live in Nomidar year-round."

I push the stick harder into the dirt. "That wicked T.B. finished Dad off two years later. We all knew he couldn't have much longer. Indigenous Peoples have always gotten the short end of the stick." My twig snaps and I toss the fragment aside.

"There is not a cure, even in your homeland?" The girl seems shocked.

"Oh, there's a cure alright, if you've got in-sur-ance." I wrinkle my nose. That's become a smelly subject.

Luz waits for me to explain, but I just shake my head. Finally, she reaches for my hand. "How do your people say goodbye to a loved one?"

"What does it matter?" I pull away. That's one memory I'm not ready to share, not yet.

The girl doesn't seem deterred. Her wide eyes study me. "What about after your father died?"

That part I can deal with. "It took a few months. The rock collection is what pulled me out of my shell." I smile at the recollection. "I named each rock like some little pet. Chaka, Bolo, Jagnose, a whole menagerie. I made them shout at each other and get into fights. In class, I wrote stories with rocks as characters."

Soothed by the past, and by the girl's apparent interest, I share my unlikely progression from lonely waif to scientist. I need her to understand what brought me to her land if I want her support when we return. "Russell McCoy's good word got me the all-expenses-paid scholarship to an elite boarding school thirty miles from home. I was grateful not to be another mouth for my mother to feed, and I wanted to honor my father's memory by going to university. I would be the first in our neighborhood, heck, the first in my clan. At sixteen, I earned a full scholarship to Athabasca Tech."

Luz tilts her head back to study my face with this last declaration. She says, "I can't imagine this much study. Onwei tradesmen will take on an apprentice at whatever age the child shows a serious interest."

"If you pursue one field for long enough, you become an expert, like your Yoka with all the tongues she speaks. We call these people savants."

"So, you are an expert in what, Savant Keltyn?"

I reach for my sample bag of the iris stone and shake it. "I stayed in touch with Russell McCoy, stopping to visit whenever I went home to Sudbury to see my mother. He saw the potential for iridium, your iris stone, to coat the hulls of our flying machines, so they could slip through the chemical pea soup of the upper atmosphere unscathed. But we needed a steady source."

"It must be scarce, or you wouldn't be here."

Bingo! This girl is sharp. "That's where craters and volcanoes come in."

"So, you pushed to get this assignment to explore a volcano on the other side of the earth?"

"You bet!" I flash a full-toothed smile.

"Was there a lot of competition?"

"There were other people qualified, but I had a leg up on them, thanks to my connections."

"Savant McCoy?"

I nod.

"You must be grateful for all he has done for you."

It always comes down to this. I turn away before answering. "I should be, shouldn't I?"

"Uh-oh."

I keep my face averted. "McCoy turned out to be a lecher."

Her hand again reaches for mine. I squeeze it in return, on the verge of tears. I hope she hasn't been put in such a bind. Some predator like Nestor, but with more guile, more subtlety, building a web of trust to ensnare a naïve fly.

"How did you deal with that?" she asks.

I lift my chin and sniff. "Not very well. I don't have Orfea's touch at flirting while keeping a man at arm's length."

"Can't you just walk away from him? It sounds like Sir Oscar has you tapped for bigger things."

"You'd think so, but Russell has too much stuff on me."

"What kind of stuff?" Luz's voice dips lower.

"Stuff that could ruin my career." I bite my lip. Can't go down that road with this girl. My past, my subversive flirtation with the Chinese.

"Like what?" She cranes her neck back, trying to make eye contact.

"I'll show you when we get back. Now try to sleep." I move around Luz's body to snug up the blanket and pull it tighter around our two forms, huddled together under the branches of the tree. The rain comes down in earnest around the tree's perimeter; now and then a few drips penetrate our spot. Leaning against my saddle, holding the girl's head in my lap, I lay my own head back and hum an ancient Cree lullaby until her eyes stay closed.

I hope her dreams are peaceful. And — though I'm not religious — I pray that she'll summon the strength to get off this mountain in one piece. Would it be too much to pray that she'll back me up when the shit hits the fan?

I try to drift off too, but the girl's question haunts me: "How do your people say goodbye to a loved one?"

***

Light flurries of snow fall. Eleven years old, I sit beside my mother, the two of us draped in thick blankets spangled with squares, pentagons and hexagons of bright red, yellow, orange, blue and green. Thirty others flank us, mostly middle-aged and elderly, in drab clothing that matches the drab winter afternoon. They intone an old Cree chant: "Wah kaw sha lomi... wah kaw sha lomi..."

The wake has gone on for several days already. It certainly hasn't been a cryfest. My father's old factory mates and my aunts and uncles have taken turns reciting a litany of his practical jokes. Before the T.B. took him down, he sure knew how to make people laugh. But now it's time to say goodbye. I take a last look at the body in the pine box. In death, his features are barely changed: the skin shriveled like a dried orange peel, the deep creases sagging, still etched with flakes of grime, despite the family's best efforts to scrub them out. The face, weary before, now appears spent.

An older man, our clan's spiritual leader, rises at the front of the group. Gray hair also braided, he is indistinguishable from the other Elders. The drumming ceases. The man leads a prayer, then a song. I try to stay in the moment, but random thoughts bounce through my brain.

I take a quick peek at my mother. It's always been hard to read her, and I'm not the only one who can't. The leader stopped by our house while my father was dying, trying to get her to share some stories about him so he could retell them now. It's part of how we heal, he had said. He couldn't get two words out of her. Even now, when everyone else is laughing or crying, she's still as a statue.

The leader finishes, and signals for my aunts and uncles to begin the last step: distributing my father's possessions to others in the clan. This is supposed to allow his spirit to depart from loved ones and, I suspect, to heal us so we don't keep grieving with each glimpse of his hat or his hunting knife. Still, I about choke when they hand off his bison belt buckle to some kid I've never seen before.

I brood over that for weeks. I would have cherished that buckle forever. I don't *want* to forget my father; his memory is the only thing that still grounds me.

Months later, my recall of Dad is slowly fading, though nothing worthwhile has come to take his place. One evening I'm holed up in my room, staring horrified at a mess on the floor. In a fit of pique, I've just finished scattering my assortment of rocks by a raging swipe across the shelf, on the verge of tossing the whole collection. What good is it? It's sure no substitute for a father.

There's a knock on the door of our home. I run downstairs. Mother has sunk into the couch, a glazed look in her eye, just like every other evening. An empty liquor bottle graces the end table.

I open the door. There stands a dour teenage kid, shoulders slumped. I recognize him. He's the one they gave the belt buckle to.

I glare at him, then notice he's holding a small enameled box. Still eyeing the ground, he extends the box at arm's length. I open it to reveal my father's belt buckle, now gleaming. By the time my eyes raise, the boy has already turned and started trudging off.

"Thanks," I manage to croak, then run up to my room, kneel beside the bed and, not the first time, bawl away. Somehow, though, this time feels different. Done with the tears, I replace each rock into its proper spot on the shelf.

***

The rain keeps falling around the edges of our dry canopy. Now I wonder what drives me on this quest. Is it justice — vengeance — for the memory of my father, taken from his family when I was but a child? Or is it for my own fame and glory, Sir Oscar tooting that horn of Bailey Science Fellow? Can I even trust my own motivation? I need to sort this out quickly, because today the stakes just shot way up.

Eventually I nod off, but vivid nightmares awaken me: I'm the one flying off Quintara's back, in slow motion. Suspended in midair, hands thrashing above my head, mouth gaping in horror, my back arches in the moment before impact.

Later, a fiend — someone I once trusted — gropes me. Pockmarks, shaggy brows, and thick-lens dialups tarnish his face. Lips pursed, he coos, "Here, here, Keltyn. Relaaaax, that's a good girl." I flail back and forth, trying in vain to push the brute's hands away.

In the wee hours, I enter a more vivid nightmare. I'm propped up, lashed to a pole, immobile and captive at the edge of a stinking volcano. I am bound hand and foot, my torso wrapped in strips of untanned cowhide, a human sacrifice to a god as yet unseen. This sadistic deity announces its impending arrival by shaking the earth, stalking its prey. The bubbling lava in the volcano's mouth is its slobber, ready to devour the tiny morsel that is me.

I shriek out, but my sounds are drowned by the clamor. My body bolts to a sitting position as I awaken. Luz reaches over her head to comfort me. Somehow, this girl, lying there paralyzed, manages to stay calm. Drenched with cold sweat, I fall back, feeling pangs of guilt. If I don't get a grip, this whole scheme will come crashing down.

15

LONG AGO, FAR AWAY

After a few hours of tortured sleep, my eyes open once more. A semblance of morning has arrived. The rain lets up and a hazy yellow circle peeks through the cloud cover.

Luz's head rests on my lap. My legs are asleep, and I realize I haven't moved them all night. She awakens when I try to shift them and moans that the pain in her back has returned. The patch must have worn off.

The long hair that I unbraided last night mats her face. Her eyes are baggy, her color pasty. She tries to turn over, but her legs won't obey.

"How is it?"

"The throbbing is intense," she grimaces, "but if it's a broken bone, I know I can live through that. Three years ago, I broke my collarbone. Quintara threw me after I tried to make her jump a gully." She flashes a sheepish grin. "I got through that okay. What scares me is not being able to move my legs."

As I get up, my own legs tingle in sympathy. I fetch water and dried apple slices and start to feed her. She wiggles her butt several times, then scowls. Tries to hide it, but I get the idea. She shuts her eyes as I remove her wet clothes, wrap a dry cloth around her bottom, and pull the blanket up to cover her legs. I rinse her leggings in a rain puddle and set them to dry on a flat rock, exposed to the morning sun.

Pinecones lie scattered around the campsite, shaken loose by the trembling. From the flat rock, I can see the mountaintop.

Luz shouts, "Is it still smoking?" She twirls her finger upward.

"Afraid so, honey." I go to check on Quintara. The poor mare's whinnies sound more muted than yesterday. How much fight does she have left?

I retrieve the phone and push the button. This time, Harry's voice comes in right away. "Still hanging in okay?"

"Best as can be expected." I gaze around our makeshift camp.

"Good. Help is on the way," he says. "Aldo is coming himself with his nephew Efrain and Joaquin, in case they have to send for more stuff to transport the girl. Oh, and Fay needs to talk with you, says it's *urgent*." Harry's voice stresses the "ur."

That gets my attention. Fay isn't one to over-react. "Which phone does she have?"

"Hit four."

"Okay. I'll update you later." I press two buttons in sequence.

Fay's voice. "Keltyn. We heard. Is the girl all right?"

"She's stable, anyway."

Luz leans up on her elbows to pay attention.

"Good. Listen. I have news to share with you." Pause. "Just you."

"Luz has an earpad. She's lying right here."

"That's okay. I just don't want this to get back to Harry or Buck." She sighs. "I can't believe how naïve I've been."

"What's going on?"

"It's about Oscar."

My head jerks back. "What about Oscar?"

"This expedition. It's not just to find iridium. It's about people."

"Well, okay. That's why you're here, Fay."

"No, you don't get it. I didn't either. Yoka's the one who put two and two together."

"Iridium. People. What's the missing link?" My free hand fans the air.

"Canadians. Colonizing. Here." Fay's voice fires off bullets.

I slump to the ground, rub a hand across my forehead to wipe the little beads of sweat popping out at my hairline, try to slow my breathing and staunch a wave of nausea rising in my gut, the salty taste in my mouth. I feel like a dead tree branch.

"He wouldn't... he couldn't." The words echo strange as they leave my mouth.

"If he could, you know damn well he would," says Fay. "Did you two find any of the stuff on the mountain?"

I gaze at my pack. "It's there, all right. Tons of it. You refine the alloy, there's enough to coat as many aircraft as Oscar can build." I think hard. "This changes everything."

"It sure does. Our little secret for now, eh? I don't know if Harry has been privy all along, but no sense fanning the flame."

"Right." My eyes bounce here, there, and everywhere.

"But listen, honey. You're the only one who can turn this around."

"Me? How do you figure?"

"They won't trust me, that's for sure. I'm the bleeding heart, biased from day one. But they trust you; you're the scientist. You can get the hounds off the scent. Too many impurities for mining to be cost-effective, that sort of thing. You've got a way to measure the stuff, right?"

"Right, but that meter, it's from China. Buck found it the other day and stuck it in my face. Harry's suspicious too." That old quicksand is sucking me down again.

"Oh." Pause. "Well, I hate to break the news, gal, but it's on you. Hey, you guys get back safely, okay?"

"Right." I push the button and set the phone down. Luz watches me, waiting for an explanation, but right now, I need to process. I camp on the ground in silence, cross-legged, chin resting on both hands, elbows on my knees, trying to figure this out.

Should I 'fess up to the Chinese connection? It's not a deal-breaker; Russell McCoy brokered my study there, and they all respect him. After a little flap, they'll get over it and we can proceed with the mission. We found a big stash of iridium; that's what we came for. I'm not a political animal, so I shouldn't much care how Sir Oscar uses the stuff. He can build a thousand planes, for all I care.

Yet, there's something about ferrying Canadians that bothers me — white Canadian farmers, to colonize this pristine rangeland. Nobody except Fay expected there would be people living down here. Even without Oscar's farm families, you have to wonder how a big mining operation will affect these nomads. Can I be part of such an enterprise with a clear conscience?

I sit there for so long that Luz lies back down. The tremors continue every few minutes. I practice breathing through my mouth to drown out the reek of sulfur. After a while, I notice Luz has dozed off.

Moments later, she awakens, sobbing and gasping. I scoot over to stroke her hair and make shushing sounds.

She can barely get the words out. "I dreamt that Ian and his father rode up while you were... changing my diaper. I was so ashamed."

Her nightmares seem pretty tame. I smile and hug her head. "That would give 'em something to talk about, eh?" After she has calmed down, I rise to a kneeling position and say, "I need to tell you something."

She turns her head to face me. "What?"

"Remember we talked about the Chinese?"

"Oh, yes. The 'bad guys.'"

"Well, I'm doing some favors for those 'bad guys.'"

Now her eyes narrow. "Is that wise?"

"Probably not." Right now, I'm so confused. My confidence in the plan I began with has become awfully shaky. "I wish I could figure out the right thing to do. Get advice from someone I can trust."

Luz gazes at me. Gradually, her eyes take on a gleam and her lips broaden. "Maybe I can help you there. Look in my saddlebags."

I venture in that direction. "What am I looking for?"

"A small bag with a few biscuit nuggets."

I ruffle around inside and pull them out, nondescript crunchy little balls. You could dunk and swallow them with one gulp.

"They are called Venga," says Luz. "Yoka Sutu dispenses them as a way to contact someone with whom you have long been out of touch." My eyes rove between her face and these little clumps of dough.

They must be some kind of hallucinogen. "So, how did you come by these?"

The girl blushes and looks down. "That bone that Flaco dug up the other day. I took it to Yoka for her to ID. Next thing I knew, we were sharing Venga."

"Did it work?"

"I got only some of the answers I sought because the effect wore off too soon. The old lady seemed to lose interest, so I grabbed some more nuggets and ran away." She gazes up at me with an impish grin. "I knew they would come in handy sooner or later."

Seems worth a try, but who do I want to get in touch with? I can think of several people. I roll the nuggets around in my hand. "How many?"

"One didn't last very long the other day," she says.

I hesitate, then keep two. Holding them in my palm, I study the girl and wonder if she'll be able to manage without me for a while. "Help will be here in a few hours, and I'm sure they'll bring extra water. Do you need another pain patch?"

She starts to nod, then freezes. "One of us ought to keep her wits intact."

I smile. "It's now or never, sister." Our eyes lock. After a minute, she shakes her head to decline the patch.

I arise to fetch my canteen, then mouth the nuggets one by one, chasing down each with a swish of water.

I wipe my lips with the back of my hand and sit down cross-legged, wiggle next to Luz, and squeeze her hand. "Sorry to abandon you for a while, but I think you'll be okay." I fold both hands in my lap and shut my eyes.

The girl reaches across to touch my knee. "Fill me in on what's happening, okay?"

I open one eye for just a second. "Okay."

Talk about crazy: I'm hoping these tasteless chunks, concocted by an ancient wrinkled hag, will shake up my mind enough to reveal answers that my conscious brain can't, and then bring me back in one piece.

I close my eyes and try to center my thoughts, but instead my mind just wanders. Not until the hairs on the back of my head tingle does my brain focus on one encounter.

***

I try to relate the story to Luz. There I am, perched in a hard chair in a small room, my feet not quite touching the floor. I squirm in a strange crisp print dress and shiny shoes, fingering a bow that doesn't belong in my hair. My mother sits with hands folded. She keeps her overcoat on. Every rustle of my dress draws a scowl from her.

Four other empty chairs spill around the room. Outside a window, people pass back and forth. Some of them wear yellow hard hats. I keep watch on the opposite door.

After what seems like hours, that door opens, and a man stands on the threshold. He wears a long white smock, script sewn on the right breast, a bunch of writing implements sticking out of the left breast pocket. His black-rimmed vision aids match his hair, which is thinning and brushed straight back. He nods and says, "Miss SparrowHawk? Come in. I'm Savant McCoy."

I turn to my mother with a questioning glance. She nods once, the corners of her mouth turned up just so. Butterflies dart through my stomach. I follow McCoy through the door, down a narrow hallway with posters depicting different rocks, past benches with real rocks: lots of them, dull ones and glistening ones, smooth and pointy, flat and round, of every color imaginable. We file past other people in wraparound white smocks. Only one person, a young woman with cinnamon skin like mine, turns and smiles.

McCoy leads me into a small room with a shiny wooden desk, points me to a straight chair. He plumps down in a swivel chair on the other side of the table. A green board with chalk script hangs on the wall. He picks up a folder on his desk and flips through its pages.

"A very well-crafted essay, Miss SparrowHawk. Crafted all by yourself, I presume."

I gulp. "My school librarian gave me a few ideas."

"But the essay itself?"

"I wrote it on my own, sir."

"Good. Now," he points at the green board, "what can you tell me of the words you see here?"

I read. "Pleistocene, Cretaceous, Mesozoic. Those are geological periods of the Earth's development."

"Very good. Tell me more."

Air puffs out my cheeks but my lips stay shut. I don't dare meet his eyes. Instead, I stare at the nickel bison clasp on his cravat. Savant McCoy is patient, asking me leading questions, teasing out the handful of facts that I know; the climate fifty million years ago was hot, most like the present-day Earth's.

The quiz session lasts another fifteen minutes before he leans back in his chair. "Very good, Keltyn. May I call you Keltyn?"

I nod, tight-lipped but goggle-eyed.

He makes a notation in the file and stands up. "Come. Let's go see your mother." He walks me out to the lobby. My mother is still bundled in her overcoat, her stoic expression unchanged.

"You have a budding geologist here, Mrs. SparrowHawk."

Her face brightens ever so slowly, as if she is not quite sure what she just heard.

Savant McCoy smiles. "I shall give her my best recommendation."

***

I'd like a few moments to digest this. Why did the Venga take me back to that particular memory, the birth of my career? I've tried to keep from dwelling on Russell McCoy so the pain of his ugly traits can't hurt me anymore. But there's hardly time to reflect, for I'm already elsewhere.

***

Now, it's years later. I'm sitting in the back seat of an ancient vehicle, bouncing along a dirt road. Five others surround me, most of them a few years younger. Their high cheekbones mimic my people's, but with a lighter, caramel complexion, their eyes almond-shaped.

The vehicle's only sound comes from wheels skidding on the dirt tracks of the road. The six of us in the carriage bounce around as the road gets rougher. Finally, the driver stops and motions for everyone to get out. The other four students and I walk to the back and grab tools, shovels, picks, chisels, backpacks and water bottles. The sun is beating down and everyone is in shirtsleeves, khaki shorts and hiking boots. Some wear canvas gloves.

The driver has black-rimmed dialups. The hair visible around his ears is graying. Like the others, he wears a pointed straw hat whose brim extends to eye level. He has symbols sewn on his tunic. I've only been here a few months and can't read or speak Chinese yet, but I know that the characters spell his name: Savant Wan Xiang. He carries this yellow cube with a screen and needle on one face.

Savant Wan consults his pocket watch and gives instructions in Chinese. Several of the students ask questions of the leader, and he patiently answers. I have not opened my mouth. He looks at me with an inquiring expression. "Have you ever seen it before?"

For some reason — it must be this Venga — I can understand him. I open my mouth, and what comes out is Mandarin Chinese, another miracle. "No. How will I know iridium ore if I spot it?"

He brightens. "You'll know, trust me. It looks like nothing else."

Our party of six walks along a path, a two-foot wide break in the grass, which has grown tall enough to block any view. Another quarter mile and the grass breaks. Here's a huge crater, as large as the one Bailey Voyager is parked in now.

Savant Wan points to an area on the opposite wall of the basin. Different colors mark the layers of rock on the crater's sides. The one he points at gleams all sorts of hues in the morning sun, but its main color is violet.

My first glimpse of the rock triggers a gasp, a stunning jolt to my brain. I don't tell Luz, but this must be what a drug addict feels like to shoot up. One glance is all it takes to hook me on the iris stone.

Luz must see the contortions of my face. "Yes," she whispers. "The stone has such power."

Still the Venga isn't done with me. It's pulling me back to this very place, on the slopes of Erebus. My mind's eye hovers above the slopes of Erebus, the same slopes we climbed yesterday, but instead of the reek and shudder of the volcano assaulting my senses once more, a whole different level of commotion greets me. I try to describe the details for Luz's benefit: a dozen earthmovers scuttle about like so many giant beetles — diggers, graders and haulers, all with their tracked hulls to navigate the steep terrain. Off to one side, a blast of dynamite spews rocks and dust for a hundred feet.

Farther down the mountainside stand several one-story buildings. The largest of these sports a sunflower logo on its front wall, surrounded by the motto of Bailey Holdings: "The Face of Tomorrow." The whole strip-mining operation is fenced in.

And the weirdest part of this whole scene? I can feel both of my savant mentors hovering over my shoulders: Russell McCoy on one side and Wan Xiang on the other. It's like a devil and an angel, both of them whispering into my ears simultaneously.

McCoy's voice is a conspiratorial gloat of approval at what my discovery has led to: "I knew you had the drive, Keltyn, the moment I first laid eyes on you."

Wan's is more cautious: "Is this really what you wish for, Keltyn?" Still, I wonder, is Wan trying to save the landscape, or just spouting sour grapes that a Chinese team didn't make it here first?

The attempt to put this wacky scene into words for Luz makes me sputter, but no matter. It fades away like fairy dust. I open my eyes slowly and blink several times. My lips pucker as I turn to Luz. "I'm back."

"So, you are." She wears a sardonic smile, like I've just told a good yarn.

I rise, wobbly as a drunken sailor, and start to pace. My mouth feels like sandpaper. I offer Luz the canteen before swallowing what little water remains. Even after the swig, my tongue and lips still feel dry. I sit back down and bury my face in my hands. How much longer until they show up? What kind of magic can Aldo conjure to save Luz or her horse?

"So, tell me what you learned." Luz's voice interrupts my despair.

I lift my head and peer at the girl through my fingers. "The Venga triggered vivid memories of my two mentors. McCoy led me into geology, Wan to your iris stone. Their impact made me who I am now. The last scene, I think, is how this place will look after Sir Oscar Bailey gets hold of it. Russell McCoy and Wan Xiang will have very different opinions about that."

It's not that hard to figure out. I straighten up. "No way. We can't let Bailey do it."

16

RUSTLERS

Aldo, his big nephew Efrain, and Joaquin were on their way to help Luz, towing her mother's old two-wheeled cart. Perhaps because his mount was shorter than the other two, Joaquin had a closer view of the ground, so he was the first to spy cattle tracks heading into a ravine.

"Horseshoe prints mixed in as well." Aldo pushed out the words with effort, between coughs. "You know what that means." Joaquin knew full well; the four missing heifers must be nearby, and not by chance.

The ravine and its creek headed into a box canyon, no more than half a mile deep. The jeaf stared in that direction for a long moment, then turned and gazed toward the mountain. He glanced up at the sun, now near its peak.

"If Luz is in bad shape we will not be able to get her back down today. Best to take care of these *mal hombres* first. Let us leave the cart here for now."

The jeaf leaned over the neck of his stallion as he rode, following the tracks. Efrain followed directly behind him, watching dead ahead. Joaquin brought up the rear.

"Were the rain any heavier last night there would be no trace left," Aldo said. Then he stopped and held his hand up, though Joaquin couldn't tell whether to rest or to listen. The three of them sat dead quiet, glancing around, straining for any sound, but aside from Aldo's labored breathing, they heard nothing.

The jeaf advanced slowly, now also watching straight ahead, pushing through dense brush. After another five minutes, he held up his hand again. This time, Joaquin heard the ripping, chewing sound of beeves grazing. Next came a clink of metal on stone.

Efrain heard it too and glanced at Aldo with his brows arched. Aldo put his finger to his lips. The three of them slipped off their horses and tied them up. Aldo motioned for Joaquin to guard them. Then he pulled out his rifle and headed off on foot with Efrain. Within a few steps, he was breathing heavily.

Joaquin lapsed into a sulk, waiting. He didn't like being left behind, but he had yet to learn how to shoot, and with his bum foot, he couldn't run if they got into a pinch.

What would happen if the bad guys shot Aldo and Efrain? He would be a sitting duck. The mal hombres would come looking for horses and find him cringing. He untied Cisco and led him up the side of the ravine, away from the main path and into the brush.

A single rifle shot rang out nearby. Joaquin froze.

A minute later, Efrain's voice shouted, "It's okay, boy. Bring the horses."

Relieved, Joaquin led all the mounts forward fifty yards. The ravine widened, showing the source of the creek as a spring, gurgling out of the rock at the far end of the box canyon.

Two scruffy men sat on the ground with their arms crossed on their knees. Efrain trained Aldo's rifle on them. The older, wiry one wore a thin mustache. He looked away as soon as he saw Joaquin, but not before he recognized the man. A wave of disgust coursed through him as the memory surfaced.

***

It was the fall before, the end of the grazing season. All the gauchos gathered at Aldo's ranch house. They came to celebrate the end of six long months in the saddle.

After each man's pay was counted out, Aldo puffed on his pipe and started mixing with the charros and the tradesmen. Joaquin sat in a corner drinking spiced maté, watching as Aldo poured his favorite cactus liquor.

Dario the butcher brought his guitar, and Matin the tanner his drum. Soriante plunged into a yodel. Those who didn't sing or play tapped their feet, while lapping up Aldo's generous store of booze. They gorged on the ribs and steaks that he and Ysidro barbequed, then moved to chat up the half dozen ladies of the extended Correon family, invited to join the fun.

The charros soon got rowdy, especially Nestor. He staggered around the room, shrieking like a tomcat, and soon cornered a couple of the younger women.

Aldo glared at Nestor with mounting displeasure, while Ysidro looked around in desperation. It was obvious to Joaquin that they wished to be rid of this pest.

He put down his drink and scurried over to Ysidro. "His cousin lives nearby. Shall I fetch him?"

"The sooner the better."

But when Joaquin arrived at Roderigo's cottage, he found the man squatting over a spot on the rough-hewn floor, playing dice with three other mal hombres whom he did not recognize. One of them sat on a low stool. Each man hoarded his own stash of coins, but Roderigo's was shrunken. A jug of pulce made the rounds. Epithets, profanities and the occasional "yes!" rolled off someone's tongue every time the dice came to rest.

Joaquin stood on the sidelines. The four men seemed oblivious to his presence. He cleared his throat several times before Roderigo looked up.

"Beat it, gimp." His speech slurred. He already knew Joaquin by sight.

"The Correons sent me to fetch you. Your cousin Nestor is causing a disturbance at their fiesta."

"Well, ain't that a shame. But, too bad. Not my problem." Roderigo turned back to his dice game.

"Please, seir." Joaquin did not expect to be turned down. He tried to think fast. "They will make it worth your while to take Nestor off their hands."

Roderigo looked up with a scowl. His mates eyed him. "Hey, a reward," said the one on the stool. "Best go collect it, Rodo. You're in the hole pretty bad here."

"The hell." His glazed eyes tried to fixate on Joaquin, but instead flitted back and forth. The scowl remained. He made no move to get up.

The man on the stool arose and lifted Roderigo by the elbow. "Go fetch your cousin and bring him. We can always use another mark."

Roderigo shook the man away, but by now he was standing. He grabbed the pulce jug for another long swig, wiped his mouth with the back of his hand and thrust his chin out at Joaquin. "Arggh."

He muttered more curses under his breath as he staggered the few blocks toward the fiesta. Roderigo's gait seemed unsteady, and he stank of drink and sweat. Hovering behind him, Joaquin chastised himself for having volunteered to fetch this pig.

Nestor seemed surprised to see his ill-tempered cousin show up at the party. With the help of Efrain and some other big young charros, it dawned on him that Roderigo was recruited to escort him away. He blew kisses to the ladies before Roderigo grabbed his arm, both of them lurching out the door.

***

Now, the cowering Roderigo would not meet Joaquin's gaze.

Aldo inspected the four missing beeves. Despite standing still, he panted.

Joaquin strolled over to him, out of earshot from the rustlers. "What do you think they were planning to do with these heifers, jeaf?"

"Wait until our herd moved on, drive them back to Nomidar, peddle them to whomever would turn a blind eye." His face appeared clammy and sweaty. "Or they might meet another tribe of gauchos along the way, make a deal with the foreman. Who knows?" Aldo's voice dropped to a coarse whisper.

Looking somber, he turned to face the two ragged men huddled on the ground. He gasped between each painful phrase. "What are your names, friends? Haven't I met you before?"

"Roderigo," croaked the older one. Beads of sweat dripped on his narrow, slanted forehead. With his shifty eyes, matted black hair, and sagged shoulders, he reminded Joaquin of a whipped cur.

The younger one was bigger than Roderigo but said nothing. Hooded eyes on his hangdog face kept watch on the ground. Every few seconds, he sniffled. Aldo stared him down until Roderigo reached over to nudge him. Without looking up, he muttered, "Uberne."

"How long have you two been following our herd?"

Roderigo's eyes flitted here and there. "Just a few days. We were camped at the edge of this valley when you entered it." He reached into his pocket, extracted a ragged red kerchief, and mopped his brow.

Aldo turned to Efrain. "Should we believe this story?" His nephew shrugged. Aldo sidled over to a rock and plopped down to study the pair, chin resting on his thumb, elbow on his knee. After a minute, he straightened up. "I remember now. You, Uberne, look at me."

The younger one inched his head up.

"You came to me months ago, looking for a job, before we set out this spring, right?" Aldo nodded at Uberne until the poor dope dropped his head once again. "I had plenty of charros with more experience, so I sent you away."

He turned to face the other. "Now, Roderigo. I never forget a face. Where have I spotted yours before?" Aldo's thumb and pointer finger pulled on his mustache. "I can't quite remember."

Joaquin gulped and spoke. "Nestor's cousin."

Aldo jerked his chin up. "Of course. The party at my house. Nestor was stinking drunk. We called you to take him home, and you were soused as well."

The jeaf dragged his frame up to its full height. He lumbered over to where Roderigo sat, cringing. "Am I to believe that you would steal cattle from the herd your cousin works for, and him unaware?"

Roderigo stayed quiet as a mouse, kept his face turned away.

"Take off your boots, both of you," Aldo rasped in a coarse whisper. No one could mistake his intention.

Roderigo whipped his head around. "Seir, no."

"You heard me." Aldo nodded toward Efrain, who raised his gun. The mal hombre's eye came to rest on Joaquin, his piteous expression that of a trapped rabbit. In the end, Joaquin twisted away.

Efrain cocked his rifle. Roderigo moved to tug off his boots; his hands shook all the while. Uberne didn't budge until Efrain nudged him with the rifle barrel.

Aldo took the gun from Efrain. "Tie their hands. Fasten the other end of the rope to that tree." He drew Joaquin aside. "Think you can herd these beeves back to camp by yourself, boy?"

Joaquin stood taller. "Of course, seir." This was the chance he had been waiting for.

Efrain finished tying up the rustlers. Aldo motioned him close. "We will take both of their horses with us. Hide their boots in the brush on the way out, but they should think the boots are gone for good." He tried to laugh but ended up in a fit of coughing. Rasping for breath, he turned to spit in the direction of his wretched prisoners.

Efrain and Joaquin mounted, shifting behind the beeves to herd them out of the canyon. Aldo, the last to leave, checked his prisoners and barked, "We have more important concerns at the moment than the two of you, but we will be back." He touched his boina in a mock salute to the shoeless duo, tied up like a couple of steers waiting to be branded. Then he spurred his palomino away.

What a pathetic pair they are, thought Joaquin.

At the turnoff to the box canyon, Efrain tied the rustlers' horses. Aldo pulled up to look Joaquin in the eye. "Say nothing of this to Nestor, hear? I wish to confront him myself. Efrain and I will return for these trash later, after Luz and her friend are safe."

He reached over with his meaty paw and gave Cisco's flank a swat. "Now go show me what you've got, boy. Get these heifers back safe."

Joaquin took a firm hold of the reins. He was sorry not to have a part in rescuing Luz, but this task gave him more responsibility. It was the first time he was directly entrusted with the welfare of any cattle. The beeves seemed docile enough. What concerned him more was Aldo's cough. His breathing seemed more labored as they gained altitude.

Heading back down the way they came, he pulled his kerchief up over his nose. Those critters kicked up lots of dust. It wasn't until they reached flatter turf that his mind could wander enough to speculate about what they stumbled upon.

There was no way Nestor could be blind to cattle rustling. He took turns at the watch. That must have been what those three whistles were for, the night Joaquin hustled back to camp after the Sky-Bornes crashed their flying machine.

If that were true, then Nestor would be suspicious as soon as he saw Joaquin lead the missing beeves back to the herd. How would the mal hombre react? Thus far, he treated Joaquin with all bark and no bite, but if his secret was at risk, that could change in a hurry. Joaquin needed to watch his back.

I7

RESCUE PARTY

Luz thrashed her head back and forth. Keltyn was nowhere in sight. A thick blanket of lava neared, slithering relentlessly down the mountain, devouring everything in its path. She tried to crawl away, her arms dragging her torso and her numb, petrified legs. The putrid stench of sulfur was overpowering.

From far down the hill came sounds: the clopping of horses' hooves, the squeak of wheels, followed, moments later, by voices. This seemed too real for a nightmare. Luz forced her eyes open. Nothing new to see; sunlight peered through the trees. But the sounds drew nearer — hoof beats, squeaky wheels, voices.

They were rescued. She lifted her head to praise the Spirits, then broke into tears.

An older man's gruff tones, wedged between wheezes and coughs, must be Aldo's. The more robust voice of a younger man sounded like Efrain. Luz turned her head to see Keltyn poised on the open hillside with her arm raised.

When they got close enough to make out Quintara's plight, they lapsed into silence. They dismounted and made their way through the woods to where Luz lay. She wiped her eyes and brushed the hair back from her face.

Aldo and Efrain stopped at the foot of her blanket. The jeaf continued to wheeze. Every bit as big as his uncle, Efrain took off his boina, somber, silent.

"This is a terrible thing, Seirita Luz." Aldo left his boina on and struggled for breath between each short phrase.

The girl rested her upper body weight on her elbows. "I hope you may cure me, seir. Or if not me, at least my horse."

"Spoken bravely." Aldo turned toward Efrain. "I told you, this one has spunk." Back to her. "Will you allow an old hand to tend your wound?"

She nodded. Aldo started to unwrap the blanket, spied her bare legs, and motioned with his chin for Efrain to withdraw. Prior to yesterday, Luz would have expected as much; now the exhibition of these useless appendages hardly seemed to matter. The younger man headed back to inspect Quintara.

Aldo wiggled his fingers: she should try moving her toes. He tested the feet for sensation. She did not weep this time, just shook her head.

From his pack, he retrieved a healer's kit, unwrapped a packet of coca leaves, and used his fingers to pulverize them. He fished out a pot of strong-smelling salve and used a twig to mix in the coca leaves thoroughly. Luz crinkled her nose. Keltyn knelt beside Aldo to watch his preparations.

"Yes, it stinks." The corner of Aldo's mouth twisted. "But this stuff will ease your pain."

He spread the paste on a dense hemp rag, handing the poultice to a surprised Keltyn. He dropped to his knees and took hold of Luz's hand to pull her upper body toward him, then motioned for Keltyn to slide the poultice under Luz's lower back.

Why did such a strong man wince from this effort? Why the labored breathing? Luz clenched her teeth in silence and lay on the poultice, the smooth grease penetrating the pores. Moments later, a cooling sensation eased through her spine.

She glanced at Aldo, who sat leaning back on her saddle. He nodded and seemed to doze off. As the minutes crawled by, Luz tried to focus on his weathered face, to search for clues to his condition. Yet the fiery pain in her back blurred her thoughts and her vision.

Gradually, the pain seemed to dissipate, and Luz tried moving her toes. Nothing. She tried to keep her cursing under her breath, but it was loud enough to awaken Aldo.

"My back feels less pain now, seir, but my feet still sleep."

Aldo's face displayed the hint of a smile. "Patience, Seirita Luz."

With the sting diminished, she could make out Aldo's features more clearly. His normally ruddy complexion appeared pale, and he continued to perspire, even in the shade. Every few minutes, he grimaced and coughed. Even the effort of shifting his weight caused his breath to labor. The stink from the volcano was annoying, but could it trigger such discomfort?

"What is it, seir? You do not sound well."

"It is nothing. Perhaps the altitude."

She didn't buy that but felt too weak to challenge him.

Efrain returned and set to gathering twigs and dried grass before using his flint to spark a flame. Aldo rose with effort, then unpacked the cup to brew what she supposed would be the gauchos' favorite maté stimulant. Instead, he fished fresh green leaves out of his pocket and pulverized them into the drink. Luz smelled the mint and flashed on the meadow from the lower slopes of the mountain. He then unwrapped a packet of brown pellets, which he held out for her to swallow.

She gagged on the first one. "Yuk. It is vile. What is it?"

"Adrenal, from the gland of a cow. It is your best hope to walk again. The mint tea will help you digest them. You must take them all."

They might cure her if they didn't poison her first. "My back is broken, seir. How can I ever move again?"

"If your spinal cord is crushed, medicine will not help you walk. But a bruised spine can mimic a crush; swelling from the shock holds your legs hostage. Adrenal is strong medicine to bring down swelling." He stopped. "We shall learn by tomorrow."

Afraid to hope, Luz uttered a silent prayer and gulped down the foul-smelling pellets. The mint did nothing to disguise their bitterness.

She plopped flat and squeezed her eyes shut. A moment later, stinging tears forced them open. She tried to look at Aldo, now squatting on his haunches on the edge of her blanket. Keltyn sat cross-legged at her feet.

"Go away, both of you. I'll be okay for a while." Luz wagged her chin at Aldo. "Please, go fix Quintara's leg."

She lay back and immediately dozed off. She awoke to the sound of Aldo's panting as he returned. He squatted down, this time removing his boina and holding it with both hands over his heart.

"Bad news, seirita. Your horse's leg cannot be fixed."

She gulped. "What do you mean, she can't stand up anymore?"

"There is no way."

"But you must at least ease her pain." She wiggled around to look Aldo straight in the eye.

"It is no use. Even if I could keep a coca poultice on her leg, the effect would wear off by tonight. You must understand. The bone, it is shattered. There is no hope."

"What are you saying?" Luz verged on a scream. "That she must be put down?" Deep down, Luz knew it would end like this. Yet she allowed herself to believe that Aldo could pull some miracle.

"I am sorry, but it is so," said the jeaf. "With your permission."

She broke into a sob. "Quintara. Oh no." She lay several minutes with her hands over her face before scooting up on her elbows. "Please, take me to say goodbye to her."

Aldo turned toward the open rocks where Quintara lay. He opened his mouth to shout for Efrain, but instead dissolved into a fit of coughs and wheezes.

Keltyn went to fetch Efrain, and Aldo gestured for him to carry Luz. She grimaced in anticipation, but Efrain's movements were surprisingly gentle for such a large man. When they reached her steed, he eased her down beside the mare's head.

Quintara's breathing was shallow. Collapsed onto her right side, all her fight quit. The culprit, that damned boulder, still sat there beside the mangled mess of her thigh. A large piece of bone stuck through the skin, surrounded by dried blood and a swarm of flies, with Quintara now too weak to swish them away.

Luz never felt so sad. Her fine steed, which but yesterday pranced through the chaparral, was now reduced to a ghost of her previous self. Luz gazed at the mare's face. No flicker of the eye, no head movement, no sign of recognition. She grasped Quintara's muzzle and held tight, barely able to feel the air crawl through the mare's nostrils.

After several minutes, Luz sat up and signaled to Efrain. "Enough. Take me back. Do what you must do."

Propped on her blanket five minutes later, Luz heard a single shot echo through the grove of trees. She slumped flat and covered her face with her hands. To the head it must have been, yes, the forehead, right above the eye.

With her own eyes still closed, an awful thought seized her: save a bullet for me. Will a single shot be enough to finish me off? Here, kneel down on your right; rest the arm holding the rifle barrel on your other knee. Position the muzzle behind my ear; don't let your hands tremble. Why should you be afraid? Even were I scared, I would not show it. Now take a deep breath. Ease the trigger finger back, don't squeeze. Bang. There, it's over.

Luz dropped her hands from her face, more drained than ever. What was the use of struggling to go on? Quintara was gone, and with her, Luz's mobility. What good would she be as a cripple? Better to be abandoned here, buried under a blanket of lava.

She lay, neither asleep nor awake, in a stage of suspended animation. In due course, horizontal shafts of sunlight coursing through the trees roused her back to the present. The rumblings soon returned, and she heard rocks bounce down the mountainside again. Despite this clamor, the frantic feelings that plagued her before now abated.

She noticed Efrain bent over nearby, murmuring to Aldo, who sat propped up against a tree trunk. Aldo croaked in a hoarse voice, words that Luz could not understand. Efrain walked away, returning a few moments later with their two mounts, tying them up farther from the open space. The shelter of a grove of trees did not guarantee protection against another boulder run amok, but the odds were less.

Keltyn gathered enough wood to keep the fire going. She and Efrain drank more maté and chewed on pieces of jerky, tortilla, and dried fruit. Luz sipped on the maté, but still felt too nauseous to eat.

Clearly, they were waiting to see if Aldo's medicine would improve her condition before towing her back in that wagon. She did not wish to disappoint all three of these people who risked so much for her sake. Now she found herself uttering a desperate prayer: Please, Spirits, if you get me out of this, I promise never to do anything so stupid again. I'll always obey Mother, too.

Efrain removed a tarp from his pack. He tied two corners to tree branches, six feet high, the other two corners to ground brush, to fashion a lean-to. Tonight, they would have shelter. He wrapped a blanket around the shivering Aldo, sitting by the tree trunk. The jeaf's loud breathing was now labored, even at rest.

Keltyn retrieved Luz's riding breeches, dried from hours on the rock. She helped Luz put them back on and changed the wet diaper. Luz could feel more around her bottom, but her useless legs were still dead. Plus, the pain, this unwelcome visitor that refused to be banished, crept into her back again. She cursed, this time in silence, reached behind, and pulled the dry poultice out, the salve absorbed through her skin.

Aldo glanced at the bare cloth that Keltyn brought him and motioned for his pack. He reached for the coca leaf and the salve, but these few movements triggered another bout of coughing. Leaning back, he used gestures to show Keltyn how to mix a fresh poultice. Luz felt strong enough to lift her upper body onto her elbows as Keltyn slid it underneath. The pain slowly retreated.

Even as the sky darkened, the tremors continued and rocks crashed down. The smell of smoke hung all around them, equal portions from their small campfire and the reek from the volcano's innards. Again, it hit Luz. Their presence was at once insignificant but also threatening, small specks perched on the side of this monstrous, malignant being. A sleeping ogre, now forced awake, groaning like thunder, drooling lava down his chin, bent on casting off those puny creatures, clinging to his chest like so many ants that dared to disturb his repose.

After a while, all she could make out were the silhouettes of Efrain and Keltyn, sitting by the fire. Efrain started to sing softly, Keltyn soon picked up the refrain. Luz couldn't quite make out the words, but the soft pacing felt melancholy. It must be about a charro's lost love.

Gradually, she relaxed, imagining the tall evergreens overhead, visible now as dark shadows, standing their guard like sentinels, ready to protect the four of them from the darker shadow of Monster Erebus. She turned her head toward Aldo, wrapped in a blanket, propped up against a tree. Too dark to see his silhouette, too much background rumbling to hear if his breathing labored on.

Suddenly, the fire sent a cascade of sparks flying high into the pines. When the fire settled, a vast emptiness surrounded her. Luz closed her eyes as the tears came. Deep inside, she sensed Aldo's spirit taking flight, and with it, some part of her as well.

***

Joaquin lay asleep in his tent, absorbed in a troubled dream.

It's barely daybreak. He rides behind Aldo, away from the herd and the other gauchos. They climb a trail leading out of the valley. They reach a pass and stop to check out the scene ahead.

The view is spectacular and bewildering at the same time. Sunlight pokes through the thin cloud cover in spots, lighting up random acres of chaparral. The pass at which they pause is the last natural barrier as far as he can see. The terrain before them slopes down toward a vast spread of water that stretches all the way to the horizon, an enormous vista. The line where the ocean meets the sky forms a faint curve.

Joaquin turns toward Aldo with his shoulders hunched, neck rigid. He wants to head back to the friendly confines of their valley. All this space ahead is too much to cope with. He flicks the reins to turn Cisco around, but Aldo shakes his head. "No, boy. You must go on."

"Where shall I go? You must lead, jeaf."

"This is as far as I come. You must proceed on your own. Trust your instincts."

"Seir, please. Do not abandon me." He realizes he sounds pathetic, but it matters not; his whining is useless. Aldo has already turned back, gone.

Joaquin sits motionless on his pony and shivers. A tear forms but he quickly brushes it away and scans the horizon again. No sign of any life, human or animal. "Well, come on, Cisco. We cannot stay here forever." He gives the pony a nudge and scans the vista for shelter, for vegetation, for any clue of what to do next.

He rides on for an hour, the wind in his face, whipped up from the great sea on the horizon. Then, half a mile ahead, he spies another mounted figure facing him, waiting.

The man sits straight, as if used to being observed. As Joaquin nears, the man looks to be nearly as old as Aldo, but shorter, on the pudgy side. He wears the clothes of a gaucho dressed formally: pattern-stitched jacket and leggings, pointed studded boots, wide-brimmed felt hat curled up at the edge. They all appear new, as if he is just trying out the trade. His face fits this notion too: clean cut, pale, eyes wide open and unlined.

The man flashes a broad smile. He speaks in a strange tongue, which, nonetheless, Joaquin can understand. "Welcome, young friend. I have been awaiting you."

Whoa. His head pulls back. "Seir, with respect, who are you?"

"I am, shall we say, your long-lost uncle. Call me Tio Hector, Joaquin." He tips his hat. "Come, let us find a spot to rest and share maté."

It takes time to locate shelter from the wind. The boy plops down cross-legged on the sand. Tio Hector tries to build a fire from twigs and brush, but he is all thumbs. It hardly seems like he could be kin if he can't even start a fire. The man shrugs, hands over the flint. For Joaquin, it's second nature; the blaze is going in no time.

Tio Hector is handier with the bombilla. Soon, they are sipping the brew, but the tonic doesn't do much for Joaquin's spirits.

"What troubles my young friend so?" Hector sets his gourd down and pulls out a small knife to clean the dirt out of his fingernails. He keeps shifting his weight, trying to find a comfortable position on the ground. He looks all the more awkward in his fancy new vaquero outfit.

"It is nothing." Joaquin tries to sit up straighter.

Hector tilts his head up and sideways. "Aldo is gone, Aldo is gone." He says it in a singsong voice.

Joaquin pulls back again. "How do you know of Aldo?"

Hector's eyes open wider. "It is my business to know these things."

"Oh." Joaquin ponders that. "So, you may tell me, what is in store for me now?"

"Ah, but you must phrase the question differently, my boy. Your future is in no one's hands but your own. You need only to recognize opportunity when it knocks on your door."

"You speak in riddles. Be clear now. Where shall I turn next?"

"Turn? Why turn?" Hector points over his shoulder, toward the sea. "Keep going straight. But..." here the man holds his pudgy finger in front of his nose. "Keep your eyes open, Joaquin, and your mind. Most importantly, your heart. A wondrous surprise awaits you, but you may at first mistrust its worth."

***

Joaquin awoke with a start, his shirt wet and the inside of the tent dark. The ground trembled softly. He listened but heard no sound except for a bawling cow and the occasional call and response of songbirds. A trace of wood smoke drifted in from the remains of the charros' campfire.

He lay very quiet, his eyes indeed wide open. Tio Hector, what a strange fellow. But what of the jeaf? Joaquin tried to tell himself that it was foolish to believe in premonitions, that dreaming about something does not make it happen. Yet he couldn't shake the thought that Tio Hector's appearance was an attempt to soften the blow of a great loss.

And this opportunity, this wondrous surprise that his imagined uncle conjured? Did it have something to do with the Sky-Bornes? Way too much was happening at once. Joaquin decided that, first and foremost, he needed to keep his wits.

18

MINUS ONE

When Luz awoke the next morning, her legs felt different, or rather, they *had* feeling. She leaned up on her elbow, pulled the blanket off, and willed her toes to wiggle. They did. Fighting back squeals of delight, she tensed every muscle in each leg for sheer joy. She pictured the array of nerves in her spine and legs, awakening from two nights of forced lethargy, and a feeling of awe overcame her, awe for the marvel that was her body on its way back to wholeness.

She turned to rouse Keltyn. Her companion rubbed the sleep out of her eyes, noticed Luz's toes squirm, and crawled over to stroke the soles of her feet. The tickling made Luz giggle. She motioned for support to try standing up. Efrain, also awake by now, helped lift her to her feet.

Luz took a deep breath. "Okay. Let me try to stand alone."

They let go, and she immediately started to crumple. They had to ease her down to a sitting position.

"It's alright." She massaged her legs. Her whole body felt lighter.

Luz turned to see whether Aldo caught the breakthrough. The jeaf lay propped against the tree, just as Efrain left him last night. The big fellow crept closer to his uncle's inert figure.

"Tio, did you see?"

No response.

Efrain leaned in closer to Aldo's face. Touched his cheek. Rattled his shoulders. "Tio Aldo. No." He shook him again, harder. Aldo started to fall to the side, but Efrain grabbed his body, laid it flat, and struggled to his feet.

Keltyn hurried over and leaned in close. She put her ear to Aldo's nose, pushed two fingers on his neck. She looked at the rest of them and announced, "He's gone." She leaned down once more to close his eyes, then slumped back.

Luz held onto her legs. She bowed her head and the tears started running again.

Efrain squatted beside Aldo's body, kept his hands over his ears, head down and eyes shut, his large torso rocking to and fro. Keltyn touched his shoulder. He moved his lips as if whispering the same phrase over and over, but his words disappeared in the rumbling din of the volcano.

After a long while, Efrain slumped into silence. Keltyn knelt and wrapped Aldo's body in the blanket. She prepared a fresh batch of maté. The previous night's shakes had rumbled worse than the first, and Luz's head pounded from lack of sleep.

Efrain remained somber even after drinking his maté. He scowled at Luz. "You must ride in the cart. It is too dangerous to stay here another night."

The girl nodded. The volcano's stench and the hissing noise of lava vaporizing snow were bad enough, but another threat loomed. During the night, rolling boulders penetrated their wooded area.

Efrain and Keltyn used the tarp of their lean-to shelter to shroud Aldo's corpse. She climbed inside the cart to steady the head, while Efrain hoisted the body up. He roped the cart to the reins of Aldo's palomino.

With everything else packed, Keltyn prepared another coca leaf poultice and tucked it inside Luz's beltline. They helped her stand; she could walk so long as they supported her. When they reached the cart, it finally dawned on her that she would have to share the space with a dead man. She winced.

Efrain's jaw was set. "There is no other way."

Luz took a deep breath as the two of them bundled her up to sit against the front wall of the cart.

Keltyn checked behind; there lay the monstrous dinosaur bone. "What a shame to leave it. Let me at least take a chunk." She pulled out her hammer and chisel, whacked off a piece, and slipped it into her bag.

That's what we should have settled for in the first place, thought Luz. The extra time spent in unearthing and roping up the whole bone had cost them dearly.

They took leave of the improvised shelter in the woods. It wasn't much, but they were alive after two days and nights on the raging mountain. Still, all bets were off if they didn't move out hastily.

With her view to the rear, Luz watched part of her nightmare come true. Real lava oozed down from the cone, half a mile up, chasing them, matching their speed. All of their hopes to return safely rested in her mother's rickety old cart. Aldo and Efrain expected to be carrying only Luz, not a second body, certainly not one as big as the jeaf's.

What if the axle broke? Luz shuddered. No way she could ride a horse, even if they tied her to the saddle. She pictured the recent nightmare, tons of molten rock oozing toward them, frying and burying everything in its path. What should she do if they got stuck?

Every time the cart hit a bump, it felt like a nail piercing her back, driving home their precarious plight. Luz gritted her teeth. If the axle broke, she would insist that Efrain use that last bullet on her, so he and Keltyn could at least save themselves.

**

By noon the volcano's rumblings lessen, as our small party distances itself from the mountain. We bounce over the rim of the crater and approach the plane. The cockpit door is open, and Buck's head sticks up inside. He can't see us yet.

There comes a roar from the plane, Buck gunning the engine. The bandage on his head is gone. I'm surprised at the amount of relief that gives me.

Now Buck sits still and watches us draw near. Harry stands nearby with arms akimbo, his gaze fixed on me. Looks like he's ready for a rumble. Buck must have filled him in about the Chinese meter. I grit my teeth, ready for the worst.

"Good to see you all made it back," says Harry. "Where is Aldo?"

Gone to an eternal green pasture. I point a thumb at the bundle in the cart. "Aldo died during the night. His heart gave out on the mountain."

"Uh-oh." Harry gulps and looks away for a moment, then straightens and addresses Efrain. "I'm sorry."

The big gaucho blinks in response.

I try to ignore Buck's stare and dismount with a sigh of relief. I turn toward Efrain and Luz and rotate my hand in front of my mouth.

The big guy shakes his canteen. "Just a cup of water. We must be on our way." He stays mounted.

I translate this for Harry, who goes to fetch the water. He forces a smile as he pours for them; it's obvious that he can't wait to vent his spleen. He whips around to face me and snaps, "You realize you're in for it now."

I tie up the mule and avoid eye contact. "Don't start on that, Harry. You knew I had to go scout Erebus."

"Another of your ill-advised decisions."

"Meaning what?"

"Meaning the not-so-smooth landing in this crater..." I start to object, but Harry isn't done, "... and, Buck told me about your little yellow box."

I face off square with Harry and open my mouth again, ready to have it out. Just in time, I glance over at Efrain on his horse, Luz in the cart, and stop myself. No sense airing our dirty laundry in public.

Efrain takes his cue, hands me the empty cup with a faint nod, and tips his boina.

I collect Luz's cup and reach down to give her a hug. "Okay. Goodbye for now."

Harry waves absentmindedly, and they're off again.

Now I've got a choice. Stand out here and argue with Buck and Harry? Instead, I heft the pack and head toward my tent. I sense Buck, still sitting in the cockpit, following my every move with his unshaded eyes, like a buzzard in a treetop.

A little part of me, the "aw shucks" part, wants to act passive. Let them take their best shot. The treasure trove of stone that we found is my best defense. Our mission is a success. The other part of me says, "Don't back down now." Sir Oscar is the one who raised the stakes. I owe it to Luz and her people to play my hand. Let the cards fall where they may.

***

Efrain, mounted on his own horse, led Aldo's palomino as it pulled the cart. It bounced back and forth as they climbed the rim of the crater. Luz, jostling along with it, was caught in her own predicament. She dreaded the upcoming display of frailty to the whole tribe, especially to those who begrudged her free time. She knew what her mother would say when they returned, aside from the obvious, "I told you bad things would happen," or more likely, "You nearly killed me from worry." Their people did not ascribe even natural events like drought to chance, let alone calamities like this one. There must be a cause, and the Sky-Bornes' appearance made them the natural scapegoat.

Luz decided her best course was to ignore her frailty, to present a brave face when they arrived at their camp. Now, as the effect of the last poultice wore off, she found her determination flagging. She tried to keep from crying out, but Efrain heard her moans, less subdued with each bump. When they got to the top, he dismounted and rummaged through Aldo's pack to make a fresh poultice.

"No, it's okay, you don't need to." Luz tried to keep her stoic bearing. "No trouble at all, seirita," said Efrain, but his tone alleged differently. He mixed the pulverized coca leaves with the salve. When he showed his face, the haggard set of his eyes and mouth still registered the shock of Aldo's death. He spread the paste onto a fresh rag and motioned for Luz to turn on her side.

"Thank you, seir." She tried to smile, but Efrain responded with a grunt. Gradually, her skin felt cooler and the pain faded. What a relief. She climbed back to a sitting position, and soon the cart again jostled along on the downward slope to their camp.

Every so often the wagon's wheel would hit a rock, and the bundle next to Luz would jerk. Each time she would jump, then peek at the shroud for further signs of life, but the faint odor of decay confirmed, if anyone doubted, that Aldo was gone for good. She took a deep, shaky breath. He died a hero; she would make sure everyone knew that. What better way could one be remembered?

As the cart bounced through the herd and into camp, Luz tried her best to sit up straight. That position, at least, would distinguish her half-functioning body from the lifeless one beside her.

By the time the cart arrived at Aldo's yurt, a string of gauchos formed the core of a crowd. Efrain dismounted and called for Ysidro to help him unload the bundled corpse. They lay it in front of the dwelling. Ysidro knelt and unwrapped the shroud before falling back in alarm.

A trio of young boys stopped kicking their ball and gawked. The gauchos removed their *boinas*. A few of the older ones' eyes glistened. He was a tough boss, thought Luz, but they all respected him. Several women gasped and broke into tears; they reached out to hug one another.

Luz watched the eyes of each person as the shock of the jeaf's death sank in. All too often their reaction was to stare at Luz sitting in her cart. She wished that she had a turtle's shell to withdraw into until this menace passed.

Ysidro pushed himself to his feet and croaked the question running through everyone's mind. "How did he die, Efrain?"

Efrain closed his eyes. "His great heart gave out. Too many bad things happened on that mountain." His lips clamped tight, reluctant to say more, but people kept pressing him. His answers came in fits and spurts. "We found rustlers, four missing heifers. Luz paralyzed. Her horse broke its leg, we had to put it down." He used his sleeve to rub the tears away. His chin trembled. "Aldo just wore out, stopped breathing."

Ysidro tugged at his whiskers. His mouth sagged into a deep frown. "Those cursed Sky-Bornes. They brought this on."

Efrain opened his eyes and ran his hands up and down his thighs. "The ground quaked the whole time." He stared at the mountain. "Large rocks rumbled down. Had we not left this morning..." He surveyed Aldo's corpse while moving his own head back and forth. "The jeaf's medicine saved the girl, but for him, the cost was too great."

Luz took a shaky breath. Please, let me just crawl away.

Silence fell like a heavy black curtain as each person reflected on the loss. Then the curtain rustled and parted as Joaquin squirmed his way to the front. He bent over and cradled his arms, the sight of Aldo's corpse evoking a numb, blank stare.

In due course, Trieste arrived, grim-faced as she bent down to hug Luz. Cheeks damp, she kept wiping her face with the back of her hand. Her mouth alternated between wide open and lips clenched, as if she could not bring herself to say what she truly felt.

You need not say a word, Mother.

Efrain removed Aldo's pack from the palomino and gave the reins to Trieste. She led the cart back to their yurt, tears running down her face all the while.

As her mother helped her into the hammock, Luz said, "Mother, don't cry. I'm going to be all right. Compared to yesterday, it's like a miracle. Thanks to Aldo. He truly did save my life."

"Yes, girl. My tears are of joy for your safe return, but also of sadness for him."

This gave Luz pause. "I did not know that you had any feelings toward Aldo. You never spoke of him."

"There is much that you do not know." Trieste turned away.

"Tell me."

"Later. First you must rest." She stepped out of the yurt, leaving Luz to wonder what secrets her mother might reveal later. Yet physical exhaustion weighed on her, and within moments she succumbed to the luxury of lying in her own hammock.

19

LOOSE TONGUES

A dank cloud of grief hovered over camp. Aldo's death started to sink in for Joaquin and for the rest of the tribe. Gauchos and camp followers drifted away from the jeaf's body, tears flowing freely. Efrain and Ysidro rewrapped the shroud, and a few women came back to drop flowers and small trinkets.

Efrain stooped down and put his hands upon Joaquin's shoulders. Joaquin stiffened, sucked in through his nose and bit down hard on his lip. Huddling next to the bundled corpse, he felt cold and dizzy.

The big fellow squeezed his shoulders, then left him alone with the body. The air was so heavy, he could hardly breathe. He fell to his knees. Were there already a hole dug to bury the jeaf, Joaquin might have slid right in there with the corpse. That dream the night before came to mind; Aldo abandoned him and this Tio Hector showed up. Where was the man now?

Just then, a breeze rattled the cottonwood leaves. A low whooshing eased through the camp like a large bird lifting free. Joaquin looked up and found another hand resting on his shoulder. Orfea. Was he imagining it, or did she know what was going on inside him? She stroked his hair and nodded.

Yoka stood alongside and peered at the shroud. "Tomorrow we shall invoke the ancestors before Aldo's burial." She stretched out her hand. "Joaquin, come along to my yurt. Find yourself a snack. We shall meet you there by and by. Right now," she turned to Orfea, "I wish for you to accompany me. I must recruit others in the tribe for the Venga ceremony, and it would be good if they met you before that occurs."

Frustrated, Joaquin got to his feet. What he really needed was time to figure out what to do next.

He stumbled over to Yoka's site, gulped down milk and nibbled a biscuit, but it did nothing to improve his mood. With his mentor and defender dead, with no Aldo to teach him, how could he become a gaucho? Efrain acted friendly enough, but none took any pains to encourage him, except for the one whose body now lay cold in the shroud.

On top of that, just as Joaquin feared, Nestor had given him the eye ever since Joaquin herded the missing heifers into camp yesterday. He made it a point to look away, but the attention rattled him. Surely Nestor must be aware that his treachery was discovered; that knowledge would make him even more dangerous than before. Now, without Aldo, who would set things right?

Yoka's fire was dying down and the sun was setting. He began to shiver. In the distance, he heard the charros gather around their campfire. They were probably into the pulce by now, mourning the jeaf in their own way.

Joaquin scouted a ways before finding dead cottonwood branches. As he limped back with these, Yoka and Orfea showed up.

"Ah, Joaquin, bless you," said the crone. She set in to fix a rack of ribs, no doubt a gift from one of the women they just called on. She rubbed in Orfea's seasonings. Her movements were more assured with the new vision aids. The smell of meat roasting on the spit soon perked up his appetite.

Yoka turned the skewer. "Joaquin, you might be interested to hear more of where Orfea is from."

"Oh yes, seira, please." He forced a smile.

"My home is a land with many mountains, Joaquin, more than here. The mountains are called Alps."

"Oh. And your friends? Is their home in these Alps also?"

"No, they come from a land far away from mine." She spread both hands away from her body.

"So, what brought you all together?"

"We all have interest in your part of the world, Joaquin."

This sounded strange. He eyed her closer. "What sort of interest?"

Yoka broke in. "Now, boy, don't ask such pointed questions."

"No, it's okay," said Orfea. "He has a right to know. My interest is the Onwei people." She eyed Joaquin, but her smile also seemed forced. "My interest is you."

He stiffened. "What is it you wish to learn?"

"You have no family, you are an orphan." Her voice dropped as she said "orphan," but she kept watching him.

"My father left my mother afore my birth." Joaquin chose his words. "Two years later, my mother also disappeared. Those of our people who knew my parents have mentioned them, but I do not care to hear more." He set his lips. "I have an uncle in Nomidar, no blood relation. He and his wife, they were childless, they took me in before she also died."

Orfea stayed silent, but Joaquin felt her eyes still on him. He shifted to watch the fire. "Uncle Fermin tried to push me into his trade, making mortar. You don't have to ride or run, so he figured I could handle it." He shrugged.

"So why...?"

Joaquin sighed, rolled the words around on his tongue. "He treated me mean, like a servant, so I wanted to leave. I decided to become a gaucho. I practiced riding a hoss every chance I could. The spring of last year, Aldo asked me to come along." He raised his head to the two women. "I would have made it as a charro, too, if..." He tried to choke back this new emptiness.

"If Aldo were alive." Orfea finished what he couldn't.

He said nothing. Every few seconds, a drop of fat fell from the ribs, making the fire hiss and flare.

She went on. "This is a sad time for all in the tribe, especially for you."

Joaquin gave a vague nod.

"It must be hard to think of the future right now." Orfea paused, offered a sad smile. "You understand what I am trying to say?"

"Well enough, seira."

"You are an intelligent young man."

"Thank you, seira." He bowed his head, frowning, confused.

"Joaquin, dear, you must use your talents, especially now," Yoka broke in. "What are your talents?"

Talents? Like juggling? Rope tricks? They were stringing him along. With half a mind to leave, only the smell of ribs kept him glued to his seat. He decided to play it safe. "I am a good rider."

Yoka closed her eyes, the corners of her mouth tight, and shook her head slowly. That must not be the answer she wished for.

"Yes, everyone admires how well you ride your pony. Ah." Orfea clapped her hands. "I wish a favor of you."

"Yes, seira."

"Tomorrow you must ride to our flying machine. You remember the way?"

"Of course."

"You shall escort Harry, Buck, and Keltyn here, so they can take part in the Venga ceremony."

He was supposed to round them up? Joaquin let out a huge sigh. "How will they learn of your wishes?"

Orfea reached in her pocket for the transmitter. "I shall tell them with this thing."

He watched her, spellbound.

"Listen." She pressed a button, waited.

After a few seconds, Harry's voice emerged. "Hello."

Joaquin's ears perked up.

"Harry, listen. You heard about Aldo."

"So sad." His voice broke.

"It is."

"How are they taking it?"

"Everyone is in shock. I'm calling because Yoka has a plan."

"What's up?"

"There's a ceremony for Aldo's funeral. Tomorrow noon. All of us should come."

"You think? I don't want to intrude. We could end up being the scapegoats. They're pretty leery of us already."

"Trust me, Harry, it's the right thing to do."

"All of us just show up?" His tones dropped a notch. "What about Buck? He's still acting kind of squirrelly."

"Clean him up and bring him along. It's important. Joaquin will come by in the morning to escort you." Orfea nodded at him.

"Is that the protocol?"

"It is."

"Well, okay then." Harry still sounded doubtful.

Orfea pushed a button to end it. She faced Joaquin. "They will expect you at..." She used her finger to trace the sun's position at mid-morning.

Joaquin thought quickly. She was using him as an errand boy, plain and simple. On the other hand, this would be an easy task. His curiosity of the Sky-Bornes was already aroused, creating a warm tingle that promised to take his mind off his sorrows.

"Very well, seira."

Orfea put the phone away. "Where were we?"

Yoka said, "We were admiring Joaquin's gifts. What are your other talents, boy, besides riding your pony?"

He shrugged. Telling stories? Tracking hoof prints? He couldn't sing or dance, if that's what she was getting at. Up to now, practicing the skills of a gaucho had consumed him.

The crone leaned toward him. "Think. What else do you wish to master?"

He pursed his lips. He was tired of being the charros' lucky charm boy. "Something others will respect."

"Well spoken. And you said before, you wish to move with the tribe."

"Yes. I have no desire to fester all year in Nomidar, stuck with the small children and the infirm." Speaking the word made him flinch.

Yoka held up a hand. "Joaquin, I have a proposition for you, one to challenge your ambition, *and* your intelligence."

He watched the crone's wrinkled black face as she handed him a plate of ribs. He took a bite, and the meat melted in his mouth. He mumbled, "At your service, Auntie."

"As you know, ever since my dear Addys died ten years ago, I have searched the tribe for another young woman to learn the Venga art. The apprenticeship is long, the reward uncertain, so no girl here wishes to commit. But, I can tell you," she leaned closer, "there is no more respected person among us, save perhaps the jeaf."

Joaquin stopped chewing and gaped at her with his mouth full. Did she really believe that? Anyone who kept his ears open would vouch the opposite. Most of the tradespeople respected her weaving skills, but they took her Venga rituals with a grain of salt. As for the charros, her antics made her a laughingstock, pure and simple.

Yoka closed her eyes and nodded casually, like there was an unspoken bond between her and Aldo. She put her hand over her chest. "And tomorrow, I hope the gauchos will attend Aldo's burial. They need the ancestors' wisdom to choose a new jeaf."

Joaquin shook his head. What did all this have to do with him? She needed to find another girl to whom she could teach her art. He went back to picking at the ribs.

Yoka let out a big sigh. "Do I have to spell it out, dear boy? I hoped you could put two and two together."

He put down the ribs and concentrated, hard.

Orfea tried to suppress a smile.

Finally, the crone's preposterous notion dawned on him. His eyes lit up and he pulled back. It was all he could do to keep from bursting out in laughter. "You want me to learn the Venga art from you. And you believe that I might influence the gauchos, being a male."

Yoka shrugged. "More or less."

Something about Yoka gave him pause, perhaps the way she now hunched her shoulders. Joaquin shook his head rapidly. No way. She had gone off the deep end for sure.

Yoka pointed her finger. "Now, boy, don't reject this offer out of hand. You haven't heard the bonus. This is where Orfea comes in." She gestured to the other woman.

"Yes, Joaquin. Yoka tells me the hardest part of the Venga apprenticeship is learning tongues of the ancestors."

Yoka nodded sagely. "Our forebears came from many lands and spoke many different languages. By means of Venga, we can learn from any or all of them. But to do that, you must speak as they did." She leaned toward the boy. "This woman can teach you many of those tongues with this machine of hers. She can teach you how to read and write, so you can learn the rest of them."

He was listening again. He picked up his ribs. As he gnawed another mouthful, he managed to ask, "What does it mean, 'read and write?'"

Orfea flashed the knowing smile of an angler reeling in her catch. "Imagine learning from someone else, without having to remember it all in your head. You can discover what the other person knew even after they are gone." She paused for effect. "And imagine being able to send your own memory to a person in another place or time."

This idea sent a thrill through Joaquin, though it sounded difficult to master. Clearly, just the telling excited Orfea. He tried to imagine himself in Yoka's position. It was a long stretch from tending cattle.

He studied these women again in a different light. Did he trust either of them enough to be part of their scheme? Suppose they had already conspired into a secret agreement among themselves? How easy it would be for two canny women to sell off his future? At the moment, he felt too confused to decide anything. He shrugged and mumbled that he would think on it.

He set down his plate to toss more wood on the embers, then found a spot on the ground to sit with hands clasped behind his bowed head. Joaquin the wizard: the charros would have a field day with that one.

***

With the fire dying down and the sun already set, Fay could no longer make out the boy's face. Yoka's shoulders wiggled as she pulled her robe tighter.

Fay expected that Joaquin was of two minds at the moment. All this talk about his future; he naturally wished to make his own choices.

Push too hard and he would fly back to his own tent to mope. Still, the fire here was warmer.

She caught his eye and winked, then pulled a flask out of her pack and let him sniff the contents. At first, he drew back, just staring at her, no doubt wondering why a grown woman would offer strong drink to a boy. She poured a finger's breadth of the brandy for him, but even after she diluted it with three fingers of water, he gasped as he swallowed it. After a few more sips, though, a contented smile spread across his face.

Yoka and Fay sipped their portions at full strength. Soon Fay found herself expounding on how her Del Campo ancestors left Argentina to go back to Italy, and later, after the sea levels rose, to Switzerland. She expected Yoka to chime in with more about her own lineage, but the old woman showed no inclination. Feeling glib, Fay launched into an account of her own early life, shared with Paul.

Yoka hunched deeper into her robe, and Joaquin's eyes began to wander. Fay stopped, stood, and held up her flask, dividing the brandy between her mug and Yoka's, with a thimbleful for the boy. She felt a bit tipsy as she sat. "Now where did I leave off?"

Yoka remained stone-faced. "Your Paul died prematurely, from a rare disease."

"His bone marrow stopped making blood cells. He lost his energy, became prone to infections. Little red bumps showed up on his skin. Nosebleeds. His skin turned pale yellow." The memories of Paul's decline whirled through her mind, but the brandy dissipated the bite. "Three years later, mercifully, he passed away." She turned to Yoka's bundled figure. "So, when you describe how your daughter died of the khokri, I know the feeling."

Yoka scoffed. "Do you? Has your child died?"

Fay jerked back. "No, I'm sorry. Paul and I stayed so busy with our careers, there was no time for children." She dabbed her eyes with a handkerchief. "But tell me, Yoka, if you don't mind, of this wasting disease that took Addys."

"Hmph. Just like with all the others, except, being black already, her skin could not turn darker like theirs did. Her bowels ran constantly. Sores appeared on her tongue and privates. She grew tired, limp but restless. She couldn't remember where she lived or what just happened. Within a year, she started hearing strange voices, fell into fits of screaming, pulling out her hair. Six months later, she breathed her last."

Fay weighed this. "What do you mean, just like all the others? How common is this malady?"

"Unfortunately, all too common among our Onwei women at midlife."

"Just the women?"

"Mostly. Many call it the curse of their sex." Yoka grunted.

"Why should they be cursed?"

"Some say it is for the sin of adorning themselves. For excess of vanity. For all the beautiful clothing and jewels that they trade for at the Rendezvous."

"But this trading is an old custom, no?" Fay pulled the blanket tighter around her legs.

"Of course, but nowadays they have many more goods to trade." Fay's eyes lifted.

"You have seen the iris stone jewelry made by Luz's mother?" asked Yoka.

"Exquisite pieces."

"I must examine them more closely. But perhaps your ancestors can explain this khokri."

"Perhaps." Yoka fidgeted, shifting her gaze to Joaquin. "Boy, throw more sticks on the fire."

Joaquin did so. As he sat down, the three of them heard noises. Four gauchos headed their way on foot. Three of them sounded drunk. Fay grabbed her translating tool and stuffed it in her pocket.

Big Ysidro led the bunch, flushed and staggering, his speech slurred. "There they are, the Venga witch, the Sky-Borne bitch, and the gimpy kid."

Stroking his side-whiskers, Ysidro glared at Joaquin like a man with a mind to step on a bug, but unsure if he wished to soil his boot. He threw his head back and laughed without mirth, then turned to his nephews, Soriante and Gabino. "See, I was right. They are plotting more designs against us."

Fay tried to relax. She had encountered this kind of bluster many times as a field anthropologist, usually among males who felt threatened by a stranger. Keeping calm usually sufficed.

Efrain walked straight, close behind Ysidro. He alone appeared sober. Fay supposed that he came along to clean up whatever mess this bunch might get themselves into.

Yoka stood up. "What is it that you wish, Seir Ysidro?"

"I wish... I wish that my brother Aldo lived. I wish that these accursed Sky-Bornes never disturbed us." He slumped to his knees.

"Do you believe that their visit caused Aldo's death?"

Ysidro gawked at Yoka, her face now at his eye level, and blinked hard.

Gabino staggered forward. "How else you explain all this?" His right arm backhanded the air. "The girl Luz would never have attempted the mountain by herself." His voice was as raspy as his face.

"Indeed, their hasty plan was ill-advised," agreed Yoka.

Fay started to nod as well, then thought better of it. Best not reveal that she could understand their conversation.

Efrain's shoulders slumped, the lines in his face etched deeper than when he pulled the cart into camp that noon. He knelt to stroke the back of the dog Mugabe, spread out near Yoka's feet. "Unfortunately, there is more bad news. Two others may be dead on the mountain."

"Who then?" said Yoka. "We heard only of Aldo."

Efrain nodded at Joaquin. "The boy came with Aldo and me yesterday. While on our way to rescue Luz, we caught two rustlers red-handed. We tied them up, hid their boots, and took their horses to prevent escape." He paused, shifted weight to his haunches. "This afternoon, Ysidro and I intended to bring them back."

The crone raised her bristled brows. "So? What happened to them?"

"We could not reach their spot. Lava from the volcano cut off the approach. The lava flow has slowed, the rumbling stopped, but too late for them. Only their horses were saved."

Ysidro lumbered to his feet. "Those two got what they deserved. Had I found them, I would not have bothered to tie them up, unlike my soft brother. Let them try running away, barefoot and horseless."

Yoka turned to Fay, asking her pointedly in Onwei, "Did you catch all that?"

No sense playing dumb anymore. "Most of it," Fay answered. "Enough to understand how these good men feel."

"How do you now speak our language?" Efrain said. All the gauchos gaped at her.

"Yoka has been very..." Fay searched for the Onwei word. She sent the old woman a pleading look.

Yoka's mouth turned down. "Patient?"

"Exactly. And the tool I brought along helps greatly." Fay pointed to her pocket but stopped short of showing the translator.

"Surely your party did not come here just to learn the Onwei tongue," said Efrain.

"True enough."

"What then?" Ysidro's tone had a hard edge.

"We came to search for..." Again, Fay beseeched Yoka.

"Minerals."

"What minerals?" said Efrain. "There is no gold around here."

"We search for that which you call the iris stone."

"Ah." Efrain brightened. "The violet rock that Trieste Hogarth fashions into jewelry."

"The same." She felt herself treading on thin ice. This was not the time to broach a deal for mineral rights with the Onwei. Besides, ever since Yoka deduced Oscar's grand design to colonize this land, Fay had no intention to serve as his mouthpiece.

"Your tribes must have many women who covet these jewels, that you should come all this distance in your flying machine to look for more," said Efrain.

Fay was dumbfounded. She eyed Yoka with a sheepish look.

The crone let Fay's embarrassed silence build before turning to the gauchos. "Their jewelers have not discovered this art. They covet the mineral for the outside shell of their flying machine, to keep it safe while in hostile skies."

The four charros gazed upward. A mass of stars twinkled. Ysidro sneered. "Surely she jests. 'Hostile skies.'"

Yoka's tiny frame straightened to its full height. She rested her hands on her hips. "You all laughed when I told you of the legends."

"What legends?" Ysidro acted baffled.

"How the Onwei people came to inhabit this place hundreds of years ago. How someday we would have visitors from a different part of the world." She raised her arms overhead. "That time has come."

Ysidro's eyes were slits. "Why did they wait until now?"

"Their land and our land are separated by thousands of miles of hurricanes, horrific storms, and caustic vapors. They could not reach us by land, nor by sea, nor by air, as the storms stretch way up high." Yoka reached her frail arm overhead. "That is what I meant by 'hostile skies.' The iris stone, forged by their smiths into a coating for their flying machine, made the journey possible now."

Fay marveled at Yoka's simple explanation, using terms she herself could have used, had she thought it through. The gauchos remained silent as they tried to make sense of this.

Gabino, squatting quietly with his jug of pulce, finally stood and stared at Fay. "But now you need more of this stone, to make more flying machines, to bring more of your people here."

Fay caught her breath. She was being forced to negotiate. "We will pay the Onwei for rights to mine the stone," she blurted in English. She caught herself and tried to repeat the phrase in Onwei, but it came out wrong and the charros just guffawed.

She turned to Yoka, begging once again for help, but this time the old woman shook her head and said nothing.

Fay slumped. Yoka was feeding her to the wolves.

Ysidro's face turned a mottled purple. He glowered at Fay until she cringed. "Do not mock us. None of you knew there were any people alive in this land when you set off. And how could any of you expect to find the stone here?"

Fay held her breath, not daring to utter another word, lest it make no sense again. The silence seemed to drag on for minutes. She could feel six pairs of eyes bore through her.

Finally, Yoka came to the rescue. "The young woman Keltyn is an expert of the iris stone. She knew there would be rich deposits near a volcano. Mt. Erebus is the sole active volcano on the planet that can be reached."

"Ha, boys." Ysidro grabbed the jug from Gabino. "Did you hear what she said? 'Active.' As in, just happens to erupt when their Keltyn goes hunting for this precious stone. Luz Hogarth becomes paralyzed; her horse and Aldo die in the process. Those rustlers swallowed by molten lava. Altogether too expensive a stone, I say." He turned to Soriante and Gabino to confirm his anger, threw back his head for a big swallow.

"These events were prophesized." Yoka's voice grew firmer. "The visit by Sky-Bornes, the eruption; do you think that your rage can change what is ordained?"

The gauchos stayed quiet, intimidated in front of this tiny witch. Yoka pressed on. "Others may share your anger. You must come to the Venga ceremony to be heard. Tomorrow at midday, before you lay your jeaf to rest. Anyone who wishes shall express his opinion."

Ysidro swayed on his feet. "You just heard our opinions, old woman. Why waste your precious Venga on dumb charros? Come on, boys. Let's go back to our side of the creek. We don't have to listen to this crap." He pushed the jug back to Gabino.

Yoka stared as they staggered off. "Think on it, boys," she called after them. "You would make Aldo proud."

They sniggered and staggered onward.

Yoka slumped down. Her voice lost its powerful edge. "What's the use? Aldo never attended a Venga ceremony in his life. Why should they be any different?"

Fay bent down to console the huddled old woman. The same dilemma tied them together now. If she and Yoka could not get the tribe to accept the Sky-Bornes' intention, the Bailey Voyager mission was doomed. Yoka deduced Oscar Bailey's true motives.

Now Fay was left with two choices, neither one to her liking: she could serve as Oscar's agent or, as she advised Keltyn, try to thwart his scheme. Her carefully rehearsed plan to act neutral, to be an ombudsman between the Onwei and Oscar, had unraveled before her eyes.

20

SINISTER SPARKLE

Despite the bright sunshine this morning, a shivering chill lingers in the air. Hey, it's early autumn in Antarctica. I've been cloistered in the women's tent since returning from the mountain yesterday, mostly lying in my sleeping bag in a state of exhaustion and funk. Now, trying to summon the energy to get back to work, I bundle up in thermal denims, a checkered red and blue wool tunic, and an oversized windbreaker.

I'm holed up alone to avoid any more arguments with Buck or Harry, at least not until I work out my strategy. Harry has been decent enough to let it go for the time being. I'm dying for a cup of coffee, but not enough to face the guys yet.

Across the tent, beyond the various-colored packs scattered on the floor, stands a folding table with a bunch of iridium ore and measuring tools of different sizes and shapes, just waiting for me. I need to test the rock samples from the mountain and mine the data for whatever they're worth. I have to keep rubbing my hands to stay warm as I set up the tools.

In between the sounds of wind whipping the tent flaps, I hear voices outside. Harry and Buck seem to be getting into their own argument. It started after a younger voice, might have been that of the boy, told them something. He must have just ridden in.

"To hell with protocol." Buck is already worked up. That can't be doing his injured brain much good. "You don't want me along,

Harry. You really don't. I might do something unpredictable, like our buddy Nestor."

"Ha. We'll have to keep an eye on him, won't we?"

"Plus, the mechanical stuff is finally coming back to me. I've got to finish repairing the VLG."

"Plenty of time, Buck." Harry's voice is muffled.

"Plenty of time? What if she doesn't fire?"

The chief keeps his cool. "We'll have to take our chances."

Buck mutters but speaks no more.

Harry says, "Come on, Joaquin. Let's go call on Savant Keltyn. She hasn't deigned to talk to me since returning yesterday. Must be scared. Maybe seeing you will cheer her up."

By the time they take the few steps to my tent, the awning flaps so loudly that Harry has to shout outside, "Morning, Keltyn."

I unzip the fly and stick my head out, hoping the boy's presence will keep us civil.

"Here's one of your fans." Harry motions toward Joaquin.

I pull back the tent fly to let them in. Harry hands me a mug of coffee, which I take in silence despite my intense gratitude. Not fair to him, but I've still got my guard up. I suck a few sips, wiggle my jaw, and smile at the boy. He finds a pack to sit on, while Harry and I stand, facing off like couple of fighting cocks.

"I've started to assay the samples," I say, by way of breaking the ice.

Harry takes another sip from his mug. "Any surprises?"

"Not really. The Erebus samples test higher for iridium content than the crater samples."

"Meaning?"

"Meaning that the Earth's core contains more of the pure stuff than the meteorites that formed the crater." The wide difference in shine between the two kinds of rocks is obvious. I put my mug down and turn my back to Harry. "Next step is to test the dinosaur bone."

I hold a lavender-gray slab in my left hand and twist my wrist inside the assay meter. It's like an antique bucket, square bottom, domed top. I'm proud of it, actually. Russell McCoy helped with the design, but I'm the one who built it and worked out the bugs to validate it.

After I turn it for two minutes, a red light flashes numbers on the dial. I make a note in my log and repeat the test twice more before letting out a slow whistle. "Fifty-nine percent iridium."

"That sounds pretty high," says Harry.

"It's incredible. It means that the calcium matrix has been completely replaced by our mineral. I wonder..." Now I face Harry.

"What?"

"Does this give us any clues into the extinction of dinosaurs?"

"Don't look at me. You need one of those dinosaur experts."

"They're called paleontologists."

"Right on the tip of my tongue." A corner of Harry's mouth turns up. He finds a pack to sit on.

"We'll just have to find one." I pull two energy snacks out of my pack and offer one to the boy. He accepts it, stays polite and quiet. He's got an earpad now, but no reaction. So far. I wink at him, peel off the wrapping, bite off a healthy chomp, and hold the bar up. "Three days on the mountain, eating biscuits, cheese and dried fruit. This chocolate tastes positively exotic."

I finish and sit hunched over for a minute, collecting my thoughts, concentrating on my next move. I've imagined it for the past two days, but can I pull off the real thing? It's my only chance to get them off the scent. I take a deep breath and head back to the table.

"Now," I cast a furtive glance at Harry before settling on the boy, "the moment we've all been waiting for. Are the rocks hot?"

I try to conceal my tremor by keeping my hands close to my body. I wrestle the Chinese meter out of the supply pack, that large metal cube, painted yellow. The face has a needle pointer and small slash marks with numbers. I hold the thing a foot away from the bone slab. There's a shrieking noise. I move the bone away from the stone samples and try again. Another screech.

"Holy buckets." I keep my face pointed away from the chief and Joaquin, worried what they'll see in it won't jive with the clear message from the machine. I go on to test the stone samples. The ones from the mountain all squawk like crazy. Those from the crater just beep.

I stand quiet as a statue for a good minute, head bowed, before turning to face my audience of two. Harry squints at me. Joaquin still has his hands over his ears. I fix my gaze on the floor.

"All right." Harry removes his dialups and squeezes the bridge of his nose between thumb and forefinger. "Let's hear it."

"It's no good, chief. The jig is up." I slowly raise my eyes to meet his, trying ever so hard not to blink.

"I'm guessing you suspected as much before we got here. Just bringing that Chinese gadget along."

"I hoped that the stuff here would be clean, but no, I'm not surprised. Not after what we discovered in Siberia."

Harry's face gets redder by the minute. His eyes bounce around. "This is going to change a lot of things."

"I wouldn't want to transport the rocks back, that's for sure."

Now his expression hardens. "More than that, young lady. The women are wearing this stuff for jewelry. You're going to have to break the news to them."

Oh, shit! "Me? Are you nuts?"

"And today is your chance. Fay radioed last night. Joaquin here will escort us to the Onwei camp."

"You should do this, Harry. You're the chief." My brain scrambles to deal with the jolt.

"But you're the scientist. You need to explain what will happen to them if they keep wearing the stuff." My fear must show because he adds, "We'll all be there to back you up."

I swallow hard and nod toward the other tent. "Even Buck?"

"He's going to come too, much against his will."

"What's the plan? A memorial service for Aldo?" I glance at the tunic lying beside my cot.

"That's part of it. Fay said that they have a communal ceremony whenever something big happens. Losing their jeaf, that's big." Harry turns to Joaquin. "I'm sorry for your loss, son."

Joaquin nods with a vacant look.

Harry gets up. "We should take off when? Half an hour?"

The boy nods again, and Harry leaves the tent. I stay slumped forward with the mug in my hands. Convincing Harry was one thing, but how can I hoodwink the whole tribe? After a while, I tell the boy to go outside while I put on a change of clothes for his jeaf's funeral: white tunic, black neo-silk leggings. Not my favorite duds, but Fay made us each pack a good outfit for an eventuality such as this.

I brush my moptop quick, slip on my windbreaker, and step out of the tent. Buck is going through the motions of saddling his mount. The gray mare has been tied up here since Nestor brought her five days ago. She appears none too happy with the way Buck yanks on the straps of her saddle and keeps skirting sideways.

"Hold still, damn you." The goose egg on Buck's head flares bright red.

I make a wish that his lump should ache, too, harder each time he tugs on the poor horse's bridle.

"Easy, Buck," says Harry.

"Hmph. Who needs this?" But when Buck spies Joaquin patiently waiting on his pony, it seems to calm him. For a minute. He stares at me as I stuff the yellow meter into my daypack. "Bringing the evidence along, eh, Missy?"

I avoid his glare and mount up. "All right, guys," I say. "Let's go take care of business." We head off.

"Clean clothes, same dirty, tired old body," says Harry to everyone and no one. "What I wouldn't give for a hot bath."

Joaquin leads us across the floor of the crater. Even though he is in charge of this little expedition, he looks pretty hangdog. Soon, his pace slows enough that Harry draws even.

"Aldo must have meant a lot to you. Everyone needs someone to believe in them." Our chief says no more, awaiting some kind of response from the boy.

"I shall get by," Joaquin mutters at the ground. Then he looks up. "But you people best watch out."

"At the ceremony?"

Joaquin nods. "Anything might happen. Especially with this news." He nods back toward me, then spurs his pony to the head of the line before Harry can draw him out further.

I'm left to struggle with how to present my "discovery" to the tribe. Unlike with Harry, I won't be able to hide my face when I tell them.

And what about Fay? Other than that bombshell over the phone a couple of days ago, she and I have been out of touch. Since she's the one who will have to convey my meaning to the tribe, she'll have to catch it on the fly.

This thing has "fiasco" written all over it.

21

BELTRAN

Just a day after Luz returned to camp in her helpless state, she now felt ready to try to walk on her own. She needed to show everyone that she was resilient, a survivor, not a victim.

She tested her weight standing up from her hammock. So far, so good.

Her recovery, she knew, was not due to any merits of her own, but rather a good night's sleep, her mother's hearty stew, and most of all, the miraculous effects of Aldo's medicine.

Aldo! Or, as Luz must now learn to think of him, Father. What a strange word to roll off her tongue. She practiced mouthing the syllables in silence as she slipped on her boots.

Her mother made the confession while Luz wolfed down her stew last night. A more unlikely pair of lovers she could not have imagined, the great roguish jeaf and the petite shy girl who, in her first season as a camp follower, plied the trade of boot cobbler.

Yet her mother allowed herself to be seduced by this man one night eighteen years ago and soon found herself pregnant with Luz. The rest of the story was a blessing in disguise, according to Trieste. She took the wisest course and retreated back to her family in Nomidar for several years, until Luz was old enough for her to bring along on the cattle migration once again. In the meantime, she developed her own craft, far better than cobbling: the unique art of smithing the piedra de yris into fine jewelry.

After shedding tears for Aldo's demise, Trieste told the rest of the story in a most matter-of-fact way. Yet Luz was still astonished; her mother always led Luz to believe that her father died before she was born. She suspected that the truth would never have come out so long as Aldo was alive. But why?

As Luz stepped out of the yurt, she wondered if her mother would have more surprises to confide later. More likely, Aldo had been her only lover. For comparison in such matters, here were her neighbors Carmen and Pilar.

"Back on your feet so soon," intoned the older sister Pilar. Her tall form leaned against the tree shading their yurt. "It's a miracle." The subtle smirk on her lips suggested otherwise. Carmen, squatting by their campfire, frowned at Pilar's feigned sympathy but said nothing.

Luz waved and kept walking. Was her mother jealous of these two? They had belonged to the camp entourage as long as Trieste had. When she alluded to certain girls who aroused the charros' passions, Luz had a pretty good idea Trieste meant to include these sisters. They must have lost count of their lovers by now. The whole tribe knew that either of them would invite a gaucho into their yurt, had he the charm or the price.

Such were the facts of life; who was she to judge? Most of all, Luz was grateful for one thing; her mother seemed not to begrudge her disobedient daughter.

This morning, Luz agreed to her mother's request that both of them should help Yoka and Orfea bake a large batch of Venga nuggets. Inching her way to Yoka's yurt, she found each of the three women hands deep in dough. She allowed herself to bask in their chatter, relieved to join in a task that demanded neither strength nor concentration.

They finished the preparations shortly before midday, and now hefted stools and trays of nuggets to a clearing in the midst of camp. The hour for Yoka's prescribed Venga ceremony was at hand. The crone acted conciliatory all morning, but Luz could tell from her attentions that she was measuring Luz for a role in the upcoming production, a role that Luz vowed to shun.

The prankish young Torme and his two buddies, who used the space to kick their ball for the past week, appeared none too eager to cede their turf.

"Go on, kids," barked Yoka. "Tell your parents that now is the time to gather." Seeing no movement, she waved her arms. "You heard me. Get a move on."

They scattered as she neared. She waited a few more minutes, hands on hips, peering in every direction. When no one ventured to the site, she turned to Luz. "Ring the bell, dear."

Shaking the cowbell made her ears ring. Flaco scampered to a safe distance. Along with the sound, a vibration spread through her body to her lower spine and unleashed a surge of pain that made her stop at once.

Gradually, people drifted toward the spot, mostly matrons in their bright shifts and straw hats, carrying stools. Youngsters mingled behind, curious but too shy to sit. A few tradesmen showed up; Matin the tanner brought his hide drum.

Soon, Joaquin arrived on horseback, leading Keltyn, Harry, and the pilot, Buck, all of them dressed in white shirts and shiny blue jackets. Harry and Buck seated themselves next to Orfea. Buck sat ramrod straight, arms crossed. Harry kept busy studying faces, appraising them, Luz supposed, for signs of hostility.

Keltyn carried her stool over to Luz and squeezed her arm. Luz wanted to stand and walk, show off her recovery, but decided it was not the moment for celebration. Keltyn soon focused on the ground, deep in thought.

Yoka gave a nod to Matin, who moved into a hypnotic slow cadence on his drum. At first, small children responded by picking up sticks and trying to strike each other to the same rhythm, until their parents intervened. In due course, a more solemn ambience settled in, everyone's attention directed to the ground. All except Luz, who could sense what the crone was up to and fretted how it would play out.

Yoka handed one of the platters to Trieste. Together, they moved through the group, now grown to thirty, bidding each person take a nugget. When all who wished were served, Yoka signaled Matin to stop his drumbeat.

The crone held up her nugget and uttered the single word, "Venga." She dropped the morsel in her mouth. Each person with a nugget did likewise.

Luz glanced around as she chewed. Keltyn, Orfea, and Harry each partook of a nugget. Buck abstained and sat as frozen as a gray stone. He was the wariest of the Sky-Bornes from the day they arrived. Like Keltyn said, it was not just his head injury.

Yoka's deep tones rumbled. "These past days have been both momentous and tragic for our tribe. Think of the prophecy." She scanned the crowd. Most of the adults nodded. "It says that strangers will descend, from another time and another place. Well, here they are." Her voice rang with the edge of command as she fanned across the front row.

Turning her back on her audience, she addressed the distant hills. "Did our uninvited guests realize the cascade of ill fortune that their arrival would beget? Or were they naïve enough to think they could come and go without disturbing the natural order? No matter. A cycle has been set in motion. We gather today for an inkling of how it will end."

Luz cast a glance at her mother and found her expression as rapt as everyone else's. Yet Yoka's speech just made Luz slump lower. Even though her mother forgave her errant behavior unconditionally, the crone's pardon came with a price, spinning Luz's misadventure into a cautionary tale.

Yoka kept her back turned and arms uplifted. "The prophecy also says that the arrival of Sky-Bornes will coincide with the Earth moving, and so it did. The mountain's eruption proved both momentous and tragic."

She turned to face the crowd again, then zeroed in on Luz. "This dear young girl, whom I relate to as my own flesh and blood, lay paralyzed, thrown from her horse. Thanks to Aldo Correon's healing powers, she recovers swiftly. Yet the jeaf sacrificed his life in the process." She paused for this to sink in.

Luz trembled, overwhelmed by a distinct wish to vanish, rather than act as a forced character in Yoka's sick charade.

A number of the tradeswomen, including her mother, wept freely. Most of them were, like Trieste, unattached to any man. How many others were Aldo's one-time lovers, wondered Luz? Could some of the other children be her half-siblings?

Yoka clapped her hands together, snapping Luz out of her musings. "Luz, dear, show everyone what you found last week."

Despite the vow Luz made to herself, she felt powerless. Perhaps it was Matin's drumbeat marking a tone of solemnity, or perhaps the sober stares of the whole tribe weighing upon her, but she felt like a puppet in Yoka's production. She unwrapped her bundle and held up the giant vertebra. Some people squinted at it, others murmured to their neighbors.

"Luz brought this to me four days ago. We believe it is from the backbone of a dinosaur, one of the monsters that walked the Earth eons ago. Have any of you ever uncovered such a bone?" Yoka gazed around and waited for a response. "Of course, you haven't. I would have heard. So, what does it mean when all of these strange things happen at once?"

No one ventured a response. Everyone seemed mesmerized by this frail hag and her imposing voice. Despite Luz's resentment, she shook her head slowly, marveling at Yoka's gift.

The witch droned on. "Events like these signal us to invoke the collective wisdom of our forebears. Many of you have Australian bloodlines like the Hogarths. You have heard of the dreaming tradition, of Songlines."

Luz saw a wave of nodding heads.

"The Songlines guide the Onwei tribes from crater to crater, finding the best pasture for our livestock. Luz dear, do you recall the name of the old woman at our last Venga session?"

"Kapujeena," The name forced its way out of her tight lips. She scowled. Yoka knew the name as well as she did.

"Just so. And what did she reveal of the dinosaur Songline?" Yoka the spider kept spinning her intricate web. Luz shook her head to dispel the image and tried to remember the details of the Songline: "The connection between craters and dinosaurs." Just four days ago, but so much had transpired since. "She said... the craters were made by giant rocks. The rocks rained from the sky and changed the Earth in a way that the dinosaurs could no longer survive."

"Changed how?"

Luz squeezed her eyes shut, trying to conceal a creeping anger. "She said the rocks stirred up giant clouds of dust. The dust storm lasted so long that it starved the dinosaurs of sunlight, of plants to eat, and finally of air. The great beasts died, and the face of the Earth changed."

"What else did she say about the rocks?"

"That... that they wear down over time, they become part of the earth, you might be able to see telltale signs around the rim of the craters. The giant rocks contained a substance that left streaks of color around the edges of the craters."

"What color is it, dear?" Yoka's voice boomed upward.

Ha! Luz flicked her eyes open. "We never found out. We lost the connection to Kapujeena."

"What other color could it be?" Yoka extended her arm, fanning around the crowd. Women started to finger the violet bracelets, necklaces or earrings of iris stone worn for the occasion. Their puzzled expressions showed Luz that, like her, they were mystified as to Yoka's purpose.

Luz's neck began to tingle just as Yoka sat down. She must have felt the tingling as well, thought Luz. Having stoked the embers, the old woman intended to let them burst into flame on their own.

***

The breeze died and the sun shone warmer. Fay noticed that many of the women removed their shawls. Harry, Buck, and Keltyn shrugged off their windbreakers, and Buck, bless him, now sat with his hands resting on his lap. Murmurs and looks traveled around the circle, but no one else stood to comment.

The ancestors' spirits might be present, but perhaps they heard enough already. Fay decided last night to use any chance she might have at this ceremony. Now she rose and said, "May a stranger ask?"

More murmurs. By now, many were aware that Yoka tutored Fay in the Onwei tongue. Yet, speaking up in public, she supposed that was pushing it.

Yoka's brows shot up, but she quickly recovered. "If you wish to expose your naïveté, be my guest," she said in English, before making a sour face and turning away.

Fay watched the scores of faces scrutinize her, expectant but noncommittal. Yoka was not the only one waiting for her to stumble.

She lurched forward in her stilted Onwei, wishing she had picked up more of the strange tongue's grammar. "I have no answer to mystery of rocks, craters or dinosaurs. But no connection between arrival of my people..." she pointed to Keltyn, Harry, and Buck, "and eruption of Mt. Erebus, I promise. We come in peace; you must believe me." She counted on her years of public advocacy to connect with these people, but their faces remained impassive.

Fay pursed her lips and studied the ground, searching for another way to bridge the chasm. After a minute, she straightened and continued her broken phrases. "Ever since we arrive here, I feel like relative to Onwei people. I told this Yoka. She say is because I am 'anthropologist.'" There was no word for this in Onwei, so Fay quickly explained. "That mean I learn from people who live in other time or other place. Nobody from where we come know for sure we find you here, but I believe it. So, I not..." she glanced at Yoka, who muttered, "surprised."

Fay nodded and fanned her hands. "But you all very surprised to meet us."

Nervous laughter broke out all around.

Fay took a relieved breath and plunged on. "Now I think some of you my kin. Yoka tell me many Onwei ancestors come from land called Argentina. Your ancestors speak same tongue as my ancestors." She bowed. "You must forgive my mistakes."

Heads wagged back and forth, and eyes rolled. Still, it seemed to Fay they appeared thankful that she drew the focus away from Yoka's stern demands of contemplation.

"One my ancestors in Argentina seek adventure and turn to life of gaucho. His name Hector Del Campo. I know nothing else of him. So, am I," she pointed to her chest, then to the group, "kin to any you?" She smiled broadly, palms splayed out, before sitting down.

More murmurs, before all bowed their heads once again. Profound silence reigned, as if three dozen-odd forms were frozen in time. Even the children hushed. They must truly be seeking a connection.

Yet as the minutes dragged on with no response, second thoughts about her challenge coursed through Fay's mind. She scanned the faces one more time. To her relief, Joaquin stood and shuffled toward the front. Several of the gauchos took notice of their mascot and wandered closer.

"May I?" Joaquin stood in the midst of the circle, arms hanging limp at his sides, posture erect, eyes squinting. "I hear the voice of one who calls himself Hector. He claims to be my distant uncle. He says that he became a gaucho in Argentina after leaving his family behind and changed his name to be accepted. He calls himself Hector..." Joaquin's brow furrowed, "Beltran."

Several of the matrons gasped. Joaquin opened his eyes and whipped his head around. "What did I say?"

The matrons turned toward each other with fingers pointing, chattering like magpies. Trieste arose, strode over to Joaquin, and led him back to sit on her stool. She placed her hands on her knees and leaned forward to look him in the eye. "Beltran. It was your father's name, Gaspar Beltran."

Fay watched him, wondering if the orphan boy heard this long ago and forgot. Joaquin held his head with both hands, studying the ground for several minutes. When finally he glanced up, his eyes shone bright.

"So, my full name is Joaquin Beltran."

Trieste nodded with her eyes closed, but Joaquin's gaze kept darting around until, torn between elation and despair, he turned to Fay. She could barely contain herself, but he must make the deduction on his own.

"And if this Uncle Hector is the same as her kin," he said, "then I am related to this woman."

"I knew it." Fay clapped her hands. She rushed over the boy, who ducked his head but allowed her to hug him to her breast. She glimpsed many of the women dabbing away tears between sobs, just as she did. Yoka alone remained unmoved, scowling.

Fay held Joaquin by both shoulders and murmured in his ear, "I can help you. Will you let me?"

He shrugged but allowed a shy smile.

Now came the hard part. The boy was her cousin; she could educate him better than Yoka possibly could. She reluctantly let go of Joaquin and strode over to Yoka, who was glaring from her perch on the stool. Fay leaned forward, hands clasped in front of her, trying to keep her voice calm but measured. "I want to take him back home with me."

The old witch shut her eyes tight and shook her head vigorously. "You know it's the only way to provide him a real education."

Yoka responded by clenching her prune lips tighter.

"Don't worry. I'll make sure he gets back to his people in due course."

Still no reply. Fay found the pitch of her voice rising, her hands waving and gesturing toward Joaquin. "Answer me, Yoka. Are you willing to throw the boy's future away? Tell me one reason why this plan won't work?"

Finally, Yoka stood with her own hands covering her ears and stomped off toward her yurt.

Fay dropped to her stool and buried her face in her hands.

***

"Get lost, old hag. Who needs that witch anyway?" Tio Hector was back, and he had a shameless side. "You found me without her help, as did Orfea. I took the risk of leaving her Del Campo clan when they returned to Italy. Instead, I joined your gauchos; I'll take the credit for bringing you two together.

"Still, the two of you make an odd pair. Not to put you down, kid, but for starters, you need a haircut. Sure, there's nothing you can do to shake the limp, but at least sit up straight, shoulders back. That's it."

Joaquin found himself paying attention, even as the more rational part of his mind told him to ignore these fevered imaginings.

Yet, his uncle was on a roll. "To think that you are related, through me, to this cosmopolitan, dare I say it, diva. Your cousin is a fashion plate, all right. She makes even the crone's shapeless shifts look good. A bit overripe for my tastes, but a lot of red-blooded men would find her figure alluring. And highlighting those dark-red curls with gray, or is the gray dyed red? I can't even tell, but she is attractive."

Joaquin tried to conjure the two of them together. He knew few couples their age, let alone any who still harbored romantic feelings.

"Now picture what she can offer you. Certainly, you need a mentor, especially now. Beyond that, think of how you would look in a decent outfit, and I'm not talking hemp here: ruffled white cotton tunic, combed lamb's wool vest, flared black breeches with gold buttons on the cuffs, red striped inlay. Top it off with a felt sombrero, gold filigree trim. Clothes make the man, my boy."

Such strange tastes this man had. These duds were even harder to picture. All that emerged was a shame-faced youth facing titters and giggles.

Tio Hector rambled on. "Still, first things first. Look at you, nothing but skin and bones."

Joaquin regarded his own scrawny figure.

"You'll need to fill out those clothes. How about some real *cucina*? Put the color back in your cheeks. Antipasto, calamari, ravioli, veal Parmesan, tiramisu. The names don't mean anything to you now but wait until you try them."

Why couldn't his uncle at least describe them? And what was the proper way to eat such things? Joaquin suspected there would be a lot of table manners to learn. He sighed. The jibes of charros were better than the scolding of women, any day.

Hector buzzed over to his next topic. "She's Italian, right? She can take you to the opera, one of the finer things in life. Actors dress up in costumes and sing their hearts out for hours at a time. 'Ombra Mai Fu.' The most sublime sounds you will ever hear."

Joaquin crinkled his nose.

"Too fancy? Well, she's also Swiss. How about yodeling? I hear the charros like that sort of thing."

Some charros might.

"And the ways of women? You say that you're not interested, but that will change in a few years, mark my words. Play your cards right, and the ladies will be falling all over you. Orfea can show you the right cards."

Joaquin tried to picture these ladies, but the only one his mind could summon was the oppressively cheerful Orfea. He would be as lost and lonely as a stray calf, unless she could impart to him her manner of charming strangers. He wondered if such a talent was born or bred.

Tio Hector rambled on. "Let's not forget what you can do for her. Don't feign surprise. What can you possibly give her, you ask? One word. Hope. The gift of youth to age. Plus, she would be the first to admit that, underneath your scruffy looks, you are hands-down adorable. Having a protégé like you would make Orfea the envy of all her friends."

Her protégé or her lap dog? *Enough already!* Joaquin whipped his head back and forth, trying to dispel Tio Hector from his mind. This strange voice that wormed its way into Joaquin's mind since Aldo's passing, he must silence it.

"I know, lots to think about." His uncle seemed to get the message that he was not wanted. Whistling a little jingle, he flitted off.

Joaquin needed to pay attention, focus on the ceremony. He waited anxiously for more distraction. Would it end now, without Yoka around to lead? The crowd sat in a hush, stunned at her walking out on her own show, but several gauchos drew closer.

22

TARNISHED GEM

Luz studied those around her. Yoka's abrupt departure stunned the crowd, but no more than this unexpected twist linking Joaquin to Orfea. One by one, heads bowed and eyes closed in deep contemplation.

She mulled over what to expect from this gathering. She came because Yoka and her mother expected her to, and in part to show everyone that she survived her brush with catastrophe. But the old witch instead turned her misfortune into a morality play, with Luz but one puny element.

Luz needed more than ever to show her clan that she was in charge of her own fate. She had in mind some kind of confessional statement, something heartfelt yet comforting. She needed to regain whatever claim to maturity that she had lost in the eyes of these neighbor women from her foolish and nearly tragic mishap. She took a breath and made to stand up, but Trieste grabbed her arm and motioned for her to stay put.

"Mama, what's the matter? I wish to show everyone that I'm okay."

"There will be time for that. Wait awhile."

Luz plopped back onto her stool and fumed in silence. Gradually, the tranquil surroundings calmed her. She became aware of the tall cottonwoods looming overhead, as if sitting in judgment, their seeds floating through the air like puffballs, helped along by a soft breeze and the heat of the noonday sun. Its light probed through the trees with a dappling effect, alternating light and shadow. Warblers twittered and leaves rustled in the high branches. Water trickled in a nearby creek. At the edge of the circle, Torme and his chums provided the only distraction, snapping willow saplings into a bright sharp crackle.

At the same time, Luz sensed tension in the air. It was not just she who had unfinished business. Things were altogether too quiet for a group this size. Normally, the women kept up a constant exchange of gossip, weighing in with firm opinions on everything from the weather to matchmaking. But today was different. Today, their jeaf lay dead.

Those with campstools positioned them under the cottonwoods. Matrons in their bright frocks and straw hats, most of them artisans like Trieste, sat alongside the few tradesmen: tanner, butcher and smith. More gauchos drifted in and lined the perimeter of the circle. They leaned on a tree trunk or squatted on their haunches, aloof but curious. They must smell a brawl, she thought.

She spied those two shameless sisters, Pilar and Carmen, standing among their charro clientele with hands on hips. Luz watched with curiosity and a dash of envy. With no other visible source of income to sustain them, they did not subsist like paupers. Far from it: in addition to being the most reliable customers for Yoka's fashions, they competed for the most ostentatious display of Trieste's earrings, bracelets, and pendants. Each of them tossed a glittering bauble into Aldo's grave, but so did many other women.

Luz searched the remaining faces of her tribe, all of them impassive. Save for an occasional hand waving to brush off a fly, each was frozen in another charged silence. The mottled light further camouflaged any expression of thought. She might as well try to read a blank wall, despite knowing each of these people by name since she was old enough to talk. All, that was, except the four Sky-Bornes in the front row.

The more Luz focused on the Sky-Bornes, the clearer it became that their presence, not Aldo's death, was the piece most in need of explanation. But with Yoka departed, who would take charge of this?

Buck and Harry appeared lost, gazing around with polite vacant smiles, trying their best to blend in. Orfea made room for Joaquin to sit beside her, and she reached over to stroke his shoulder. Keltyn alone acted preoccupied, hunched forward and rubbing her fist into her palm, as if to burnish it for a fight.

If she had something to say, she should get up and say it. Luz closed her eyes, trying to will this gathering to move toward its destined goal. Soon her head ached from forced concentration. She again felt an overpowering urge to rise from her stool. Not only she was wounded, she now realized, it was the whole tribe. To heal, they needed to talk to each other, out here in the open. If no one else would take up where Yoka left off, it needs to be her. She felt her mother's arm again try to pull her back down, but this time brushed it off. Her new mission was more important than simply reassuring her neighbors of her recovery.

Eyes wide open and glaring, features contorted, Luz reached out and spread her fingers as she addressed the crowd. "As you all know, I almost died on the mountain. I feel extremely lucky and grateful to be alive and regaining my health; I owe an immeasurable debt to our jeaf Aldo Correon." It felt wrong to exalt this man, who saved her life while sacrificing his own, without acknowledging that he was her father, but she promised her mother to keep her secret.

"While I lay paralyzed on that mountain for two nights, the question that haunted me was this: Did our misguided search for the iris stone cause the volcano to erupt? Who among us can tell me?" Luz turned to scan the baffled faces of her tribal neighbors, awaiting an answer from whom she knew not. She caught her mother's reproachful look yet knew that the same question coursed through her mind, despite being too timid to voice it before the crowd. Indeed, were Trieste the one to utter it, others besides Luz would have chalked up the thought to superstitious imagining.

A man's voice rang out from several rows back. It was Dario the butcher. Luz recalled the Sky-Bornes' first afternoon in camp. Harry pulled a burnished fiddle out of his pack, trying to break the ice with dance music. After he attracted an appreciative crowd, Dario disrupted the concert with purposely raucous squeals from his own primitive fiddle.

Now, standing with his fist raised, Dario demanded, "Sky-Bornes must answer." He looked around, raised both arms and shouted once more. "Answer!"

A chorus of voices responded, "Answer!"

Luz gritted her teeth. Her wish, to draw out her neighbors and begin the process of healing, had backfired. Instead, the game had turned into finding a scapegoat. She dropped onto her stool in a slump.

***

Perched across from me, Harry leans forward to get my attention. He wiggles his fingers, palm up, signaling that now is my time. I waver, squeeze my fist again, and grab a deep breath before arising.

Standing up, that's all it takes to hush the crowd. Fay hovers beside me, ready to translate my words. But what words will they be? I've never been any good at speeches; hell, I could be the poster child for stage fright. Plus, I'm still pissed at Harry for making me do this. Oh well, here goes nothing.

I try to keep my voice measured, since that seemed to work with the media back home. First, I focus on a spot in the distance. I lean forward as if reading a message, etched across the sky in cloud formations. I'm afraid that if I engage anyone in eye contact they'll see through me and the whole thing will blow.

I try to convey how Luz and I discovered each other's fascination with the iris stone, how I willingly assumed the risks involved with scouting the mountain, how we found the stone, more than we could dream of, how the mountain rumbled, raining down giant boulders. Out of the corner of my eye, I detect faces hardening or weeping.

I gulp and stand straighter, ready to deliver the coup-de-grace. "It gets worse. I discovered more bad news this morning." I light on the girl. Her face registers surprise, probably wondering what else could go wrong. My eyes jump away once more, now unable to come to rest on anyone.

"Radioactive." I stretch the word out, leaving Fay slack-jawed, unable to come up with any way to translate this. "There is no word for it in your tongue. It is a poison that seeps out from the stone, forever. It will kill you if you are close to it, but slowly, without any clue. It gives no warning that you can see or hear or smell or taste. In your hand, it feels the same as any other rock."

I reach into the bag by my stool and hold up the yellow meter. Its red needle wavers to and fro. "This device measures the poison."

As I pick out a sample, there's the sound of women sucking their breath through clenched teeth. I flip the meter's switches on. The needle jumps, and the box emits a noise like a crow's caw, squawking loud enough to startle even those sitting in the rear.

A lot of the women sport jewelry made from the iris stone, but I'm hoping they are confused enough by the whole premise so that they don't connect the dots. No such luck. The ones wearing jewelry spring up and tug at their dresses, their ears, necks, and wrists, ripping off their pieces in a tortured frenzy, elbowing each other aside to thrust them at my meter. Most of their gems light it up, and their owners throw them on the ground in disgust. They storm off, howling, but not before several of them pause to scowl and spit at me, the bearer of bad tidings.

The good news is that I seem to have convinced the two people who matter. Harry's Adam's apple bobs up and down as he surveys the crowd. Buck keeps his eye on the needle of the yellow meter, engrossed in the Chinese technology more than its implications.

Now with the tribeswomen and my chief pissed, I cast around, looking for my own private hole to crawl into. How am I going to get out of this mess?

***

Luz surmised what the rest of them must have, all but the Sky-Bornes: this must be the cause of the khokri that plagued so many in their clan. No one knew the cause of the disease, but that didn't stop her mother's fevered imagination, and Keltyn's revelation would only stoke it further. Mother fretted on lots of things, but every time she forgot a piece of trivia, every time a little rash popped up or she felt tired, it must be the start of the khokri.

Once it started, she was convinced, it could only degenerate into the full-blown disease. Her bowels would run constantly, sores would pop up in her mouth and down below, and strange voices would plague her while she lost her mind. When that time came, she would have to retire back to Nomidar for the few miserable years left to her.

Now her mother hung her head and wept as Luz tried to comfort her. Those exquisite pieces, her passion and their livelihood, lay scattered in the dust at her feet. First the tradesman disappeared, now this. Mother's nightmare of contracting the khokri had taken a macabre twist. Instead of coming down with the living death herself, she had become its unwitting agent.

Luz chewed on her lip while stroking her mother's hair. Was the iris stone really to blame for the wasting disease? She had her doubts. Keltyn was unable to hold her gaze as she made her declaration. Judging from the panic that spurred her solo Venga trip, she was up to something. From the conversation Luz overheard on the mountain, Orfea was involved as well.

Yet, if the iris stone was not the cause of the khokri, the only way to prove it, with the tribe so alarmed and her mother devastated, would be to discover the true culprit.

People started to drift away, grumbling among each other. Luz helped her tearful mother to her feet. Keltyn appeared out of nowhere and attempted to guide Trieste by her other arm, but her mother shook her off with a scowl. Nonetheless, Keltyn hovered nearby on their entire way back and stood by the yurt's entrance. Luz eased her mother onto her cot and knelt to soothe her brow. Trieste continued sobbing, on her way to collapse from exhaustion.

Luz took a deep breath. To find the true cause of the khokri, she would need Keltyn's help. Both of them had much at stake, but could they trust each other anymore? Luz would first demand to hear the full truth about this so-called poisoning of the stone.

She turned to face Keltyn, but the Sky-Borne was gone. Was she afraid to confide? A sinking feeling weighed on Luz. Instead of confronting Keltyn, she was stuck in her yurt, tending to her feeble mother. Yet by now she knew Keltyn's nature. She had as much at stake as Luz; she would be back, and together they *would* find the answer.

23
STUNNED

Matin's drum, this time with a more urgent beat, aroused Joaquin. Big Ysidro stood next to the drummer, waving his hands toward the gaucho camp. Joaquin glanced briefly at Orfea, still standing in the midst of the circle, seemingly in shock from the crowd's reaction to Keltyn's pronouncement. Best to let her be. For now, he needed to join the charros to say farewell to his jeaf and mentor.

Groups of three or four turned and stumbled across the shallow creek towards the gaucho camp. Joaquin caught sight of the shrouded corpse with a freshly dug grave next to it, and he again felt the gnawing hole in his gut. All of the gauchos clustered around, boinas off, everybody quiet for a change. The crowd behind them stood two and three deep.

Ysidro cleared his throat and waited for silence. "My brother Aldo distinguished himself as a great and wise jeaf." He stood straight, jaw clenched. "I shall have large boots to fill." Charros exchanged glances, nodded to themselves.

Ysidro bit his lip. He acted tongue-tied when sober. His darting eyes lit upon Harry, standing at the edge of the crowd, hands clasped. Ysidro lifted his head. "A good jeaf will do his best to keep his people safe and avenge them if they come to harm." He opened his mouth to elaborate, but more words seemed to fail him. He jerked his head down and stepped back.

Big Efrain eased forward. He fidgeted with his boina, but his voice rang clear. "Uncle Aldo adopted me when my father died twelve years ago. He was wise beyond words, taught me everything that is worth learning, showed me the meaning of courage and honesty. I shall miss him more than I can express. Farewell, tio." He bowed, stepped back.

Now Heriberto Paz shuffled up. His long bony frame reminded Joaquin of a scarecrow. He studied the ground. "The jeaf was not happy with my performance lately, and for good reason. Yet he put his grudge aside to save my wounded horse, which stands on its own feet today. Were it not for his efforts, I would be a destitute man, worthless. Thank you, seir, thank you." He wiped his eye and retreated.

Heriberto's words, as heartfelt as they were few, struck a chord with Joaquin. He expected he could pay homage to Aldo just by being here, but now came a strong urge to express something of his own. He ambled forward and clasped his hands behind his back. He wanted to say simply that Aldo gave him a chance to make something of himself, and he would try to be worthy.

Yet, when he opened his mouth, the words would not come. He cleared his throat and tried again. Nothing. Feeling flushed, his heart pounding in his ears, Joaquin retreated. This time there was no one to embrace him or pat him on the back. Everyone seemed lost in a well of sadness, but Joaquin felt shame as well. He had let down the jeaf's memory by failing to voice any tribute.

Ysidro checked to see if anyone else wanted to speak. No one did. He signaled to Efrain, Soriante, and Gabino, who threw ropes underneath the bundle. The four of them lowered Aldo's corpse into the ground, moved back, and stood with their hands clasped.

Several women pressed in to toss bits of bright cloth. A few who kept their jewels earlier now took them off, dropping them into the grave. When the women finished, other charros went to work, shoveling dirt to fill that big hole.

Joaquin's knees wobbled. Part of him, the part that aspired to become a gaucho, again wanted to slide into that hole alongside his mentor. Despite his silent pledge of a few moments ago, his chances of reaching that goal now were about as likely as Aldo climbing out of his grave.

But Orfea's promise enticed him. What else did she have to offer? Some of those creature comforts and exotic encounters that Tio Hector conjured, could she deliver on those? Above all, he wanted to see if the Sky-Bornes could extract themselves from the deep doo-doo they slipped into. Maybe *he* could help them.

The crowd started to break up again when Joaquin felt the ground rumble. He whipped around to find a lone bull trotting toward them. It pawed the earth, head jutting back and forth, grunting every few seconds, breath steaming. The bull's skin showed no sign of moisture from sweat. Joaquin knew immediately that this one had also eaten locoweed, and that sureness gave him confidence. Here was a chance to put to use some of the jeaf's knowledge, and perhaps redeem the humiliation of his previous silence.

Yet this beast was bigger and more aggressive than the one that had gored Heriberto's mount a few days afore. Its bloodshot eyes, jumping around the crowd, showed the creature to be clearly spooked, ready to charge anything. Joaquin knew what he must do. He stood taller and focused his thoughts.

If the bull could be lured away from the crowd, its threatening behavior would abate in a few hours. He needed to convey this to someone before the bull was needlessly slaughtered, or worse, before someone was gored. He cast around, trying to find Ysidro or Efrain. He spied Nestor on the run for his rifle.

"Wait," Joaquin shouted after him, but he knew that trigger-happy Nestor would see this as an opportunity to become the hero. The villainous charro did not look back.

Mothers grabbed their small children, holding them tight behind. Everyone froze. The bull was no more than thirty feet away when a rock hit it on the ear. Joaquin whirled and spied Torme taking off. *Idiot.*

The crowd started to bolt; the bull charged. Yet a moment later, it stopped in its tracks as if it hit a brick wall. It slumped to the ground, but the grunting breaths kept on.

A few people tiptoed forward. Joaquin heard no shot, saw no sign of blood, but there stood Buck, a head above most of the crowd, as frozen as the animal he just dropped. His right hand held a teeny gray gun.

Joaquin stared at him. Where had that gun come from? He must have carried it in the pocket of his windbreaker. He clearly fired it, but where was the noise, the smoke?

Nestor reappeared with his rifle ready. He took in the bull on the ground, glanced around, and spied Buck holding his weapon. The rogue charro clenched the rifle tight, ready to point it but wavering. Joaquin froze, bracing for the worst.

This delay seemed to wake Harry up. He paced over to Buck, held out his hand, and said a few words. Buck looked down at the gun, like it just dawned on him that he held it. He handed it to his chief, who tucked it in his jacket pocket.

Nestor's mouth turned to an ugly sneer. He raised his rifle to waist height and pointed it at Buck. The big pilot stared straight back at him, unflinching.

His heart pounding, Joaquin deliberately stepped between the two of them.

"Nestor, not now," Ysidro growled. "Put it down."

Ysidro was quite a bit bigger than Nestor. The younger man shrugged and lowered his weapon. No one moved, all watching the bull in stunned silence. The only sound came from the beast itself, snorting and heaving, its red eyes casting all about, but now harmless. Finally, Ysidro turned toward Joaquin. "Does this bull not behave like the one that gored Heriberto's horse?"

The adrenaline rush of a moment ago passed, leaving Joaquin limp and shivering. The words stuck on his tongue. "Yessss. After I led Aldo to it, he figured out that eating locoweed poisoned it. We found the plant growing nearby. This beast acts just the same as the other one." He rubbed his arms.

"Get a grip on yourself, boy." Ysidro turned back to study the fallen bull. "The other one recovered by the next day. The poison should leave this one's body also, but," he pointed at Buck, "will it be able to stand again?"

Orfea translated. "Effect of shot wear off four hours."

"In that case, we shall watch closely." Ysidro scanned the frozen crowd. "Go now. We must prepare to move the herd to the next valley, lest the locoweed that grows here crazes more of them."

People drifted apart, but Nestor stayed put. He fixed his stare on Joaquin, stuck his head forward, and contorted his face into a snarl. He again grabbed the rifle with both hands but relaxed it under Ysidro's withering stare. Another shiver zapped through Joaquin; he whipped his head away. He had to focus his breathing to keep from fainting.

When Joaquin finally raised his eyes, everyone was gone except Efrain and Ysidro. They wandered off together, out of earshot. Ysidro kept striking the back of one beefy hand on the other palm as he made his point. Efrain nodded, his gaze fixed upon a rock, shuffling it back and forth with his boot. Ysidro finished, jerked his head down for emphasis, and stormed off.

Efrain turned to see Joaquin standing by, huddling. He checked to make sure Ysidro left, then walked over and put an arm around his shoulder. "You saw?"

"Ysidro is angry."

"He blames our recent misfortunes on the Sky-Bornes. I expect that he will persuade other charros of this belief."

"What are his wishes?"

Efrain's mustache bristled. "He would take action to rid us of their presence."

A chill ran up Joaquin's spine. "But they plan to depart soon. Why not just let them leave?"

"Ysidro wishes to demonstrate his leadership skills, to enhance his reputation as the new jeaf." Efrain's jaw set as he watched the gaucho encampment. Ysidro's nephews gathered together, and Nestor sauntered over to join them. Several times, Ysidro pointed in the direction of the crater.

Efrain said, "I cannot tell if he is bluffing about bringing harm to the Sky-Bornes. Maybe he just wants to scare them. But now, with Nestor and his rifle lined up..." He turned back to Joaquin. "The Sky-Bornes have brought us nothing but ill fortune. Yet, they say an eye for an eye leaves everyone blind. One of us must warn them to stay on guard."

"You wish me to do so?" Joaquin tried to keep from shivering.

"Perhaps." Efrain studied him. "The bull scared you, eh?" The big gaucho tousled Joaquin's unkempt hair. "C'mon. It's okay now."

At least he could be open with Efrain. "Nestor knows we found the rustlers."

Efrain straightened, then again eyed the distant figures of Nestor and Ysidro's clan in close counsel, no doubt plotting.

Joaquin's wits returned. "Orfea still shares Yoka's yurt. She can warn the rest of them with her machine."

"Then let us go first to warn her."

This was surely the best plan. As long as Yoka did not dismiss her, Orfea would be safe. Last night, with Ysidro and his nephews in their drunken state, the old woman more than held her own.

At Yoka's yurt, they found Orfea gathering branches for the campfire. Joaquin could not recall seeing her so glum afore. He felt a twang of pity. "Good day, seira."

Orfea dropped the branches and dusted off her hands. She flashed a tight-lipped smile but said nothing. Now Yoka came out, looking equally frazzled.

Efrain squeezed his clasped hands and nodded to Joaquin, who said, "Auntie, we need your help."

"Do you now?" She straightened, eyed the big gaucho, and bid them both sit. "I am not surprised. The gauchos need a new jeaf."

"Exactly," said Efrain. "And Ysidro expects to be the one."

"Hmph. Too coarse a person, in my opinion."

"He seeks to bolster his standing by enlisting his fellows to scare away the Sky-Bornes."

Yoka turned to Orfea. "You are leaving soon?" It sounded more like a demand than a question.

Orfea grimaced. She pulled another earpad out of her bag and showed Efrain how to use it. "As soon as Buck finishes his repairs."

"You said he struck his head. One wonders if he can think straight," said Yoka.

"Indeed, but he says his memory has returned, and he is anxious to complete the task." Orfea turned to Efrain. "And Ysidro realizes that, no?"

"It matters not what day you plan to leave. That talk of 'hostile skies,' of transporting the iris stone, and now learning the stone is poisoned, all this puts fear in their minds." Efrain pinched the bridge of his nose.

Joaquin eyed Orfea. "You have a way to alert the others."

She pulled out her speaking tool.

"You must warn them to be on their guard."

Orfea pressed the button, but nothing happened. She tried again; got only silence. Her brows knit. "It's not working."

Efrain gave a quick shake of his head and motioned to Joaquin.

"Ride to their camp. They trust you. Tell them to take precautions. I shall keep my ears open and let you know if an attack is imminent. Ha. Ysidro's lot will need to find their courage from a jug of pulce." He rose to head back toward the gaucho camp.

Joaquin jumped up. He followed Efrain until they were out of earshot of the women. "The Sky-Bornes will need your help if an attack comes. They have nothing to defend themselves with."

Efrain barked a laugh. "Have you forgotten their pilot's little hand weapon? It felled the bull with one shot." Seeing no reaction from Joaquin, he said, "Helping the Sky-Bornes defend themselves would put me in a difficult position with my uncle." The corners of his mouth drooped.

Joaquin nodded, his palms breaking into a sweat as he watched Efrain leave. Nestor still lurked out there somewhere. Efrain was aware of the danger, but for now, keeping the gaucho band from self-destructing would be his first priority.

The old woman beckoned him. He accepted a mug of warm milk but passed up her offer of stew. His appetite was gone. He remembered the run-in with the bull and again shivered. He knew that would pass, but something deep inside told him that the problems with Nestor would not.

Joaquin avoided Orfea's glances, finished the milk, and headed cautiously back to his own tent to ready Cisco for the ride. He bundled up in extra layers. It felt like the cold season again.

He also needed to prepare himself. To do it right, he needed to be armed, but unlike Nestor, he owned no gun, just a puny knife, barely big enough to dig out a thorn. He had nothing to rely upon save his wits.

24
STAY HERE

As if my confession to the tribe hasn't put me in enough hot water, on the ride back from Aldo's funeral, Harry makes it clear that he and I need to have a chat. How deep is he going to dig this time?

By the time we get to camp, it's getting on to evening. Harry plops down onto a pack in my tent, looking as wilted as last month's flowers. He studies the floor and massages his scalp. "You never mentioned studying in China when we recruited you."

I gulp, try to keep the monotone that makes me feel like I'm in control. "Would it have made any difference? Oscar wants this stuff so bad he can taste it."

There's a long silence before Harry comes back. "Better tell me the whole story," he says in a much softer voice.

He's got to be fishing. "What's to tell?"

"Oh, I bet there's plenty."

Ah, hell. No sense spinning any of this. He'll check it all when he gets back. "You know my mentor, Russell McCoy."

Harry's ears perk up. "Of course. Russ recommended you for the mission."

I try to recite, like I'm reading off my C.V. "Five years ago, I start graduate school and need a research topic. Iridium is just hitting the big time. McCoy learns that the head of geology at the Sino-Siberian Academy of Earth Science in Irkutsk is set to explore a big new meteor crater. This could be my chance. We contact him, and yes, he would be pleased to sponsor a Canadian for a student visa."

"Especially one touted by the esteemed Savant McCoy, I'll bet. It's all about connections."

I squirm. Harry just triggered one of my hot buttons: the reason I can't dump that lecher McCoy. It's all I can do to let the remark pass. "Three months later, after the usual background checks from the Chinese bureaucracy, I get my one-year visa. As my research progresses with Savant Xiang's team of trainees, the pass extends for a second year, but with a catch."

Harry's brows furrow.

"In my dissertation, I am to share credit with the SAES team. Meantime, Wan Xiang stays in contact with Russell McCoy."

"So, you became a goodwill ambassador." Harry spits out the last two words.

I stop, stare at him. Should I tell him the whole story, fling myself at his feet and beg for mercy? Would he shield me or just feed me to Oscar? "Call it that if you want, but it really doesn't change anything outside of the small world of academic geology."

Harry waits. "Is there more?"

"Actually, yes. Two years ago, 2313. Time to defend my dissertation on iridium assay methods. Coincidentally, Savant Xiang is granted a one-month visa to Canada to deliver guest lectures at Athabasca U., and they ask me to translate. He sits in as my research committee grills me, keeps nodding encouragement. I pass, and for that," I pause and take a deep breath, "I owe him a lot."

What I don't reveal is that now he would love to collect on the favor.

"No doubt you're in debt, ma chère, but this arrangement with him, you've overstepped your bounds."

Dammit. He's passing judgment on me and he only knows half the story. "So you say." My tone rises involuntarily, which I regret as soon as the words leave my mouth.

"Yes, so I say." Harry flushes. "And last time I checked, I'm your boss, for the duration of this mission. Now I'm going to insist that you hand over that yellow meter and your data."

The evidence. "For what? No one here can make any sense of it but me."

"For safekeeping. I'm sorry, ma chère. This is non-negotiable."

"Everything's negotiable, Harry." I feel the blood rush. "Isn't that your main job for Oscar, when you're not leading a wild lark like this? Negotiating deals for Bailey Enterprises?"

"Been doing it for thirty-some years. What of it?"

"A few deals everyone wins, but most deals, there's a loser. Ever stop to think when your deal puts someone out of a job, Harry?" My skin starts to tingle. Maybe he's too hardened to feel guilty, but I need to get this off my chest.

"What's that got to do with anything?"

"Remember the Bailey nickel mill in Sudbury?"

"Sure. We had to close it. Nickel smelting isn't cost-effective anymore. So, what? Closings happen all the time."

"My dad worked there." I spit it out. "Twenty-three years, then goodbye. One month's salary for severance."

"I'm sorry. Couldn't be helped."

"Then he came down with silicosis and TB. A few years later, he's dead." The words still sting as I fire them. I wait to see if they hit their target.

Harry's mouth opens and closes. He can't seem to figure out what to say to that, so I press him. "Negotiating deals for Oscar, putting out all those fires. You must do lots of traveling, Harry."

"Goes with the territory." His voice is more subdued now.

"How does that leave things on the home front? What does the little lady say about all the time you spend away?"

He takes a deep breath and slumps. "You got me there. Celine left me ten years ago. Claimed that my career was a jealous mistress." He gazes at me sideways. "Not that her job let her spend any time at home either, mind you."

No wiggle room there. I need to find out if he's got a conscience, to see if I can shake him from those thirty years of "yes sirs." "Sir Oscar must be a terrific boss. You've given your whole life to him."

"He's a decent boss." Harry squares his shoulders. "I don't follow where you're going with this, ma chère."

"Has he ever asked you to go along with something that you didn't agree with?"

"Of course. We have disagreements all the time."

"I mean, something wicked. Illegal, or at least immoral."

"Such as?"

I go for broke. "Such as building iridium-coated transports to colonize Antarctica with Canadian farmers."

Harry freezes, says nothing for a minute. "Where did you hear that?"

Bingo. I feel back in the driver's seat. "Let's say a little birdie told me."

"Even if that rumor were true, which I'm not saying it is, there's nothing illegal or immoral about it."

"Difference of opinion there."

"Enough speculation. Will you hand over the meter and data now, or is this going to become unpleasant?"

"Okay, okay, I'm not going to fight you for the meter." Not to pat myself on the back, but I saw this coming, light years away. I try to smile and pass the yellow box to him. "You can have the data, too, soon as I finish crunching the numbers."

"And what's to keep you from cooking those numbers?"

Oh, puhleeze. "Look at me, Harry. I'm a scientist, right? You said so yourself this morning, before you threw me under the bus. A scientist, a real one, does not cook the numbers. We go wherever the data leads us."

"Spare me the speeches, Keltyn. I'll expect all of the data before we depart." Harry struggles to rise and skulks out of the tent.

A minute later, I hear him talking inside his own tent. "Well, if it isn't Joaquin. You and Buck must have heard the whole thing."

I tense, a little. What will the boy make of our spat? He must have just showed up.

"Maybe you like to hang out with Sky-Bornes, son. We get into nasty fights all the time. Or maybe you're here to deliver another message. What's up?"

"Efrain sent me to warn you," Joaquin says. "Ysidro is gathering other mal hombres. They plan an attack."

Harry grunts. "Why am I not surprised? Buck, you're our security detail. Are you prepared for this?"

"Depends on how many of 'em. 'Member, all we got for weapons is my little-bitty stun gun. Actually, boss," Buck loudly clears his throat, "you're the one's still got it."

A moment of silence during which Harry doesn't bite. "Listen, son, it's too late to ride back to your camp. You're welcome to spend the night, but you'll have to share Keltyn's tent. Fay's still with Yoka, huh? Maybe it's for the better."

My tent flap is half-open. Sure, the kid can hang out with me. He sticks his head in the opening, looks bummed. I point at a pack for him to sit on. I'm already busy on another project, encrypting data from my notebook.

Five minutes later, I'm done. "That's my backup." I pat the little tool. "Another copy, just in case..."

"In case what?"

"In case I get framed when we get back. Maybe Fay can help..." I stop myself abruptly. Help with what? Who am I kidding?

Poor kid. Just a blank look. I say, "You don't get it, do you? What's at stake here, why Harry is so upset that I trained in China?"

He shakes his head.

How and what should I tell him? That I'm juggling loyalties between two nations? He doesn't even know what a nation is, or that he's better off without one. That I'm trying to double-cross the man who gave me the opportunity of a lifetime?

Sure, I'm walking a tightrope, but I've thought this strategy through. Something more primal weighs on me now; everything I touch seems to be cursed. The crash landing, leading the girl up that mountain to disaster, inciting the tribe to panic, ruining Trieste's trade and striking her down. How else to explain all that's happened since we showed up here?

But I can't just dump my bad karma on the poor kid. We end up sharing candy bars. I pull out a small checkerboard and teach him how to play. He promptly kicks my butt. The presence of another human being with whom I have neither an agenda nor an obligation, that's the ticket. Be here now.

That night, I sleep well for the first time since we got here, fully confident in my chosen course.

***

The next morning, Joaquin is up before me, early enough to share Harry and Buck's coffee and pastry filled with cherry jam.

They're all sitting under the wing of the plane when I come out of the blue tent. I'm ready to make my move. "Guys," I say, "It's time to talk."

"Uh-oh," mutters Harry. He nods toward Joaquin. "What of the boy?"

"It's okay if he hears. In fact, I'd be curious of his reaction." I pull up a chair and wiggle my hands. "I've been thinking."

Buck rolls his eyes. "You do a lot of that, Missy."

"Take it easy, Buck," says Harry.

"Maybe I will and maybe I won't. We've got unfinished business." I sigh. Can't he stop obsessing about that damn radiation counter?

Harry squares up. "You ready to fess up, young lady?"

I suck in a breath as I face Buck, but I can't seem to look him in the eye. "If you must know, Buck, I did my first iridium research in Siberia."

"So I heard." He shakes his head. "It's like you had a clue beforehand that the rocks were gonna light up. That's why you brought the thing along. Am I right?"

I try to play it cool. "Who knew? This is the other end of the world."

"Now I get it. The Siberian rocks are contaminated too, aren't they?" His deep blue eyes bore into mine, gleaming like cold steel.

I nod and avert my gaze, so as not to betray glee that he's fallen into my trap.

"But that counter," he says. "It's Chinese technology. You wouldn't have been able to take it out of the country without permission."

I nod again.

"Which means, you must have made a deal with them."

"Says you."

"Missy, are you a spy?"

Once Buck discovered the yellow meter, it was just a matter of time before the spy angle would come up. I'm sure Joaquin's earpad has no way to translate that word, but the cunning tone in Buck's voice leaves no doubt that its meaning is vile. I parry. "That would depend on how you define a spy."

Buck forces a laugh. "The Chinese are just as interested in iridium as we are. Anything you pass on to them would be spying."

The back of my neck tingles. God, I hate stereotypes. "Oh, quit calling them 'the Chinese.' They're individuals, just like the three of us." I gaze out toward the crater wall. "It was a favor for Savant Wan, the mentor for my graduate work in Siberia. I guess I just have a soft spot for him."

"What kind of favor?" Buck's bushy blond eyebrows knit together.

"He sent an innocuous message a month ago, one that wouldn't alarm the censors. 'Best wishes for glorious mission,' that kind of stuff. I sent back a thank you note, and mentioned the data I hoped to collect, thinking he might find that useful for his research."

Buck sits back and points at Harry, like he's taking credit for this confession. "Now we're getting somewhere." He eyes the chief. "Good Lord, Harry. Aren't the Bailey security boys supposed to do thorough background checks?"

Harry ignores him, keeps his gaze straight on me. "I hate to tell you, ma chère, but if you think this Savant Wan is just going to file your data away in his notebook, you're naïve. Ten to one, someone in the Presidium found out you were headed here and leaned on your trusted mentor for leverage. Of course, they're scared what we might do with this stuff."

He pauses, looks from one face to another before returning to mine. "You're a bright young woman, Keltyn. How could you let yourself get into this mess? Whether or not you realized it, you were spying. Anyone of your caliber has to understand the implications. You may well get the book thrown at you when we get home."

Sitting on my hands, I snap up straight. "Meaning?"

"Prison versus..." Harry takes a deep breath, "exile."

My nose wrinkles as I weigh these options. "I admit to being naïve. What I don't admit is that the Chinese are evil. Aside from all the geology I learned there, aside from the friends I made..."

Buck tosses his hands in the air. "If you're so in love with the Chinese, why not just defect?"

Oh, Buck, you're such a sap. "That would be too flip," I say. "I'd be just another dupe in the disinformation wars." I lift my chin. "No, I'm charting a different course."

Harry leans forward. "What would that be, ma chère?"

"I'm planning to stay here, with Luz and her mother."

"You're what?" The chief jerks back and gawks at me.

Buck guffaws and lifts his chin, eyes raised to the sky. Even Joaquin looks baffled.

They don't get it. Did I expect them to? "Of course, you guys wouldn't understand; you'd have to be me. Iridium is my fate, has been ever since I took up geology — before I even heard of the stuff. And where are we right now? Sitting in the midst of the biggest stash of iridium ever discovered..." I pause, feel a quiver to my voice, "whose beauty, ironically, poisons the Onwei women."

I clear my throat. My voice steadies. "So, the best course for yours truly is to stay on. To assay the stuff, to test which fields are radioactive, and maybe, just maybe, to help these folks come to terms with their destiny." I'm trying to show them the big picture, but I don't see any lights flashing on.

"What is that supposed to mean?" Harry still gawks.

I point at him. "That 'wasting disease' of theirs, how were we supposed to know about that? You made me explain radiation to them, Harry. Hell, it practically caused a stampede."

"Ha. We got blindsided, all right." He runs his fingers through those receding gray curls.

I plunge on. Now comes the worst part. "Half the women in this tribe are probably going to develop leukemia, which they've never heard of and have no way to cope with." I try to picture this scene, and it's not pretty. Fevers, headaches, sores, spontaneous bleeding. "Caring for them will be a big drain on their loved ones, every bit as bad as their wasting disease." I reach for a kerchief and blow my nose to emphasize the point. "As for Oscar Bailey, if he wants to mine anything here, he's going to need a geologist around."

Buck barks. "How convenient. You can work both sides."

I wipe away tears; I'm not going to rise to that bait.

Buck presses on. "These poor Onwei folks will need an advocate, or better yet, an agent."

"Good point."

"Thank you. While I'm at it, I'll make another observation."

"Hmm."

I pocket my kerchief. "Staying here beats doing hard time."

"There is that." I rock my head back and forth. "You may think it's about saving my own skin, guys, but I really feel for these people."

"They feel for you too, Missy," Buck sniggers. "Rage. After yesterday, you've got plenty of fences to mend." His hands make a curt wave.

I turn for Harry's reaction, but he just shrugs.

"Come on, Joaquin," I say. "Let's us ride back to your camp." We rise to get our mounts, which are grazing on clumps of grass fifty feet away. I wipe my nose again as we return to the plane. "As far as I'm concerned, there's just one fence I'll need to mend for this plan to work out."

"Whose is that?" Harry shields his eyes from the sun behind me.

"A person whom I've wronged deeply."

Harry has no clue. I adjust the saddle and pat Cozuel. "This mule belongs to her."

25

CHAR'S CAL

All was quiet inside Trieste's yurt. Luz sat hunched over, rocking back and forth, next to her mother, asleep on the cot. Flaco curled at her feet.

Once the news about the stone sunk in yesterday, Trieste sobbed for hours until mercifully fainting from exhaustion. Her sleep now should have come as a welcome respite for Luz. Instead, she obsessed on their future options, each of which gave her a headache.

Would her mother bounce back, or was her soul so tied to the piedra de yris trade that its loss would be fatal? Luz doubted that wearing the stone could cause something as devastating as the khokri malady, but it didn't matter what she herself believed. Her mother was convinced of the link, and so were most women in the tribe, her mother's main customers. The only way out of this hopeless muddle was to find, no, to prove, a different cause. All of this, and Luz still must pack their goods and break camp.

Her reflections collapsed as Flaco's head snapped to attention, ears pointed. Soon she heard hoof beats, slowing as they approached the yurt. Keltyn's figure appeared at the entrance, hesitating, lips clamped, sweaty.

Luz fished in her pocket for the earpad. Somehow, after yesterday, she did not expect to need it anymore. Fumbling to put it on with one hand, she motioned with the other for Keltyn to stay where she was.

Luz approached, keeping her voice low. "Mother has stayed in bed since yesterday, sleeping fitfully or lying awake sobbing."

"I'm sorry." Keltyn bowed her head. She appeared surprised at finding Trieste no better than when she left her the day before.

"Plus, we are supposed to strike camp tomorrow morning. I've been trying to pack things during Mother's naps." Trieste would never tolerate the disarray were she not ill. Clothing, bedding and cookware lay scattered throughout the yurt.

Keltyn squeezed Luz's arm as she watched the sleeping woman, then turned to face her. "Let me stay on with you. I can help you pack and take care of your mother." She nodded for emphasis.

A little wave fluttered inside Luz. "Your flying machine is supposed to leave soon, no?"

"True, but I won't be on it."

What had happened between her and the others? Luz considered the possibilities. It must have to do with the iris stone being poisoned and Keltyn's guilty feelings. Whatever the reason, Luz needed all the help she could get right then. She flipped her braid back and gave Keltyn a hug.

Suddenly awake, Trieste demanded from across the yurt, "Why has the Sky-Borne returned?" Her body remained flat,z but her head rotated toward them. The look she directed toward Keltyn was one of utter scorn, and her friend hastened to turn away.

"Mama, Keltyn has come to help us. She feels terrible about her discovery. She begs to make amends."

"She can make amends by leaving us alone. I wish never to see or hear of her again." Trieste shut her eyes. Small gasps echoed across the enclosure.

Luz fought to hold her own tears back. "Mama, you know not what you say. We must depart from this camp. You are too weak to sit up, and I cannot strike the yurt alone."

"Our neighbors will help us," Trieste muttered.

"Please, Mama. Keltyn is a wonderful nurse. She took care of me on the mountain when I lay paralyzed." Luz nodded at Keltyn for confirmation. "She will help you get back on your feet in no time."

"I do not wish for this strange one to nurse me." With great effort, Trieste propped herself up on her elbows. "You delude yourself, girl, if you think I shall recover in a few days. Do you not realize why I collapsed?"

"Of course, Mama, from the shock of hearing what Keltyn discovered about the stone."

"A great shock, yes, but I have been feeling weak for months."

Luz said nothing. The signs of her mother's decline were all there, even before the Rendezvous: weariness, mood swings, poor memory, loss of appetite. Luz was too wrapped up in her own quest to pay them mind, convinced that finding a new source of the piedra de yris would rejuvenate her mother's spirits.

"Now I understand why," said Trieste. "The khokri has struck me."

"No, Mama." Luz ran over to squeeze her mother's hand. "It must be something else."

"It all fits now." Trieste's voice took on a grim quality. "This malady fells our Onwei women. No one could explain why we are cursed. Now we know." She let her head fall back down. "The iris stone is poisoned." She reached for the string of violet beads lying by her cot and contemplated them with nostrils flared. They rattled in her grasp.

After several minutes, the shaky hand holding the beads dropped back down. Trieste lay back and closed her eyes again, drained, clutching the rosary to her chest.

Luz rose and motioned Keltyn to follow her outside. They sat on stools at Trieste's worktable, Keltyn hunched forward with her arms folded, staring at the ground. Luz studied her friend. What if Mother and Yoka were right? What if the Sky-Bornes were the cause of this run of bad luck?

Several minutes passed before Keltyn straightened up. The look on her face was desperate, the look of someone caught between no-win choices. "It's okay," she said, almost in a whisper, head again bowed. "You don't have to take me in. I'm a big girl. I can handle whatever's coming."

"What do you mean? Are you being punished?" It must have to do with the two of them climbing the mountain without permission.

"Naïve me. I imagined I could serve two masters at once."

"You said that before, but you never explained what you meant by 'masters.'"

"It's a manner of speaking. Someone you work for is called your master. Bailey is the one who employs me on this mission."

"And your other master?"

"Savant Wan Xiang. He kept in touch with me for the past three years, even though we're not supposed to."

"His country and your country are enemies?"

"Right, they distrust each other."

"And you hoped that somehow you could overcome this distrust?" Luz knew none of the details, but this wish did seem naïve.

"It's not like I'm flying a personal peace mission, but I agreed to share my research findings with Savant Wan, and even brought one of his instruments along, the one that detected radiation in the stones."

"Oh, my."

"Harry thinks I'll be sent to prison when we return. People will consider this as spying." Keltyn saw Luz's blank face. "Working for my other master."

"I can see why you would rather stay here."

"Just an idea. You and your mother could use the help." "We'll manage. I can't force her, you know." Luz blinked hard, trying to stanch a new round of tears.

Keltyn reached out to take her hand but Luz felt too bleak to respond. Then Keltyn jumped up and stepped back abruptly, as if she saw a ghost. Luz turned to see Pilar and Carmen approach. The sisters had taken pity on her and her mother and agreed to help them prepare for an early departure the next day. Plus, Luz hoped they would help resolve a dilemma: how to dispose of her mother's wares.

They nodded to Luz, ignored Keltyn, and scanned the table on which Trieste lately strung a necklace. Doe-eyed Carmen began pawing through her stash of jewelry, scattered in baskets around her workbench, while haughty Pilar pulled her head back and regarded Keltyn with a sneer. The petite Sky-Borne stood aside, her hands behind her back, as Carmen pawed through Trieste's collection.

Luz winced. They had no regard for how much work went into making each piece.

A dozen cuts of the ill-fated stone, of different shapes but each roughly an inch in diameter, lay spread out. Each passed through her mother's furnace in Nomidar over the past few winters, the pure stone separated from the ore to bring out the finest gem qualities. Dozens of smaller gems lay piled in baskets at the foot of the table, along with different sizes of awls, hammers and chisels.

Carmen picked one of the gems, perfectly spherical. She held it up to the sun at arm's length, using her other hand to clear the auburn curls from her face. "What a shame to waste such beauty."

Pilar leaned against a pole of the yurt with her arms and legs crossed. The taller and older of the two, plain speech was her habit. "And how would you now salvage this beauty, dear sister? Do you not believe what the Sky-Borne said?" Pilar inclined her head toward Keltyn. "Would she lie about such a thing?"

Carmen straightened and eyed Keltyn. "I don't know. Would she?" Both sisters smirked, as Carmen returned her attention to the stone.

Keltyn flushed but kept silent.

"Of course, there must be some truth to it." Carmen turned her wrist to examine all sides of the gem, craning her neck to get a better look.

Perhaps these sisters could help Luz figure out the mystery of the khokri. Unlike the rest of the women, they did not panic at Keltyn's shocker, and continued to flaunt their Rainbows. Neither Pilar nor Carmen showed any signs of the khokri.

Luz decided to jump in. "So why is not every woman who wears the piedra de yris struck down by the khokri?"

Carmen put the piece down and faced Pilar. "It is true what the girl says. You and I, for instance, have been spared. Yet who displays more of Trieste's Rainbows than we two?"

Luz moved to sit at her mother's workbench. Everyone knew that the khokri picked its victims at random. The most common explanation was that the victim deserved her fate, that the Spirits demanded payback for one's vices. But how would that idea explain the continued vitality of these wonton sisters?

Pilar puckered her lips and nodded slowly. "We must be doing something right." Both sisters threw back their heads and issued the full-throated laugh they shared.

Flaco picked up his ears.

"Now what might that be?" added Carmen, tilting her head side to side.

"Well, for starters," Pilar said, using her right pointer finger to bend back the left one, ticking off their virtues, "we bathe every day."

That was true. No matter how cold the day, or how primitive the conditions in camp, Pilar and Carmen could be counted upon for at least a sponge bath from the local waters.

"We watch our diet," offered Carmen. "No greasy foods, no sweets to rot your teeth, Char's primo tortillas..."

Pilar broke in. "And nothing to rot your brain, none of that pulce or cactus liquor that the charros wave under a girl's nose," she crinkled her own, "as if that would get her into the mood."

"That goes for Venga too," said Carmen. "Who wants to get buzzed to talk with your dead grandma? Let her rest in peace, I say." They both sniggered again.

True again, thought Luz. Pilar and Carmen disdained to partake at any of Yoka's Venga ceremonies, but, being such good customers of her wearables, Yoka forgave them this lapse.

As Carmen continued to rummage through Mother's pieces, Luz dug through her memory and came up short. "Which others who sport Trieste's Rainbows have been spared from the khokri, besides the two of you?"

Carmen and Pilar looked at each other.

"No one," shrugged Pilar, "unless you count Char, which you really shouldn't." She guffawed. "The poor woman has always been feebleminded. How could anyone tell if the khokri were to strike her?"

Luz pictured Char, who often wandered over to her mother's workplace and sat in silence for hours, watching Trieste assemble her Rainbows.

Carmen lifted her chin toward Luz. "Why did your mother gift that gaudy pendant to Char?"

"Out of pity, I suppose."

"The poor woman displays it constantly," observed Pilar.

Luz smiled. "I think Mother considers Char an advertisement for her wares." She stood and faced the sisters. "Please, take a few pieces for yourselves, then help me pack the rest. My mother may never work this trade again."

Carmen and Pilar exchanged glances. The older sister raised her head, shrugged, and moved in for a closer look.

Keltyn, standing aside, looked puzzled. Now she motioned for Luz to follow her behind the yurt. "What's so great about that Char's tortillas?"

Luz was taken aback that Keltyn should interest herself in something so mundane, but seeing that her friend's look remained dead serious, she told her what she knew. "Char uses an old-fashioned recipe that calls for slaking the maize with lime. She learned this craft as a girl and made it her calling."

Keltyn appeared skeptical. "Lime is dangerous stuff. You said this Char is feebleminded."

"Her husband handles the supply end. He hunts for the limestone and prepares it for slaking. Then he sells the finished product by the dozen, for a handsome profit, to his pal the gaucho cook, to his fellow tradesmen, and to these sisters."

"Is she the only one in camp who makes tortillas?"

"Two other women make them as well." Luz considered this twist. "Funny thing is, they despise the dangerous extra work of slaking lime, and they can easily undercut Hortensio's price."

"So why would anyone buy Char's?"

"You'll have to try them, see for yourself."

Keltyn nodded, then looked around. "Which is her yurt?"

Luz pointed it out. "She's probably making a batch now. The gaucho cook always wants a bunch before they move the herd, so they don't run short before we find the next grazing site."

"Take me there." It sounded like an order.

"Not now. I need to watch Mother." Luz checked Pilar and Carmen, both of them now scouring the gem pile. "And I need to keep an eye on these two, lest they plunder Mother's whole collection."

Keltyn reached out to grab both of Luz's arms. Her eyes, boring upward into Luz's, flashed like never before. "Listen, sister. You and I are in this together. We're going to find out what's really behind this khokri."

"But... you said it was the stone."

"No, I didn't. I said the stone was radioactive, and that radiation can make you ill and even kill you."

"Same thing."

"Not. I lied." She spit the words out. "The stone isn't radioactive, but I need Harry and Buck to believe that it is. Long story, back to my two masters." Keltyn shut her eyes and whipped her head to and fro, as if trying to escape the hole into which she sunk. She stopped abruptly and eyed Luz again. "You and I both need your mother to get well, and the key to that is learning the truth about your khokri. We don't have much time. Now let's go find this Char."

Luz checked to see what Carmen and Pilar were up to. Sure enough, they each set aside half a dozen fine pieces for themselves. Yet Keltyn was right. What did her mother's collection matter if she was no longer well enough to ply her craft? They would have to tuck tail and retreat to Nomidar year-round, trying to eke a feeble living in their own small village, like others unfit to carry their trade abroad. The thought made Luz shiver.

She signaled the sisters to keep an ear open if her mother cried out. Then she turned and led the way toward Char's yurt.

***

Luz and I approach Char, the tortilla queen. She is an eyeful, a skinny toothless creature of indeterminate age, sitting cross-legged on a blanket. She's draped in a loose-fitting faded shift, set off by the sparkling pendant from Trieste around her scrawny, deeply lined neck.

With her mouth muscles in constant motion, she gums a wad of tobacco. She peers over her shoulder and lets fly a wad of spittle, which lands in a brown puddle of a spittoon, six feet away. With total focus, she returns to tortilla preparation and barely bothers to glance up as Luz introduces me. We plop down beside her.

Char may be feebleminded, but she's obviously methodical. I notice a large earthenware bowl behind her left arm, full of husks and cobs from which she has cut off the kernels. Next to that lies a mortar and pestle, which she uses to pulverize the kernels into maize paste, ready in another bowl. Directly in front of her she tends a cook-fire. To its right lays a water gourd and a rag. On her far right sits a lump of limestone. I couldn't line things up any neater if I were preparing a chemistry experiment.

Char pours several cups of water into a cauldron, then makes a big show of drying her hands on the rag. Signaling to the two of us to keep our distance, she reaches for the block of powdered rock and mumbles.

"'Cal,' she calls it," Luz explains. "That's her secret ingredient for making tortillas taste better. That's the way her mother taught her, that's the way she's always made them."

Char crumbles in chunks of powder. The water bubbles furiously. When that quiets, she uses a long wooden spoon to add the large bowl of maize paste to the cauldron, mixing slowly and carefully. She covers the cauldron with a lid and suspends it on a bar, inches above the meager flame.

Now she sits back, cradles her knees with her arms, and mumbles more trade secrets for Luz to explain to me. She cackles at letting the cat out of the bag. Char must be pretty sure that no one else is going to beat her recipe.

"She says the two other women in camp who make tortillas are too lazy to use cal, but it's not just that. The stuff is dangerous, strong as lye. Hortensio carries those chunks around in a tightly sealed pouch. She must be very careful when she adds water."

The girl points back to Char, who holds the backs of her hands out for me to inspect. They're full of burn marks from spatters. How sad.

She has the right instincts, just not the stuff she needs to do the job safely. In a different world, I could train her to be a damn good lab tech.

Then she points to her right eye.

Luz says, "She wants you to understand that the fumes can go to your lungs, and God forbid if it gets in your eyes."

The milky blue-white pearl near makes me gag.

The two of us sit there, numb. Char shares nothing more, content to gum her wad of tobacco until the cal has done its job on the maize. After maybe fifteen minutes of simmering, she strains the maize slurry from the cal, rinses it with water numerous times before dumping it out to dry on a cloth. She flashes her toothless smile at us, placing her palms together with a brief bow of her head.

We arise to leave. I bow out of respect, yet I'm still half in shock at the price this woman has paid for her "calling."

As we walk off, Luz explains, "Later she will combine the paste with lard and roll out the mixture to make tortillas, but the other two women who make them do that part the same way. Any ideas?"

"The lime caused a chemical change in the maize, but darned if I can figure out how that relates to your khokri." I bang my knuckles together. As we head back to Trieste's yurt, the options ricochet through my brain like a billiard ball. We've unmasked a key piece of a big puzzle. Now we need to find the rest of the pieces, pronto.

26

A BAD HAND

Joaquin sat back against a willow tree. If he simply watched Cisco munch red clover at this creek, his mind might be put at ease. They were half a mile downstream from the gaucho camp, a spot he discovered two weeks before, soon after the tribe settled in. Cisco had a thing for clover, and that patch was the only place that it grew anywhere around here.

Yet Joaquin found himself scanning right and left for signs of Nestor. He was thankful not to have run into the *mal charro* since yesterday, but was he really gone, or just biding his time? He hoped that Efrain would be around if and when Nestor surfaced, but what kind of a plan was that?

The best case would be if that crow flew to the camp of their neighboring tribe from Sarume. His ugly secret was not yet exposed, but Efrain was on to him. Joaquin tried to picture how that scumbag would hold up under questioning by the Sarum. Why was he looking for a new job in the middle of the grazing season? Savvy enough to come up with a plausible excuse, Nestor would blame the chaos from Aldo's death and the Sky-Bornes' arrival. No one would suspect anything of rustlers.

All wishful thinking. What if he was still around, allied with Ysidro as his protector? The new jeaf needed to find another charro who owned a rifle if he was serious about attacking the Sky-Bornes.

Would Nestor risk killing him? Only if he could corner him away from camp, and then hide his body somewhere. Yet even that seemed implausible, unless he planned to dispose of Efrain the same way. Could Nestor be so brazen? Efrain too now had a rifle, and he was smart enough not to leave himself alone with Nestor.

The best plan for Joaquin was obvious. Stick close to Efrain. When the Sky-Bornes left, Ysidro would cool off, then Efrain could expose the truth about Nestor and his gang of rustlers.

So, what was he doing here now? Why was he taking such a foolish risk for the sake of his pony? He needed to hustle back to camp, but as he made to get up, Joaquin heard hoof beats behind him. Too late. He turned to behold his worst fear, as if just the thought caused the man to turn up. Joaquin's fingers turned to ice.

The loathsome charro casually climbed off his piebald and moseyed toward the boy. No need to run when your prey couldn't.

"See if your witch or your Sky-Borne friends will help you now, you little jerk." Nestor's lip curled into a snarl. He drew out his knife. The length of its blade matched the span of two hands. Joaquin once watched it sever a beeve's hindfoot tendon with a single swipe.

Joaquin clambered up and inched backward. If he could make it to the creek, Nestor would have less of an advantage in the water. Instead, his bad foot stumbled on the pebbles, and he fell on his butt.

Nestor lunged at him, straddled his chest, and poised the blade's edge at his throat. Joaquin's instinct was to gulp, but he dared not move a muscle.

"Who have you told, gimp?"

"Nobody. I ain't told nobody." He tried to squirm away.

"The hell you hain't. You herded those heifers back to camp the other day. Don't tell me no one asked the score." Nestor drew the blade ever so gently across Joaquin's neck. It chafed like a rope burn. "Better spill it before I get clumsy."

Nestor's weight suffocated him. "I can't breathe."

The rogue gaucho backed onto his haunches, clamping the boy's knees with his own, and moved the knife into a clench grip. The point stuck right up against Joaquin's Adam's apple. "Now talk. Who else knows?"

Joaquin's heart pounded in his ears. He struggled to get into position for the mean trick that his Uncle Fermin once showed him. He spread his arms overhead and made a few moaning sounds.

"What's that, gimp? You're not making sense." Nestor moved his sneering mug closer to Joaquin's but doing so lifted his weight off his haunches.

This was the moment Joaquin was waiting for. He quickly thrust his left knee up into Nestor's groin. Caught off guard, the mal hombre convulsed into a ball.

Yet Nestor, momentarily disabled, still clutched the knife in his right hand. As Joaquin reached out to push Nestor's weight off of him, the blade sliced the back of his left wrist like butter. Joaquin felt the sting immediately, and his hand went limp. It took all his remaining strength to wiggle out from under Nestor. He pulled off his kerchief to stanch the blood gushing from the wound and stumbled to his feet.

Nestor still writhed in agony. He lifted his head and bared his teeth. "You little bastard."

Joaquin grabbed Cisco's reins and scrambled atop, clinging for dear life as he pointed the pony back to camp. At this dire moment he could think of only one safe haven.

Orfea rushed to help him down. She gasped and turned as pale as he knew he must look. The rag wrapped round his left wrist dripped with blood.

"Ay. What is this?" Frantic, she turned to Yoka, who took one look and waddled away.

Joaquin said nothing. He tried to act brave. Still, a few tears and whimpers escaped. Orfea hugged him and pulled him to a stool. She brought maté with extra sweetener. He sipped while they waited for Yoka, watched her appear with soap and a bowl of water.

Gradually, he settled down. Orfea stroked his hair while Yoka removed the makeshift bandage. A wide gash splayed across the back of his wrist, like a blood orange sliced open. He tried to move his hand and his heart sank. Though he could make a fist, the three middle fingers would not straighten on their own. This couldn't be. Joaquin's lips turned numb. His body was falling apart in front of his eyes. He needed to regain control. He slowed down his breathing and whimpered, "Aldo."

Yoka nodded. "Yes, if Aldo were with us, he could fix your hand."

"The tendons must be severed. He needs a surgeon," Orfea said.

The corners of Yoka's mouth twisted. She made a show of scanning the camp. "Sadly, I see none." She went back to cleaning the wound.

Orfea held the boy's head close and whispered, "You were attacked?" He nodded.

"By whom?"

"Ne... Nestor." He clamped his eyes shut. "He sneaked up on me at the spot where Cisco's favorite grass grows. He must have known."

"But you got away."

"I used my knee."

Orfea eyed him hard. "He is quite a bit bigger than you."

"I kneed him in... a special place." He felt better just saying this. Uncle Fermin once showed him how, when a bully neighbor boy, hired to help make a batch of mortar, attacked Joaquin for not keeping up with his pace. The smaller and weaker must use their cunning, his uncle said, and Joaquin remembered that lesson when he needed it most.

Yoka adjusted her vision aids, surveyed her sewing equipment. "I am no curandero like Aldo, but I can stitch. The skin, anyway. The tendons are a different story. We'll have to splint your wrist and hope for the best."

Joaquin grimaced as Yoka set to work. Now he knew what Heriberto's mount felt like. At least the mare had a coca poultice to ease her pain. He had but a few swigs from Orfea's flask.

She scanned the camp. "Nestor may come back. We've got to find a way to protect you."

Why had he been so foolish, to wander away from camp alone? Joaquin gritted his teeth each time the needle pierced his skin.

When she was done with her sewing, Yoka took an old blouse and rigged up a sling for Joaquin to rest his arm in. Orfea spread out a blanket and pillows under the cottonwood tree. He eased down.

He tried to picture how this would affect him. At first, nothing came to mind but a dull blur. What chance did he have to make it as a gaucho now, or anything else, for that matter? Was he consigned to be a cripple?

Yet Orfea and Yoka were sympathetic enough. Their offer from several nights ago might be his only option. He wished Aldo were still around to ask. Meanwhile, here he was, bum foot, bum hand, no Aldo, and still in Nestor's sights.

Joaquin started to shiver again, and this time he could not stop. Orfea brought a blanket and spread it over him, rubbing his shoulders from behind and making shushing sounds. He turned over and tried to drift off, but every time he moved, a shot of pain from the mangled wrist woke him. He ground his teeth and blocked it out.

"Courage, Joaquin."

Tio Hector again? Not who he had in mind.

"The darkest hour is just before the dawn."

"Why do you keep bothering me?"

"Nothing of value ever comes easy, my boy. You must first believe in yourself, then these trials will turn into mere bumps in the road."

"Everyone is giving me advice. Whom should I trust?"

"Trust me, of course. Aren't I your favorite uncle?"

Joaquin pondered this. "If I trust what you tell me, you are my only real uncle." He studied this strange man in his brand-new gaucho outfit.

"Once upon a time, I was faced with a tough choice too, my boy."

"Is that so?"

"I had to decide whether to stay with my people, who were headed back to their native Italy, hoping for better conditions. I chose to be a gaucho instead, even though I knew nothing of life on the pampas. The wind, the heat, and the cold were bad enough, not to mention my crude mates. Charros are merciless on rookies."

They sure were.

"There are times when you have to take a leap of faith."

"And where would you have me leap now?"

"Why, into the deepest water, of course."

Tio Hector vanished as abruptly as he appeared. As always, he spoke in riddles, but a couple of things seemed clear; Joaquin's fate was somehow wrapped up with the Sky-Bornes', and there was no safe haven for him at this moment.

***

When I saunter over from Luz's yurt, I spot Joaquin dozing on a blanket, mumbling in his sleep. His left arm is bandaged, not a good sign. I kneel beside him, and his eyes list open.

"What happened? Did junior gaucho fall off his pony?"

"Nestor stabbed me." He says it so matter of fact that I suspect he knew it was coming.

"Show this to Efrain, and Nestor will be ground beef."

The corner of his mouth lifts an inch.

Fay comes closer. "I'm not so sure. You said you didn't tell him anything."

He shakes his head.

"So, unless Efrain rats him out... and right now Efrain and Ysidro don't exactly see eye to eye, am I right? Ysidro wants revenge, and Efrain just wants us to keep everyone safe."

"Will Efrain help us?" I wonder.

"He promised to keep an eye out for their movements," Fay says. She looks at the boy. "This attack on the boy, though, that might be enough to enlist his help."

"Let's hope so." Right now, I need to state my case. "Listen up, both of you. I'm in a pickle."

Fay knows this already. She just shakes her head slowly. The boy studies me but says nothing.

"I could help Trieste if she would let me," I venture.

Joaquin reaches out to pet Mugabe with his good hand. "She doesn't want your help?" His voice is almost a whisper.

"She thinks that the Sky-Bornes brought this streak of curses on her people."

Joaquin nods, as if that's a fair conclusion.

"I can't stay here. Luz won't go against her mother, and I don't see Trieste changing her mind, unless..." I stop and turn to Fay, "unless we can find a way to prove that radiation poisoning isn't the cause of khokri."

The two of us lock eyes. Fay says, "Any alternate suspects?"

"Have you met those tarts, Pilar and Carmen? Gaudy, always sporting lots of makeup and baubles." Brazen is the word my mother would use.

Fay angles her head back. "Oh, yes. Those two are hard to miss."

"They're Trieste's neighbors. They came over this morning. Bragged on how healthy they are, despite sporting tons of Trieste's jewelry. Started ticking off all their items of clean living. Got me thinking what could really be behind the wasting disease."

Fay's lips take a funny twist. "Not our radioactive stone?"

I sigh. "You saw right through that, didn't you?"

"I'm starting to figure out how your mind works, dear." Fay has a far-off look. "The skin damage, the mouth sores, loose bowels, losing your marbles. Yoka says that the khokri may have plagued the Onwei since the time that their ancestors first set foot on this continent, though some generations were hit harder than others. Funny thing is, when I tried to draw her out, she changed the subject."

That gets my attention. Is the crone hiding something?

Fay settles a hand on her chin. "I wonder if one of her ancestors could shed light on the cause."

My eyes widen. "And how do you propose to find that out?"

Fay brightens. "Talk to her."

"Her? Who?"

"M'Bine. Yoka's forbear, who first discovered Venga. And I think I've figured out how to get through to her." She casts a sidelong glance at the crone's yurt. "Yoka is used to me poking around inside by now." She puts her finger to her lips and says, "Wait here."

Minutes later, Fay returns. With one hand, she displays, then quickly pockets, a few Venga nuggets. In the other hand, between thumb and pointer finger, she holds a dark bead, the size of a grape. "From her necklace. I doubt if she'll miss it. She's still snoring her way through a siesta." Fay gazes around the campsite. "Now we just need a bit of privacy."

Joaquin raises himself up on his good arm. "Go to my tent, Seira. The charros are all busy elsewhere. No one will bother you."

I tag along with Fay. She's going to need help on this ancestor hunt. I'm the one who has the most at stake here. I need to be front and center.

27

DISTANT MIRROR

Fay and I plop down on a dusty blanket in front of Joaquin's hide tent. Fay crushes the bead from Yoka's necklace between two small stones, then divides the thick contents among two cups of the crone's sun tea. We force the bitter potion down in a few gulps and I shiver mightily. Fay spreads her dress and fans her legs into a lotus position, hands palms up in her lap. I start to mimic her, but end up in a sitting-kneeling stance, close my eyes and began to meditate.

"You think we'll both see the same thing?" I ask.

"Oh yes," Fay says. "Think 'M'Bine.'"

It seems like forever before anything comes up. Then I perceive a small house, thatched roof, set upon red clay earth. Two people sit in an outdoor kitchen, covered with only an awning. An ebony-skinned girl in her teens, hair plaited in a dozen long rows, gold spirals in her earlobes, mixes up some kind of batter. She looks at us, points at her chest and says her name. Sounds like M'Bine, all right.

A shriveled old woman sits beside her, holding a jar full of some murky speckled lather. She pours some into the girl's batter. The girl mixes and spoons the batter into a cake pan, slips the pan inside the oven.

That's all we get of that scene. A flash of light blurs it into a new one. M'Bine wears a black shift, weaves her way through a crowded room inside the small house. Along one wall lies an open casket, with the body of the old woman. The dozen middle-aged guests wear black mourning clothes and sip from foamy mugs.

M'Bine enters the kitchen, pulls her freshly baked cookies out of the oven, serves them to her guests. Long, nodding faces alternate with short bursts of laughter as they listen to stories. They steal furtive looks into the casket.

Soon, the voice of the old woman fills the room. Her tone is sweet, but the guests look at each other with alarm, and appear flustered even after the voice ceases. A few more minutes of forced chitchat and they depart, leaving the girl with her mother. M'Bine places her hand on her mother's arm, but the woman retreats to a chair and slumps down.

Abrupt end of that scene. Venga doesn't waste any time, I'm learning. Another bright light, and now M'Bine has become a tall woman nearing thirty, but instead of filling out, her cheeks are sunken, her skin blotchy.

She huddles with two girls, about seven and nine, on a shallow hill behind a wharf. M'Bine tethers an emaciated cow, tugging up shoots on a hill behind. They've got a rickety cart, stuffed to the brim, and a cage with two skeletal chickens.

The sky is cold, windy, and gray. Just watching this scene makes me shiver. Choppy greenish-gray ocean waves batter a row of wooden piers. Half a dozen small fishing boats moor at each dock.

Other struggling families crowd the wharves, along with soldiers on patrol. M'Bine watches anxiously as her own husband walks down a pier. He wears nothing but a knee-length threadbare coat, tattered breeches, a battered straw hat, and open-toed sandals. When he's halfway down, M'Bine shouts his name — sounds like 'Shakon' — and raises two fingers as a good luck sign.

Shakon returns her salutation and heads toward the end of the pier. A particularly rundown fishing boat, barely twenty feet long, peeling paint, rocks with the waves. A grizzled man in yellow rubber overalls – the only fisherman in sight – sits hunched over on the pier repairing his nets. He glances at the young man's approach and waves him away.

Shakon won't take no for an answer. He takes off his hat, bows his head, and tries to engage the fisherman's attention. The old man swears, uses both hands to shoo him away and spits into the water before picking his net up.

Shakon is undaunted, pursues his plea with expansive gestures. In due course, the fisherman drops his net and listens. Shortly, he invites the young man to board the boat, and Shakon in turn signals for M'Bine to join him. In the boat's tiny galley, they discover a compact cast-iron oven. Shakon pantomimes placing a nugget in his mouth and cocks his head in the direction of the stoic fisherman. Then he grabs the hand of their surprised new captain and pumps it up and down.

I open my eyes and try to catch Fay's, but she's all caught up in the trance. So far as I can make out, Shakon leveraged his wife's Venga recipe into a boat passage for their family. The fisherman must have wished to reach the spirit of some family member.

I need to pay attention though. Just in those few seconds with my eyes open, the old beat-up fishing boat has already finished its voyage. Shakon and the older girl, hunched over from the cold, grasp the railing, the girl bent forward with one hand on her stomach. M'Bine scans the shoreline as she clasps the younger girl to her breast.

In front of them lies a small harbor. Two dozen squalid huts nestle in the flat, backed up by cliffs. Smoke trails up through the roofs of the huts, none of which have a chimney. Not a soul to be seen.

The fisherman throws a gangplank onto the makeshift pier, helps Shakon push his overloaded cart onto the walkway and wheel it down. Then comes the cow, followed by M'Bine and the two girls. Down the dock they make their way and step off the edge onto a pebble-strewn beach. There a driftwood signpost reads 'Welcome to Destiny.'

The family trundles up the beach until they find a hut with no smoke trailing from its roof. M'Bine peers inside and quickly jerks her head back in disgust. Yech. I can smell it too. Dung smoke and rancid butter. There's a ring of rocks in the middle of the dirt floor, directly under a little hole in the roof, that serves as a fireplace. Chips of dried cow dung are stacked for fuel.

Shakon builds a smoky fire, leaving the front door open until the blaze catches, but the pungent smell of burning dung permeates everything. M'Bine spots a table and chair, pieces of paper piled underneath a stone. She leafs through the notes, eight of them, all with different handwriting, perhaps from previous occupants who have overwintered here. M'Bine's face turns forlorn as she reads them. She holds up one page. "Destiny," it reads. "This place should be called 'Misery'."

The family goes about trying to settle themselves in this meager hut. By late afternoon, the sun disappears behind a rocky cliff. They tire of breathing smoke from the dung fire, and wander outside to scout for more fuel. Now they notice other inhabitants, two dozen people huddling around a brazier burning driftwood.

It turns out the commons fire ring is lit for but an hour each morning and evening, the better to stretch the scant supply of wood. M'Bine hears stories of Destiny's downcast inhabitants. She asks if anyone has an oven. No one does, but one person suggests burying an enamel pot in the fire.

M'Bine mixes her slurry into portions of rancid cornmeal, water, sugar and baking soda. The chickens have stopped laying and the cow has dried up during the turbulent voyage, so this batch of nuggets may be edible but not choice. She coaxes her neighbors into sampling them. They report visions of Aunt Lassi or Grandpa Moshi and are strangely at peace after the experience.

The seasons shift. The sun feels warmer, the shadows shorter. Families gather their belongings, making ready to depart, probably to claim their own land. M'Bine's friends surround her. She holds up her small jar, just a couple of ounces of slurry left. The other women offer their containers, and M'Bine spoons out a little into each. She hugs each of them as they go their separate ways.

Now the poor woman stands alone, shoulders slumped. She's emaciated, unkempt, her eyes blank, her face disfigured by sores, barely recognizable from before. No bright light this time, as her vision, and ours, fade to nothing.

When I open my eyes, Fay is staring at the mountain.

"What do you make of all this?" I shake my head. "Such a resilient woman, she weathered years of exile and sustained her family through the hardest of times. Why did she fall apart so quickly after reaching the promised land?"

Fay doesn't turn, keeps that faraway look. "Whatever the cause, it started before her family left Africa. It's not something she picked up after their exodus to Antarctica. When is the last time I saw that, where?" She squeezes her eyes shut, opens them, sticks her tongue out, points to a spot above her ear. "It's buried back here."

I lean forward. "Those sisters said one thing that intrigued me." I fill her in on Char's tortilla recipe.

"You're proposing that different tortilla ingredients make some of the women sick? What? Contaminated maize? Rancid tallow?" Fay tilts her head. "This is like Epidemiology 101."

"Or maybe Char adds something to hers that protects her customers from getting the khokri."

"Like what?"

"She uses caustic lime – cal – to slake the maize kernels. Her skin is full of old spatter burn scars and she's been blinded in one eye."

Fay shudders. "No wonder the others don't want to use the stuff." She stops. "But somehow this cal must be protective. That may explain M'Bine's decline. We'll need to confirm that her African staple was corn, but I'm pretty sure it was. Then, just like with Venga, you can see how all of their forced moves led to shortages of the proper ingredients." She points at me. "If the other women who make tortillas are using shortcuts, it would all tie together. The khokri may well be a deficiency of something, rather than poisoning."

I nod. "Makes sense, but we gotta prove it." Or the tribe won't buy it and I'll be sunk.

***

Fay had no idea how to prove her theory. She stayed in her lotus position, leaning forward with her head between her hands, racking her brain. What kind of nutritional deficiency could cause the symptoms of khokri? It certainly was nothing she remembered from her own field studies.

Keltyn motioned that they should head back. Fay took one more look around Joaquin's sparse tent. It was little more than a string of untanned hides, leather thongs run through holes poked in the edges of the hides. The thongs tied to staves no taller than Fay, but that was enough space for a bedroll and pack. The whole bundle could be easily pitched, and just as easily furled and stuffed in any space left on the gauchos' gear wagon.

Witnessing the squalid nature of Joaquin's everyday existence was a jolting reminder for her. She needed to rescue him from this sinkhole before he suffered any more physical or emotional trauma. She knew at once what her next step must be.

By the time she and Keltyn made it back to Yoka's yurt, they could hear rustling sounds from within. The crone must have awakened from her nap.

Keltyn seemed strangely upbeat as she neared Joaquin. He leaned up on his elbow to watch. She started to speak, but Fay waved her hand and put her finger to her lips.

Yoka shuffled out of her tent, glanced at the three of them, and moved to get on with her packing.

Fay approached her. "Can we talk, Auntie?"

Yoka scowled at Fay and Keltyn in turn, then shrugged and waddled over to her rocker. "So?"

"Keltyn has decided to stay here. She wishes to help Trieste and Luz."

"Have you now?" The crone looked Keltyn up and down. "Are you sure Trieste wants your help?"

Keltyn shrugged.

Fay bit her lip. Trieste must have spurned Keltyn's offer.

"That would change things, wouldn't it?" Yoka removed her vision aids, squinted at the two of them.

She backed down. "It... it would mean an extra seat on the plane."

"I understand exactly what it would mean," snapped Yoka. Her booming voice rattled all of them. "It would mean a chance to take the boy with you."

She had to make her plea. "He could be treated by a surgeon. Fix the tendons in his hand. Even repair his clubfoot..."

"Enough." Yoka's roar made even Joaquin sit up with a start. She eyed him and turned back to Fay. "Have you bothered to ask the boy?"

Yoka waddled over, stood over Joaquin and laid out his choices. Fay squeezed her eyes shut and reached for a hankie. Why did it have to become a contest? How could she, someone who only met the boy a few days ago, compete with one from his own tribe? She kept her eyes closed and whispered a silent prayer.

By the time Fay opened her eyes, the boy had managed to get up, stand in front of her, and hold out his good hand. Could it be? He was choosing *her*. Tears welled up again, dissolving into blubbers. Half-blinded, she reached out to hug the boy and caught his bad arm in her squeeze. He winced. Fay felt a strange sound emit from her throat, somewhere between a laugh and a sob.

Yoka sniffed and shook her head. She tossed her dialups aside, pushed herself up, and busied herself packing.

But was the boy sincere? "You must pack your things, dear. Are you sure you wish to take this step?"

The boy hesitated. "Yes, seira."

"Call me Fay."

"Seira Orfea." He ignored the hand she offered him and headed back toward his tent; the wounded arm cradled in a sling. No doubt he wished for more time to prepare, but time was running out, for all of them.

Fay wondered if she had truly won the boy's heart. He was so vulnerable at this moment; it was hardly fair to make him commit. Yet she wouldn't have a second chance.

A line from Kipling came to mind: "If you can keep your head when all about you are losing theirs..." She needed to stay positive. No more petty arguments.

She whistled some bars from a yodel, *sotto voce*.

28
JOAQUIN'S FATE

Joaquin felt more upbeat as he, Orfea and Keltyn approached the Sky-Bornes' camp next morning. The place had begun to feel like a second home, but why? Was it because of the escalating chaos and danger at his own gaucho camp, or was it because the four Sky-Bornes appeared more focused, more resourceful? Keltyn seemed to be in trouble, but Joaquin liked that she was actively trying to fix it. Too often his own people simply accepted whatever hand fate dealt them. He needed to take a lesson from Keltyn: buck up and take control of his future.

The flying machine appeared even more bizarre than before. Sleek pointed craft, tall vertical silhouette, poised on its tail, ready to shoot upward. Harry peered into a small gadget and pointed it at the plane. Buck sat in the cockpit, all smiles, his arm raised like a statue in salutation until Harry put down his device. A moment later, the machine's bowels rumbled, and it returned to horizontal.

Harry acted puzzled to see Joaquin among the threesome. Then he brightened. "Ah. Joaquin, you came along to take the horses back. Lucky you, you'll get to meet our chief, Sir Oscar Bailey." Harry turned to Orfea and Keltyn. "The daily reports are way overdue. He's going to want input from both of you."

Their great jeaf, thought Joaquin. How would he address such a powerful man? Yet, first someone needed to set Harry straight on Joaquin's status. He looked to Orfea, but she was engrossed in Buck's feat.

"You fixed the VLG." Orfea nodded approvingly.

The big pilot smiled from the cockpit. His tongue flipped a toothpick as he tapped his skull. "Just a matter of gettin' the noggin back in shape. You have to be able to think like the machine."

"Well." Orfea turned back to Harry. "Chief, request permission to bring another passenger, to fill the vacant seat."

Harry tilted his head ever so slightly.

Joaquin imagined what went through their chief's mind as he checked him out: Are you kidding me? Not this scruffy scarecrow kid. He stopped at the sling cradling the bandaged hand, opened his mouth to object, but instead took a slow, deep breath. Finally, the chief turned to Keltyn. "So, you've made arrangements to stay on. What did the girl's mother say?"

"We're working it out." Keltyn's lips clenched.

Harry waited, but Keltyn kept mum. He turned back to Orfea, shook his head rapidly. "What? So, you and the boy are distant cousins. You think you can just go and adopt him?" But when he faced Joaquin again, his stern look softened. Joaquin's heart settled back into his chest.

"Well," said Orfea, "it's not like there are any authorities here to ask permission. For all intents and purposes, Aldo was responsible for him. Aldo's dead, so I shall be his guardian."

"And what do you propose to do with him, if I may be so blunt?"

"Get him proper medical care, for one. Nestor attacked him this morning, sliced open his wrist. The tendons need repair. They can fix his foot too."

Joaquin pictured a beat-up chuck wagon, its owner casting about for spare parts.

"That's ambitious." Harry took another deep breath. "What else?"

"Schooling. He has remarkable intelligence. Think what he could do here by learning other languages."

Buck broke in. "Come on, Fay. A boy's main prospect here is to be a gaucho."

"Oh, really? Take a good look at this kid."

They all stared at Joaquin. He stood next to his pony and tried his best to smile. These people, he hardly knew them, yet here they were, debating his future. Did they even remember that he could understand every word they spoke? Or did they simply not care?

Orfea threw an emphatic hand in the air. "How could he ever make it as a gaucho with two gimpy limbs, especially with Aldo gone? No one but Efrain has encouraged him, and that big guy's got all he can handle for the time being."

They all moved to sit down, everyone watching Joaquin, who felt too awkward to shift.

Buck shook his head. "Poor kid, you're stuck in this mess. What good is it gonna do you to speak a bunch of languages?" He whipped around to Orfea. "Say, you're not thinking of sucking him into anthropology?"

Orfea laughed. "That would be too much culture shock, as they say. No, Yoka and I hatched a plan for him, and he sounds interested."

"Double, bubble, toil and trouble," said Harry. "What's the Onwei word for witch?"

"*Bruxa.*" Orfea spoke the word with a quirky grin. "We bruxas propose to groom Joaquin to become the next Yoka. Truth be told, she's pissed right now that he's leaving. She expected I could find a way to tutor him here."

"What makes you think he'll want to come back after seeing the bright lights? Or that you'll be willing to let him go if he does?" Harry's vision aids slid down his nose.

Now Joaquin sat down too, leaned forward, rested his chin on his palm, curled fingers covering his mouth. This might get interesting. Should he speak up? Better to stay quiet. The momentum was turning in his favor without a word on his part.

***

Fay reached over to tousle the boy's hair. "It's his life. Right now, Yoka has him hyped on becoming the first male brux of the Nomidar Tribe.

That is, after I've taught him those languages and the three R's." She lifted her chin. "Naturally, I would want to come back here to visit him too."

"Ha," sneered Buck. "What a career. Leading séances with hallucinogenic cookies."

Fay sniffed. "Call it what you wish. All I know is that now I'm connected with my kid cousin. He's bright, he wants to take advantage of an opportunity, and I aim to help him."

Harry checked for Buck's reaction; the pilot shook his head slowly. Harry turned back to Fay. "Have you factored in the immigration and adoption hassles?"

"I'm hoping Oscar can grease those skids."

"We'll need to get Oscar's okay for sure. Remember, he wasn't too keen on bringing you along in the first place, Fay. For exactly this reason, as I recall. Getting chummy with the locals."

"This is not the time to drag out dirty linen." Fay bit her lip.

"Why not?" Buck scowled. "Missy fessed up this morning. Now everything's cool with her. Right?" He gave Keltyn a sly look.

"Sort of," Keltyn muttered, heading over to sort gear beside her tent.

"I've been curious from day one, Fay." Harry moved back on the attack. "What did you have to do to get a seat on the plane? Oscar fancies himself a ladies' man."

"You flatter me." Fay smirked at the thought. "No, we were not intimate."

"What then?"

The wind picked up. Fay pushed her hair away from her eyes, watching a distant hill. "It was Paul."

"Paul?"

She spun to face Harry. "My husband, Paul Buchschreiber. He died from chemical poisoning."

"I know that name." He shut his eyes a minute. "He did research at I.G. Farben."

"Oh, and what else do you know?" Her gaze bored into the chief.

"I read his report, what, ten years ago, when Bailey Holdings absorbed them. All the poisons they needed to bury."

"But Oscar claimed never to have seen it." She felt her fingers clench.

Harry flicked a crumb off his sleeve. "There's a lot of stuff that Oscar never sees."

Fay kept her eyes glued on him. "Well, someone has to decide what gets kicked up to him."

He took another minute to answer. "All right, it was my call to suppress it."

"I knew it!" Fay crossed her arms. "I'm glad we got that out into the open. So, that report, Harry, I found a copy of it after he died. When the right time came around, I brought it to Oscar's attention."

Harry's brow darkened. "You blackmailed Oscar, is what you did."

"I did what I needed to do." Fay searched each of their faces. "What's so wrong with that? No one got hurt."

No response.

She snapped her fingers. "Come on. Let's do the transmission and bring Oscar up to date. I'm sure he's going to be shocked to hear about the stone." Fay turned to Joaquin. "Would you like to meet Sir Oscar Bailey?"

***

Joaquin nodded slowly at first, then more vigorously as he looked up. He wanted to see how the Sky-Bornes behaved in the presence of their great jeaf.

From his tent, Harry pulled another of the crew's endless stash of metal boxes. This one came with a shiny front. When Harry flipped a switch, it shone a soft fuzzy light. He set the box on a little table so the front faced three stools. Harry pointed to one for Joaquin. Buck busied himself with further checks on the plane, while Keltyn kept sorting her gear.

On the table, just in front of the lighted box, Harry arranged half a dozen iridium pieces collected by Keltyn. He glanced at Orfea and the boy. "Ready?"

"Ready," said Orfea.

Joaquin kept his eyes fixed upon the shiny box and nodded. He had no idea what to expect. He knew the legend of the genie, a powerful spirit that one could summon out of a teapot with the right incantation. Was this such a summons?

Harry flipped another switch. Nothing for ten seconds, but then the screen flickered, and there was the cool, calm, collected image of the man they called Sir Oscar Bailey.

Joaquin was astonished. Certainly, the emergence of this image out of thin air was a feat of magic. What struck him more, though, was the simulation of this man's features, compared to what he imagined the real Sir Oscar Bailey would look like, were he sitting across the table. For one thing, his silver hair seemed overly lit, like a halo. His skin shone as smooth as glass, not a single wrinkle.

Strangest of all were the eyes. They glinted like burning coals, as if they could blaze straight through to the soul of the beholder. Joaquin felt a small shiver.

"There you are, Harry," came this ringing voice. "I was ready to give up."

"Where do I begin, chief? It's been a heck of a week." Harry did his best to dish out the straight story, but he struggled. Several times, he reached for a sip of water. When he got to the part about the stone being radioactive, he choked. He must be greatly disappointed, thought Joaquin. Perhaps he has failed in his mission and fears rebuke.

"Take it easy, Harry, get a hold of yourself. Where's Savant SparrowHawk? I want her account."

Harry signaled to Keltyn. She pointed at her chest with a questioning look. When Harry jerked his head, she trudged over. By the time Sir Oscar could see her, she was composed.

"Ah, there's our geology prodigy. I hear you have bad news for me."

"Afraid so, sir. The best stones, the purest ones, are hot."

"That's shocking. Savant McCoy never mentioned it as a possibility. Good thing you brought the equipment along to test for radioactivity. I wouldn't want my whole crew exposed, to say nothing of my lab people."

"Yes, sir. You can't be too careful with unknown ores." Keltyn's glance flickered back and forth.

Sir Oscar studied her. "No chance the machine could be in error?"

Harry jumped in. "We're bringing that back for independent verification, chief."

"So, you're not sure the result will hold up, is that what you're saying?"

"We're not taking any chances, is what I'm saying." Harry nodded for emphasis.

"Whatever." Sir Oscar's edgy gimlet eyes danced around the screen until they settled on Joaquin. "Fay, it looks like you have made yourself a new friend."

"Yes, Oscar, this is my distant cousin Joaquin Beltran. Joaquin, this is Sir Oscar Bailey, who made our trip possible."

He nodded toward the spectral image. He could feel those hot coals probe the inner recesses of his mind, sifting through all its secrets.

Orfea went on to explain her proposal. She mentioned nothing about Keltyn staying behind, but the fact that their craft had room for only four seemed to escape Sir Oscar's notice. By the time she finished, his fleshy pink face beamed. "Well done, well done, Fay. Of course, you will feel at home in Canada, Joaquin. I shall see to the arrangements personally. You shall be a goodwill ambassador for your people."

"Thank you, seir." Joaquin gulped. "It will be an honor."

Sir Oscar turned to Orfea. "I couldn't have envisioned a better solution myself."

She lifted her head. "Solution?"

"Canadians will wish to learn what these... Onwei people are like."

Joaquin startled. Did speaking the word "Onwei" just make this man gag, or were the images on this box playing tricks on his own mind?

"Of course," muttered Orfea. She flushed. Her next words seemed to come with effort. "But tell me, Oscar. Do you expect to send Canadians to settle in Antarctica?"

His color darkened ever so slightly. "Why, what gave you that idea?"

"Actually, the tribe's old witch deduced as much, without even having met you."

Orfea's smile was tight-lipped. "Well, it may have merit. I'll have to confer with Harry, in a few days, after you've rested. Really," he inspected them closer, "you folks look bushed. Let's get you back here and settled in."

Orfea gave Harry a pleading look. He took a deep breath. "Oscar, just a minute."

The face on the screen raised its brows.

Harry continued, "I think what Fay is trying to say..."

The gimlet eyes flitted back and forth between Orfea and Harry. "Well?"

"Can I be blunt, Oscar?" said Orfea.

"That has been your constant virtue, Savant Del Campo." Oscar's nostrils flared.

"We have no business colonizing Antarctica. This land belongs to the Onwei, Joaquin's people." Orfea put her arm around Joaquin. Finding himself embraced by his newfound cousin still felt strange, but not nearly so strange as the idea that the land belonged to anyone.

Sir Oscar pulled back at this display. "Oh, please, Savant." He rocked his head back and forth. "I should have listened to my better judgment. I knew sending you along would be a mistake."

Orfea's jaw set. She took a deep breath, but Harry cut her off. "If it's all the same to you, chief, I think it's best if we sign off now. See you in a couple of days." Before Sir Oscar could object, Harry flipped off the switch and faced Orfea. "You near blew it there, Ms. Bleeding Heart. You realize that?"

Orfea reached for her hankie with one hand and drew Joaquin closer with the other. "I can't help it. These people need protection from Oscar's schemes." She blotted tears and eyed Joaquin, while still sniveling.

"But I must do what's best for Joaquin as well, even if that means playing ball with Oscar. What a dilemma." She paused. "I never had children, no doubt a blessing for doing all that field research. Since Paul died, I've often wondered, what do I have to show for my life? Who will miss me when I'm gone?" She squeezed Joaquin's good hand in both of hers.

Damn. There she was, poised on the verge of tears again. He had begun to feel confident in Orfea's judgment, but this self-pity was too much. Joaquin had gritted his teeth this whole time, feeling more embarrassed each moment. Up until this morning, he didn't notice any disputes between Harry and Orfea, let alone their boss. He wiggled his hand out of Orfea's grasp and turned to look at Harry, now standing with his hands on his hips and jaw set.

Keltyn emerged from her tent and reached to dig a pebble out of her shoe. Buck raised his eyebrows; that was all.

Joaquin started slowly, with no idea of what to say. "With respect, I wish not to hurt anyone's feelings. You have all treated me well and opened my eyes to many wonderful things."

Orfea's cheeks were damp. She bit her lip.

"This lady wants to do what is best for me," he said. "We are cousins, and I am an orphan; she feels an obligation."

"No, Joaquin, no obligation at all. It's what I truly wish to do, with all my heart." The lines on her face sagged.

He plunged ahead. "I do not wish for anyone's sympathy, but I fear that is how your people would react to me. For many in my tribe, I am already an object of curiosity from my foot and being an orphan. Now they will have another infirmity to gossip about." He held up his bandaged wrist and smiled grimly. "But at least they are my people."

Orfea snuffled, shook her head back and forth. "'My people.' What does that really mean, Joaquin? Have you thought about it? You have no family..."

He hung his head.

"Your mentor is dead..."

He squeezed his eyes shut to stop the tears. Above all, he would not let anyone see him weep.

"...and now you have a bum hand to go along with your bum foot. What do you think 'your people' are going to do for you now? Look at me, Joaquin."

Slowly, he lifted his head to meet Orfea's gaze. Her complexion turned blotchy, but her voice was still strong. "I want to help you."

Joaquin tried to picture himself with two good hands, two good feet. On winter nights in Nomidar, people gathered at a great barn by lamplight. The guitar, fiddle and panpipes would strike up a tune and, slowly, couples would drift out onto the dance floor. Could he ever hope to dance with a girl? Were he to approach a girl displaying his two bum limbs, she would either hide from his gaze, or accept his offer out of pity.

Yet, were his chances any better with Orfea's people? Certainly, she would introduce him to her friends. Some of them would have young people his own age. He tried to picture Orfea's home, with himself sitting in a fancy chair, dressed up in an outfit like Tio Hector described, trying to chat up a highbrow girl sipping tea. Or worse, be the subject of unending awkward questions about his dismal origins. The kind of questions he spent his entire youth trying to ignore.

It struck Joaquin that he would be better off to sit with the musicians in Nomidar. He could play rhythm on the tambourine, keep time by tapping the floor with his good foot. Sooner or later, a girl would notice him, overlook his defects, and ask him to dance.

He searched Orfea's face, her fountain of tears. He shook his head slowly but firmly.

Orfea straightened and wiped her eyes. "If you're sure..."

"As sure as I can be." Doubts already raced through his head.

"But do you not wish to learn languages?"

That part appealed. He nodded.

Orfea fished the translating box out of her bag. "Then take this."

The offer stunned him. "No, seira. How can I use such a thing?"

"The settings are arrived at by trial and error. It took me two days of listening to Yoka to get them right for Onwei. I'm sure she can help you with the tongues of the ancestors."

Joaquin hesitated.

Orfea extended her arm. "Take it. It will save you years of sitting at Yoka's knee as she withers away."

Since she put it that way... He took a deep breath and accepted the box.

"Just let the sunshine hit it, keeps it running. And you'll need spare earpads." Orfea searched through her bag. "Ha." She held up a handful of Venga nuggets. "Say, these will come in handy back home. Maybe I can get in touch with Paul." She brightened. "You and I might be able to stay in touch too."

"How, seira?"

"Through our mutual ancestor, Hector Beltran."

"Oh yes, my crazy Tio Hector." Between those chatty two, there would be no need for Joaquin to say much at all. He pocketed the earpads and studied the nondescript cube sitting in front of him. Was this really where his future lay? Channeling dead family members for the bereaved? A junior wizard to expound Onwei ancient history?

Worse, could he accept the harsh tutelage of wizened Yoka for the few years left to her? It would mean a clean break with the gaucho life. Yet that path vanished the moment Aldo breathed his last.

Joaquin tapped the box with a staccato beat of his fingertips. He needed to apply the same diligence to learning its secrets as displayed by these four Sky-Bornes and their cunning sponsor.

29

THE MAIZE CIRCLE

Fay is generous, I'll give her that. She put a lot of work into the lang-synch before gifting it to the kid on a whim. But the translator gadget gives me an idea. I signal Joaquin. "Hey, scout, mind if I borrow that contraption for a while?"

No objection. I think he wants more pointers how to use it.

I hit up Fay for some of the Venga nuggets she lifted from Yoka. She reaches into the pocket of her frock but hesitates. I follow her gaze. Buck and Harry pretend to busy themselves, but in fact are watching our every move. As if Ysidro's bunch didn't give them enough to worry about.

We retreat to our blue tent, Joaquin trailing behind. I wave him in to join us. The boy and I sit cross-legged on the floor, while Fay rests on a stool. She starts heating water for tea and says, "So you think your ancestors grew maize? It wasn't native to Canada."

"But they learned how to cultivate it. I need to question some of them. And I want you around to confirm if I'm on the right track."

"What you described before, from that Char, sounds like you've already got it worked out," says Fay.

"Maybe, but I need more proof before I confront Yoka."

She waits for the water to boil, pours it into a small cup with a tea bag, then fumbles in her pack for a needle and reaches for my hand. I squeeze my eyes shut and try not to wince as Fay withdraws a drop of blood into the teacup. She fumbles for nuggets to mix them with.

Joaquin watches the ritual with a novice's curiosity. I ask him, "Can you see making a trade out of this, scout?"

He shrugs and holds up his bandaged hand. "How many choices do I have left?" He lifts his chin. "Shouldn't you ask the old woman for guidance?"

Fay and I catch each other's eye. "We think she may be holding out on us," I say.

Joaquin's mouth curls, as if he's not too surprised at this. He points to the lang-synch and asks, "Why do you need that thing? Can't you speak the tongue of your forebears?"

I feel a hollow space in my gut. "I'm ashamed to say that the Cree language is now extinct. I won't understand a word they say."

Fay finishes marinating the Venga nuggets in the bloodstained tea. She shivers as she hands me the dish. I wolf down the whole mess and chug the tea as a chaser. Then I slow my breathing and wait.

And wait.

After ten minutes that seem like an hour, the hair on my neck tingles. Instead of sitting on the floor of my tent, now I'm camped out in a clearing in the woods. Buzzing, must be mosquitoes around. Three figures sit on the ground, middle-aged women. They're dressed like the First Peoples used to. Hides, black hair in braids, gathered around a circle cross-legged.

They're preparing maize. One shucks the husks; the second cuts the kernels lengthwise off the cob. The third tends a small fire. Beside her lies a water gourd and, several feet away, a lump of limestone. Her preparations look much like Char's.

I sense Fay, poised beside me at the controls of the lang-synch. "You'll have to get their attention, honey," she says.

I clear my throat loudly. The three Cree woman glance in the direction of their strange uninvited guest and nod to each other knowingly. Then they continue their tasks.

"Not enough," mutters Fay. "You need to get them talking."

I lean forward, rest my chin on my knuckles, elbow on my knee, as I ponder how to spark banter among these three matrons. Any of them might be my ancestor, but I have no clue to their tongue. As if this is some kind of game in which only they know the rules, the three of them take turns glancing and smirking at me in my helpless plight.

Should I try to imitate the circle dance from our Pow Wow's when I was a kid? No. I really doubt these folks ever did that dance, way back whenever.

I end up standing as straight as I can, to my full runty height, my lips clenched and my right arm raised way overhead in a fist. If this doesn't get their attention, I don't know what will.

Sure enough, these matrons drop what they are doing and sit, mouths agape. After satisfying themselves that little old me can't harm them, they laugh and jabber all at once. I sense Fay tweaking the dials for several minutes as I continue to dance, until the words of these women resonate.

"Clearly, she has the features of kin," says one of them as she shucks the maize, "so she should know that our people never behaved in such a manner."

At this, I drop my stone-cold pose and squat on my haunches to face these tribal ancestors at eye level. "My apologies, sisters, for this unseemly exhibit. I needed to hear you speak, so I could decipher your tongue."

"Well?" says the second woman, slicing the rows of kernels. Now, with the raucous dance ceased, all three act wary again.

"I am indeed your kinswoman, come from a distant place. I have a simple question, then I shall leave you in peace."

The three matrons glance at each other, shrug and turn back to me.

"The question is how you prepare your maize."

They all snicker again. "As you see here," says the second one, holding up her knife. "Why? Have you some better way?"

"No, not at all." I bow my head and point toward the block of limestone. "But I know not the purpose of that powder."

The one who sits by the fire wipes her hands dry and picks up the block. "This powder, dangerous as it may be to handle, is a blessing. It enhances the taste of the kernels cooked in it, to be sure, but there is more."

I lean forward, conscious of being but a few feet from these three distant kin. Not since childhood have I felt so blood-connected and secure. I may be way outside my comfort zone, but I'm only the most recent in the long line of people who have made this same journey. In some crazy fashion, despite my hide flaying out here in the wind, I feel more firmly anchored than ever.

"In the old days," says the one by the fire, "before anyone learned how to prepare the maize in this way, our people suffered."

"How did they suffer?"

"Oh, girl, are you sure you wish to hear the gruesome details?"

I force myself to nod.

"All right, picture this. Your skin shrivels and blisters as if burnt. Sores show up, on your tongue and in your privates. Your bowels run day and night. After a while, you become listless, confused, forget things, unable to sleep. You start hearing voices, seeing things that are not there. A few years of this agony, then one day you mercifully curl up and die."

Throughout this description, I am aware of Fay, watching the dials with one eye, leaning forward to catch every word. Now she sits bolt upright and interjects, "Aha! Same symptoms as the Onwei khokri."

I slam my palms together in victory and reach out to hug the woman by the fire, who I am so sure is my direct ancestor. But these abrupt moves cause the vision to dissolve. All three gone, just like that.

I should feel bummed to lose them but instead, I'm ecstatic, because now I've got the goods to take on Yoka, to shake the truth out of her.

And then, and then... I stop in my tracks, as the end game washes over me, like a cold shower. What good will it do me to uncover that truth? This whole sleuthing expedition will only pan out if hearing it is enough to convince Trieste and the other tribeswomen. Even then, will knowing the truth allow Trieste to recover her strength, and the toughest test of all, will she forgive me within the short time the tribe still has here?

Yet the alternatives are so bleak I can't even picture them. Return to Canada to face trial, then prison? Exile to China? Heading off on my own here, an even worse form of exile. How many days would I last? I've really got only one card left to play, so I'd better play it well.

***

It's mid-afternoon when I ride back to the Onwei camp, still figuring out my moves after I settle this score with Yoka. Fay wanted to come along, but she and the old witch are past the honeymoon stage. They've already come to loggerheads over the boy's future, and what I'm going to lay on her wouldn't bring them any closer.

I stop Cozuel just before the creek, dismount and begin to walk him back to Trieste's hut. Maybe, just maybe, she's changed her mind about me. Even if she hasn't, I need to fetch Luz, so she can bear witness when I go to confront Yoka.

Efrain spies me and waves me down. He speaks in somber tones. "You should not stay here, seirita. It is too dangerous. There is talk that tonight will be the night when they attack."

Ysidro's gang, he must mean. I crane my neck up. The sky is clear and there will be moonlight. That bunch will have no trouble finding the plane. Oh, why does the world have so many Ysidros and so few Aldos?

Efrain dwarfs me by over a foot. I search his worried face. "Listen. I need to ask you a big, big favor."

The tall guy says nothing.

"You know Ysidro well."

"I should. He is my uncle."

"Is he a superstitious man?"

"How do you mean?"

"That yellow machine I showed everyone, the one that measures poison in the stone. How would he look at that?"

"I saw his expression when you displayed it, seirita. He watched the box as if it might have magical powers." Efrain removes his boina and scratches his thick black curls. "He has mentioned the box, in fact all the different machines that you people use. He does not understand them, so he fears them, as do the others who ride with him."

"So, they may wish to destroy these machines?" The glimmer of an idea flits through my brain.

"It would not surprise me."

"Well, I'm going to tell you where they are, in case you wish to pass this information on to them." I purse my lips and nod. "They're in the orange tent at our camp."

Efrain peers down at me long and hard. "I do not understand why you would wish Ysidro to find this out. Are you saying that you also want these devices to be destroyed?"

"If Harry or Buck ask, I will deny every word." I try to look sincere.

"But why?"

"It's a long story. Harry is guarding that yellow box now. If it goes back with us, I will end up in prison."

The big guy's features soften. "I would not wish that."

As decent a guy as Efrain is, it shames me to hook him into a conspiracy. "So, will you help? All you have to do is mention it casually to Ysidro. Tell him that on your way back from the mountain the other day, when you dropped me off, you saw the guys move equipment in and out of the orange tent."

Efrain inhales through his teeth. "He will not trust that information coming from me. He understands I am not one for vengeance."

The two of us stand silent until Efrain shakes his head. "You cannot clue Ysidro without arousing his suspicions." He plops the boina back on. "I must ride to the Sky-Bornes' camp and warn them an attack is imminent." He moves to retrieve his horse.

So much for that inspiration. I remount and head towards Trieste's yurt at Cozuel's usual clip-clop pace.

Luz takes the mule's reins as I climb off. She looks at me with a question in her eyes.

"It's still up in the air," I say. "I have to choose by tonight. All my gauges and transmitters are in Harry's tent. He'll have all the measurements I made, in case I don't return." I look past her, toward the inside of the yurt. "But it's your mother's call. No way I can stay here on my own."

"Mother hasn't said anything since this morning. I can't go against her wishes."

She appears as glum as I feel. The past few days seem to have taken all the fight out of the girl. Her former self, that impetuous ball of fire who spurred me to tackle Erebus, risking Yoka's wrath and her mother's sanity in the process, lies somewhere up on that mountain, along with her mare.

"It's okay," I say. "Whatever happens, will. But I've got one more favor to ask."

She nods absently.

"This one involves you, me, and Yoka."

She grimaces at the prospect of another session with the crone after all the recent drama. It must be the desperation in my face that makes her shrug okay.

"Bring one of your mother's tortillas. I have a hunch."

30

HOUR OF THE WITCH

Yoka bustles around, making ready to leave the next morning. She glances at us for just a second, then returns to her packing.

Luz and I stand ill at ease for several minutes before the crone, her back still turned, flicks two fingers downward, in a motion to sit. When she finally faces us, her shriveled hole of a mouth stays clamped shut. The black furrow of her brow hasn't lightened since yesterday afternoon. A brief incline of her chin serves as a curt invitation to state our business.

I begin. "This has to do with your forebear who first learned the Venga art. Orfea told me her story."

Her stone face softens the least bit. "You refer to M'Bine, from eastern Africa."

"Orfea said that the story ended when M'Bine was but in her thirties."

"Sadly, yes. She begat what became the Onwei people's greatest asset, but never survived long enough to see it spread."

"What illness brought her down?"

Yoka flips her wrist back. "Exhaustion, physical and mental. The climate, the day lengths, they were too extreme for her frail constitution."

I might have believed that once. "But no one knows for sure, do they?" I motion for Luz to unwrap the tortilla. "Could this have been the reason?"

Yoka frowns at the tortilla. In a slow metamorphosis, like a kettle coming to boil, she spills into her deep, gurgling laugh, shoulders bouncing up and down. "Whose fool idea is this?" She stops abruptly and squares toward me. "The report of your pronouncement at the Venga ceremony has reached my ears. You have ruined Trieste's trade. Now you propose to incriminate the staple of our diet as well?"

I swallow hard and glance at Luz before answering. It's a confession I owe them both, owe the whole tribe. "I made a huge mistake. One thing led to another. The stone is not poisoned, not really. I was trying to protect your people from Sir Oscar Bailey's designs."

Yoka purses her lips, lifts her head until her chin sticks out. "Ah, yes, your great chief back in Canada. Hmph. So, young woman, how would you escape the deep hole you have dug yourself into? And why should the tribe believe a word that you say now?"

"They shouldn't and they won't. That's why I need you, and Trieste, and Luz, all of you, to help clear me."

"Fat chance of that."

"What if we found the true cause of the khokri?" Just saying this pumps my adrenaline.

Yoka raises her bushy brows, measures me over the rims of her dialups. "You would have to prove it, and that's not so easy. It doesn't fell its victims overnight."

"That's where your Venga comes in."

The crone's expression freezes, so I backpedal, explain our suspicion that the answer lies in how maize is prepared.

"Interesting theory." Yoka twirls the thumbs of her folded hands.

"Was maize the staple food where M'Bine came from?"

"Quite likely," the crone concedes.

"Then tell me this. With all the upheavals her people went through, would she have been able to get the lime to cook the maize with?"

"Hmph. They were lucky to get maize at all, let alone prepare it properly."

Fay was right about that. So far, so good. I take a deep breath and relate the Venga encounter with my three Cree ancestors. I repeat word for word their description of the symptoms that befall those who partook of maize prepared without slaked lime.

Yoka remains sober faced. "A breakthrough, to be sure, but not the whole story."

My blood starts to boil. How much more proof does the old hag need?

She waits until I calm down. "Part of the khokri mystery is the random nature of its attacks. My daughter Addys, did you know she died from the disease?" She slumps down. "Why could it not have been me, so at least the Venga tradition could be carried on in our tribe?"

I feel a note of pity for her. "You have won a disciple after all. The translating box belongs to Joaquin now. Orfea's parting gift, to help him learn the tongues that you will tutor him in."

"Oho." Yoka brightens. "He decided to stay with his people in the end."

"An especially mushy performance by Orfea clinched it. Her flood of tears unnerved him."

"Hah." She pauses to picture that. "Still, the question remains. Why would the khokri strike its victims at random?"

"Perhaps not so random. Tell me, who makes the tortillas you consume?"

"Why, Char, of course. I've always been partial to them. They taste better, worth the extra coppers."

"And Addys, do you remember which kind she ate?" The muscles in my jaw tense as I pose this question.

Yoka freezes again. "Why would I remember that? Addys died ten years ago."

"Think, Auntie, please think." It's Luz's plaintive voice.

"But yes, I do recall." Yoka spits this out. The veins in her temples bulge. "Addys despised the feebleminded Char, figured her habits must be foul. She went out of her way to get her supply from another woman, always made a point of keeping hers separate from mine."

We all three sit, frozen. After a minute, I whisper, "Now you see?"

"Oh yes, I see." The crone stretches her arms. "The khokri has come and gone for generations. You know, I have done plenty of sleuthing on my own, ever since Addys died."

I should let it go, give Yoka the benefit of the doubt. After all, she did lose her daughter. Yet, right now, I'm pissed. "You've suspected the cause all along, haven't you, old woman?"

She glares at me. "What do you imply?"

"So long as the cause of the khokri remains a mystery, your power over the tribe is enhanced. If no one discerns the answer, they will seek whatever solace Venga can provide, and only you can provide the Venga."

The crone's lips pucker like she's sucked on a lemon. "You have quite an imagination, girl. A few things you haven't considered, however."

"Such as?"

As she answers my question, Yoka watches Luz. I notice confusion in the girl's face. "You believe that I would allow your fool theory about radiation in the stone to kill Trieste's trade, if I knew the true cause of the khokri all along?"

Yoka's answer is clearly a bid to gain sympathy from Luz. The girl stares straight ahead, like a deer caught in the headlights. I have to call the crone's bluff on this one. "I don't know. Would you?"

Yoka doesn't answer.

I signal Luz. We get up and leave the old witch to whatever version of the truth she wants to believe.

It's a risk, perhaps a dumb risk. I should act sympathetic and try to enlist Yoka as an ally in spreading the truth about the cause of the khokri. Yet I'm afraid she'll put on conditions, somehow try to bend this twist of fortune to her own ends. It's enough that Luz is convinced. Now we need to see how her mother reacts to the news.

***

Darkness has fallen, but a rising moon lights our path as Luz and I start back to Trieste's yurt. I stuff my hands back in my pockets and hunch forward. "Do you think what we just learned of the khokri will improve your mother's opinion of me?"

Luz kicks away twigs in her path. "Mother is a great fan of Char's tortillas, which means her illness can't be the khokri. But she'll be skeptical of any new theory. Who knows how she or the other women will react to another shock?"

My friend won't look me in the eye anymore. I didn't let her in on my radioactive ploy with the stone back up on the mountain. I was afraid she would blab, and that would get back to Harry, and there would go my whole game. Now, for the first time since we've met, I feel the tension. We walk in silence, descended like a wall between us.

"Well, at least say a prayer for me to your Spirits, like you did for your dying horse." I blurt out this phrase from pure spite, but a rotten feeling comes over me as soon as it leaves my mouth.

Luz stops abruptly, turns toward me, nostrils flared, and stares down at my face, trying to read it in the dark. She shakes her head slowly, turns away and marches forward, like she's determined to leave me behind. So much for shaming her into being my advocate. My fool attempt just backfired.

We're fast approaching Trieste's yurt. I speed my pace to catch up with the girl, so I can apologize.

But Luz has already stopped. She's watching something in the dark between the trees. I follow her gaze and notice a saddled horse grazing.

That's strange. I glance around for its rider and spot a mounted figure on a second horse, lurking in the shadows under a cottonwood. He swings out to block our path. A rifle rests on the horn of his saddle. Nestor!

"Well, looky these two birds, out for a moonlight stroll." He sways in the saddle.

"You are blocking our way, charro," scowls Luz. "Who do you think you are?"

I gather that gauchos are supposed to follow an unspoken rule: do not disturb the camp followers, stay away from their space unless invited. "Oh, so sorry, seirita." Nestor cocks his head in mock sympathy.

"Important business. Boss sent me. Deliver bruxa Keltyn."

A shiver courses through me. Deliver me? To whom? Ysidro? For what?

"A few of us goin' for li'l ride to Sky-Bornes' camp tonight. Tell her, she stay calm, so will we." Nestor's speech is slurred, his sneer the same as always. "Tell her mount up." He flicks his finger toward the other horse.

Should I try to make a run for it? The rising moon is still nestled behind the trees; I can dart through them. How good a shot is Nestor, anyway? He acts like he's dipped into their pulce, which won't help his aim. Probably doesn't have enough bullets to get much target practice either.

On the other hand, even if I do manage to elude him now, where could I hide out? The only one who can stop this trigger-happy kid is someone else with a gun. That would be Efrain or Buck, which means hustling back to the plane. On Cozuel? What a joke. Or through miles of open field on foot? Nestor would catch me, tie me up and drag me back without needing to fire a shot.

I feel knee-deep in that old quicksand again, utterly powerless. Nestor senses my hesitation and waves the barrel of his rifle.

I try to show no sign of fear and mount in silence. Luz reaches up to grab my hand and I squeeze it. "Be careful, she says." Her recent flash of anger is history. With this twist, the differences between us seem trivial.

I act nonchalant while loosening the reins. "Oh, don't worry about me." I'll be a model prisoner, until the right moment comes to make a move.

31
THE POSSE

As he trails the reins of my horse, Nestor leads across the creek toward the gaucho encampment. We don't need the moonlight or their campfire to guide us; the charros' shouts and hollers advertise their position. Whatever may happen tonight, it's not going to be a stealth operation.

Sounds like they want me for a hostage, but is that all? I'm not pin-up material, but who knows how long these guys have been without a woman? If the rest of them are as liquored up as Nestor... Ugly thoughts swamp my mind.

Turns out there are four of them, all standing around the fire. Gabino yammers away to Ysidro, who unleashes an epithet every few seconds as he stares at the flames. Soriante spreads his hands at arm's length — one hand grasps a bottle — and belts out a yodel. One other lean gaucho, whom I don't recognize, stands by himself, grasping what looks to be a branding iron, as if on guard.

Ysidro spies the two of us. "Good work, charro. Did the Sky-Borne girl give you any trouble?"

Nestor glances back at me and flashes his spiteful grin as he pats the rifle, still resting on his saddle horn. "No, boss, she is too smart for that."

Ysidro digs out a length of rope. He walks over to my horse and regards me with a sneer. Then he points to my ear. "I know you can understand me. Listen very carefully, seirita. You're going to be our safe passage tonight when we pay a visit to your mates. You try any funny business, it will be your little hide to pay."

He points his thumb at Nestor. "This charro has one itchy trigger finger." Leaning forward, he lowers his voice. "And some other itchy parts, too. You catch my drift?"

I can barely force a nod.

"Good. But just in case you got any funny ideas..." Ysidro grabs both of my hands in one of his meaty paws. With the other, he lashes the rope around my wrists, none too gently, and secures it to the saddle horn. Then he turns around. "All right, boys. Let's mount up and get this thing done."

Soriante trots over and tips his boina at me. He purses his lips in a kiss, and says, "So sorry, seirita," as he grabs the reins and pulls my horse in line with his.

The posse of five, with yours truly as their ace-in-the-hole, heads out of camp. Nestor rides in front to show them the way, then Ysidro, Gabino, Soriante, and me. The tall, morose fellow with his branding iron tails behind.

I try to imagine how this will play out. Efrain has almost certainly stayed with my crew after delivering his message about the attack, so that means one more gun for our side. He has taken pains to act neutral in Ysidro's vendetta against us, and I doubt that anyone on this posse expects to run into him when they attack. Buck has his stun gun. Still, Ysidro's boys outnumber ours.

I wish I could just holler out, stop everyone in their tracks right here and now, and explain away all the misunderstandings. But these guys don't have earpads, and besides, I get the sinking feeling that it's too late for explanations.

As we head across the valley toward to the crater, I test the rope. The passes binding my wrists are plenty tight, but in the loops around the saddle horn, Ysidro left just enough slack to afford some wiggle room. Pretending to hold firm to the saddle horn with both hands, I use the slack to move my fingers down to the knot and start digging to loosen it.

Soriante hasn't let up on the yodeling even by the time we've reached the crater's rim. Gabino still jabbers away at his uncle, the new jeaf, and Ysidro responds with scattered groans and affirmations. Best I can tell, the younger charro is projecting all the future miseries that may befall the tribe, should the Sky-Bornes not be dealt with once and for all. A spread of the khokri to the male population heads his list, along with an invasion of more Sky-Bornes in their flying machines, soon followed by enslavement of all the Onwei tribes.

Though I wonder at Gabino's overly fertile imagination, I have to concede that his prediction about more Sky-Borne landings is entirely possible. In fact, his dread mirrors my own, and it stokes my resolve to use any opportunity that comes up. Heck, at this point, what have I got to lose?

You would think the charros would quiet down as they near the plane, to favor some element of surprise on the off chance that their targets are asleep. Or maybe Ysidro expects my mates to show their faces. Either way, there's no sound from their side as we pull up. Ysidro motions for the posse to stop, halfway between the plane and the tents. Soriante and Gabino fall silent.

The jeaf signals Nestor to fire his rifle into the air. What a joke. All that clamor and he expects his quarry to sleep through it?

Facing the tents, Ysidro shouts, "Come on out, you cowards," not knowing or caring that only Fay and I understand his tongue. "We've got your girl hostage."

When no one answers, he motions to me. "Tell them it's their last chance if they want you back alive."

I lean toward the tents. "Guys, they mean business," I try to shout, but it comes out as a croak.

Still no answer. Damn. Did our crew abandon camp for a safer hideout after Efrain warned them? If I'm the only one left to vent their frustrations on, who knows what kind of ritual sacrifice they would make of me, just to teach my mates a lesson?

Wait. There's no way our guys have left. Leaving the plane unguarded would jeopardize their only way out of here.

All five charros stay mounted. Nestor keeps his rifle trained at the tents. Ysidro motions to Gabino, who reaches into his saddle pack and unwraps a clay pot with soaked rags sticking out. He takes his flint and strikes a spark. The rags burst into flame. Gabino heaves his homemade torch at the orange tent. It bounces off the top and hits the ground at the edge of the fabric, which catches fire just like that.

I gasp. Oh geez, even if — I hope — Harry and Buck have vacated their tent before we showed up, that's where my data and meter are stored. An irrational urge to protect my work overwhelms me.

Soriante fixes his own bundle of rags to set the other tent afire. Just after he lights the flame, he freezes, crumples, and drops the clay pot. His ample body topples off his horse, landing right next to the flaming torch.

Buck's stun gun! Good job, big guy, wherever you are.

Ysidro and Gabino jump off their mounts to help Soriante. He screams as his shirt catches fire. Ysidro runs to grab a blanket from his horse.

In the commotion, here's my chance. I've already managed to loosen the knot that binds my wrists to the saddle horn. I wiggle off the mount, run toward the orange tent, and holler, "Guys, get out." They probably already are, but where's my stuff?

Wrists still bound together, I fumble with the tent's front flap. The flames lick my feet, but I can't shake this sudden need to save my stuff.

Somewhere behind me, I hear Orfea shout, "Keltyn, we're all okay."

From a different spot, Buck hollers, "Missy, back off before you're toast."

A tiny but very strong fist punches me in the ribs and knocks me to the ground.

***

Joaquin watched the scene in enforced safety, his face pressed to the pane and his hands clawing the frame of the flying machine's cockpit. He wished to be out amidst the action; at least then he could warn the others.

He spied Nestor licking his lips and raising his rifle. Here was the charro's chance, yet he hesitated, apparently unable to decide between his three Sky-Borne targets. He settled on the smallest but closest one. Just as he fired at Keltyn, a shot popped from the other direction. Joaquin whipped around to see Efrain's rifle pointed, smoke trailing out. Nestor fell off his horse, his rifle beside him. His piebald galloped away.

Joaquin glanced back at Nestor's body. It lay frozen, spread-eagled, face up. Joaquin wanted to breathe a sigh of relief, yet he half expected that, like some diabolic cat, Nestor would jump up any second to settle this lingering score. Joaquin kept his eyes glued on the corpse for minutes, before finally convincing himself that his nemesis was truly dead.

Joaquin felt smug just yesterday morning at Cisco's favorite spot by the creek, having believed that Nestor fled. But Nestor turned up with the knife that mangled his wrist. Now that the mal hombre was dispatched for good, Joaquin could feel a big weight alight from his shoulders.

Yet Nestor did not go down alone. Keltyn lay on her side, writhing in pain. Joaquin scooted over to climb out of the cockpit, but Orfea grabbed his arm.

"Not yet. It's too dangerous."

He brushed off her arm and scrambled over the side of the plane, crouching in the shadows, waiting for his moment. He saw Buck motion to Harry, pointing toward the blue tent. The chief hurried his chubby frame to find a blanket. He ran back and swatted with both hands, trying to smother the orange tent blaze.

Efrain hunched down from his cover behind the plane's other wing, his eye on retrieving Nestor's rifle. Ysidro whipped around, cussing, as if that would douse the flames rising from his nephew. He also spied the rifle. Meanwhile, with his horse blanket spread out at arm's length, Gabino cast his body into a belly flop on top of Soriante, who lay twisting in agony.

The only charro still mounted was the bloke Onofre, he with the branding iron. He spurred his mount, heading toward Efrain as he tried to collect Nestor's firearm. Joaquin's heart dropped as he watched this mal hombre light on Efrain from behind. Onofre held the branding iron tucked in his armpit like a jousting stick.

Joaquin jumped out of the shadows, ran toward Efrain, and shouted his name, but with all the commotion, the big guy had no clue that he was about to be impaled.

As Efrain bent to retrieve Nestor's gun, he sensed Onofre bearing down on him, just in time. Efrain grabbed his own rifle barrel with both hands. His huge arms swung the butt over his head and knocked the branding iron flying. Onofre screamed and shook his arm. He barely managed to stay mounted but couldn't rein in. He and his mount streaked off into the night. Good riddance.

Taking advantage of Efrain's distraction, Ysidro snuck up behind him and lunged for Nestor's rifle. Joaquin scrambled as fast as his legs would carry him, diving the last few feet, and managed to grab the gun barrel with his good hand at the same moment that Ysidro seized the butt. Joaquin landed on his bandaged arm, yelped and grunted to hold on, but Ysidro yanked it away with one good heave.

Joaquin's cry alerted Efrain, who quickly trained his own gun at Ysidro's midriff before he could gain full control, leaving him with no choice but to drop the rifle.

Efrain jerked his chin toward Joaquin. He picked up Nestor's rifle and carried it to Buck, who in turn kicked it behind the plane. Then the pilot ran toward the facedown Keltyn and hollered for help. Joaquin stumbled toward her and Orfea clambered out of the flying machine. The pilot's long arms gently rolled Keltyn to face upward, but not before Joaquin spotted a dark stain pooled on the side of her windbreaker. That did not look good, not at all.

Buck pulled up the layers of clothing to examine the wound. It made a sucking noise every time she took a breath. "Damn," he said. "The bullet must have entered her chest." He probed around. "But here's an exit wound. That's a plus."

Her eyes stayed shut.

Buck used one arm to prop her head up and the other to wipe her airway with a rag. "Come and hold her head, Fay."

He pushed two fingers on the side of her throat. "Racing pulse. Hold 'er just like that. I've gotta find the cylinders, the oxygen bottle and suction." He noticed the rope tying Keltyn's wrists and motioned for Joaquin to cut it, then sprinted toward the plane.

Orfea's chin quavered as she cradled Keltyn's head. Her hands jerked to and fro while trying to wipe away the sticky red foam bubbling from Keltyn's mouth. When Joaquin finished cutting the rope, she handed him the soaked rag, wiping away tears with the back of her hand. "Keltyn, honey, can you hear me?"

Slowly, Keltyn opened her eyes and tried to whisper. Joaquin couldn't make it out from the froth. Orfea reached in her pocket for a dry rag and gave it to the boy. Tears gushed down her cheeks. Her bloodstained hand pushed the hair out of her face.

"Keep wiping, every few seconds," she told Joaquin. She turned to Keltyn. "Say it again, honey."

This time, they could barely make out a coarse murmur. "The yellow box, the data, gone?"

"That's a good bet." Orfea glanced at the charred remains of the burnt tent. Harry was able to douse the flames after five more minutes of swatting. He stood bent forward, hands resting on thighs, gasping for air.

Keltyn closed her eyes and whispered, "The stone is pure."

"That's what you said before... but the machine measured something." Orfea frowned. "All the buzzing, the needle jumping."

Keltyn opened her eyes slowly. She glanced at Buck as he hurried back, lugging two small metal cylinders and a blanket. This time, her murmur was clear. "Measures iridium purity..." She reached for Orfea's hand, lapsed into a feeble cough.

Joaquin used his good hand to drape the blanket over Keltyn's torso. Buck dropped the cylinders. A clear tube poked out from one, attached to a mask. He turned a dial and the mask hissed. He strapped it over Keltyn's mouth.

The other cylinder attached to more clear tubing with a hollow metal wand on the end. Buck turned it on to emit a hissing noise, louder than the one from the hole in Keltyn's chest. He poked the wand into the hole, sucking up blood and froth from her wounds. As Joaquin watched the gruesome scene, it put him in mind of Aldo's efforts to aid Heriberto's gouged horse. Buck, despite his crude humor, also possessed the unflinching but delicate touch of a curandero.

After clearing as much as he could, Buck eyed Joaquin. "Think you can handle this?"

Joaquin tried to conceal a shiver as he nodded.

Buck handed him the wand. "Keep up the suction. It's her only chance." He dropped his voice and muttered, "Probably a tension pneumo." He bent his head and rubbed the back of his hand across his brow. "Missy, you damn fool. Why did you have to play the hero?"

Keltyn's eyes remained closed.

Joaquin sucked harder. That was his job. Orfea held Keltyn's head just so; that was her job. And Buck? Joaquin watched to see what miracle the Sky-Borne curandero would perform next.

The big pilot sat back on his haunches. "She's stable for now. I better go check on our pyromaniac friend."

He rose and moved toward a moaning Soriante. Wait, thought Joaquin. Buck needed to do something more for Keltyn first. Her breathing seemed shallower. How did he know she was stable?

The smell of Soriante's burnt flesh floated over to where Joaquin knelt. A wave of nausea swept over him, but he focused his breathing and kept on with his task.

As his hand steadied, Joaquin snuck a look toward Harry. The Sky-Borne jeaf caught his wind and now stood bent over the first aid kit, digging around for wound supplies. His hands bounced tubes of burn ointment and dressings around at random.

"Whoa, pardner." Buck leaned close to Harry. "Chief, take a break. Let old Buck look after the burns."

"No, I got it," Harry croaked. "You take care of Keltyn."

Buck said nothing for a minute. "I've done all I can, chief. You better go decide what we're going to do with her."

Joaquin listened closely to catch their exchange, his heart sinking with every word.

"What are her chances?" Harry squinted at Keltyn's now immobile body.

"Could go either way. It'll take a few days to tell."

"Can she tolerate the flight back?"

"Next week, maybe. Tomorrow, no way."

Harry winced and shuffled his way over to Keltyn. Joaquin never saw their jeaf look so ill at ease, not when he downed the charros' pulce around the campfire, not when he forced himself to watch Aldo repair the horse's wound, not even when Nestor and Buck almost dispatched each other in their prior confrontations. Harry's look at this moment confirmed Keltyn's desperate prospects.

Joaquin pulled his gaze away from Harry's forlorn face to focus on his suctioning duties. What else could he do to improve Keltyn's odds of survival?

He heard Buck warn Ysidro and Gabino to step aside so he could help their hollering kin. Even the man's groans sounded musical, thought Joaquin, and allowed himself a glance.

Soriante lay flat on his back, wailing, with his face lifted toward the sky. Every so often, he stopped to give Buck a suspicious stare. Buck struggled to peel off what was left of the charro's shirt, since Soriante's bulk was dead weight from the stun.

The big pilot turned to Orfea, still squatting by Keltyn's body. "Fay, I'm gonna need soap and water and rags to clean this boy up." He pointed to the gear, rummaged through the first aid kit until he found a small cartridge. He jabbed the pointed end into Soriante's hip, none too gently. The charro let loose a wave of choice cuss words.

Buck gave a barking laugh. "He'll thank me for that in a few minutes."

Orfea hurried with a jug of water. She ran back and retrieved a cloth from the blue tent. Buck tore strips and poured the soapy water on. Cleaning off the charred, fried skin didn't seem to bother him. When Buck moved, Joaquin caught another glimpse of Soriante. His whole stomach wall was red as a beet, a big blister the size of a grapefruit popped up in the middle.

"Too bad there's no more ice in Antarctica. This burn could use some." Buck picked a small blade from his first aid kit to lance the blister. Yellow stuff that looked like pee gushed from the wound. Buck sponged it up with gauze and slopped on burn ointment with the motion of spreading butter on a yam. He motioned for Ysidro and Efrain to lift Soriante's butt and wrapped a big wide roll of gauze around his middle.

Done. Buck stood. "That ought to take care of our torcher buddy for now. They'll have to wait here four hours until he can stand on his own and mount a horse." He eyed Joaquin. "You'll have to explain that to them."

The boy took a gulp. He looked up from his suction. "Soriante must rest here until the stun wears off."

Ysidro glared at him. "How long?"

"Four hours, says the man." Then Joaquin's memory sparked. "Just like locoweed."

Ysidro let out a short laugh, then a longer one. Soriante frowned. "What's so funny?"

"What's funny is you, as useless as a bull poisoned by locoweed." Abruptly, Ysidro stopped laughing and shouted Gabino's name without even looking at him.

"Seir?"

"Ride back to camp and fetch the wagon to carry your useless brother."

"Seir." Gabino eyed Efrain for permission. The big guy's gun now pointed downward. He gave a curt nod. Gabino arose and fetched his horse. Joaquin glanced once more at Keltyn's face. Her eyes were closed, and Harry and Orfea knelt on each side of her head. The wand of the suction machine still pulled pink froth. This could not be good.

Buck leaned down to show Joaquin how to adjust the suction pressure: using his fingertip to close a hole in the tubing. Then the pilot knelt once more to check for a pulse in her neck. "Fast, but not racing like before."

He pulled open her eyelids, shone a little pocket torch around them. "Missy, can you hear me?" No response. "Pupils react OK. She must have lapsed into a coma from the shock."

Harry struggled to his feet, removed his vision aids, and pinched the bridge of his nose. "This is going to be a tough one."

He turned to glance at Ysidro, who glared right back at him. "We stay here, it gives Ysidro's boys another excuse to harass us. And we just lost half of our remaining supplies." He faced Buck. "You say it could take a week for her to tolerate the flight back?"

"Roughly. But you're making one big assumption there, chief."

Harry stared numbly at his pilot.

"That she makes it at all. A tension pneumothorax is seldom fatal if, big if, you get the right medical care. Most important thing is suction, to keep her lungs from collapsing while the chest wound heals."

"So?" said Harry. "You've got her on suction now."

"Right, but it runs off a battery generator. Needs to be recharged within three days."

"Damn." Harry scrunched his lip.

A tiny spark flickered in Joaquin's brain. He tried to recall what ingredients Aldo mixed in his poultice for the horse wound. Efrain should still have that curandero kit somewhere.

"Fellas, someone's got to play devil's advocate," Orfea chimed in. "What would Keltyn want?"

Harry frowned. "I assume she'd rather survive, if that's what you mean."

"That's not what I mean, and you know it. She told you her wishes yesterday."

"You mean, stay here? After what they just did to her?" Harry turned to Efrain. "Besides, who would take care of her, may I ask?"

Joaquin cleared his throat. "I will explain it to Yoka when we return to camp. She bandaged my wound." He held up his arm.

Efrain nodded. "She will nurse Keltyn as well as any one of your people could."

Harry tilted his head. "And when the suction runs out?"

Efrain held his hands up and crossed his fingers.

Buck shook his head. "How you gonna get her back to your camp?"

"She will need to share the wagon with the body of her would-be killer and her former captor, the yodeler." Efrain showed the trace of a smile, nodding at Soriante. "But of course, in his present state, he can do her no harm. In any case, I will escort all my errant kin back, and the boy will help me."

Joaquin's eyes roved over the bunch of them: Ysidro glaring, Soriante groaning, and Nestor's silent corpse. Would Ysidro or his nephews resent his role in helping Efrain and the Sky-Bornes? Probably, but Efrain would be the main target of their bile. He would have to stand tall until this blew over.

Buck flashed Efrain a thumb's up sign when their eyes met again.

Ysidro must have noticed this signal. He barked at Efrain. "What gave you the right to shoot Nestor?"

The big gaucho's expression turned to scorn. "The right? Should I have stood by while he killed this woman? Do you have any idea what kind of scum this punk was? Are you blind to the filthy secret he tried to protect?"

"What secret?"

"The identity of the rustlers. One of them was Nestor's cousin."

"Who, that Roderigo?" A look of disgust came over Ysidro.

"The same."

"Worthless scum."

"The boy here recalled the connection. When we returned to fetch the rustlers the other day, I told Nestor their names to see his reaction, but he betrayed no sign of complicity. I might have believed in his innocence, until he attacked Joaquin yesterday."

Ysidro lapsed into a speechless frown, then blew out a breath and shook his head, as if to rid his mind of the whole mess.

Harry paced around what remained of the orange tent and pawed through to remove the flakes of its shell. Everything inside appeared totally charred. Clothes, packs, and sleeping bags smoldered, all worthless now. Keltyn's notebooks were but scattered ashes. Harry tried to wipe soot off the instruments. Everything lay blackened, the glass faces cracked. Telling one box from another was impossible.

Joaquin felt an ache in his good arm, but he had stuck out worse than this before. As Aldo sewed up the wound of Heriberto Paz's horse, every muscle in Joaquin's limbs cramped. Now Keltyn's life lay in his hands. He was not about to cry for mercy. Joaquin could not will the ache away, nor could he dispel the fatigue that crept through mind and muscle.

A change in the hissing tone of the suction jolted him awake. His hand must have lost its grip. He quickly repositioned the wand tip into the wound, glancing around to see if anyone had noticed.

Sometime later he became vaguely aware of another person gently removing the wand from his hand. By this time, he was too exhausted to struggle. Someone else — Harry, perhaps — covered him with a blanket and stuffed a pillow under his head. He slept in fits and spurts, jolted awake as each dream turned into gunfire and falling bodies.

Yet toward the end of this restless night, the germ of an idea formed in his brain: how to save Keltyn when they returned to camp. He knew whom he had to convince to help, and what it would take to do so.

32

UP AND GONE

The sun rose, but the flying machine's shadow kept the light out of Joaquin's eyes. He awoke to the sound of Gabino pulling up with the wagon.

Ysidro cursed. "What took you so long, charro? We have been sitting here shivering for hours."

"I was dead tired, uncle. I had to start a fire and brew maté, just to gather the strength to free a wagon."

Ysidro and Gabino each grabbed an end of Nestor's corpse and tossed it in like a side of beef. The jeaf regarded his other nephew, now leaning on one elbow. "At least your worthless brother can sit now." He barked at Soriante. "Can you ride?"

"Yes, seir." Soriante clambered to his feet, wincing from the pain of his burn.

Efrain studied him. "Good. This will free up room for the girl." He turned to Joaquin. "It will be a bumpy ride. Can you still tend to her wound?"

Joaquin nodded vigorously. He cast a look at Keltyn. She still lay on her back, but now a blanket was wrapped around her. Orfea looked haggard. It must have been she who relieved him during the night. She handed over the suction with a brief nod, winced as she pushed herself up, and stumbled over toward the coffee Harry brewed.

Efrain sat with the Sky-Bornes in the shade of their flying machine, also drinking coffee.

Harry sat slumped forward in his stool, arms resting on his knees. "What a night. My head feels like it hit a brick wall."

"Now you can appreciate what mine's been feeling like all week," said Buck. "Thanks for covering the watch, chief."

"I admit to nodding off." Harry rose to pass around a box of pastries. Buck reached his long arm for a couple of sugar crusts. With the stun gun tucked in his belt, he stood and brought one over to Joaquin. "How are you taking it, son?"

He grunted, aware that his mouth and nose were already covered with jelly. Though still tired from a restless sleep, he was aware that some here had not slept at all.

"Beats tortillas, huh?" said Harry. "Here." He pointed to the pastries. "You can take the rest of these back with you."

Orfea huddled with her coffee. "That reminds me. Keltyn figured out what causes their wasting disease."

"Not radiation poisoning?" Harry turned to her. "How do you know?"

"The symptoms don't fit. Keltyn and Luz narrowed it down to the tortilla preparation. You have to slake the maize with lime."

She squeezed her eyes shut. "I've been trying to remember since yesterday morning, about maize preparation..." The eyes jumped open. "It just came to me. It's a vitamin deficiency. Niacin. The maize contains niacin, but you have to cook it with slaked lime to make it available for human digestion. If your staple is maize, like here, there's your sole source of niacin. No niacin, eventually you get the wasting disease." Orfea wiped her hands. "There used to be an English name for it, but it's been hundreds of years."

Joaquin knew that the gaucho cook bought his tortillas from Hortensio. Was that why none of the gauchos ever developed the khokri?

Harry's lower lip stuck out. "Good job, but rotten luck for Keltyn. This could have ended a whole lot better..." He slurped the last of his coffee and dragged himself up. "We need to get going before anything else happens."

"I wish we could stay, explain everything to the tribe," Orfea said.

Harry glanced at the rogue gauchos, off to one side nursing their maté. "Think on what you're saying, woman. Are you going to be the one to convince them that their wasting disease is from a vitamin deficiency? Right now, most of them will say good riddance to all of us."

"I guess you're right." She stood and headed toward the blue tent. A moment later she reappeared, dragging out bags.

Buck carried the packs to the plane, and Harry stuffed them behind the back seat. Then they folded the tent and stuffed it in a sack that one of Cisco's saddle packs might easily hold. Joaquin's own tent stood but half as big when it was raised yet took twice as much space when furled.

Again, second thoughts hit him. The marvels that the Sky-Bornes carried — Buck's stun gun, Harry's magnifiers, Orfea's translating machine, Keltyn's magic meters, as well as these bright compact tents — all were but a small sample of what he might discover back in Orfea's homeland. He watched closely as they stuffed the tent.

Harry looked over at him. "How did you like sleeping in this, son?"

"Oh, very much, seir."

"Beats the one you have, I'll bet."

That it did.

Harry glanced at Buck and Orfea. "What do you guys think? Souvenir for the kid?"

Buck flipped his toothpick. "He'll put it to good use, that's for sure."

Joaquin smiled in gratitude, then realized he was collecting quite a haul. Would this fuel more jealousy among the charros? Too bad.

Hands on hips, Harry eyed the charred remains of the orange tent. Whatever chunks of iris stone might be buried in the pile, no one could pick them out now. The chief shook his hands, palms down. "Oh, the hell with it. There's no way we can clean this mess up. Let's just get out of here."

Orfea returned to Keltyn's side, while Joaquin stuffed the blue tent and the pastries into Cisco's saddlebags. He untied the spare horses and handed the reins to the already mounted Efrain. He looked up into the big gaucho's face. Efrain winked and flashed a thumbs-up. Joaquin flushed with pride.

Harry and Buck both reached up to shake Efrain's hand.

"Good man," Harry said. "You saved our hides." Then he grabbed the boy's hand. "So did you, son. Good luck. No doubt in my mind, things are going to work out."

"Yep, kid," Buck tousled his hair. "You got what we pilots call 'the right stuff.'"

Joaquin smiled to himself as he scrambled back onto the wagon to resume his suctioning duties. Orfea gave him one more plaintive look, kissed him on the forehead, and turned to scoot off the back of the cart. A knot welled up in his throat. Half of him wanted to shout, "Wait, seira. I have changed my mind. Please take me with you." Yet, the other half knew that what's done is done. If he wanted to be treated like a man, he would have to stick with his decisions.

By now, the bubbling from Keltyn's chest wound was quiet. Gabino shook the reins, and the wagon lurched forward. Joaquin raised his limp hand to salute the three Sky-Bornes as the gaucho party set off.

The cart kicked to and fro as it climbed the side of the crater. By the time they reached the rim, Efrain signaled for a halt and climbed down to adjust Keltyn's huddled body. Her eyes remained closed, but on the way up, Joaquin saw her grimace each time one of the cart's wheels hit a bump. He decided that, in her condition, a wince of pain was better than no reaction at all.

Ysidro and Gabino stepped down to confer with the still-mounted Soriante. He had refused Buck's offer of another injection of pain medicine before they departed. His grimaces, as he rubbed the dressings over his abdomen, now suggested second thoughts. Joaquin could not help but feel for the boisterous charro.

Facing backward in the cart, Joaquin studied the flying machine in the midst of the crater. The longer he watched its shiny silver form, the more convinced he became that his first notion was right; a bird, a giant mother bird that carried her children from a distant place. A low humming noise started up. The bird slowly, slowly tilted backward on its haunches, until it pointed straight upward. The humming sound stopped.

Next came a different sound, more like whooshing. Then a bright light shot out of the bird's tail. It perched like that for several seconds before lifting off, barely moving at first, as if just testing. Picking up speed, the airborne silver beast leveled and headed in the gaucho party's direction. By the time it reached the crater's rim, the bird gained several hundred feet of elevation.

The gauchos lifted their heads to watch. Just as she passed overhead, the bird rocked her wings side to side, gentle-like. She headed northward and slowly faded away to nothing.

Should he be cradled in the belly of that bird now, like Harry and Buck and Orfea? Joaquin imagined himself strapped into the same seat that he dozed in last night. He watched out the window as the ground disappeared below him. He heard Buck and Harry in the front seats, congratulating each other on a successful lift-off. All the tension of the past week, wondering if they were ever to depart alive, and now they were on their way home.

Then, in his imagination, he turned to Orfea, sitting next to him. She flashed her motherly smile and reached over to smooth his curls and brush some dirt off his collar. At this, Joaquin snapped his eyes open; don't treat me like your plaything. He focused on Keltyn's wound, and on the upcoming bargaining that would spell the difference between her life and death. Better to be with his own people. He had made the right choice.

33

KELTYN'S KEEPERS

Word about the shootout spread the next morning. The Sky-Borne woman, they said, was shot in the chest, gravely wounded. Yet Luz had one consolation. Nestor, the mal hombre who had done this, lay dead. Praise the Spirits.

Not until Keltyn was abducted did Luz realize she still valued their friendship. Did she have any chance to recover? Luz needed to do whatever she could, for this woman saved her own life. Now, as the cart carrying the inert Keltyn rolled past her through camp, Luz followed it toward Yoka's yurt.

The crone emerged. Efrain explained their circumstances.

"The hell you say." Yoka stood, hands firmly planted on her hips. The Sky-Borne lay quite still in the wagon, only an occasional groan betraying any sign of life.

"You expect me to nurse her back to health, after all the disrespect she has shown me? To say nothing of the chaos she spread among our tribe with her wicked self-serving lies. Ffft." Yoka made a brushing-off motion and turned away.

"Auntie, please," said Luz. "It was thanks to Keltyn that we finally learned the khokri's true cause."

"Ha. Save your breath, girl. First you must convince your ailing mother of this 'truth.'"

Joaquin stepped forward. "I too beg for your help, Auntie."

Clearly surprised, Yoka turned to face him. She tried to stare him down, but he kept his gaze firm.

Yoka frowned. "Hmph. They tell me that Orfea has gifted you her translating box, boy. Are you prepared to learn the Venga art, then?" Her frown softened.

"I might be, if..." The boy nodded toward the cart.

Luz smiled; Joaquin knew how to strike a bargain. Yoka's lips puckered into the trace of a snarl. "I see. Another tit for tat, eh."

Nodding slowly, her stare morphed into a squint. "Very well, it seems that I must swallow my pride and care for this pathetic creature. But," she peered up over her vision aids at Efrain, "I don't relish the thought of her and I being the only ones left behind in this valley, in the shadow of the volcano so recently erupted. The herd, the whole tribe is to move on today, no?"

Efrain removed his boina and dug his knuckles into his scalp. "The Sky-Bornes say that she has only three days in which to recover, otherwise the machines that keep her alive will quit running. I believe that we owe her enough to bide our time here for three more days. In his present state of contrition, I think Ysidro can be persuaded of this as well."

"Three days, eh? Well then, let us get the girl unloaded."

Luz cradled Keltyn's head with both hands while Efrain held her body. Joaquin carried the suction machine with his good arm, Yoka the small pack that produced enriched air for each breath. In rather awkward fashion, they settled her onto Yoka's cot.

Efrain departed. Yoka plopped down on her knees and peeled away the blanket covering Keltyn's torso to inspect the wound. She motioned for Joaquin to use the suction wand, watching intently as he did so. Clearing the bloody froth only changed the noise escaping the hole in Keltyn's chest from a soft gurgle to a loud sucking.

Yoka rocked back on her heels and turned to Joaquin. "Sadly, Aldo is the one you need now, not me. It's the right poultice that will heal a chest wound, and no one knew poultices like your jeaf."

"I know. I watched him mix one for a horse's wound, but it seemed like magic. I paid no attention to which of his many herbs he mixed in." Joaquin waved his bandaged hand at the crone. "But you mustn't act so modest, Auntie. Your dressing did a fine job for my gash."

Despite this reassurance, Luz could tell from the chagrined look on Yoka's face that her self-confidence was shaken. Yet Joaquin's words gave Luz an idea. The crone did not seem too surprised when she asked if the crone could spare a few Venga nuggets.

Luz ambled over to the gaucho encampment as fast as her newly healed legs would carry her. She found Efrain emerging from Ysidro's yurt. He signaled for her to wait while he distanced himself from the new jeaf's earshot.

"Ysidro is spent from his misadventure of last night. He craves a day of rest." Efrain studied the ground, avoiding eye contact.

"Only one day?" Her stomach knotted. Keltyn could not possibly recover that quickly, even if Luz's plan worked to perfection.

"We bargained. I got him to agree to wait three days, no more. He is sick of this place." The big gaucho looked around and shuddered. "Can't say as I blame him."

Luz studied him, newly concerned. "What's wrong? What did you have to give up to get Ysidro's agreement?"

"He wants Nestor's rifle. Hah. Good riddance. The thing is cursed." He tried to smile, but the furrows in his brow only deepened more. He eyed her. "But how goes it with Keltyn? I should think you would be helping to tend her. And what of your mother?"

"Mother is well enough to sit up on her own now. I'm hoping these extra days will give her enough strength to ride in the cart. As for Keltyn's wound, Yoka claims it is beyond her meager healing powers. She thinks that only Aldo could have fashioned the right kind of poultice to close it."

Efrain sighed. "So, what are we to do?"

Luz reached into her pocket and produced four Venga nuggets.

Efrain registered no expression.

"Did you pack Aldo's curandero kit when we came down from the mountain?"

"Of course, though what good will it do anyone now? Only he knew how to use it."

"Did he never offer to teach you?"

Efrain cleared his throat. "He did, but like a fool, I never showed the patience. The jeaf discerned that Joaquin might have the right temperament, but it would take years to learn."

Luz swallowed. Efrain, she sensed, still faulted her for his uncle's demise, and right now she needed him if her plan was to work. "Can we go to Aldo's yurt? I need to tell you something. Best you should be sitting."

Luz eased down cross-legged on the braided wool rug that comprised the floor of the dead jeaf's shelter. The yurt was spacious, tall enough for someone as big as Aldo or Efrain to stand in. Without ever having set foot inside before, Luz felt at home immediately. Perhaps it was the earthy smells that permeated the yurt: untanned leather, fleece, pipe tobacco, the hint of manure tracked in by the jeaf's boots.

She turned to Efrain as he also sat. "Is this yours to inherit?"

"I suppose so. Aldo had no other heirs." He studied the walls, flapping in the breeze.

"He did have one other, it turns out." Luz gave a sly smile.

Efrain whipped around to look at her. "How could he? He never married."

Luz shook her head slowly. "Perhaps, but when did that ever stop a man?"

Efrain snickered. "What? Now one of his paramours claims him?"

"Not at all. But his daughter does." Luz stared straight at the uncomprehending gaucho until his eyes slowly widened and he nodded.

"I should have guessed. Did he know?"

"Perhaps." Luz did not wish to lie, but she was mindful of the promise to her mother.

Efrain's eyes turned vacant. "That explains much." He would not elaborate.

Finally, Luz said, "Let us see what the curandero kit contains."

Efrain opened the main pouch and Luz spread out the various packets of smelly salves, herbs, barks, and pulverized leaves. Side pouches contained twigs for mixing the various ingredients, flat and rolled lengths of hemp gauze to apply the mixed poultices, and a packet of another vile-smelling sticky substance to adhere the dressings.

While Luz sorted through all this, Efrain busied himself brewing a batch of maté. He needed the stimulant badly, she decided. His eyes puffed from lack of sleep.

"Here." Efrain took a sip from the bombilla and handed it to her.

"Ready?" She tried to hand a Venga nugget to Efrain, but the big gaucho shook his head. She felt miffed. "How can you mix the poultice if you can't hear what Aldo says?"

"Just repeat everything he tells you. I can hear you just fine." Efrain wafted a tired smile.

Luz consumed her nugget and waited until her neck began to tingle. She sensed Aldo's presence before she could glimpse his form. "Father." The word felt strange to Luz even as she uttered it.

Aldo's rough-hewn roguish face now stared back at her. His stern look softened. "Your mother told you? Then she broke her promise."

"What promise, Father?"

"She wanted me to help support you. But she never approached me until years later. What tale did she tell you when you first asked who your father was?"

"She said never I should mind, that he left our tribe before I was born."

"A likely story. I did agree to contribute to your upbringing, so long as she would not broadcast my role. After all, I was hard pressed to remember our brief fling. For all I knew, any one of these charros could have sired you."

The thought of someone like Ysidro consorting with Trieste made Luz gag and laugh at once. It was, after all, Aldo whom the Venga led her to channel. "Don't worry, Father. Mother said she never told anyone else, and it was only your death that opened her lips to me."

She took a deep breath. There was something else she needed to ask. "Father, was it you who procured Quintara?"

Aldo's voice sounded robust once again. "Yes, I arranged the whole thing. I could see how fast you grew, how headstrong you became. You needed the horse to channel your energy. You would not have the patience to learn your mother's painstaking trade. She wished to avoid having you constantly underfoot."

Learning that her mother placed a higher priority on her trade than on nurturing her daughter sent a small shock through Luz.

Aldo said, "What was your mother's story of how the mare had come to you?"

Luz shook her head. "She said my uncle had made a deal with someone."

"Hmph." Aldo closed his eyes. "It most broke my heart to put Quintara down."

"But you saved me, and now I have come to beg you to help save the life of Keltyn."

The jeaf's eyes snapped open. "What sort of trouble has the Sky-Borne gotten into now?"

"Nestor shot her, and your nephew in turn shot him dead."

Aldo growled, "Nestor, that pig. Good riddance."

"Keltyn has a sucking hole in her chest, and grows weaker each day. The other Sky-Bornes have left her here. Actually, Keltyn wished to stay behind, not to return with them." Luz felt flustered. She was getting off track. "So, you must describe what kind of poultice will speed the wound to close."

Aldo considered this. "Putting together the right poultice for your Keltyn's wound is not difficult, but does the girl really think she can just become one of our tribe? She will need to attach herself to someone." The jeaf regarded his daughter. "Is that someone to be you?"

Luz hesitated.

"You wish to answer yes, but it is not that simple, is it?"

Luz shook her head.

Aldo went on. "Your mother resents the girl. Why?"

"She thinks Keltyn ruined her trade." Luz explained the Sky-Borne's ploy and how it backfired.

Aldo emitted clucking sounds. "So, your mother wants nothing more to do with her."

"Yes, but for no good reason. Keltyn, in her shame, tracked down the true cause of the khokri. It has nothing to do with the piedra de yris," said Luz. "Within the next few days, everyone in the tribe will understand this. Keltyn and Mother will both be cleared."

She paused, chewed her lip. How much of this was wishful thinking on her part? It might take weeks or months to allay the suspicions of the tribeswomen, let alone to change their ingrained tortilla preferences.

Aldo smiled gently. "You must give your mother a message from me. Tell her that if the Sky-Borne girl survives her wound and your mother does not take her in, she will have me to deal with. Ha, ha, ha!" A belly laugh escaped him, deeper than any she remembered during his life.

Luz smiled too. Mother, with her superstitious nature, would take pains to avoid being haunted by Aldo's ghost, even if it meant sheltering the Sky-Borne girl whom she so recently despised. The thought gave her comfort as she repeated Aldo's recipe for the poultice.

"Thank you, Father," Luz managed to say. The word now felt natural, rolling off her tongue. She suspected it would not be the last time she would utter it. She tried to reach out and touch Aldo's image, but all her hand could feel was the soft breeze rustling through his yurt.

34
NOMADS

My eyes flutter as I try to open them. My whole body feels stiff, like I've been harnessed too long in the Bailey Explorer. I try to turn on my side, but a sharp pain in my left ribs puts a quick halt to that notion. I yelp and again struggle to open my eyes. When, finally, I glimpse my surroundings, all I can see are shadows, save for a slit of daylight peeking in ten feet away.

I must be in a tent or yurt. Whose? The slit of daylight widens, and a familiar short, squat silhouette stands at the threshold.

"Oh ho." It's Yoka's booming voice. "So, you have decided to rejoin the living? Took your sweet time, I must say."

"How long have I been asleep?" My mouth feels like it's stuffed with cotton.

Yoka leans down and holds a cup of water to my lips. "Four days, five nights. You didn't get here until the morning after you were shot."

I remember the shot, the punch in my side that felled me instantly. I look up at Yoka. My last contact with the crone ended badly, with myself as the accuser. "Why did you save me?"

The crone harrumphs. "I had very little to do with your salvation, girl. Only provided the cot, and frankly, I wouldn't even have volunteered that, save for the boy."

"Joaquin?"

"He's quite fond of you." Her brows lift. "In case you're curious, your other saviors are Luz, Aldo's spirit, and your big pilot, Buck."

Yoka gestures to the tubing, the oxygen and suction machines, lying discarded by the wall of the yurt. She lifts my tunic to expose a poultice covering my wound. "Oh, and Efrain is the one who brought you here. He has stopped by each day since. You needed every last bit of help to close that wound, otherwise you'd never have awoken."

I lie back to take this all in. It feels good to have friends, even if they are teenage kids, a ghost, and a crude chauvinist. But Efrain? I misjudged him too. I wonder if the big guy has a soft spot for li'l old me, and if I'm ready to indulge it. Opposites attract, they say, and he and I are about as opposite as they come.

As far as that goes, I'm literally the opposite of everyone here. Other side of the world, other features, other language, you name it. How am I gonna fit in? Guess I'll have to start with being more polite, which has never been Keltyn SparrowHawk's calling card. But, as they say, when in Rome...

***

Just like on the plane coming here, I'm encased like a mummy, this time ready to take my turn in Trieste's bumpy cart. My body is squeezed between blankets, pots and pans, and boxes containing what remains of Trieste's iris stone jewelry.

One problem remains. Cozuel the mule balks at having to pull the overloaded wagon. Trieste sits in the driver's seat, whipping the reins, while Luz stands and tugs at the mule's bridle. No use. The creature will not budge.

Most of the other camp followers, including Yoka, moved on earlier this morning, not far behind the gauchos and the herd. They're pointed in the direction of Nomidar, though I understand it will be another month — with two, perhaps three, more campsites — before the grazing season ends. Then comes the long, dark winter in their village. The thought triggers a quick, nervous pang, but I dismiss it. I will be fine.

Besides us, Trieste's brood, the only others not yet departed are Carmen and Pilar. They share the driver's seat of their own cart and watch with amusement the scene of Cozuel's work stoppage. I notice that their cart includes a trove of Trieste's wares.

Pilar addresses Trieste as one wagoner to another. "Dear woman, you've overloaded the poor beast. No wonder it won't move."

From my angle, it appears that the sisters' cart has spare room.

"And what, pray tell, are you volunteering to relieve me of?" Trieste calls.

Pilar and Carmen exchange glances.

"Surely not your household furnishings," says Carmen. "Unless you wish to give up more of your fine gems, it would have to be the Sky-Borne."

Trieste sighs. "No, the Sky-Borne is mine. I have made a promise." She turns around to watch my bundled form. "Anyway, she's on the mend. Soon she'll be able to earn her keep." She points to the kitchenware. "I would rather send the heavy stuff with you. I'll consider it the return of a favor, considering Luz invited you to cherry-pick my wares while I lay ill, thinking that I could never ply my trade again." She brightens. "The poor girl underestimated her mother."

We all underestimated each other. I roll over to settle myself for the long journey ahead. Sounds like the mule and I are destined to become bosom buddies, even after I heal up. Plus, I'm gonna need to learn Onwei; there's not enough earpads for the whole tribe.

And, just like on the Bailey Voyager mission, I'm the newbie once again. Except this time, the newbie aims to get it right.

THE END

ACKNOWLEDGEMENTS

Curtis Walters pointed out the unique properties of iridium, and its connection to volcanoes and craters.

Catherine Reed suggested the name "SparrowHawk," and was a generous sounding board in the eight years it took me to write this story.

Paleontologist-in-training Madeline Marshall clued me to research showing that dinosaurs lived in Antarctica.

Doug Aretz put me in touch with Marie Zhuikov, my first editor.

Catherine Adams, my second editor, imparted the author's need to respect the sensibilities of female YA readers.

Michael Neff's seminars helped teach me the craft of writing fiction. They also gave insights on how the publishing business works, and of having realistic expectations.

David Bischoff led me to discover the narrator's voice.

Adrienne Sinclair inspired me to redirect the story as YA sci-fi, saw Joaquin's arc as strong enough to be a co-protagonist, and lent me Elizabeth Lyon's wonderful book on writing fiction.

Loren Oberweger, my last editor, guided me through four re-writes over the final two-plus years, until this story became publishable.

Kaitlin Littlechild proofread the manuscript and provided insight into Cree funeral customs.

ABOUT THE AUTHOR

Patagonia 2011

Norman Westhoff is a physician and geography buff.

He has visited all of the ice-free continents, and lives in Lawrence, Kansas.

Stone Fever is the first volume of a trilogy, *Erebus Tales.*

Lightning Source UK Ltd.
Milton Keynes UK
UKHW010637251120
374072UK00002B/426

Selections from Harry Potter AND THE GOBLET OF FIRE

Music by Patrick Doyle

Except for
HEDWIG'S THEME by John Williams
DO THE HIPPOGRIFF by Jarvis Cocker and Jason Buckle
THIS IS THE NIGHT & MAGIC WORKS by Jarvis Cocker

© 2005 by Faber Music Ltd
First published in 2005 by Faber Music Ltd
3 Queen Square, London WC1N 3AU
Printed in England by Caligraving Ltd
All rights reserved

ISBN 0-571-52510-5

To buy Faber Music publications or to find out about the full range of titles available,
please contact your local music retailer or Faber Music sales enquiries:
Faber Music Ltd, Burnt Mill, Elizabeth Way, Harlow, CM20 2HX England
Tel: +44(0)1279 82 89 82 Fax: +44(0)1279 82 89 83
sales@fabermusic.com fabermusic.com

CONTENTS

FOXTROT FLEUR

By PATRICK DOYLE

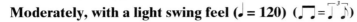

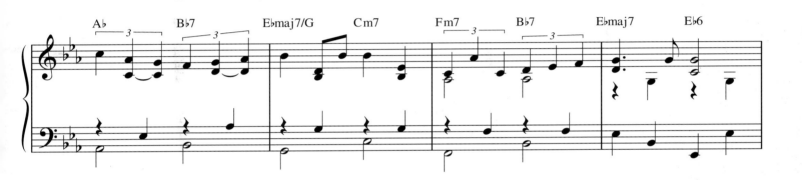

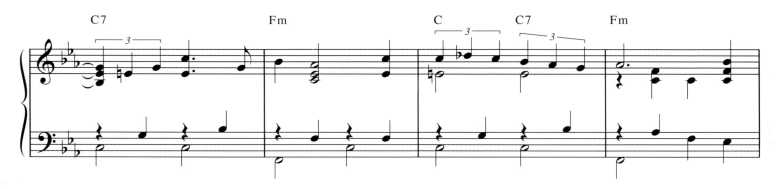

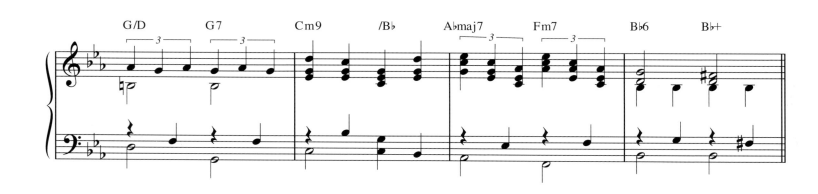

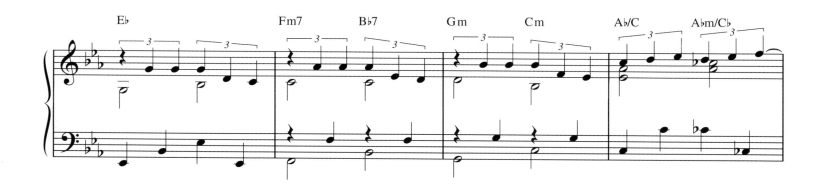

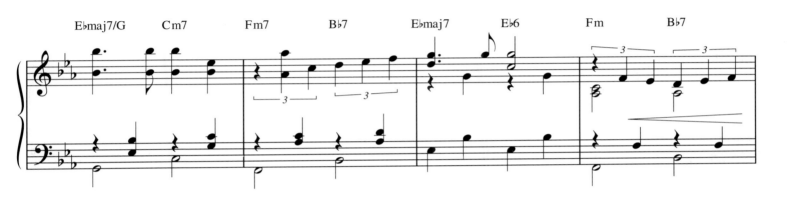

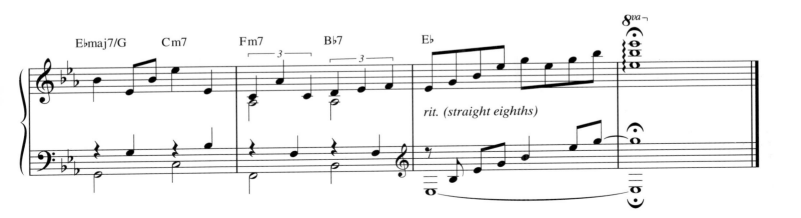

DEATH OF CEDRIC

By PATRICK DOYLE

Funebre, serioso (♩ = 84)

DO THE HIPPOGRIFF

By JARVIS COCKER and JASON BUCKLE

Bright rock ♩ = 152

1. Move your

Verse:

bod - y like a hair - y troll,_____   a - learn - ing to rock and roll.

round_ like a scar - y ghost,_____   a - spook - in' him - self the most.

HARRY IN WINTER

By PATRICK DOYLE

HEDWIG'S THEME

By
JOHN WILLIAMS

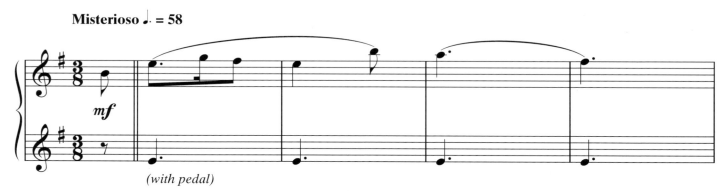

Bright ♩ = 80

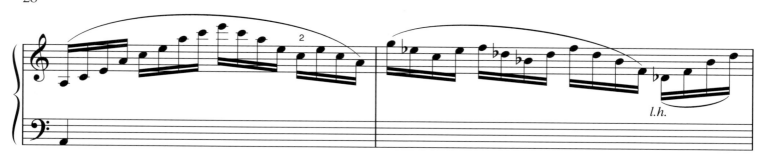

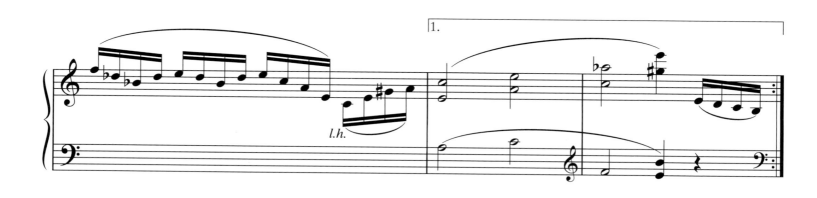

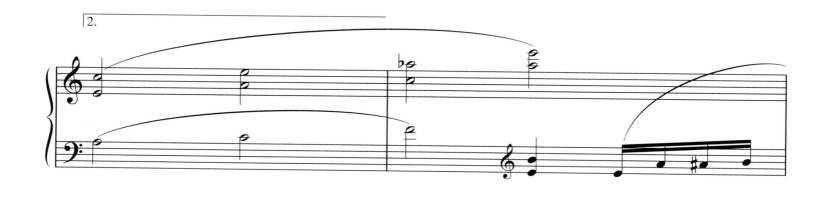

HOGWARTS' HYMN

By PATRICK DOYLE

Nobilmente con expressivo (= 69)

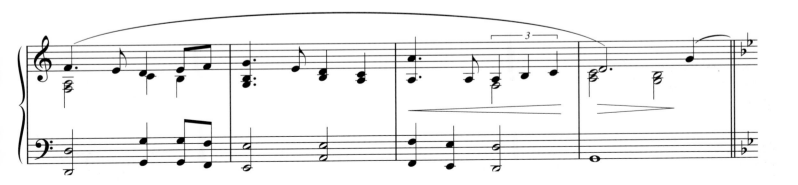

HOGWARTS' MARCH

By PATRICK DOYLE

D.S. % al Coda

NEVILLE'S WALTZ

By PATRICK DOYLE

POTTER WALTZ

By PATRICK DOYLE

Bright waltz (♩ = 176)

THE QUIDDITCH WORLD CUP
(The Irish)

By PATRICK DOYLE

MAGIC WORKS

By JARVIS COCKER

Spoken: This one's going out to all the lovers out there.

(with pedal)

Hold each other tight, and keep each other warm.

1. And

Verse:

dance .... your fi - nal ...... dance. ......
make .... your fi - nal ...... move, ...

THIS IS THE NIGHT

By JARVIS COCKER

Moderately slow ♩ = 76

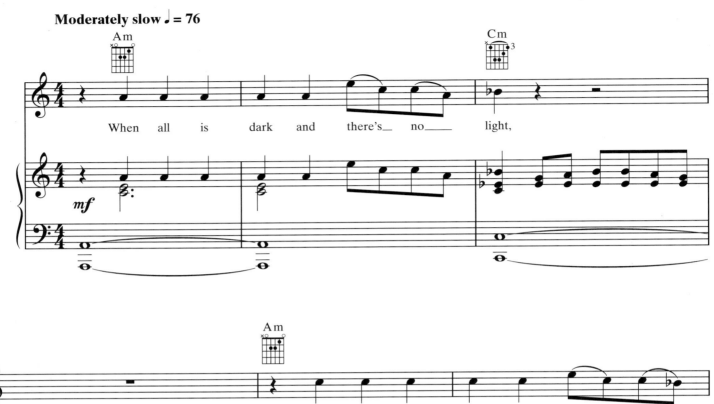

When all is dark and there's__ no__ light,

lost in the deep-est hour__ of__

night, I see__ you.

Chorus:

Verse 2:
There was a time I would have walked on burning coals for you,
Sailed across the ocean blue,
Climbed the highest mountain just to call your name.
The moon throws down its light and cuts me to the quick tonight.
A change is in the air and nothing will ever be the same.
You still look good to me,
Ooh, but you're no good for me.
I close my eyes and squeeze you from my consciousness.
And in the morning when I wake,
I walk the line, I walk it straight,
But the morning's so many miles away.
Good God now!
(To Chorus:)

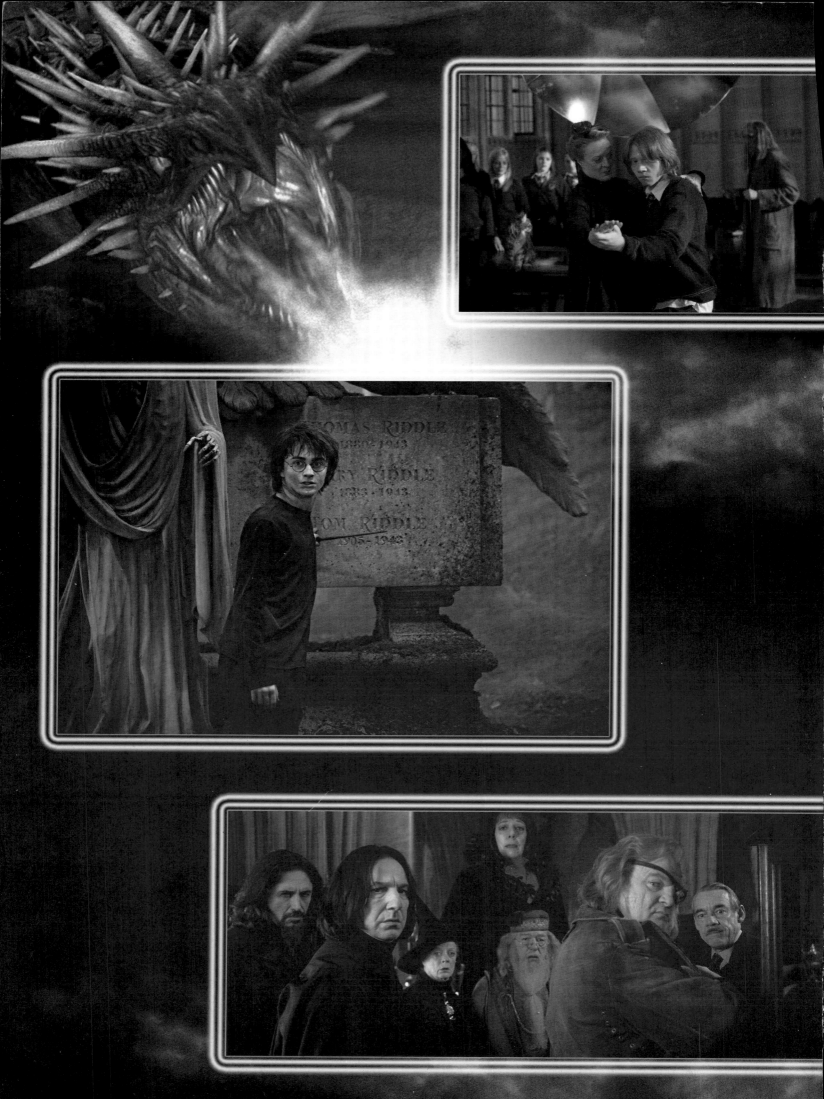